Date Due

D1505200

LOVED HONOR MORE

AN ELIZABETH PEPPERHAWK/
AVIVAH ROSEN MYSTERY

LOVED HONOR MORE

SHARON WILDWIND

FIVE STAR
A part of Gale, Cengage Learning

GALE
CENGAGE Learning·

Detroit • New York • San Francisco • New Haven, Conn • Waterville, Maine • London

GALE
CENGAGE Learning

LIBRARY OF CONGRESS CATALOGING-IN-PUBLICATION DATA

Wildwind, Sharon Grant.
    Loved honor more : an Elizabeth Pepperhawk/Avivah Rosen
mystery / Sharon Wildwind. — 1st ed.
      p. cm.
    ISBN 978-1-4328-2619-2 (hardcover) — ISBN 1-4328-2619-0
(hardcover)
    1. Vietnam War, 1961-1975—Veterans—Fiction. 2. Military
nursing—North Carolina—Fiction. 3. Murder—Investigation—
Fiction. I. Title.
PR9199.4.W542L68 2012
813'.6—dc23
                                      2012020679

First Edition. First Printing: November 2012.
Published in conjunction with Tekno Books and Ed Gorman.
Find us on Facebook– https://www.facebook.com/FiveStarCengage
Visit our website– http://www.gale.cengage.com/fivestar/
Contact Five Star™ Publishing at FiveStar@cengage.com

Printed in Mexico
1 2 3 4 5 6 7 16 15 14 13 12

For Ward
Brothers in arms are well and good,
but nothing beats the real thing.
Thanks, brother.
And for our brothers gone before, John and L.J.

ACKNOWLEDGMENTS

Ken, usually you get last billing, but this time you're at the top of the list. You are my joy and delight. Thank you for everything from researching Shanghai to doing the dishes so that I could write.

Final roll call: Wes, Darce, Harry, Bill, Jim, Dennis, Rick, Jan, Spider, Bob, Braun, Joe, and David. I could never have created Benny and Darby without knowing you.

Brian and Barbara, thanks for all the Saturday mornings in the store on Haywood Street and for your continued friendship. I think you can guess where Yanni's store is. Also, if it's okay with you, Avivah and Saul want to buy your house.

It's a long, long trail a-winding to the end of a book, and it's been a lifesaver to have company along the way. Thanks to all of my fellow travelers:

Avivah Wargon for help with her namesake's grandmother, and for reading and commenting.

Cate Prato for information on Greek culture.

Elizabeth Zelvin, Jeff Cohen, Lisa Black, Pamela Ridley, Robin Burcell, Sheri Gaia Chapin, and Susan Whittig Albert for reading, comments, answering questions, and generally keeping me on track.

Hank Ryan for information about television weekend talk shows in the 1970s.

John Metzer, who runs Metzer Farms in Gonzales, California, for information about hatcheries and guard geese.

Lee Huynh for help with the Vietnamese words.

Kaye Barley, who said it was okay to use her name, as long as she got to wear cowgirl clothes at some point. And Mary Jane Maffani, who came up with the idea of having Kaye pop up on the page.

Zoe Rhine from Buncombe County Public Library for information about John Walter Boyd's part of Asheville.

Thanks as always to my agent Janet Benrey, my editor Alice Duncan, and to Five Star™ for believing in me.

It's time to thank the musicians who have been in the background daily as I wrote all of these books:

James Taylor, for "Carolina in My Mind," and the late John Denver for "Take Me Home, Country Roads," and "The Night They Drove Old Dixie Down." These three tunes have been the series' signatures.

Simon and Garfunkel for lots of music, especially "Homeward Bound" and "Bridge Over Troubled Waters," two tunes that could, in an instant, flash Pepper back to the emergency room in Qui Nhon.

Yo-Yo Ma, Mark O'Connor, and Mark Edger for *Appalachian Journey,* and Anonymous 4, for all of their albums. They were the wings of music I used to travel from my living room to North Carolina, and to stay there long enough to write five books.

All of the artists on the original soundtrack recording of the PBS show *The Civil War,* most especially Jay Ungar, Molly Mason, and friends; and the late Tennessee Ernie Ford for a collection of bittersweet Civil War songs. Darby spins this music in his head a surprising amount of the time. So does Pepper.

Benny, Avivah, and Saul have different music tastes. Benny loves cheating and hurting country-and-western, and Texas swing. Avivah thinks music sounds best played in a New York City piano bar, preferably on a wet Sunday afternoon. She

Acknowledgments

adores Gershwin's "Rhapsody in Blue."

Saul, who played clarinet in both high school and the famed Marching Hundred at Indiana University, still has an unfortunate tendency to do brisk pivot turns when he hears any John Philip Sousa music. Anyone who has marched in a high-school band or a precision-drill team will understand that.

Likewise, any of you who are dedicated blues fans probably know why a man named John Walter Boyd goes by the nickname of Leadbelly.

And for all of the readers: Peace, thank you, and welcome home.

INTRODUCTION

I know exactly where I was on April 30, 1975. Like Pepper I was glued to my television, watching images that in retrospect I would have been better off not seeing. I'd made it through the previous six weeks of *Newsweek* and *Time* articles, and through the television coverage as Saigon fell, but it was a month later, on May 31, 1975, that I came apart when I opened the morning paper and saw the famous Doonesbury cartoon strip of B.D.'s reaction to Saigon falling. Looking at that cartoon in the Doonesbury archives still moves me to tears.

When I began this series, I knew that the last book would center on the immediate aftermath of the withdrawal from the US embassy in Saigon. The problem was, how was I going to have events, which happened half a world away, resonate in North Carolina? My solution was to bring the war home to Pepper, Avivah, and Benny.

This is a book where real life, in this case the horrific final weeks before the fall of Saigon, intersects with fiction. I made sure the dates were correct. But, after that, fancy and imagination took over. Any historical inaccuracies are mine alone. This is a work of fiction. Any similarity between characters and real people or events is purely coincidental.

All things come to an end. The characters have assured me that they are ready to get on with being civilians without me looking over their shoulder. I wish them God speed, and I hope they will drop me a line every few years to let me know how they are doing.

CHAPTER 1

Sunday, 4 May 1975, 2200 hours
The Homestead
Madison County, North Carolina

Ex–Army Nurse Elizabeth Pepperhawk burrowed deeper under her quilt. If she could stop the images, she could sleep. Both Saul and Avivah had warned her not to read every issue of *Time* and *Newsweek,* not to linger over each gruesome photograph coming out of Vietnam and Cambodia. If Avivah really were her best friend, she would have snatched magazines from her hands. That wasn't fair. Avivah was her friend, not her mother or her watchdog. It wasn't Avivah's fault that Pepper now shared sleepless nights with images of dead children and burned vehicles.

Pepper weighed the quality of her tight, hard stomach knot. If she concentrated on feeling nauseous, she could make herself ill. If she were lucky, she might vomit. A good upchucking would be a hell of a lot better reason for booking off sick tomorrow than "We lost the Vietnam War five days ago. My country's honor is a shambles, and I don't have enough energy to get out of bed."

The doorbell's shrill ring cut through the dark, cool night. Who came calling at ten o'clock at night? Pepper pulled a pillow over her head. Her housemates, Avivah Rosen and Saul Eisenberg, were out; she was alone. She wasn't answering the door. Whoever was there could ring until hell froze.

13

The ringing persisted. Pepper threw back her quilt. She didn't bother with a robe or slippers. Her pajamas were decent. If fluffy baby ducks on blue flannel bothered this unexpected and unwanted visitor, tough luck.

She pulled a heavy walking stick from the umbrella stand by the front door, and without turning on the porch light, looked through the peephole. Her yard light, on a pole beside the graveled parking area, illuminated a middle-aged woman. Gray hair framed the woman's face; she wore wire-rimmed spectacles. A baby blanket covered part of her chest. Under the blanket, something small wiggled.

Pepper's Madison County neighbors made it their business to know who had a tow truck, who knew about electrical repairs, who was a nurse. Neighbors being available to neighbors were part of rural life. She turned on the porch light and unlocked the door, but kept the chain in place and a firm grip on the gnarled stick while she opened the door a crack. Her heart pounded. "Yes?"

Fussy baby sounds—very young baby sounds—came from under the blanket. "My name is Edith Filmore. If you are Elizabeth Pepperhawk, I've come to see you."

The woman's accent was "not from around here."

"Is the baby ill?"

"No."

"Are you ill?"

"No."

"Then why are you bothering me this late at night?"

Edith Filmore awkwardly extended her tight hand. In it she held a small black notebook that had a piece of elastic built into the cover to hold it closed. "This will explain."

Pepper opened the notebook. The dim light was enough for her to read the first page.

Darby R. Baxter
Begun: 5 March 1975

It was Darby's handwriting. Pepper whispered, "Where did you get this?"

"From a man in the American embassy in Saigon."

Darby was on a goodwill tour with a US congressman. How dare this stranger frighten the wits out of her by suggesting otherwise? Pepper braced herself against the door, lest the woman try to break in. "I don't believe you. Go away. I'm calling the sheriff." She started to close the door.

Edith Filmore rattled off a string of numbers: Pepper's unlisted phone number.

"He made me memorize your phone number and address. He insisted I had to know them 'without reference and without error.' "

Almost the first words that Pepper had heard Darby Baxter say were "without reference and without error." Those words had become their private mantra. Only Avivah, Saul, and Benny knew that; none of them would arrange this morbid practical joke. The tight knot in Pepper's stomach disappeared. The black hollow that replaced it wasn't an improvement.

"Stand away from the door."

The woman stepped away. Pepper scanned her empty yard through the small door opening before she slid off the chain and opened the door. The yard looked empty. Edith Filmore walked in, leaving a black leather purse and a baby's diaper bag on the porch. Pepper brought the bags inside and relocked the door.

Her unwanted guest was a large-boned, pigeon-breasted woman who either sewed her own clothes or had the world's best dressmaker. Her gray shirtwaist dress fit her corseted body perfectly.

Baby-duck pajamas had been a bad idea. Pepper pulled the

collar tight around her neck. "Come into the living room."

Edith Filmore sat in the upholstered armchair. Across the room, Pepper turned on the tri-light lamp to its highest setting. She turned to the next page in the book.

5 March 1975/0630 hours—Air America: Camp Zama, Japan, to Seoul, Korea, and Seoul to Saigon

Darby had lied to her, allowed her to believe he wasn't going anywhere near Vietnam. She should have suspected something was up when she got his last letter. It had been a little too breezy, a little too pat.

She rifled pages, skimming through lists, hand-drawn maps, and notes in several inks and handwritings. Some of the entries were in Vietnamese, but most were in handwriting she recognized all too well.

In her bedroom she had a cigar box full of love letters written in the same hand by Darby Randolph Baxter, Colonel, US Army Military Intelligence and US Army Special Forces. She was never sure exactly which one he belonged to. Some days she thought he didn't know, either.

This was Darby's field diary. All officers were supposed to keep them; Darby kept his religiously. Even when he was on leave, he carried a black notebook identical to this one, in case World War III broke out, and he had to take command of something, somewhere. She'd seen him write an occasional note in it.

Back a coon's age ago, when she was Captain Elizabeth Pepperhawk, US Army Nurse Corps, she'd held a security clearance. It hadn't been the top-secret clearance that Colonel Baxter held, but it had been enough for her to learn what did and didn't belong in civilian hands. An officer's field diary was classified information. Pepper skimmed the pages once more, afraid to allow her gaze to rest anywhere too long, least she read something she shouldn't see. She was a civilian now and had no more right to this notebook than Edith Filmore did.

The baby fussed. Miss Filmore, or was it Mrs. Filmore—the woman wore no wedding ring—Miss Filmore reached into the diaper bag and pulled out a small bottle. She plunked the nipple into the baby's mouth.

The baby had Vietnamese features. It wasn't very old, maybe five or six weeks. A down of fine black hair covered its head. Pepper couldn't decide if the baby was a boy or girl.

Miss Filmore said, "Read the last two pages in the book."

Near the book's end, writing and a rust-brown stain covered two pages. Reading the first lines drained blood from Pepper's head. Her living room contracted into darkness. She sat down hard on the couch and lowered her head between her knees until returning blood pounded in her head. From very far away, Miss Filmore asked if she was all right.

Of course she wasn't all right.

When color came back to her vision, Pepper stared at the stain that partially obscured some of the words. It wasn't a stain; it was a baby's footprint. The footprint's red-brown color was unique to dried blood.

Darby had written her a letter, then pressed an infant's foot— probably the same infant Miss Filmore held in her ample lap— into blood and made the footprint. A fingerprint, also in dried blood, had been pressed beside the footprint. Had Darby wanted to establish a macabre evidence chain?

Pepper read the letter slowly, taking in the shape of each word, trying to understand its meaning before moving to the next one.

Dearest,
There was no pooh-bah, and no elephant train. You're smart enough, and you've enough of a military background to figure out the rest.

Things weren't supposed to end like this: not us, not the war. I'm sorry. If we had had decades together, it would have never been long enough to show you how much I love you. Thank you sounds lame, but it's all I have time and strength to write. Thank you for everything.

The baby's mother once worked for me. I failed to save her, but her daughter deserves better. Please find Vietnamese parents to raise her. I promised Miss Filmore three thousand dollars from my estate if she delivers the baby safely to you. I know I can trust you to see that she is paid.

If a West Point graduate gets himself killed in a war, they write his name in a memorial book. I would be grateful if you made sure they put my name in that book.

October was my favorite time of year at The Point. The fall colors are beautiful and that month was always so full of promise for the coming year.

Don't waste time tying yourself in a knot over me. I want to die believing that I brought you more joy than tears. I could not love thee, dear, so much, loved I not honor more.

All my love—forever—Darby

Wasn't she supposed to faint? Scream? Burst into uncontrollable sobs? Pepper held her breath, waiting to see which one her body would choose. In the end, it chose verifying the initial intelligence report. A small, sarcastic voice in her head said that Darby would have been pleased that he had trained her so well.

"Who gave you this notebook?"

"An American."

"What did he look like?"

"Mid-thirties, blond, curly hair."

Stay calm. Lots of soldiers besides Darby were in their mid-thirties, blond, with curly hair.

"How tall was he?"

"I don't know. He was sitting on the floor. The electricity was

18

out, and my flashlight batteries were almost dead."

"Did you actually see him write the last pages in this note-book?"

"Yes."

Pepper leaned forward and wrapped her arms around herself. She pushed her fingernails into the soft spots at the back of each elbow. Her body was taking a recount, and it appeared that crying might win after all. Don't cry yet, she commanded herself. Listen. Get it right. Get every detail right. Darby always said that knowing a truth was better than not knowing. She bent her head and closed her eyes, prepared to focus on Miss Filmore's voice. "Tell me exactly what happened when you met this man."

"It was the night before Saigon fell. None of us had slept for two nights. The air-conditioning and most of the lights were out. The embassy's top floor was hot and dark. A hall ran the length of the building. People sat on the floor, waiting. The lights were on in a conference room at the end of that corridor. It was one big square of light in the distance.

"I tripped over a man's feet. His legs stuck out of a small alcove into the corridor. When I shined my flashlight on him, I saw a knife sticking in his side. He'd been stabbed."

Darby couldn't even get killed like a normal soldier. He had to embellish death by getting stabbed in the middle of a war. Pepper willed herself to remain absolutely still. And breathe. It was very important to keep breathing.

"I bent down; he grabbed my hand. When I saw he was hurt, I told him I would find a medic, but he wouldn't let go. He asked to borrow my flashlight. When he moved so he could sit up and write, I saw the baby. He'd laid her behind him, so his body protected her. He wrote what you read, then handed the notebook and the baby to me. I held her while he unwrapped her foot and made her footprint over what he'd written. Then he added his own thumbprint."

This wasn't just blood; it was Darby's blood. For the first time since nursing school, Pepper felt queasy at the site of blood.

"He made me memorize your name, address and phone number; promised me three thousand dollars to deliver the baby to you; and ordered me to go to the roof immediately to get on the next helicopter."

Even dying, Darby's last act would have been to issue an order.

Pepper rested her forehead on her palms, unable to stop the tears. She could live with crying quietly. She wasn't going to embarrass herself or Darby's memory with body-wracking sobs in front of a stranger. She eventually pulled in a ragged breath, and wiped her eyes unceremoniously with the heels of her hands. "Did you?"

Miss Filmore's image was blurred. "Did I what?"

"Did you go to the roof, or did you stay with him until he died?"

"I found a Marine and told him there was an injured American who needed a medic."

"An injured American? Not an injured soldier?"

"He wore civilian clothes; I assumed he was a civilian."

With the North Vietnamese literally at the outskirts of Saigon, a military intelligence officer pretending to be a civilian made sense, if you disregarded the fact that, out of uniform, Darby could be shot for spying. Darby was good at disregarding minor details like that. "Did you go back to him with the medic?"

"I went to the roof and waited for a helicopter."

Miss Filmore hadn't seen him die. And a Marine medic had gone to him. Pepper knew firsthand how skilled corpsmen were, how many men they'd brought back from the brink of death. Warm, blessed relief flowed through her. All right, somewhere in that mad confusion of abandoning the American embassy,

Darby had been hurt, not killed. He had to be somewhere in the military medical evacuation route from Vietnam to the States. "When did this happen?"

"Last Wednesday."

That was the day that Saigon had fallen. "What time?"

"The middle of the night. I wasn't keeping track of the exact time."

That was Wednesday; today was Sunday. Six days was a long time to be in medical transit, but with the whole Pacific Military Command coming unglued, who knew where Darby was or when he could get to a phone. He might call at any moment. Now she had a wonderful reason to stay home from work; she had to wait for Darby's call.

Miss Filmore said, "I know he died. His body was on the helicopter."

Pepper's carefully constructed medical evacuation scenario splintered. "What?"

"Just before my helicopter arrived, two Marines came up the stairs carrying a body wrapped in a blanket. I caught a glimpse of the man's shoes when they loaded him on the helicopter. The Marines told the pilot they weren't leaving an American's body behind."

Pepper scrabbled for one last, faint hope. "You're sure he was dead, not just wounded?"

"He was in a body bag. One of the Marines gave the pilot an envelope. He said to give it to Graves Registration."

"Where did your helicopter land?"

"The USS *Blue Ridge*."

The *Blue Ridge* was a Navy ship. That meant Darby's body was somewhere in the military Graves Registration system. Why hadn't the Army notified her? Pepper's shoulders slumped. She knew why: Darby's parents were listed as his next of kin. They'd sent the telegram, or the chaplain, to his family in Macon, Georgia.

Why hadn't his parents called her? She'd never met them, but surely Darby had told them about her? Maybe they didn't want to be the ones who broke the news to her. Maybe they didn't have her unlisted phone number. More likely, they were too grief-stricken or thought the Army had notified her, or any number of reasons that meant she'd had to learn about Darby's death from a stranger.

Miss Filmore set the empty formula bottle on a small table. The inexpert way she tried to burp the baby would never work.

Pepper stood. "Give her to me."

The baby felt so tiny; a sack of potatoes weighed more. Pepper walked around the room with the infant on her shoulder, gently patting her back. The baby gave a loud burp. "Good girl," Pepper said, moving the baby from her shoulder.

She stared into a pair of smoky blue-gray eyes. Not blue, not gray, but a combination of the two colors. She'd only seen one other pair of eyes like that in her life: Darby's eyes.

Pepper scrambled to remember her maternity nursing. All newborns had blue eyes. Blue eyes, not blue-gray. Newborns' eyes changed color at what age? She couldn't remember, but she could do arithmetic and count backwards. A nine-month pregnancy plus a six-week-old baby equaled ten and a half months. Ten and a half months matched exactly when Darby had made a clandestine trip to Vietnam, a trip even the Army didn't know about.

While she'd been in North Carolina worried sick about him, half a world away he was banging this baby's mother. Wait until—

A lump rose in Pepper's throat. *Until* would never happen again. "What's the baby's name?"

"I don't know."

Pepper held the baby with one hand while she picked up Darby's field diary and held it to the light. "The baby's mother once worked for me." How hard would it have been to use the baby's name in that sentence?

Blast Darby. The first two rules of military intelligence were (1) keeping quiet was better than telling a lie and (2) release information on a need-to-know basis. Need-to-know had lost its charm.

This baby was Darby's daughter. Pepper ran her finger over the baby's cheek. He would have loved her so much. He had loved her so much that he'd given up his life to get her to safety.

Miss Filmore squared her substantial shoulders. "I lost everything when I left Saigon: my clothes, my mother's jewelry, my books, my records, all of my souvenirs. I have nothing left except the clothes I'm wearing. I've washed and ironed this same dress every night. I have to have money. I want my three thousand dollars tomorrow morning."

Pepper wanted to scream, "You didn't lose everything. You're alive." Instead she managed, "I don't have three thousand dollars. You'll have to wait until Darby's will is probated."

"I want the money tomorrow morning, or I phone child welfare and tell them that you have this baby illegally."

"I have Darby's letter. That gives me the right to this baby!"

"Does it? Even if child welfare eventually agrees, they will pick her up and she'll be in foster care for months while they consider the matter."

Pepper knew she was right. Darby had given her a sacred trust and she wasn't about to give his daughter to strangers. "I can give you three hundred."

"Three thousand in cash by tomorrow noon, or I make a phone call."

She'd find a way to raise the money, even if she had to risk losing her homestead in order to get it. "Meet me in the lobby of the Pack Square Library at noon tomorrow."

Avivah Rosen fumbled with her house keys, finally opening the front door. Her shoulder bounced off the door frame. The Sleepwalking Policeman. It sounded like a bad British mystery novel.

Every muscle ached and her eyes burned. Was she coming down with something? She'd come down with something all right: butt-kicking anger toward the Army, the US government, and the world in general.

Pepper's reaction to losing Saigon was to hide in her bed, but Avivah preferred pounding out reports on the sticky keys of a manual typewriter she'd found tucked in an unused corner of the police station. Her "to do" basket had never been so clean. If she were lucky, tonight she'd fall into a deep sleep, and wake up in time to go to work.

The house was dark, but by the light coming through the windows from the yard, she saw an outline of Pepper sitting in the dark at the kitchen table. Avivah sniffed the air but didn't smell booze. Be thankful for small mercies.

Pepper looked up when Avivah walked into the kitchen. Sheets of tears covered her cheeks. "Darby is dead. This is his daughter, and if I don't raise three thousand dollars by tomorrow at noon, child welfare will take her away from me."

Obviously, staying late to finish reports hadn't been a good idea.

CHAPTER 2

The next morning, Avivah scrawled her name on the loan application, putting her car and her bank account on the line if Pepper defaulted on loan payments. She handed the pen to Saul. She didn't know what he had put up for collateral. Pepper had been determined to put up the homestead for a second mortgage. It had taken Avivah and Saul a long time to convince her that trying to keep up two mortgage payments was insane. Pepper had settled for putting up investment bonds she'd bought while she was in the Army.

The banker hooked his thumbs in his vest and beamed at Pepper. "Renovating an old house is always a good investment, particularly for a growing family, though I'm surprised your husband isn't the one countersigning the loan."

"I'm single."

The banker stiffened.

She shifted the baby from one hip to the other. "I'm babysitting for a friend. Her mother—"

Avivah nudged Pepper. They'd gotten the loan, and one of Pepper's protracted stories could queer the deal. Pepper looked at her, and said simply, "Her mother is out of town for a few days."

The banker, acting a degree cooler toward them, ticked the papers against his desk to straighten the edges. "One of our tellers will set up a separate account for the loan funds. That way you can keep track of your building costs in one place."

Pepper said, "I want the money in cash: fifties and twenties."

"I beg your pardon?"

"Cash. I can have cash, can't I?"

"We don't usually handle loans that way."

"You have three thousand dollars in cash on hand, don't you?"

"Of course we do."

"We'll wait in the lobby until it's ready."

In the lobby, Avivah said in a low voice, "I wish you'd told me you were getting cash. I'd have come armed."

Pepper said, in an equally low voice, "Miss Filmore said cash. Besides, all we're going to do is walk a few blocks to the library and hand over the money."

Half an hour later, a teller escorted them into a tiny carrel used for viewing safe-deposit box contents. She expertly counted out three thousand dollars in fifties and twenties. It made an untidy pile. Pepper stuffed the money into a pink-and-gray cosmetic bag. The bag's sides bulged; on the second try, she managed to close the zipper. She hid the bag at the bottom of the diaper bag covered by diapers and bottles.

When they came out of the bank, Avivah scanned the tree-shaded street in both directions. It was a perfect spring morning, except for having a baby illegally in tow and three thousand dollars in a frayed cosmetic case. She couldn't think of a better definition for a policeman's nightmare.

They walked three abreast down the street toward the Pack Square Library.

The baby fussed and Pepper jiggled her. "Sweetheart, you have the attention span of a gnat. You have to learn patience."

Avivah had babysat a flock of younger cousins, most of whom were now close to voting age, but she recalled that patience wasn't an infant's strong suit. "How are you going to care for her?"

"My boss carries on about the sanctity of reproductive choice and women being allowed to breast-feed in public. Letting me bring a baby to work will give her a chance to practice what she preaches. She won't be trouble. You make her comfortable in her basket and she stays until you come to retrieve her."

Pepper never had been a person who learned new lessons the easy way.

Saul said tentatively, "I could take care of her."

Both women stared at him.

"I work at home. I could see to her while I'm writing."

Saul was a lovely man who lost track of time when he was doing a phone interview or rushing to meet a deadline. They'd already sacrificed two teakettles and several casserole meals to Saul's headspace wandering off into journalism.

Avivah offered, "Maybe Lorraine could take care of her. She has a nursery ready to go, and she lives next door."

"Lorraine is due to deliver any day. Pregnant women rarely arrive on the labor-and-delivery unit with a newborn already in tow."

Saul asked, "Do Lorraine and Benny know that Darby is dead?"

Pepper quietly said, "Not yet." When Avivah frowned, she added, "I didn't want to wake them in the middle of the night, and I didn't get a chance before Benny left for school this morning."

Avivah said, "Benny won't be happy that you didn't ask him to contribute collateral toward the loan."

"Benny's got enough money worries."

"He'll be unhappy that you didn't let him decide that."

"Then he's going to have to be unhappy."

Avivah opened her mouth to protest, and then closed it. Pepper and Benny would have to work this out between them. Twenty minutes later, she pushed open one of the library's heavy glass-and-brass doors. The lobby was empty.

Avivah said, "We wait ten minutes. If she doesn't show up, we go back to the bank, and deposit that money in an account."

A few minutes later a taxi pulled up outside and a woman got out.

Pepper handed the baby to Saul. He asked, "That her?"

"Yes."

Edith Filmore wore the same fitted gray dress and the black purse Pepper had described. The dress was clean and ironed, but it had a fine white soap line near the hem. For a moment Avivah felt a degree of sympathy for the woman. It evaporated when she thought about risking her car and savings because this woman refused to wait until Darby's will had been probated.

Miss Filmore hurried toward Pepper. Her breath came in deep, gulping gasps. "You're early." She made it sound like an indictment.

"You're late."

A library patron passed between the two women, looked at each face in turn, and then hurried double-time through the heavy doors.

Pepper led them into a deserted reference section near the front door. Placing the diaper bag on a waist-high empty shelf, she dug deep into the bag for the cosmetic case. "Count it, then get out of my life. I never want to see or hear from you again."

Avivah escorted Miss Filmore to a ladies' washroom and stood guard outside a stall. She heard the case's zipper open, the flipping of pieces of paper, and the zipper again. The stall door opened. "It's all there," Miss Filmore said, with obvious relief.

Avivah held her badge open in front of the woman's face. "I'm an Asheville City Police detective. The man in the lobby with us is a journalist, Saul Eisenberg. Maybe you've read his stories in the *New York Times*?"

Miss Filmore's voice wavered. "I don't think so."

"This is all you're getting. If you ask for even one dollar, or if a child-welfare worker ever shows up on Miss Pepperhawk's doorstep, I'll have you up on extortion charges. Is that clear?"

"I wanted what I'd been promised."

"I advise you to go straight to a bank and deposit that money."

Pepper didn't protest when Saul and Avivah offered to take the baby. Maybe Avivah was right. She had friends who wanted to help, and something important—something only she could do—was best done quickly.

She found an old desk by a radiator in the most deserted section of the library. From her backpack, she removed a box of note cards, a fountain pen, and a slightly creased business card. Like a blind person reading Braille, her fingertip traced the embossed General Zachery S. Fairclough, US Army (retired), and the Tennessee address.

Darby had given her the card last July, on his last visit to the homestead before he shipped out for Camp Zama, Japan. "If you need anything while I'm gone, contact him. He knows all about you."

Never in her entire life had she imagined that she would have the private address of a person like Darby's friend. Darby had brought both love and power into her life. A fat lot of good it had done him.

Using the general's first name was beyond the pale. Finally she wrote:

Sir:

She stared at the single word for a long time.

I regret to inform you that Colonel Baxter died in the evacuation from Saigon. As he lay dying . . .

The pen made a ragged sound, and a blob of black ink spread over the pure white paper. Pepper's eyes blurred. The Dewey decimal numbers, marking the end of the nearest book stack, was watery through her tears. Who the hell was going to waste a fine spring day on *122 Causation; 123 Determinism & Indeterminism; 124 Teleology?* She could die back here without anyone knowing or caring. She surrendered again to tears, allowing them once more to wash down her face and into her clothing.

She tore the soiled card into pieces. Damn it, she should have seen this coming. Darby had spent over twenty years in the military, if she counted the Georgia Military Academy and West Point. He'd been wounded twice; the second time had almost killed him. He who lived by the sword, died by the sword. What stupid cockiness had possessed her to expect Darby to leave the military alive?

And a baby. At least, that she could understand. Being in a war zone reset libido over the red line. Attractive guys in sweaty fatigues had always set her hormones flowing, but she'd been too entrapped in a net of Catholic guilt to do anything about it. Darby had cut her free from that net. If she'd gone back to Vietnam, met those men again within the sound of gunfire, well—she wasn't going to cast stones in Darby's direction. She whispered, "I forgive you. I'm damned furious, but I forgive you."

She reached in her bag for a cotton handkerchief and dried her face. She clutched her fountain pen, and began a fresh card.

> *Sir:*
>
> *I regret to inform you that Colonel Baxter died in the evacuation of Saigon.*
>
> *As he lay dying, he wrote the last two pages in this notebook. They are a private matter, which I will handle.*
>
> *I once had enough of a security clearance to know that a military intelligence officer's field diary doesn't belong in civil-*

ian hands. It is my personal belief that the last two pages do not belong in military hands.

This notebook, Colonel Baxter's eyewitness account of the war's last weeks, is his final gift to the military. Life would be much simpler if I could razor out the questionable pages. I hesitate to admit that Colonel Baxter's paranoia reaches to me from the grave, but it does. He said, "Altering or destroying any part of a classified document gives people who want to destroy what the military stands for a golden opportunity to assume that something nasty was swept under the rug."

I don't want his legacy to be tainted by the slightest suspicion. I am confident you have resources to ensure that the relevant military information—minus the last two pages—reaches the appropriate people.

Colonel Baxter valued your friendship immensely. Thank you for all you did to guide and advise him.

Elizabeth Pepperhawk, formerly Captain, US Army Nurse Corps

You bastard, your guidance and advice got him killed. She slid the field diary into a padded envelope, and addressed it. On the walk from the library to the post office, warm spring sun cleared her head.

Avivah was right. Benny was going to be angry and hurt that she hadn't told him about Darby's death. The truth was that she couldn't face Benny's "I told you so."

Benny once served in Darby's command and had a grudging respect for him—sort of, most days, when he wasn't worrying about Darby being a prat who would eventually break Pepper's heart.

Benny, Lorraine and their boys lived next door. It was a matter of hours before one of them wandered over to visit and saw the baby; then the whole story would come out. The longer she waited, the more hurt they would be. Benny would be at his part-time job by now.

After she'd mailed the diary, Pepper walked the few blocks from the post office to Skoufalos Electronics Repair on Haywood Street. The shop occupied a tiny two-story, nineteenth-century storefront squeezed between two much larger renovated buildings.

She pushed the door open and a bell tinkled in the back of the shop. Seventy-five years ago, the store sold dry goods. Now, secondhand radios, record players, toasters, and vacuum cleaners filled the shelves and glass-fronted cases. Pepper waited for Yanni Skoufalos to appear from the workshop in back. "Mr. Skoufalos? It's Pepper, Benny's friend. Hello?"

Silence. She'd dropped in to visit Benny enough times that she felt okay walking to the back of the display area and pushing aside the heavy black curtain that separated the store from the work area. "Mr. Skoufalos? Benny?"

A key and a hand-printed cardboard sign—"*Back in 15 minutes. You wait, please*"—hung from a nail beside the curtain. Mr. Skoufalos always locked the front door and posted the sign, even when he stepped out to buy a paper from the sidewalk box down the street.

Maybe he was in the cavernous basement storage room. Pepper didn't want to leave the front door open and the shop unattended. She went to the front door, flipped the placard from *Open* to *Closed*, and locked the door.

A moment later, she stood at the top of the pitch-black basement stairs. Nothing happened when she flicked the light switch. She yelled, "Hello," several times into the blackness; her voice echoed. The hairs stood up more on the back of her neck. She wasn't going into that darkness alone.

Mr. Skoufalos's apartment was over the shop. She went out the back door and quickly climbed the white, wooden stairs to the apartment's door. A set of keys dangled from the door lock. Not good. She touched the keys. They were hot, the kind of hot metal gets when it had spent hours in the sun. This was more than not good. Tentatively, she tried the doorknob. The door was unlocked. Not good moved to really not good.

Yanni Skoufalos was in his late forties or early fifties, solidly built, a man who ate hearty meals, drank wine, and never exercised. What if he'd come out of his apartment, felt a heart attack coming on, went back inside, and collapsed? Pepper mentally reviewed the steps of CPR before she opened the door. The apartment was silent.

"Mr. Skoufalos, it's Elizabeth Pepperhawk. Are you all right, sir?"

Silence answered. Pepper went in and closed the door behind her. The apartment was surprisingly open and airy for a second-story apartment wedged between two other buildings. Stark white walls and light-colored wooden floors compensated for the lack of windows along the long walls. The oilcloth on the kitchen table was spotless, clean dishes sat in the dish drainer. Nothing was out of place in the living room, the bathroom, or the first bedroom. Each empty room lowered the possibility she would have to do CPR.

In the second bedroom, the one Yanni obviously used, a closet door stood open. On the shelf above the clothes were two matched suitcases: a small one, and a train case. The shelf next to the small case was empty, a hole the right size to accommodate the large piece of a set of matched luggage. Several empty wire clothes hangers hung tangled around one another. Maybe she wasn't the only one who had received bad news recently.

A small box was attached to a corner of one bedroom wall. A faint outline inside the box showed where something rectangular had been tacked to the back of the box for a long time. This had been some kind of a home altar or shrine for a religious icon, candles, beads, or whatever Greek Orthodox used. The box held a five-by-seven black-and-white photograph of a woman. A laminated obituary was tucked into one corner of the photograph's dime-store frame.

Mrs. Marta Skoufalos. Dead two years. Survived by her husband, Yanni, and a list of brothers, sisters, aunts, uncles, and cousins. Likely Yanni had been called away suddenly to tend to one of his deceased wife's relatives. Pepper let out a long breath.

She locked the apartment's door and went down the stairs and in through the shop's back door. She was halfway through the workshop when a man's voice said from a dark corner, "I have a gun and the skill to use it. Stop where you are."

Pepper's heart leapt in her chest. She put her fists on her hips. "Benny Kirkpatrick, you'd better not have a gun or Lorraine will be furious."

A shadow moved from behind a stack of boxes. "Pepper?"

Benny, holding a length of pipe, moved into a dim light circle made by the forty-watt bulb. Sweat glistened on his bald head. His round face was creased. "What are you doing here? Where's Yanni?"

"I don't know." She dug the keys from her pocket. "These were in his apartment door. They were hot, like they'd been in the sun for a long time. The apartment was unlocked. Everything is in order, but some clothes and a suitcase are gone. Maybe he had a family emergency."

"Yanni has no family."

"His wife's family, then. I saw her obituary and photograph in the little shrine."

"He hasn't kept in contact. Did you check the basement?"

"The basement lights aren't working."

"They worked on Friday." Benny walked to the top of the basement stairs and flipped the switch. It didn't work for him either. He reached for an industrial-strength flashlight at the back of a high shelf, held it in one hand and the length of pipe in the other. "Stay here," he said over his shoulder to Pepper. He called in a louder voice, "Yanni? It's Benny. You down here?"

Pepper followed him down the stairs. Dark shapes towered over them. "What is this stuff?"

"Yanni's version of spare parts. He haunts flea markets and garage sales for anything he can cannibalize."

Pepper wished he'd used other words beside haunts and cannibalize, which had unpleasant associations in a black basement.

Benny shined his flashlight at a fuse box. "Here's why the lights won't go on."

Half the sockets were empty. A printed sign, taped below the box, proclaimed in big, black words:

Buncombe Electrical Systems

Danger! Repairs in Progress!

Do not replace fuses!

The basement smelled of dust, machine oil, damp cardboard, and old brick walls. At least Yanni was neat. Old vacuum cleaners were all together; old televisions were arranged neatly on industrial metal shelves; sagging boxes of unknown parts were arranged in some order that escaped Pepper. All was in order except for one missing owner. Ten dusty minutes later she followed Benny back up the stairs. "What do we do now?"

He laid down the flashlight and pipe. "I'm going to ask the other shopkeepers in this block if they saw him this morning. Phone Buncombe Electrical Systems and see when their repairman was here. I know the basement lights worked Friday because I was down there scrounging parts."

She watched his retreating back moving toward the front of the store, and suddenly didn't want to be alone here, even for a few minutes. She called out, "Darby is dead."

He whirled around. "What?"

"Darby died in the American embassy in Saigon last Wednesday."

"Son of a bitch!"

Benny came to Pepper and collected her into his arms. Under his T-shirt, his burn scars along the right side of his chest pressed into her skin. A different kind of silence surrounded them, one that had included the tropical smell of rice paddies. Vietnam kaleidoscoped through Pepper's head, the images flitting too fast to name, but not nearly fast enough to avoid leaving impressions on her soul. She found the courage to say the one thing she'd been holding back since Sunday night. "I fucked up, didn't I?"

"What do you mean?"

"You tried to warn me. You said that Darby would break my heart."

He hugged her again, his body moving in a small rocking motion. "You didn't fuck up. I may not have always been complimentary about Darby, but I had this secret hope that I was wrong and that you two were right for each other. I am so sorry."

"Thank you."

"For what?"

"For not saying 'I told you so.' "

Benny brushed damp, stray hair from her forehead. "Do Special Forces know yet?"

"I don't know."

Special Forces—Green Berets—had been Darby's Army family. Benny had been part of that family, too.

The United States Army had had two hundred years to perfect the process for notifying blood kin: the telegram, the chaplain or family liaison, and the letter from the commanding officer. They had also had two hundred years to perfect the unofficial notification—which, instead of somber men appearing at a front door, took place in bars—starting with the Special Forces bar on Smoke Bomb Hill at Fort Bragg. A beret or other headgear would be slapped down on the bar, followed by, "Baxter's dead." The inevitable stunned silence. "When? How?"

Darby would die in a dozen different ways, in twice that number of places before the news spun around the world. Details didn't matter. What mattered was that enough of a representative military contingent showed up at his funeral.

She didn't want to think about Darby's funeral right now, but she would have to soon. She didn't dare miss it. "Will you take me to his funeral?"

"Of course, and I'll make sure the word is out on the Beret grapevine."

"Don't mentioned he died in Saigon, okay?"

Benny let her go. The front of his T-shirt was damp from their basement excursion and from the close way he'd held her. "Why not?"

"I think he wasn't supposed to be there."

"How did you learn he had died?"

"From unofficial sources."

He frowned. "Reliable sources?"

"Eyewitness."

Benny held up his hands. "Don't tell me. I have no need to know. Hell, pretty lady, words can't—"

"They can't, and don't call me pretty lady anymore, okay?" She choked on the words. It was a joke left over from an Army recruiting campaign that used the phrase *the most beautiful girl in the world is an Army nurse.* Darby had shortened it to calling all Army nurses *pretty lady;* Benny had learned it from Darby. Code words for things about honor and caring that none of the three of them could afford to take too seriously and keep sane. "Darby would expect us to pull up our socks and keep going."

"I expect so."

"Buncombe Electrical Systems is probably in the phone book."

"Try the Yellow Pages."

Only after Benny left to talk to the other shopkeepers did Pepper realize she hadn't said anything about Darby's daughter.

CHAPTER 3

When Pepper came from using the phone, Benny stood in front of the open cash register. He said, "Anything?"

"Nobody named Skoufalos or matching Yanni's description has been admitted to a hospital today. Should we ask Avivah to check the morgue and the jail?"

Benny massaged the back of his neck. "I can't imagine Yanni in jail. This is all so weirdly normal. The electrician claims to have arrived at eight thirty. When he left, Yanni was opening the store. The usual float is in the cash register. Apparently Yanni didn't do any business between the time he opened and when he left. None of the other shopkeepers saw him leave. He washed his breakfast dishes, made his bed, and packed, but he left Marta's photo behind."

"It looks like he took something from the shrine."

"Yeah, it does look like something else was pinned there, but I have no idea what. I was never in Yanni's bedroom before."

Benny reached under the counter, pulled out a ledger in which he wrote something, and then slammed the book shut. The money he counted out from the cash drawer wasn't very much. "I hate to do this, but Yanni pays me on Monday. He owes me for last week."

Pepper ran her fingers over the smooth side of a wooden radio cabinet. It was easier to look at wood grain than Benny's embarrassed face. "It's your money for work you already did."

"It feels like robbing the till."

"It's not."

Benny shrugged and closed the cash register.

"How many more GI Bill checks do you have coming?"

"One."

Pepper consulted her running bank balances that she carried in her head. She didn't like the figures, but even having to pay a mortgage and a loan payment, she was in better financial shape than Benny. "I'm making your mortgage payment next month. Call it a graduation present."

Benny slammed the cash drawer shut. "Let's call it what it is, okay? I can't afford to support a wife and two kids, much less three."

A little imp Pepper never liked whispered in her ear that Benny should have thought of that before he got Lorraine pregnant. Blast the Catholic Church's antipathy to birth control. She shooed the imp away. "Give it a rest. You won't be a student forever. Lorraine will have the baby; you'll graduate and get a full-time job. A few months from now life will be better."

"Paid attention to the news lately? Highest unemployment rates since nineteen forty. There are precious few full-time jobs, especially for a thirty-two-year-old guy fresh out of tech school."

"A thirty-two-year-old veteran who did two tours in Vietnam and earned a couple of medals for valor and a Purple Heart. Your best bet, hire a vet." The old public service advertisement sounded worn around the edges.

She did pay attention to the news. Instead of being first in war, first in peace, and first in the hearts of their countrymen, veterans these days were most often first in the food-stamp lines. "You don't have to solve the whole unemployment mess. All you need is one job."

Benny placed both palms on the counter and leaned forward, his head drooping. "I know. It's so damned hard. If your clinic hadn't sprung for free prenatal care for Lorraine, I don't know what we would have done."

His school backpack lay on the counter. From it Benny removed a slick tri-folded brochure, which he handed to Pepper. She opened it, and her stomach went into free fall.

Are you a veteran?

Did Uncle Sam teach you skills that are going to waste?

Executive civilian advisors needed immediately. We pay top dollar for what you know, and are willing to teach. Six-month, one-year, and two-year contracts available immediately. Earn full medical benefits, free airfare, and subsidized quarters. Call us today to find out how much your skills are worth.

At the bottom of the page was an address and phone number in New York City. Pepper handed the brochure back to Benny. Her mouth tasted sour. "Executive mercenaries are more like it. I can't believe you're even thinking about this."

"I wouldn't be wearing a uniform or carrying a gun. They want me for my electrical knowledge: how to repair radios and set up communication networks."

"You've already called them."

"Only to get information. A six-month contract, starting the week after I graduate, will get me back here by Christmas with enough money to pull us out of the hole. If I can't find a job after I get back, they will guarantee me another six-month contract, starting after a month's leave."

"What does Lorraine say about this?"

Benny zipped his pack closed.

"In other words, you haven't told her."

"Like I said, I was collecting information."

"I already have to bury Darby. If I ended up burying you, too, it would kill me. Think about that before you sign some stupid contract."

41

★ ★ ★ ★ ★

Pepper arrived home to find baby things all over her kitchen. "What did you do, buy out the store?"

Avivah hoisted a case of baby formula into a kitchen cabinet. "Buying case lots was cheaper."

Saul carried a stroller in through the back door, and set it in the middle of the kitchen. "Watch how clever this is. Set it up this way and she can sit in it; set it up the other way, and it's a bed. We got two things for the price of one. Isn't that clever?"

Pepper agreed that it was. "What do I owe you?"

Saul grinned. "Nothing today. Have you seen what they're selling for babies? I've got an idea for a magazine article on shopping for babies, something like 'The Cradle of Consumerism.' "

Avivah shut the cabinet door. "Enough about money for today. When Saul's credit-card bill comes in, we'll sort this out. Saul can go to his dinner alone, if you'd rather I stay home."

Saul was guest speaker at a North Carolina newspaper awards dinner. "And deprive you of banquet food and lengthy thank-you speeches? I'm fine, really I am."

An hour later, after her housemates had left, Pepper wandered around the house, holding the baby against one shoulder. The baby. She couldn't keep calling her that.

Darby had been in pain and shock when he wrote his last letter. Shock did funny things to people. Maybe Darby couldn't remember the baby's name, or he thought he'd included it in the letter.

Under the living-room window was a low bookcase where she and Avivah stuck the old books they'd carted around for years. *Anne of Green Gables.* Anne was a fine name. She held the baby out in front of her. "You want to be Anne?" The baby didn't object.

Anne of something. Anne of Madison County? Anne of

Saigon? What sounded Vietnamese? Duc To did. Duc To was a Special Forces A-camp near Pleiku in the central highlands. Benny talked about it. If there was an Anne of Green Gables, why couldn't there be an Anne of Duc To?

She said the name out loud. "Anne Duc To." It sounded Vietnamese. It would do.

Darby wanted Vietnamese parents for Anne. Pepper had no idea where to start to give Darby what he wanted.

She'd encountered plenty of indigenous workers on the hospital compound in Qui Nhon: the mama-sans who did her laundry and cleaned the wards; the cooks' helpers, a young amputee who ran the tailor's kiosk. He had sewn Pepper's new rank on her fatigues when she made captain. She hadn't known his name. In the year she'd been in Vietnam, she'd never once been inside a Vietnamese house, church, school, or store. Everything she knew about Vietnamese culture came filtered through her GI experience and was, in other words, useless. She'd have to start from scratch.

She looked up *Vietnam* and *Vietnamese* in the phone book, but without success. The emergency room's interpreter had been named Mr. Than, or possibly Mr. Tieu. She checked both names, but found nothing.

A big, black limousine pulled into their parking area; a young man in a dark suit got out. He gave a steadying hand to help an old woman get out of the backseat. The old woman was swathed entirely in black.

Pepper ran through a list of neighbors, local busybodies, and extended families—her own and Avivah's—without a clue about who this woman was. Saul's family didn't come calling unannounced.

An old woman dressed in black fit one person: Nana Kate, Darby's formidable doyenne grandmother! So the Baxter clan had sent a representative after all. She didn't know whether to

43

be pleased or terrified.

Darby really, really had intended for her to meet his family, but every time they planned a trip to Georgia, someone got murdered.

Would the matriarch of the extended Baxter clan travel all the way from Macon, Georgia, to make a condolence call? You bet she would. Nana Kate was a Southern woman "of a certain age." It was an age that had absorbed proper Southern behavior through its pores.

Pepper laid Anne in her stroller/bed. Anne made happy, squealing noises, and jiggled her arms and legs. All she'd done since she arrived was eat and sleep, but now she seemed fascinated by the toy that Saul had hung from the stroller's canopy. This was one hell of a time for Anne to perk up. Even if Pepper shoved her stroller in a bedroom, she had a feeling Anne wouldn't lie quietly until Nana Kate left. What in the world was she going to say to Nana Kate about the baby?

The doorbell rang.

Pepper scooped up stacks of magazines from the coffee table and shoved them under her couch. She grabbed a milk-stained glass, brushed her sweatshirt sleeve over the table, and ran to the kitchen to deposit the glass in the sink.

The doorbell rang again. Pepper was grateful that the patchy discoloration on her baby-stained jeans was formula and not something earthier. She opened the door. "Yes?"

The young man wore a plastic name tag that said *Dave* and underneath *Atlanta Limousine Service*. Nana Kate had not only come all the way from Macon, she'd hired a car and driver.

Nana Kate tapped her cane once on the porch. "You may wait for me."

Dave touched his fingers to his cap brim. "Yes, ma'am."

She must be baking in her black wool coat, black gloves, and veiled hat. The one spot of color was her gold-headed cane. She handed Pepper an engraved card.

Mrs. Katherine Wright
Macon

"I've come to call on Miss Elizabeth Pepperhawk. Is she receiving?"

All Pepper had to do was say, in an appropriately sepulchral voice, "I'm sorry, Miss Pepperhawk has gone into seclusion," and Mrs. Katherine Wright—aka Nana Kate—would leave her calling card and go away. Even in a shiny black car with a driver named Dave, five hours here and another five back to Macon would be a long trip for an old woman.

The nuns at Pepper's convent school had taught her how a proper Southern woman handled all social situations, including condolence calls. Pepper extended her right hand and Nana Kate shook it. Through the suede gloves, the old woman's hand felt bony and birdlike. Pepper randomly strung together stock sentences from Southern Etiquette 101. "I'm Elizabeth Pepperhawk. Darby told me so much about you. I am indebted to you for coming all this way. Please, come in."

Once inside, Nana Kate divested herself of her gloves and coat. She lifted the veil and set it expertly on top of her hat.

Pepper gazed upon the Sphinx, and found that she was after all only a very old woman. She was a beautifully aged woman whose clear skin probably never faced the sun without a parasol or sunbonnet. Her white hair was pulled into a bun at the back of her neck. She smelled of face powder and a light, flowery eau de toilette water. Jet-black earrings dangled from enlarged holes in her pierced ears. Her eyes looked sad, but not grief-stricken. Nana Kate had been born twenty years after the Civil War ended. She was probably a lot more accustomed to grief than Pepper was.

The women had just entered the living room when Anne let

out a juicy squeal.

Nana Kate stopped in the arch that separated hall from living room. "There is a child."

Her cane thumped forcefully on each second step. She bent to peer into the stroller and her body seemed to collapse.

Pepper hurried forward and guided her to an armchair. Nana Kate had survived Reconstruction, supported votes for women, organized Red Cross work parties through two world wars, and endured the Great Depression. If she died here, in this dusty living room, Pepper would be left to explain to Darby's family how a pair of infant's eyes killed her.

She tried to surreptitiously count Nana Kate's pulse, but the old woman withdrew her hand from Pepper's touch. The brief contact had at least assured Pepper that her heart was not only beating, but that the beat was strong and regular.

"May I offer you coffee?" Coffee would be a lot easier than "May I explain to you how your grandson came to father that child?"

Nana Kate straightened. "That would be most thoughtful. My driver would appreciate a cold drink."

Always remember the hired help.

Pepper had a porcelain coffee service that she'd inherited from her grandmother. By the time the coffee perked, she'd supplied Dave with a hastily made sandwich and iced tea, and set a tray with newly washed coffeepot, cups, sugar, cream, and a plate of lemon cookies. When she returned to the living room, Nana Kate had moved a straight-back chair closer to Anne's stroller and was jiggling the handle in a practiced motion.

Pepper willed her own hand to be rock-steady pouring coffee. "Her name is Anne."

Nana Kate set the cup and saucer on a side table without taking a sip. "I owe you an apology. When I saw the baby, I harbored a wicked hope that you and my grandson had been indiscreet. I am sorry. This is obviously not your child."

All Pepper had to say was four words, "Anne is Darby's child," and Nana Kate's life would change forever. So would hers, and Anne's. Nana Kate thought that she and Darby producing an illegitimate child would have been indiscreet. What would she consider Darby and a Vietnamese woman producing a child? Pepper didn't know which frightened her more, that Nana Kate would reject Anne, or that she'd sweep her up and take her away in a big, black car to be raised by Darby's family. If Darby had wanted Anne to go to his parents, he would have sent her there.

"I'm babysitting. Her parents are away."

She'd told the banker that the mother was out of town. Now she'd created two fictitious parents. If she kept this up, Anne would acquire siblings, aunts, uncles, and a family dog. Pepper sought refuge in one Southern certainty—being a good hostess. "Cream or sugar?"

Nana Kate picked up her cup and held it out. "Cream and one sugar, please."

Pepper's heart stopped tap-dancing in her chest. The living room light wasn't the greatest; at her age, Nana Kate likely had less-than-perfect vision. Thank goodness the old woman hadn't noticed that the baby had Darby's eyes.

Nana Kate sipped her coffee, and then set her cup down again. "My grandson was fond of you. Fond is too mild a word. He loved you deeply. I assume he made that clear to you?"

Pepper tried to ignore the hard knot in the middle of her chest. "He was very clear about that."

"He implied that you drove him crazy."

Pepper smiled. It was the first time she remembered smiling in the past twenty-four hours. "That feeling was mutual, too."

"Darby was a difficult child; he knew his own mind from a young age. We must comfort ourselves that God called him home while he was doing what he loved most. Those young men in his command will profit from his exemplary behavior in the aftermath of that tragic accident."

Tilt. No matter how the Army sliced, diced, or compressed it, dying of a stab wound in the American embassy in Saigon could not be described as a tragic accident. She had told Benny that Darby wasn't supposed to be in Saigon. If she were right, what cover story had the Army concocted for Darby's family?

Nana Kate rested both hands on her gold cane head. "I assume shipping his body from Japan is contingent upon the Army completing its investigation of the training accident. It will be a military funeral, of course. I trust you won't find that distasteful."

Tilting moved into reeling. If the Army's official story was that Darby died in Japan in some mythical training exercise, his name wouldn't go into the West Point memorial book. Pepper had taken that West Point stuff to be a dying man's poignant musings about his golden youth. What if he did want his name, spelled correctly, in that book?

Even dying, had Darby suspected that the Army would lie about his death? He loved codes and ciphers. Had he been trying to get a coded message to her?

"Miss Pepperhawk, are you all right?"

Pepper blinked and Nana Kate came back into focus. "I hadn't thought about Darby's funeral. Of course it must be a military funeral."

"You will sit as part of our family, and join us in the receiving line at the wake."

Pepper had never imagined meeting Darby's extended family for the first time at a funeral home. Darby Baxter owed her big-time; if God gave them the chance to be together in the hereafter, she intended to take it up with him. "That's very kind of you."

"He should have made you part of our family a long time ago." The old woman's voice softened. "After he came home wounded from his second tour in Vietnam, I was afraid for him. After he met you, he regained a lightness and hope I had despaired of seeing again. I came to thank you for that."

Time passed before either woman could speak again.

After Nana Kate and Dave left, Pepper got Anne ready for bed, but the baby wasn't sleepy. She was content to lie in Pepper's bed, and have Pepper play this-little-piggy on her toes.

Pepper's fingers were going to market, but her brain was bound for a lot darker place.

According to Nana Kate, the Camp Zama commander phoned Darby's parents personally. During routine field exercises, some enlisted men had become trapped in a truck under a damaged high-tension wire. Darby, who had been an umpire for the exercise, saved them, but he had been electro-cuted in the process. CPR failed to revive him.

It was perfect. Anyone who had known Darby more than ten minutes would believe that story. She would have, too, except that the Army didn't know she had three aces in the hole.

First ace: she knew the military. Colonels weren't umpires for routine training maneuvers. That duty fell to less senior officers.

The second ace rested in her dresser, in a cigar box full of Darby's letters. In his last letter from Japan Darby had bitched about being assigned to escort VIPs on a tour of Pacific military bases. A cover story, Pepper saw now, that included a coded message about elephant trains.

The Viet Cong used elephants on the Ho Chi Minh Trail. While Viet Cong soldiers moved silently through the jungle, elephants didn't. They made so much noise that US artillery easily zeroed in on them. In Vietnam parlance, "to ride an elephant train" was to be ordered to do something distasteful, in some cases, downright dangerous.

Bother! Darby had told her that he was heading into danger, and she'd missed it.

Her third ace was Darby's field diary and his daughter. That was more than an ace; that was the winning hand.

If some senior officer was covering his ass because he'd messed up by sending Darby to Vietnam, she wasn't about to play along. The Army's fabricated story allowed Darby to die a hero, but in a training exercise. He'd died in combat, in a real war, and she intended to see his name where it belonged, in the West Point memorial book.

If you are captured or killed, the secretary will disavow any knowledge.

It was a line from an old TV show. How much of this mess had been Darby's own doing?

Congress had forbidden further US military involvement in Vietnam. Was sending one officer further involvement? To congressmen who'd voted vociferously against further aid, it would be. If Darby had been in Vietnam with the Army's blessing, someone was in deep doo-doo. The questions were how many someones and how far up the chain of command? Darby taking leave and going to Vietnam without the Army's blessing also created a lot of doo-doo options.

Nine months and six weeks ago Darby *had* taken leave and gone to Vietnam for personal reasons without the Army's knowledge or permission. That ruse had worked too well, considering the piggy-toed baby now falling asleep on Pepper's bed. If it worked once, Darby would be tempted to use it again.

She had proof the Army had lied. All she had to do was tell Saul that Darby's field diary existed, and where she'd sent it. Saul looked tall and gangly, but he had killer instincts when it came to investigative reporting. He would get at the truth.

I will support and defend . . . I will bear true faith and al-

legiance . . .

Elizabeth Anne Pepperhawk, senior nursing student, had raised her right hand in front of an Army nurse recruiter in the Biloxi Army Recruiting Station and taken her enlistment oath. Darby had taken the same oath. So had Benny, and Avivah, and every soldier who'd come through her care.

She had resigned from the Army years ago, but some things, like her enlistment oath, didn't expire. The Army must have some reason for that cock-and-bull story. She'd keep quiet for now, but after Darby's funeral, she'd go to West Point. Darby's name was going in that book.

The phone rang. Pepper scooped a sleepy Anne into bed and ran to the kitchen. "Hello."

"Miss Pepperhawk?"

"Yes."

"John Ferguson from Marshall."

Lawyer Ferguson had been Avivah's lawyer, on and off, for years. Why was he calling her?

"I wanted to express my condolences on your loss. Colonel Baxter was a fine man."

"Thank you." How had he known that Darby was dead?

"I expect you know that I'll have to wait for a death certificate before going to probate."

"I'm sorry, I'm lost here."

"I'm Colonel Baxter's executor. I assumed that you knew that."

"Why would I?"

"You are his primary beneficiary."

The Queen in Alice in Wonderland had it easy. She'd had to believe six impossible things before breakfast. Pepper didn't dare count how many impossible things she'd had to believe in the past day. She had trouble swallowing. "I wasn't aware of that."

"He provided well for you."

Pepper thought about Benny's mortgage. "How well?"

What was she saying? She was Darby's lover, his friend. Their relationship hadn't been based on money. What about his family? Was it legal for him to name a friend over his family in a will? Especially now that he had a daughter. "I don't think I can—I mean, I can't—I mean I shouldn't—"

"This is obviously something of a shock."

"Mr. Ferguson, my life has been one shock after another for the past twenty-four hours."

"I imagine so. I can't divulge all the details before probate, but I think Colonel Baxter would want you to know that your house and land will be paid for. He took out a second life-insurance policy specifically designated for that. If you'd prefer to donate the rest of the money to charity or set up a memorial fund in Colonel Baxter's name, I can help you do that."

The rest? Money to pay for her house and land plus some left over? It had never occurred to her that Darby was wealthy.

Benny could give up that fool notion of an overseas contract. Darby and Benny might circle one other like wary dogs, but Darby would never begrudge helping another Beret in need. She could pay back the loan and maybe qualify for another one, a real loan this time to renovate the homestead.

Pepper let out a sad breath. Darby wasn't even buried yet, and she was spending his money. Her mother would have called a woman who did that a cheap gold digger. Possibly the Baxters would feel the same way.

"Miss Pepperhawk?"

"I'm sorry. Do I have to sign papers or something?"

"Eventually, but for now—"

The phone clicked. A woman's voice came on the line: "This is the Southern Bell operator. I have an emergency telephone call for Miss Elizabeth Pepperhawk. I must ask the caller to relinquish the line immediately."

John said hastily, "I'll phone you later in the week." He hung up.

An emergency call? Oh, God, Darby was alive after all. She was getting used to him being dead; now she'd have to get used to him being alive. Her house and land wouldn't be paid for after all; she wouldn't be able to help Benny and Lorraine. She mentally slapped her hand. Gold-digger.

The operator said, "Go ahead, madam."

Avivah's voice asked, "Pepper, is that you?"

Not Darby after all. "It's me."

"Brace yourself."

Any more braced and she'd be stainless steel. "I'm braced."

"Miss Filmore has been strangled."

An image of three thousand dollars in a pink-and-gray cosmetic case floated before Pepper's eyes. "Was it robbery?"

"I don't know. Your janitor found her body in an exam room at Laurel Ridge Clinic. The place is a mess. We haven't been able to reach your boss. Can you come and help us sort out if anything is missing?"

CHAPTER 4

Avivah stood in the Laurel Ridge Clinic's waiting room, studying a fuzzy black-and-white photo enlarged from an old negative. The thin woman's bonnet shaded most of her face. A tall bean trellis filled the photo's background. The engraved brass plaque underneath read, *For my mother, Velma, in loving memory.*

Avivah knew the story from Pepper. Velma Teague had married at fifteen, delivered her first child at sixteen. One miscarriage and five more children had followed in the next six years, and then she'd died from tetanus at twenty-eight. The oldest child, Pat, had just had her twelfth birthday. Pat's brother, aged ten, had walked a day and a night to bring back the Frontier Nurse. By the time the nurse arrived, all she could do was help bury the mother and send the children to be cared for by neighbors until their father returned home.

"My grandmother would have had you sterilized for your own good," Avivah said to the photograph.

Her chest tightened. Why hadn't her sister let well enough alone? A New York publisher had already accepted her sister's biography about their grandmother. Doing more research, visiting one more archive was her sister's inability to leave well enough alone. Her sister's frantic letter had sat on Avivah's desk for a week; she didn't know what advice to give her.

The gurney, bearing Edith Filmore's body, bumped over the linoleum floor and stopped when the morgue attendant encountered Pepper and the baby stroller at the door. After a few dance steps, Pepper pulled back and allowed the gurney right-of-way. Once the doorway was clear, she wheeled the stroller inside and parked it in a corner. "Why are you here? You should be with Saul."

"I'm on call tonight. The duty-sergeant paged me while Saul was speaking."

Even though they were alone, Pepper moved closer and said in a low voice, "I won't have to identify her at the morgue, will I? I never liked morgues."

"Identification has to be made by a relative, friend, or someone who knew the deceased. Right now, we're calling her Jane Doe."

"But we know who she is."

"We know who she said she was."

"What about ID? Did you find her purse?"

"Yes, but the only useful thing in it was a key from a motel down the street. My driver is there right now."

"Did you find the money?"

"She had about twenty-five dollars in her purse."

"How much trouble are we in for having paid blackmail?"

"Some."

"I'll have to give a statement, won't I?"

Avivah knew that Pepper wasn't a killer. Knowing that and proving it were different things. Please let Pepper have an ironclad alibi. If she didn't, Avivah would have to tell her that she couldn't leave town to attend Darby's funeral because she was on their suspect list. "Yes."

"Do I have to include that you and Saul countersigned the loan, or that we all met her at the library?"

Thank goodness she and Edith Filmore had been alone in the women's bathroom. Avivah had meant her lecture to be a stern warning. Under the present circumstances it sounded like a threat. "For my sake and yours, don't hold back anything.

Trying to protect me will make things more difficult for both of us."

Pepper removed a bottle from the diaper bag, shook a little formula onto her wrist, and popped the nipple into the baby's mouth.

Avivah frowned. "Aren't you supposed to warm that?"

"It's at room temperature. It won't hurt her."

At Fort Bragg, she'd seen Pepper care for her GI patients with great care and affection. This baby got cold efficiency. If Saul were dead and she were feeding his baby by another woman, Avivah didn't know that she'd behave any different. "For me to interview you would be a conflict of interest, but unofficially, what did you do after Saul and I left home?"

"I had a visitor: Nana Kate, Darby's grandmother."

Avivah had never met any of the Baxters, except for Darby, but she couldn't imagine that they'd send a frail old woman all the way from Georgia. "Isn't she old?"

"She's old like a five-hundred-year-old oak tree is old. She's not nearly as unapproachable as Darby said. Our visit was—emotional." Pepper's body drew inward, like a balloon losing air.

Pepper ran her life at a hundred and fifty percent. It was easy to forget that a normal human being lay buried somewhere inside. "You okay?"

"Everything is starting to sink in. Darby isn't coming back, is he?"

"No, he's not. What did you tell Nana Kate about the baby?"

"That I was babysitting. Her eyesight isn't good. She couldn't see the baby's eye color."

Small mercy. At least Pepper wouldn't have to contend with the Baxter clan descending on her, telling her what she must do about Darby's daughter.

From the homestead to the clinic was a forty-minute drive. If

Pepper had never been alone for more than an hour, it would have been impossible for her to drive to Asheville, kill Edith Filmore, and drive home. "How long after Saul and I left did Kate arrive?"

"About half an hour."

"Was she with you when I asked the operator to break into your phone call?"

"She left about seven thirty."

The clinic janitor had discovered the body at a few minutes after eight. If Pepper's story could be verified, she wasn't on the suspect list. "Did she come alone?"

"She had a chauffeur."

"Chauffeur? Darby's family must have more money than he let on."

"Oh, Avivah, he left me money. I was talking to his executor when you called. The homestead will be paid for, and I'll have more than enough money left over to pay the loan. I was so happy when I heard that. I'm such a rotten person."

Next to Darby, Pepper loved her little piece of Madison County above all else in the world. The prospect of owning her homestead, free and clear, would go a tiny way toward healing Pepper's grief.

Darby dressed well, but not extravagantly. He drove a four-year-old car. He had no hobbies, and his vacations for the past few years had centered on coming to see Pepper.

Two decades of officer's pay, plus a few infusions of combat pay would have set him up comfortably, but if he'd more than enough to pay Pepper's mortgage, he'd either made great investments or—

She didn't want to think about *or*. A smart but unprincipled Army officer could make a lot of illegal money in Vietnam. Pepper loved the homestead, but she would never accept tainted money to pay for it. "You have a right to be happy about a windfall, even if it comes via horrible circumstances."

Pepper wiggled Anne back into her stroller. "Maybe I'll believe that one day. What are we going to do about Jane Doe?"

"You'll have to come to the police station tomorrow and give a statement. Tonight I need you to go through the clinic and decide if anything is out of place or missing. Do you have any idea what Edith Filmore was doing here?"

"None."

"Did you tell her that you worked here?"

"No. Darby made her memorize my home address and phone number. Maybe he made her memorize the clinic's address, too. That would account for her getting a motel room near here."

Avivah could believe that a dying man might ask someone to memorize one address and phone number, but not two. Not even Darby Baxter could manage that and die at the same time.

Pepper said, "There wasn't a car!"

"What?"

"When she came to our house Sunday night, there wasn't a car in our parking area. I don't remember hearing one pull up."

"What about when she left?"

"I was crying too hard to hear anything, but I don't remember hearing a car leave."

Edith Filmore had likely flown into Asheville. Checking the airlines, car rentals, and taxis was the place to start.

"Stand aside. This is my clinic."

Avivah recognized that voice: Patricia Teague, Pepper's boss. When Pepper had gone to work for Laurel Ridge Clinic, Avivah had run a background check on Pat Teague, who "intended to win a victory for all poor women by going against the hydra-headed paternalistic white, male-dominated health-care system." Ms. Teague's own words from a *Ms. Magazine* interview. Self-proclaimed feminists who spouted jargon were tiresome and pretentious. Pepper had been so happy about her new job that Avivah had kept her opinion of Pepper's new boss to herself.

Ms. Teague barged past the door guard. She was middle-aged, padded rather than fat. Black hair, cut in short wiry spikes, framed her face. She wore jeans, a long-sleeved cotton shirt, and a hand-dyed vest. Avivah had seen one like it in a natural-fiber clothing store. It was expensive. So were the turquoise and silver earrings from the same store dangling from Ms. Teague's earlobes.

Holding out her hand, she headed straight for Avivah. She had an ultra-firm handshake. "It's been far too long, Avivah. How nice to see you again, though I wish it were under different circumstances."

"So do I."

"I hope Pepper conveyed to you my delight in your promotion to detective?"

"She mentioned that you were pleased."

The baby let out a gurgle.

Pat's voice changed completely. "Who do we have here?"

Pepper said, "Her name is Anne."

Avivah blinked. How had Pepper found out the baby's name?

Ms. Teague smoothed her hand over Anne's soft black hair. The baby eyes widened, and then squinted. She either giggled or passed gas. Lots of things sounded the same at that age.

"Is Ahn her first or last name?"

"First. Anne Duc To."

Avivah knew where Duc To was and she had a horrible suspicion Pepper had made up the name—and who knew what else—in order to feed Nana Kate information. Sometimes Pepper's imagination became a freight train barreling out of a tunnel. Smart people got out of the way until the train was a memory far, far down the track. Avivah had learned to stand aside a long time ago.

"Shouldn't her name be To Duc Ahn? I thought the Vietnamese used their last name first?"

Pepper didn't falter. "Her mom prefers to use the American form, now that she's in the States."

"Where is Mom?"

"Womack Army Hospital, Fort Bragg. She had to have emergency surgery."

"Is Dad in the picture?"

Pepper's face colored. "Of course! He was one of my corpsmen in Vietnam. Poor guy, his unit left on maneuvers this morning."

Storm clouds gathered on Ms. Teague's brow. "You mean his wife just had surgery, he has a new baby, and he can't get excused from stupid soldier games? Isn't that what chaplains are for?"

The freight train wobbled on its track.

"Everything happened too fast. She had surgery yesterday afternoon, and he was already on standby for an R-and-D mission to the Arctic Circle testing a new cold-weather vehicle."

"You said he was a corpsman. Why is he testing a vehicle?"

"All Special Forces are cross trained. His primary MOS is Ninety-one B, but his secondary MOS is mechanic."

The film rewound, the train returned to the track and continued across the gorge. Good old Army Four-B: If you can't blind them with brilliance, baffle them with bullshit. Pepper could still sling the lingo. Avivah concentrated on sending out waves of stop-while-you're-ahead thoughts.

"Anne is staying with me for a few weeks. I'm bringing her to work."

It was a statement, rather than a request for permission.

Ms. Teague pulled a blanket over the now-sleepy baby. "Fine." She straightened. "My apologies, Avivah, but these little ones always come first. The constable who phoned said that Mr.

Boniface discovered a body. Where is he?"

"The victim was a woman."

"I meant, where is Leon Boniface."

"At the police station, giving a statement."

"Surely you can't suspect him. He's the kindest, most nonviolent man I know."

First she'd shown concern for the baby, now her janitor. In Pat Teague's book, the dead must wait on the living. "What time does Mr. Boniface usually start work?"

"Eight o'clock on Monday, Wednesday, and Friday evenings, and ten on Tuesdays and Thursdays."

Mr. Boniface's phone call had come in to dispatch at eight-oh-three. Before coming to clean the clinic, he had been at a church event all evening. Avivah didn't suspect Leon Boniface of anything other than discovering the body. "A woman's body was found in one of your examination rooms. The technician is working in there, so I'd like to start by going through the rest of the clinic. Tell me if anything is out of place or missing. Start here in the reception area."

It was interesting to watch the different ways that Pat Teague and Pepper surveyed the room. Pepper stood in the middle of the room, faced the front door and moved in a slow, clockwise circle until she again faced the door. Ms. Teague walked around, peered in the trash can, bent to check under tables and chairs, and leaned over the receptionist's counter to peer at the desktop that couldn't be seen over the counter. She said, "The photocopier shouldn't be on."

"Who was the last staff member to leave this afternoon?"

"I was, and the photocopier was definitely off when I left."

Avivah called down the hall, "Jake, I need the photocopier dusted." Photocopiers always had layers of prints. Maybe she would get lucky and find it had been wiped clean. That would tell her that someone hadn't wanted to risk fingerprints being found.

"We found no sign of forced entry. Who has keys to the clinic?"

Pat Teague said, "Me, Pepper, our receptionist, and Mr. Boniface."

"What about your landlord?"

"It's a management company. I imagine they have a set."

"Are these the original locks?"

"I had the locks changed and dead-bolt locks added on both front and back doors when we opened the clinic."

"Do you two have your keys?"

Pat and Pepper pulled identical key rings from their pockets. She'd already seen Leon Boniface's key ring. That left the receptionist's keys to be verified.

"Do you have an alarm system?"

"We're too strapped for cash for extras." Ms. Teague pointed to a locked metal grill in front of the charts. "Leon rigged a fake alarm for the chart grill. A siren goes off and a light flashes, but it's not connected to the police station or a security company. We hoped noise and light would scare off anyone who activated it. Medical information is the most valuable thing we have here."

"What about drugs?"

Pepper said, "I'll show you."

She led them down the corridor to the first door on the left, which was marked *Storage*. Along one wall of the room, medical supplies lay neatly stacked on industrial gray metal shelves. On one shelf was a small collection of vials and bottles. "We stock a few antibiotics, cough medicine, Tylenol, and lice shampoo. Antibiotics have a small street value, but we figure if someone needs penicillin enough to steal it, let him have it. We keep nothing of street value, including narcotics, on the premises after closing."

"That implies you have narcotics here during office hours."

Pat said, "Our narcotic supply is kept in a red toolbox. When we close, the box goes to the pharmacy down the street. The pharmacist stores it for us in his drug safe. I took it to the pharmacy when I left."

A man in coveralls, carrying a black case, came out of the examination room. "I'm done back there."

For the first time, Pat Teague looked a bit unsteady. "Is she in there?"

"Her body has been removed. It appears that she was strangled, so there's no blood either."

The three women moved to the examination room door. The room was a mess. Shattered glass jars, Q-tips, rolled gauze, and other medical supplies lay scattered over the floor. Yards of exam table paper lay in great torn and crushed loops, and a straight-back wooden chair was overturned. Miss Filmore hadn't gone gently into that good night.

Avivah asked, "Is anything missing?"

Pat studied the room for a long time. "I won't be able to say for certain until it's cleaned up, but I'd say no. Pepper?"

"I agree."

The rest of the clinic—a second examination room, two bathrooms, a staff coffee area, the furnace room, the doctor's office, and a double office belonging to the nurses—appeared untouched. Whatever had happened here had happened at the copier and in the one exam room. Pat Teague removed a tissue-wrapped object from her desk drawer. She unwrapped it and held a gray-green grass braid out for Avivah's inspection. One end was singed.

"A sweetgrass-and-sage braid. We'll need to do a proper emotional cleansing later, of course, to reestablish a positive environment, but this will help. May we burn it in the exam room?"

Why not? Jake had finished.

They went back to the examination room. Pat entered first. She lit the end of the braid. The grass flamed briefly, then smoldered. A pleasant odor filled the room. Pat held the twisted grass in front of her, and moved her hand in an arc, wafting smoke around her head. She said, "Blessed be," and handed the grass to Pepper who repeated the ritual and the words.

Avivah's stomach felt queasy. Pepper never did rituals, other than toss spilled salt over her left shoulder. She hadn't checked Pat Teague's religious affiliation, but she was concerned about a woman who'd suckered Pepper into doing a spiritual ritual, a feat that two decades of Catholic priests and nuns hadn't managed.

Pepper held out the braid to Avivah. "It's optional, and it's spiritual rather than religious."

Her eyes held such hope that Avivah accepted the braid and repeated the motions she'd watched. To herself she said, "For Pepper, and for Darby."

Pat lit the braid again to produce more smudge. She walked into the room, stopping in each corner. She returned to the center of the room.

"How old a woman was she?"

Pepper said, "Middle-aged."

If Pat thought it was odd that Pepper answered, her face didn't show it. She bent her head and closed her eyes. "Mother, your work here is finished. Your spirit is passing through to us, your daughters. Go in peace. Safe journey."

Live and let live was Avivah's motto, except when it came to her housemate. Pepper was too spiritually vulnerable. Avivah wanted to do what she could to protect her from crap.

Pat went to the sink in one corner of the room and ran water over the lacy, black braid ends. Ash floated in the water.

Avivah handed Ms. Teague a Polaroid photo. "You recognize this woman?"

"I'm afraid that's privileged information."

Avivah retrieved the photo. "Can I assume then that she had been a patient at this clinic?"

"You can assume anything you want."

If Edith Filmore had arrived in Asheville on Sunday, this morning was the only time she could have visited this clinic. "When was she here at the clinic?"

"I never said she was."

"I can get a court order to view her medical record."

"Not tonight you can't."

Avivah could, but it would mean waking up a judge, and sleepy judges were often cranky. It was after midnight. She was tired and Pepper looked exhausted. "Pepper, you and Anne go home. Come to the police station tomorrow to give a statement. Ms. Teague, I know it's late, but I would like to interview you right now. And I'll need your receptionist's name and home address."

Pepper drove home with her car window open. She would have sung to keep awake, except that Anne was finally asleep and she didn't want to risk waking her.

Stumbling, she locked the garage door, and pushed Anne's stroller along the uneven grass toward her kitchen door. Pepper suddenly sensed a small air-pressure change. Someone was behind her.

She spun around. Her brain had enough time to register that the person was too tall to be Benny and too short to be Saul. She shoved the stroller hard to get it out of the way, dropped her center of gravity and, in one fluid movement, whirled and raised her leg at what she hoped was the person's groin. Her knee connected with soft, squishy bits. Definitely male.

The man went down on his hands and knees, and vomited. Pepper clasped her hands together with her fingers interlocked, and brought them down hard on the man's neck. He fell forward into his own vomit.

She screamed and screamed again. A few seconds later, a light went on in the kitchen. Help was on the way. She positioned herself between the fallen man and Anne's stroller.

He managed a strangled, "Jesus, pretty lady, you kick like a mule."

Pepper forgot how to breathe. Ghosts weren't supposed to have soft, squishy bits. "You're dead."

Slowly, awkwardly Darby Baxter rose from the ground. "Pretty near."

The waning moon moved from behind a cloud; Pepper's kitchen screen door banged against its frame. Pepper saw Saul run barefooted toward them holding a baseball bat as if ready to hit a ball out of Yankee Stadium. In the pale light, Pepper realized that blood as well as vomit covered Darby. She ran past Saul into her kitchen and phoned the rescue squad.

CHAPTER 5

Dawn outlined the mountain ridges in pastel pinks and blues as Pepper and Darby drove away from the Pisgah Mountain Veterans Hospital. Darby fell asleep immediately after they left the parking lot.

An ulcer! He had a whopping duodenal ulcer. Colonels were supposed to give ulcers, not get them.

Pepper gripped the steering wheel with both hands. Prayer hadn't been her strong suit for a long time, but likely she owed someone—or something—big time for Darby's deliverance. There was no such thing as a free lunch. She glanced at Darby, who slept, open-mouthed, with his head thrown back. "Thank you," she said in her head. It would have to do for a prayer.

Darby's head rocked gently from side to side in time with the car's motion. They had so much to talk about. Where to start?

He hadn't asked once about Anne, or whatever name he knew her by. The baby had screamed the whole time the rescue squad worked on Darby. It was just possible that being kicked in the balls, then vomiting blood, and then being the object of intense ministrations—first of the rescue squad, then of assorted doctors, nurses, and technicians—hadn't left an opportunity for him to think about Anne. They would have to talk about her, but not while he resembled Dracula's lunch. She'd let him get his bearings first.

Should she tell him about the loan? No, Darby shouldn't have to worry about her bad decisions. She should have been stronger and refused to pay. She'd have to convince Avivah and Saul to agree not to talk about the loan either.

Edith Filmore's death could also wait for now.

For weeks, Pepper had lain awake nights, enhancing magazine images with her Qui Nhon memories. The *Newsweek* cover of a man carrying his dead child reminded her of how long it took a body to cool in tropical heat. She smelled burned, melted rubber when she saw photos of burning military vehicles. Vietnamese sweat smelled like fish. Those crowds of fleeing Cambodians and Vietnamese would have stunk to high heaven.

Darby had been in the middle of what she'd only read about. He'd stayed until the very last day, had come within a hair's breadth of being the last American casualty in Vietnam. Never mind the West Point memorial book. Being the last casualty would have gotten his name in the history books.

She reached over and brushed a wisp of his hair with her fingertips. "Well done, young warrior," she whispered. "Fucking well done."

She'd done well, too. When Edith Filmore had told her how Darby supposedly died, she hadn't screamed, fainted, or done a thing that would have tarnished Darby's memory had he really been dead. She wanted to believe that she would have done well at his funeral. After the funeral, she would have come home, found adoptive parents for Anne, and then—?

The steering wheel wobbled. She loved her homestead, but wasn't a homesteader. She didn't grow food, sew clothes, or scour the hills for medicinal plants. She couldn't sing, clog dance, or play a musical instrument. Unlike her friend Frannie, she never wove or threw clay pots. Her life revolved around working out at the gym, hanging around the homestead, writing long letters to Darby, and nursing. If writing Darby letters were out of that equation—if Darby was out of the equation completely—what did she have left? Nothing that truly excited her except nursing.

If Darby had died: she would have come home from his funeral, found adoptive parents for Anne, turned over the mortgage-free homestead to Saul and Avivah's care, and reenlisted in the Army Nurse Corps. With a nudge in the right direction, she would turn into a military lifer. Darby knew that about her; she suspected Benny knew, too.

She sneaked another glance at Darby, the man whose deliverance had saved her from making a colonel of herself. Even asleep, he appeared ill. She should she have sided with the internist, who wanted to admit him, but she believed Darby when he threatened to sign himself out against medical advice. She'd rarely seen a man more determined to resist medical care. His attitude hadn't been his usual slap-on-a-Band-Aid-and-I'll-be-on-my-way bravado.

It had been—not naming it wouldn't make it go away. It had been fear. He had been piss-ant terrified of staying in the hospital. Hospitals, in the abstract, didn't scare Darby. Having lived through two Purple Hearts and the occasional football injury, he grudgingly admitted that hospitals were useful. Why did staying in one tonight scare him? She hadn't found an answer by the time her car rumbled over the cattle guard at her gate.

Darby jerked awake. "What?"

She smoothed her hand over his thigh. "We're home."

He tried to focus on his watch. "What time is it?"

"After six."

"What time do you have to leave for work?"

"Noon."

Except that Anne needed feeding, and Avivah expected her to go to the police station this morning to give a statement.

Pepper locked her car and followed Darby across the yard. "Where did you end up after Saigon?"

"In a Bangkok hospital."

"How?"

"Air America."

Air America: the Central Intelligence Agency's private airline. Darby had CIA connections. Big surprise.

Obviously, the Saigon to Bangkok trip had taken a while. If it hadn't, the Army wouldn't have had time to notify Darby's family that he was dead, and Nana Kate wouldn't have made her condolence call. "How did your family react when you called them?"

Darby stumbled.

"You have phoned your family?"

"Not exactly."

"Darby!"

"Give me a break. I spent most of the past six days unconscious or on airplanes."

"The Army told your family that you died in a training accident!"

"The Army did what?"

"Their cover story is that you died a heroic death in Japan."

"How do you know this?"

"Nana Kate told me."

"Nana Kate?"

"She hired a limousine and paid a condolence call. Come on, you are phoning your parents this minute."

"I can't wake my parents at six in the morning to tell them I'm not dead."

Pepper unlocked her back door. "Have you thought for one minute that they aren't sleeping because they are grieving over your death?"

The note on the kitchen table—*Anne is in our room, Avivah*—told Pepper that Avivah had finally made it home. She moved a kitchen chair under the wall phone. "Sit."

Darby sat.

She held out the receiver. "Dial."

Darby rubbed his hand through his short, curly hair. "I can't."

She was close enough to him to smell his body odor: a rancid, dark smell like rotten garlic. She'd never smelled fear on him before. What had President Roosevelt said? The only thing we have to fear is fear itself. How right that was.

Pepper dialed Darby's home number. She'd memorized it a long time ago, but never used it before. Her heart was racing. What was she going to say? Hi, did I wake you? Your son is sitting in my kitchen.

Darby grabbed the phone out of her hand. With his other arm he reached up and pulled Pepper to him, pinning her ear against his chest. His heart raced, too.

Three rings, then a man's sleepy voice said, "Hello."

Pepper absolutely did not want to hear both sides of this conversation. She tried to pull away, but Darby's arm held her in a chokehold. Like it or not, she was going to listen in.

"Dad, it's me, Darby."

All sleep left the man's voice. "You bastard, when I find out who you are, I'll have the law on you."

"Don't hang up. On your thirtieth wedding anniversary you, Uncle Toady, and PawPaw Wright missed the anniversary party because you got lost dove hunting. Mama, Aunt Heddie, and Nana Kate were so mad that they made you sleep at the Oc-mulgee Hotel."

"That story was all over town."

"Uncle Toady and PawPaw shared a room and you had a room to yourself. I snuck Mama and a bottle of champagne past the desk clerk at two in the morning because she said she'd be damned if she'd sleep alone on her anniversary, and what the hell good was it having a Green Beret son if he wouldn't use his fancy training to help his mama. My mama does not say damned and hell, but she did that night."

Silence, then a tear-filled voice said, "Boy, is that really you?"

"The Army made a stupid mistake. I was hurt, not killed, in the accident."

He hadn't flinched while confirming the Army's lie about the mythical accident. There had been an accident all right; the proof was in Avivah's room.

Darby's father asked, "How bad are you hurt this time?"

"A few stitches in my left side. Nothing serious."

In addition to having an ulcer and bruised balls, Darby had been stabbed. He had twelve stitches in his side. Everything else considered it was hardly worth mentioning.

"Where the hell have you been for the past week?"

"In a hospital. I got out an hour ago."

Technically, that was true. They'd left the VA hospital an hour ago.

"Why didn't you call us sooner?"

"I didn't know that I'd been reported dead. You know the Army: the left hand never talks to the right."

"Where are you now?"

Darby grimaced and his gaze darted around the kitchen. "Trying to sort out one hell of a mess here."

Here implied that he was in Japan. She'd never realized before how easily Darby bent truth. Not that she expected him to tell his parents the real story. The Army had concocted their cover story for a reason, and his parents were, after all, civilians.

He'd better not lie to her. She'd been a captain to his colonel, served three years to his seventeen, and she'd never been in combat, but she'd been a soldier, too, and that counted between them. There had never been lies between them, and never would be.

Darby asked, "Where's Mama?"

"In her sewing room."

"Get her for me, will you?"

He had to let go of Pepper to place his hand over the receiver. Pepper stood.

"When Mama can't sleep, she quilts for the premature nursery."

Considering the past week, Pepper suspected that Mama Baxter had had a record-breaking quilting week.

She tiptoed into Avivah and Saul's room. A jealous pang went through her when she saw the easy way they slept huddled under the covers. Avivah's hand rested against the back of Saul's head and he had his arm around her shoulder. If she did sleep today, it would be alone. Darby would be in the guest room. Sleeping alone had nothing to do with Anne or Darby. She was exhausted and needed sleep.

She sneaked out of the bedroom with Anne in her arms. Pepper whispered in the baby's ear, "Your daddy is alive." Anne seemed unimpressed.

Darby was alive. The three of them were a little family. Except that Pepper wasn't about to raise Darby's daughter. When he'd thought he was dying, he'd wanted Vietnamese parents for her. For whatever reason, he hadn't thought Pepper good enough to raise his daughter. Fine. Vietnamese parents were his original plan, and he'd better stick to that plan. She walked into the kitchen in time to see Darby hang up the phone.

Pepper held out Anne to him. "She's safe. Risking your life to get your daughter out of Saigon was a very brave thing."

"My what?"

"It's okay. I've forgiven you. You don't have to pretend that she's not your daughter."

Darby eased back the blanket with one finger. Anne reached up, wrapped her tiny fist around his finger and gurgled. Darby's Adam's apple bobbed.

"The bad news is that the woman who brought her here has

been murdered. Avivah is the investigating officer."

"What woman? What are you talking about? I've never seen this baby before."

Pepper stared into Darby's eyes, then into Anne's. She'd been right: the color matched. He'd lied to his parents, but he wasn't going to get away with lying to her. Pepper laid Anne on the counter by the phone, holding her in place with one hand and dialed with the other. Dialing took an eternity.

"Kirkpatrick." Benny's voice sounded groggy and pissed-off.

"Darby lied to me. He said he's never seen Anne before, and I know he has. I need you. Rock-and-roll, Benny."

Silence, then Benny said, "If you've been drinking, I'll have your hide."

"Not a drop. Darby is alive. He's in my kitchen, feeding me a line of bullshit."

"Who is Anne?"

Bother, she'd never told him about the baby. "Darby's daughter."

Darby said into the receiver, "She is not."

A click sounded, then a dial tone. Five minutes later Benny—bleary-eyed, his hair tufted around his head, and his clothes askew—burst through the kitchen door. He pointed a finger at Darby. "Don't you ever get yourself killed again!"

The two men fell into an embrace so fierce that Pepper had to look away.

CHAPTER 6

Avivah had moved from being late for work Tuesday morning, to being very late. From the extension phone in her bedroom, she called her office.

Her driver answered. "Where are you? Lieutenant Alexander wants you."

"Crisis at home. I'm on my way."

"First thing this morning I went to interview that Hood woman, the receptionist. I didn't get an answer at her house so I tried the clinic. She wouldn't let me in. Pointed to a sign that said the clinic opened at one this afternoon. Shall I go haul her out at one and bring her to you?"

Hauling employees out of her housemate's work site wouldn't be good public relations. "Be at the clinic when it opens and ask her to come to the station. If she refuses, call me. In the meantime, I want you call the airlines and find out when two people, Edith Filmore and Darby Baxter, flew into Asheville. They were probably on separate flights."

She hoped they'd been on separate flights.

"I want flight numbers, where the flights originated, and time of arrival. Baxter might have been flying on a military ticket. Did they rent cars or take taxis from the airport?"

"How soon do you want this?"

"Yesterday."

"What shall I tell Lieutenant Alexander?"

"That I'll be at my desk in an hour."

She hung up and sat on the edge of her bed, worrying at a small hangnail. What was she going to do about Anne?

Yesterday, she'd helped pay blackmail in an attempt to assuage Pepper's raw grief. Today, with Edith Filmore dead and Darby insisting that he'd never seen Anne, the rules had changed. So much for buying a three-thousand-dollar conscience.

Unless a child was in imminent danger, a police officer couldn't apprehend her; that task fell to child-welfare workers. Was Anne in imminent danger?

Anne might be irrelevant to Edith Filmore's death, or at the center of it. The second possibility constituted imminent danger. Avivah had no desire to walk into her own kitchen and snatch Anne from her housemate's arms. That would be even worse than hauling Miss Hood out of her workplace. If Anne was in danger, she was safer with a houseful of adults who'd done military service than in your average foster home.

She reached in her bedside table, found a nail trimmer, and cut off the offending hangnail. If she discovered one iota of a connection between Edith Filmore and Darby Baxter, she'd call child welfare. Until then, Anne stayed where she was.

Unlike most mornings, the old farmhouse kitchen didn't smell like coffee or breakfast. Three men and a baby sat around a bare table. Pepper sat on a chair in a corner as far away from Darby as possible. Earlier, Benny had quieted Pepper's hysteria with one question. Was Darby willing to submit to a blood test to prove he wasn't Anne's father?

He was, but from Pepper's sour expression and rigid body, his agreeing to do so hadn't satisfied her by a long shot.

Darby now held a sleeping Anne against his right shoulder and stroked her back, seemingly by rote. She'd taken to him immediately, screaming and resisting all comfort until he held her. Avivah had read that babies liked deep voices. This morning Darby's normally low voice practically croaked with fatigue.

Darby said, "By early March, a Pentagon pooh-bah had concluded that Vietnam was going to hell in a handbasket. He wanted the Army to insert a man covertly on the ground; next thing I knew I was on the elephant train. Ban Me Thuot, Pleiku, Da Nang, Saigon."

Saul's groan was almost sexual. "Any journalist would sell his soul for access to an American eyewitness who'd been in every city that the North Vietnamese captured. I've got you and I can't print a word. I'm walking away from a Pulitzer Prize here."

Benny said, "Keep walking."

Saul got up from the table, encircled Avivah with his arms, and kissed the top of her head. "Call me."

She snuggled into the warmth of his flannel robe. "This may be a long day. Don't wait up."

Over Pepper's protests, Benny insisted on taking Anne with him. Darby went to the guest room. In her own room, Pepper tossed her clothes in a pile, climbed into bed, and fell asleep. Cartoon elephants squirted her with water, which turned to napalm, setting her skin on fire. She sat upright in bed, gasping for breath. Sweat dried sticky on her skin. She hadn't felt this bad since she stopped drinking.

Elephant trains and pooh-bahs.

Pepper stumbled out of bed. She dug in the bottom drawer of her dresser for the old cigar box where she kept all of Darby's letters. The last one she'd received from Japan sat on top. She opened the single folded sheet, written on military stationery purchased at the post exchange.

3 March 1975
Camp Zama, Japan
Dearest,
I'm up to my ass in packing so this will be short and sweet. A Washington pooh-bah decided to forgo the cherry blossom

festival in Foggy Bottom (aka Washington) for the real thing in Japan followed by a congressional inspection tour–cum–shopping spree for Mrs. Pooh-bah. This guy had latched on to me when I was stationed at the Pentagon. He considers me the all-knowing, all-seeing oracle on US military interests in Asia. Being stationed in DC taught me that not all congressmen have good sense.

Orders came down this morning assigning me to be his military point man. For the next few weeks, my life will be walking two paces behind him, attending tea ceremonies and formal dinners, and protocol up the ying-yang. It's a good thing I just bought a new dress uniform.

Our elephant train leaves in two days. Keep writing to the Camp Zama address. Looking forward to a stack of letters when I return will keep me focused.

Yours in service to our country, (blah!)
Darby XOXOXOX

She was certain that Darby had written the letter she held in her hand. The paper, his handwriting, the way the sentences read matched every other letter from him. Was the field diary that Edith Filmore had given her really Darby's field diary? Maybe. Likely. It was the same kind of notebook he carried, and the entries looked like his handwriting. Faking a whole diary would have been a lot of work. Why would someone have bothered?

If she believed that the field diary was genuine, had he written the last entry, the letter about Anne? Her throat tightened. It was exactly the kind of letter he would write if he were dying. Anyone who wanted to forge the last two pages would have had a whole book full of examples of his handwriting to copy. But the handwriting wasn't exactly his, a fact she'd attributed to shock, pain, and bad lighting. The other possibility was a not-quite-perfect forgery. The blood, baby's footprint, and fingerprint had further obscured the writing. Pepper wasn't convinced that Darby had written the letter. Faking two pages would have been a lot easier than faking a whole diary. The strongest link connecting Darby to that letter hinged on three words.

Dearest. The word burned her throat. Darby had started every letter he wrote to her with that word. Anyone who had seen other letters would know that. He'd better not have been showing his private letters to anyone else.

The only places she'd ever heard him use *pooh-bah* and *elephant train* were in his letter from Japan, in the letter in his field diary, and in conversation this morning. They could be they new words that he'd picked up, or some kind of code.

If the letter was faked, did it have something to do with Edith Filmore's death?

Pepper hid the cigar box in her bottom drawer and went back to bed with a stomachache so bad that she could legitimately call in sick. Except that today she didn't want to stay home. The more people around Anne and herself, the safer Anne would be. Darby might not have sent Anne to her, but that baby was now her responsibility.

Avivah came out of a hole-in-the-wall café balancing coffee and a breakfast bagel.

"Avivah!"

Benny ran across the street, giving a nod and wave to cars that jerked to a stop inches from him. He eyed the coffee. "Share?"

Avivah raised the cup out of his reach. Before a mission, Sergeant First Class Benjamin Kirkpatrick, US Special Forces, always wound himself up like a cat about to spring. Benny had been out of the Army for years, but this morning, his body showed the old pre-mission tightness. Black coffee was the last thing he needed.

She was suddenly, inexplicably, nostalgic. A military post seemed so orderly compared to civilian life the past forty-eight hours. She had a hunch Benny felt the same way. She handed him the coffee. "Why aren't you in school?"

"Finals week. We're on a different schedule. You and I need to talk."

She nodded toward the lawn in front of City Hall. "Let's sit on a bench. There will be fewer interruptions than in my office."

They snagged a bench shaded by a large flowering dogwood. This late in the spring, green leaves had replaced most of the white blossoms.

Benny ran his finger over the cup's rim. "Darby is tired beyond exhaustion. I've seen the signs in other Berets. He's been too many places and seen too many things. Remember the proverb 'A pitcher that goes to the well too often ends up broken'? We have one broken colonel on our hands."

"I agree; I recognize the symptoms."

"He needs help, maybe even a psychiatrist."

When things had come apart for her, the last thing on her mind had been to ask an Army psychiatrist for help. Even though she was long out of the Army, safely away from a psychiatrist's report that would have ended her military career, Avivah felt cold at the thought. Darby was still in the Army. Seeing a psychiatrist would mean kissing his career good-bye. "Darby isn't going to surrender himself to medical care voluntarily. Which leaves what? Ship him back to Japan, labeled *Damaged in Transit?*"

"Sounds good to me. I'm going to talk to Pepper. She spent years reassembling guys like Darby."

"She's too close to him."

"She's going to have to find a way around that, because right now she is Darby's only hope. He will listen to her when he won't listen to the rest of us."

"You always said that Darby would break Pepper's heart."

"I hate being right." He handed Avivah a folded piece of paper. "This is something else I don't want to be right about."

She glanced over a military-style compilation of facts about Benny's boss, Yanni Skoufalos: age, height, weight, hair color, and so on. Paper-clipped to it was a snapshot of a wiry, bearded man. "He's not back yet?"

"He wasn't when I left the shop a few minutes ago. The police won't activate a missing person's report for another twenty-four hours. I'm afraid something has happened to him, but I can't do a thing about it. Lorraine is due to deliver. Mark feels pushed aside by baby preparations. Randy is suddenly behaving too secretively for my liking. I'm worried about Pepper and Darby. I'm juggling final exams and trying to keep Yanni's business open. I need help. Please."

Benny rarely asked for help, and never pleaded. "What do you want me to do?"

"Whatever it is the police do when a person goes missing, but do it now instead of waiting another twenty-four hours."

"I'll do the best I can."

Her driver was waiting in her office. "I called the airlines. Edith Filmore booked a package deal through a travel agent in Hawaii. Honolulu to San Francisco on Saturday, stayed Saturday night in the airport hotel, and flew from San Francisco to Atlanta on Sunday. The flight included a thirty-minute stopover in Dallas. In Atlanta, she changed planes for Asheville."

"That would have been an expensive trip. How did she pay for it?"

"Cash."

Where had a woman who washed out her one dress in motel rooms every night get enough cash to fly halfway around the world?

He continued, "She arrived on Piedmont flight two-three-one out of Atlanta at seven forty-three Sunday night. She didn't rent a car. A couple of the taxi companies are rechecking their records, but I don't think she took a cab, either."

It was about an hour's drive from the airport to the homestead. If Edith Filmore had come directly to Pepper from the airport, she should have arrived at nine o'clock instead of ten. What had she done during that missing hour? And she'd checked into her motel a few minutes before midnight. How had she gotten from the airport to Pepper's place and from Madison County to the motel?

"The only Baxter flying into Asheville in the week was a Randolph Baxter."

Avivah winced. Randolph was Darby's middle name. Was he playing stupid identity games? But if he'd wanted to do that, why travel under the name of Baxter at all? "Could be him."

"He bought a first-class ticket at the Seattle-Tacoma Airport early Monday morning. Before that, no airline had a record of him."

They wouldn't have if Darby had flown Military Air Transport Service out of anywhere in the Pacific to Fort Lewis, Washington. Fort Lewis and the Sea-Tac airport were about thirty miles apart.

So Edith had been in Asheville before Darby climbed on a plane. That was a relief.

A first-class ticket on short notice would have cost Darby an arm and a leg. If he'd flown military standby, it would not have been in the first-class cabin. She hoped he'd spent the extra money because his battered body had wanted a more comfortable seat. The other option was that he was flying under military radar for a reason, and she's rather not dwell on that.

"He flew Seattle-Tacoma to Atlanta with two stops: Denver and Dallas. Changed to Piedmont flight two-oh-four in Atlanta.

Arrived in Asheville at five-oh-four Monday evening."

So much for him arriving in Asheville well after Edith's body had been discovered.

"Is he a suspect?"

Avivah hated saying what she had to say. "He is now."

She wasn't looking forward to asking Pepper if Darby had duplicates of her office keys. She couldn't figure out why he would, but stranger things happened all the time.

"He rented a car at the airport at five twenty. Gave a military APO for his home address and a local phone number where he'd be staying. Here's where it gets weird."

Gets weird? Avivah braced herself for more bad news.

"At nine o'clock this morning, the owner of a feed-and-seed store called the rental agency. A rental car had been left in his parking lot after he closed last night."

"What time did he close last night?"

"Six."

"Where's his store?"

"Highway Seventy-four, north of Fairview."

The opposite direction from where Pepper lived.

"The agency sent a tow truck, in case the car had had mechanical trouble or had been in an accident, but it's working perfectly. Rental papers were in the glove box. They called the local contact number on the rental form, but that number isn't in service." He handed Avivah his clipboard. "Is that number familiar?"

If she reversed the fourth and fifth digits, it was her home number. Had pain, exhaustion, and jet lag caused Darby to make a simple mistake, or was disguising Pepper's home number more of his military intelligence games? That unwanted call to child welfare now hung on how honest Darby would be with her.

Lieutenant Nate Alexander, Avivah's supervisor, finally came to her office just before lunch. "You were late this morning."

Avivah slid the blank *Request for Child Apprehension* form into a folder. She didn't want Nate asking questions. Darby was on her shit list right now, but Benny was right. Darby was broken and even broken soldiers, maybe especially broken soldiers, protected one another.

"One of those nuisance home emergencies."

"Everything okay?"

"Yeah."

Nate sat beside her desk. Since he'd reconciled with his wife and been promoted to lieutenant, he'd stopped dressing like a 1950s television detective. Today he wore a navy suit, fresh white shirt and an orange-and-gold-streaked tie. He asked, "What do we know about last night's victim?"

She grabbed the corner of a piece of paper and pulled it from the stack. "Female, apparently strangled, discovered last night at twenty hundred hours in the Laurel Ridge Clinic in West Asheville. She registered at a local motel under the Edith Jane Filmore with a Racine, Wisconsin, address. In her room, we found a letter from the US State Department, saying that she was in transit back to the States, and that her identification and passport had been lost.

"This morning, I talked to the State Department's personnel office. They do—did—have an employee named Edith Filmore who fits our victim's description. If our Edith is their Edith, she was forty-five years old. Single. A career government employee. Spent a number of years working for the Wisconsin state government before she joined the State Department. Next of kin is a cousin; she has the same Racine address the victim gave the motel."

"Is the cousin coming to identify the body?"

"I talked to her, too. She's in ill health and can't travel. I'm waiting for the State Department to send us a photograph to confirm Miss Filmore's identity." It was better that Nate knew the truth now instead of later. "Miss Filmore's last posting was the US embassy in Saigon. Her position was Administrative Assistant, Finance. She was evacuated from the embassy on April thirtieth."

"What a disaster."

Avivah wasn't sure if he meant the evacuation or Miss Filmore dying on their doorstep. Both qualified. "Miss Filmore was logged onto the USS *Blue Ridge,* at zero-one-zero-five hours Wednesday, April thirtieth, Vietnam time. On Thursday, May first, a group of State Department employees were flown to Hawaii, then it gets complicated."

Nate frowned. "When isn't murder complicated?"

Just wait.

"State Department people met the plane in Hawaii and provided transportation to a private estate where they housed them. Like Miss Filmore, many of them had lost ID and passports in the evacuation. They gave everyone a letter that would give them permission to enter the continental US. Edith Filmore picked up her letter and fifty dollars in pocket money—gift of the State Department—walked away from the estate and never came back. Forty-eight hours later, on Saturday, the State Department filed a missing-person report with Honolulu Police Department. By then, Edith was on a plane to San Francisco."

"Why did she come to Asheville?"

"She was escorting a Vietnamese refugee, a child, to a family here. She delivered the child Sunday night. Monday, the family paid her three thousand dollars, which was what she'd been promised."

"Promised?"

"The person who asked her to bring the child to the US

Sharonenefef俊

contracted with her for that amount."

"Dodgy business for the State Department."

"I agree." Except that this business had nothing to do with the State Department.

"Any possibility of this Vietnamese family being involved in the murder?"

"It's an American family, and they have alibis."

Except she hadn't heard Colonel Darby Baxter's alibi yet.

"Crap, it's that Baby Lift thing again."

The Baby Lift had been a disastrous attempt, including a horrific plane crash, to evacuate hundreds of Vietnamese orphans to the US during the closing days of the war.

Nate looked as if he'd tasted sour milk. "They're treating these Vietnamese kids like war souvenirs. People aren't going to forget or forgive this war, and they won't want reminders growing up next door. I suppose the kid is half GI. Black or white?"

Anne had Vietnamese features, but those blue eyes hinted that she wasn't one-hundred-percent Asian. "If I had to guess, white."

"Small mercies. We've got a murdered State Department employee who was involved in something dodgy. A racial angle would be another complication."

Nate didn't want complications? Try adding blackmail. And that she'd helped pay the blackmail demand. And that her friends were, once again, up to their necks in murder. *Oy vey,* he was going to get complications.

Nate asked, "What's Edith Filmore's connection to Laurel Ridge Clinic?"

"She may have been a patient at the clinic on Monday. The nurse-practitioner who runs the clinic isn't volunteering information, so I'm applying for a court order for records."

"Ms. Teague won't be happy about that."

He said *Ms.* without smirking. Nate came from good ole boy

stock, but the past two years had shredded that worldview.

Avivah leaned back in her chair. "You know Pat Teague?"

"I'm afraid so."

He got up and Avivah assumed he'd say the usual, "Keep me informed." Instead he opened the office door, and called softly, "Ash?"

A tall, middle-aged blonde walked into the office. Avivah had met Ash Alexander—wait, she went by her maiden name—Ash Morgan at the police department's Christmas party. In December, Ash had been thin; today she was gaunt. Avivah wondered if she had an eating disorder.

Avivah stood and held out her hand. "Good morning, Ms. Morgan, I'm Avivah Rosen."

Her handshake was damp. "Silver-sprinkled sugar cookies."

"Pardon?"

"That's what you brought to the Christmas party."

Nate held out a chair for his wife. "Ash has recently become the volunteer coordinator for Laurel Ridge Clinic."

Ash's head snapped around. "I can speak for myself."

Nate backed a step away from his wife's chair. "Sorry."

Why did anything involving her housemates have to be this complicated? Why hadn't Pepper or Pat mentioned that Nate's wife volunteered at Laurel Ridge Clinic? Maybe Pepper didn't know who her volunteer coordinator was. Ash was testy enough about speaking for herself that she might not have confided in anyone at the clinic that she and Nate were married. Since she used her maiden name, Pepper wouldn't have made the connection on her own.

Ash and Nate had endured their daughter's unexpected death and a year's separation when Ash went off to "find herself." Avivah didn't believe the search had succeeded.

One of the things Ash apparently had found was Pat Teague for a fashion advisor, but she didn't appear to be a very apt advisee. Her silver earrings were genuine—a familiar dogwood pattern—but her jeans came from a discount store and, unless Avivah missed her guess, the folk shirt and down vest were homemade. The clothes were well made, but far from the upscale versions that Pat Teague paid handsomely to wear. Pat was round and solid; this kind of clothing fit her body. On Ash's thin frame, the clothes might as well be on a scarecrow.

Avivah assumed her professional police officer voice. "What can I do for you this morning, Ms. Morgan?"

Ash clasped her bony hands together. "I want to make a statement."

Nate said, "I know I can trust you to keep Ash's name out of the investigation if that's at all possible. She has an alibi for the time of the murder."

First Benny and now Nate had asked her for favors. "I'll have to interview her without you present."

"That's the way I want it."

He kissed his wife on the cheek, gave her clasped hands a gentle squeeze, and left.

Ash fidgeted. "Nate used to talk about work, so I know about interviews. Do I have to prove I'm who I say I am? I have my driver's license. Do you need to see it?"

Avivah removed a fresh pad of paper from her desk drawer. "Telling me your full name and address will be sufficient. I assume you know that you have a right to a lawyer."

A blush started at the base of Ash's long neck and quickly worked its way up her face. "I couldn't have our lawyer here. Nate and I have known him for years. His wife and I were in our bridge club."

"Ms. Morgan, try to relax. If you do want a lawyer, I can help you find someone other than your family attorney."

"Will Nate read your notes?"

"He'll read my report, which will contain what I consider

relevant information from my notes."

"Does that mean you can leave out things?"

"The best I can offer is to downplay aspects of what you say that aren't essential to my investigation."

She rubbed goose bumps on her arms. "All right."

Avivah wrote down the essential preinterview information. "For the record, what is your connection to the clinic?"

"I'm the director of volunteers."

"What does that involve?"

"I recruit, train, and supervise volunteers, and do volunteer work myself."

"How often are you at the clinic?"

"Two or three times a week."

"Were you there yesterday?"

"All day."

"Do you remember a middle-aged woman with salt-and-pepper hair? She wore a well-fitting gray dress and carried a black purse."

Ash pursed her thin lips. "Laurel Ridge Clinic maintains a strict confidentiality policy."

In other words, if she'd seen Edith Filmore, she wasn't going to be any more forthcoming than Pat Teague.

"Is the name Edith Filmore familiar to you?" She watched Ash closely for a tell, body language that bespoke a lie.

"I never met anyone by that name."

Ash had shown no tell.

"In spite of your clinic's confidentiality policy, you came in this morning to give a voluntary statement. Why was that?"

Boney hands twisted again. "I can't answer any questions about clients, but I've been concerned about something at the clinic. I was told it was none of my business, but murder changes things, doesn't it?"

It certainly did. "What are you concerned about?"

"Drugs."

Avivah visualized the sparsely stocked shelves of cough medicine and lice shampoo. Street value zilch. Unless the clinic had other drugs that Ms. Teague neglected to mention.

"The nurses encourage clients to bring in old drugs for disposal. They dump them into a big glass jar in their office."

Avivah couldn't remember seeing a glass jar of drugs. "Why?"

"Ms. Teague takes that jar with her when she speaks about waste in the health-care system."

"What concerns you about this jar?"

"It's always two-thirds full."

"You're saying that the nurses add drugs to this jar, but it never gets full?"

"That's right, but it does get rearranged."

"You mean that Ms. Teague moves it to different places in the clinic?"

"I mean that the pills inside the jar get rearranged. Do you remember sand art?"

"Layering colored sand in bottles to create patterns?"

"The pills are always arranged in pretty layers. I think someone is stealing drugs from that jar and covering it up by rearranging the remaining pills."

"Did you ask the nurses about it?"

"I mentioned it to Ms. Teague." Ash fidgeted again. "She said drugs weren't my concern. I can't help if I notice things."

Notice and remember. She'd remembered what cookies Avivah had brought to a party months ago. "Is the drug jar the only thing you've noticed at the clinic that seems out of place?"

"Yes."

Drugs were a big deal, but Avivah couldn't think of a single possible connection between missing pills and Edith Filmore. "This is a formality, but I have to ask. Where you were between four and eight o'clock last night?"

"In a tutoring session. I attend UNC-A part-time. Nate dropped me at the library between four thirty and five. He picked me up about ten thirty. I usually drive myself, but my car is in the shop, and the bus connections to the university from where we live aren't that good. I didn't want him to bother, but he insisted."

It was too much information, recited by rote. For some reason, Ash Morgan had known she'd need an alibi on Monday night. Illicit sex was a timeworn reason for which a wife fabricated an alibi. Women experimenting with feminism sometimes explored their sexual orientation. Avivah picked up the phone. "I'll need your tutor's name and phone number."

Ash's hand went to her mouth. "Please don't."

"I must know where you really were."

Ash straightened her long spine. "My tutor and I *were* together. We were with eleven other women honoring the goddess for Beltane. We had a potluck supper, wove Beltane wreaths, and danced around a bonfire."

Avivah had picked up a smattering of goddess lore. She couldn't resist asking, "Sky-clad?"

"Yes, Detective Rosen, neither my tutor nor I had on a stitch of clothing."

CHAPTER 7

Pepper stirred a package of chocolate breakfast drink into milk and gulped it down. The cold sticky liquid coated the back of her throat. Through the kitchen window she watched her friend and tenant, Frannie Maddox-Doan, down on her middle-aged belly on a blanket facing Anne, who also lay on her stomach. Frannie raised her head and chest and waved a toy at Anne, who attempted to raise her head. Frannie looked like a multicolored, silk-draped seal. Anne looked happy.

Benny had taken Anne to his house. How had she ended up with Frannie?

A cold wave flooded through Pepper. Decades ago, Frannie had started her social work career in child welfare. What if Frannie asked questions about Anne?

What was that story she'd concocted for Pat Teague? Mom in hospital—doing well, Pepper had called this morning for a progress report—Dad on maneuvers. Don't embellish; don't volunteer information. Stick to those two facts.

She stuffed her supper and an unopened can of formula into her backpack, picked up Anne's car seat, and bolted out her kitchen door, straight into Kaye.

Kaye. The problem. The enigma. The temporary boarder. Temporary for three weeks now. She'd arrived at Frannie's art studio without a last name or a history. A battered suitcase full of faded clothes were all she brought with her. Kaye could be about Pepper's age, but that was a guess.

Pepper used her best nurse-voice. "Good morning, Kaye."

"Good-morn-ning-miss-pep-per-hawk." Kaye always spoke in a singsong voice, like a first grader.

"May I see what you have this morning?"

Kaye opened her threadbare apron, which she carried by the bottom corners. Pieces of shattered clay rested on the faded cloth. Pepper wasn't sure what the shards had been originally: something intricately artistic and beautiful.

Pepper held a fragment to the light. The fired pottery shined with a gray opalescence, akin to mother-of-pearl. "This glaze is beautiful."

"Not-right-not-right." Kaye said, holding out her apron to indicate that she wanted the piece back. Pepper replaced the shard. Kaye closed her apron and continued on her way toward the refuse bins around the side of the house.

Pepper walked across the wide expanse of level ground behind her house, toward the trees that sheltered Frannie and Anne. Her property contained her own house and a smaller, older house, which had been the original homestead. In the past two years, Pepper's contribution to property development had been having a three-car garage built, and scattered groupings of plastic, discount-store lawn furniture placed around the back-yard.

It was Frannie who had the real vision for the property. She'd rented the small house and renovated it into an art studio. Behind the studio, she'd built an outdoor pottery kiln, and turned a large patch of earth into an herb garden. A carved wooden sign hung over the studio's front door.

Fran-tastic Art: for women moving on

A few weeks ago, Frannie had bought Lorraine's trailer when Lorraine and Benny moved into their new house. The second-hand trailer rested on gray cinder blocks on the far side of

Pepper's backyard. Now that Frannie had a place for students to sleep, she planned to offer workshops that lasted more than one day. Right now, Kaye was staying in the trailer, and Frannie was being very closemouthed about Kaye. Pepper couldn't help wondering if Kaye had recently been discharged from a mental hospital.

She plopped down beside Frannie, who had placed Anne on her back and who, to Anne's obvious delight, was brushing the end of her hand-painted silk scarf across the baby's skin.

"How much pottery has Kaye made and smashed?"

Frannie watched Kaye meticulously deposit shards into the garbage can. "I've lost track."

"I know you're a good therapist, but she needs something more."

Kaye shook out her apron and carefully replaced the lid on the can.

"I'm waiting for some small sign that she's ready to trust me."

"Maybe you shouldn't wait much longer; we'd see her at the clinic."

"I know. Thanks. Lorraine said that you had the weekend from hell."

"It was okay up to Sunday night."

"How come you didn't phone me?"

"Every time I turned around, a new twist complicated my life. Phoning anyone fell off of my to-do list."

"How is Anne's mom?"

Bless Benny! He had paid attention when she outlined their cover story.

"Better. Had what we call in the trade a comfortable night."

Frannie leaned toward Pepper and said in a low voice, "It's not a good idea for me to babysit Anne."

"Why not?"

"Kaye became hysterical when she saw me holding Anne."

Pepper wasn't surprised, but she was disturbed. She didn't want Anne around anyone who became hysterical. "What do you think is going on with Kaye?"

"My first guess is that she lost a child recently. Gray glazes. Breaking every piece of pottery she throws as soon as it comes out of the kiln. Wearing faded clothes. She's in sackcloth and ashes, doing penance for a whole lot of guilt."

Two voices, one male and one female, drifted from where a small footpath, which connect Kirkpatrick and Pepperhawk land, emerged from the trees. Lorraine and her older son, Randy, came down that path.

Whatever man thought up the idea that being pregnant made a woman glow had never seen a woman in the last week of pregnancy. Lorraine Kirkpatrick, who normally resembled a tall, white-and-gold ice queen, was now an overweight, exhausted, waddling duck. That wasn't fair. If Pepper ever became pregnant, she'd resemble a duck; Lorraine was more an overweight, exhausted, waddling swan.

She wore black maternity pants and a yellow-and-white maternity smock that she'd bought at a secondhand store. Lorraine could give Kaye a lesson about wearing secondhand clothes with style.

Her son Randy had reverted to the nineteen fifties. Pepper had seen photographs of Randy's late father. The boy was built like his dad, had the same facial features and, by choice, sported the same close-cropped hair, the same jeans, white socks, penny loafers and a tight, white T-shirt. Even the same teenage scowl. The one thing missing was a package of cigarettes rolled into his shirtsleeve, an affectation that Benny would never permit.

It was Tuesday morning. Randy should be in school. "Why is Randy home?"

"Broken water main. The health inspector closed school for

the rest of the week while repairs are done. Bad luck for him. He stepped off the school bus fifteen minutes after Lorraine got a letter that sent her through the roof. It would have been better if she'd had time to cool off before Randy came home."

"Is that how you ended up with Anne?"

"She wanted to give Randy her full attention."

Lorraine said to her son, "We'll talk about this again when Ben gets home. Stop pestering me. There's a list of chores on the refrigerator. I want you to work on that list until three o'clock."

"Come on, Mom."

"I need those chores done."

Randy stomped back toward the path. He said over his shoulder, "How about what I need? This is first grade all over again."

Lorraine waddled to the tree-shaded area. Frannie got up to help her into a chair, but Lorraine waved her away. "Don't bother. I'd only have to get up again. I'll lean for a few minutes." With a groan, she rested her back against an arched tree trunk. "I hate motherhood."

Pepper said, "I don't believe that."

"Today I do." She handed Pepper a folded piece of paper.

Randall Fulford, Jr. had been accepted into a summer camp at a nearby art school. Even nonartistic Pepper recognized the school's name. "This is terrific."

"Read the last paragraph."

The cost would make any parent woozy.

"Ouch."

She handed the letter to Frannie. After she read it, Frannie said, "I'd contribute to support a fellow artist."

"I'd contribute, too," Pepper said. Except that her mortgage and loan payments would take all of her spare cash. Blast.

"Thank you, but that's not the point. We told Randy months

ago that we couldn't afford this. He applied anyway and used our signatures on his old report cards to forge Ben's and my signatures on the application. I wouldn't let him go now even if we had the money."

Frannie shoved Anne's toys in her diaper bag. "What did Randy mean about first grade?"

Pepper couldn't decide if Lorraine's expression was frustration or guilt. "Mark had an ear infection the day Randy started first grade. Randall was on a field exercise. Our neighbor drove Randy to school while Mark and I went to the pediatrician. He was the only kid in first grade without a parent."

Military brats learned to survive things like that.

"We were transferred from Panama to Fort Bragg six weeks after he started school. He's always thought first grade was so hard because we didn't get the juju right on the first day. Now he thinks that if he doesn't go to this art camp, he'll never become an artist."

Pepper asked, "Was first grade the year that Randall went missing in action?"

"That happened the week before Randy began second grade."

Both Pepper and Frannie groaned.

"Motherhood sucks." She struggled to right herself from the tree. "Ignore me. I have a new house, a wonderful husband, and two normal—if irritating—kids. A week from now, when I pop this baby, we'll be a bigger and better family. Assuming I don't kill Randy first. I came over to make sure that you didn't need me to babysit Anne this afternoon."

Pepper buckled Anne into her car seat. "Thanks, but I'm taking her to work. We have to go. I'm late."

Pepper let herself in through the clinic's back door. She was half an hour late. Hopefully Lillian and their volunteer doctor had held the fort.

From the wave of sound that hit her, they hadn't. She dumped the diaper bag and her backpack on her office chair, and Anne's carrier on the desk. "I'll be right back," she said to the baby before hurrying down the hall. Their waiting area had become another country.

About sixty people, most of them Vietnamese men and women, crowded into the tiny room. The men slipped into their expected place in Pepper's memory. In Qui Nhon, Vietnamese men wore the same kind of slacks, short-sleeved shirts, and baseball caps. But Vietnamese women wore tight silk dresses and black silk pants. Seeing a couple of dozen Vietnamese women in white sundresses and perky green-and-yellow canvas hats couldn't have looked any stranger if they had been giraffes in tutus. All of the clothes looked new, down to their spotless white canvas shoes.

Lillian Hood, the clinic's receptionist, was trying to hold simultaneous conversations with two Vietnamese men and several of their regular clients. Behind her, the doctor who volunteered on Tuesdays held a handful of charts over his head. He yelled, "Everyone, sit down."

No one listened to him.

The calm spot was Ash in her pink volunteer smock. She smiled, bowed, and handed out cups of coffee to all comers. Bless Ash.

Pepper worked her way through the crowd to the reception desk. She yelled at Lillian, "What's going on?"

Lillian pushed a gray curl from her face. "I don't know. A school bus was parked outside when we opened. These people marched in here, and the bus drove away."

"Where's Pat?"

"Gone to the police station."

That was odd. Avivah had asked Pat for a statement last night. All right, if Pat wasn't available, she was on her own.

One of their regular clients shoved a Vietnamese man; he shot her the finger. Background chatter turned ugly. Uh-oh, powder keg time.

Pepper boosted herself onto the desk and clapped her hands above her head. She didn't know the Vietnamese word for quiet, but she frowned and raised her finger to her lips. In a few minutes noise dribbled away to a hostile silence.

Her legs protested when she sank into a squat, something she hadn't done since she left Vietnam. She wasn't sure she could get up again. She moved both of her hands in a downward gesture. One by one the Vietnamese sank into squats, flowing with more grace than Pepper managed. That left ten clients standing: tall white trees in a forest of brown bushes. Sixty people looked at Pepper with various degrees of curiosity, anger, or confusion. She bowed her head slightly. *"Cám on."*

The words felt funny. Her tongue had forgotten how to fit around one of the few Vietnamese words she knew. She hoped she'd remembered the words correctly and hadn't insulted someone's parents.

"Thank you," she repeated in English. "I apologize for the confusion. Our regular clients will be seen first. Please take a chair and form a line down the hall."

The women picked up chairs. A few Vietnamese rose to their feet and picked up chairs, too. Ash circulated through the crowd, gesturing for the Vietnamese to leave the chairs alone.

Pepper tried to stand, but Qui Nhon had been too long ago. Her muscles weren't as limber as they had been then. She rocked back on her heels, and landed hard on her butt. Some of the Vietnamese women giggled behind their hands.

Pepper laughed, too. The Vietnamese believed in saving face, but they appreciated a pratfall. And they respected someone who could laugh at herself.

She grabbed paper and marker and wrote *Closed until 3:00*

because of a medical emergency. Sorry for the inconvenience. She taped the paper to the front door, locked the door, and pulled blinds down over the two big windows. She didn't want passersby to gawk at the Vietnamese. Besides, a secured perimeter was a good perimeter.

After their regular clients had settled in a crowded line down the hall, Pepper turned her attention to the Vietnamese. Some of them were squatting with an ease that said they could hold that position for hours. She patted her chest. "*Đại uý* Pepperhawk." Except that she hadn't been Captain Pepperhawk for a long time. She'd never learned Vietnamese for Miss Pepperhawk or Nurse Pepperhawk, so Captain would have to do. "*Đại uý* Pepperhawk. Sixty-seventh Evac Hospital. Qui Nhon."

One of the men at the front of the room stood and patted his chest. "*Trung uý* Bach. Da Nang."

Lieutenant Bach. An ARVN officer from Da Nang. Pepper pushed away all of the derogatory names that GIs had called Arvins. Old grievances or soldier's humor wasn't what she needed today. She was grateful for someone who would understand the importance of discipline and order.

A ripple passed through the room. Half a dozen men stood, pointed to their chests and said their name, rank and unit. The one unit Pepper recognized was LLDB. *Lực Lượng Đặc Biệt.* South Vietnamese Special Forces.

What she wanted to do most was apologize. *I'm sorry we didn't come to your aid. I'm sorry we lost the war. I'm sorry we made such a cock-up of it in the end.* Signaling for the men who had said they'd been soldiers to *come here* with the fingertips pointed at the ceiling would be an insult. Instead, she waved her fingers back and forth, careful to keep the fingertips pointed at the floor. *"Lại đây! Lại đây!"*

The ex-soldiers grouped themselves around her.

"Does anyone speak English?" She'd learned a long time ago

that yelling didn't make her more comprehensible, but sometimes speaking slowly did.

The man who had said he had been LLDB said slowly, "I speak some English."

Pepper had an almost uncontrollable urge to ask him if he knew Darby, Randall Fulford, Benny, or any of the other US Special Forces she knew. It would be so much of a relief to have a connection with someone in this group. Instead she held out her hand. "What is your name?"

The man shook her hand. "Nghiem Tho Huyna."

Okay so far. "Mr. Nghiem, why are you here?"

He said something in Vietnamese to the other men. There was nodding and guttural agreements. One of the men took a brochure from his back pocket and handed it to Pepper. On the cover was a photograph of a plump brown-and-white goose.

Charles Tu
Ducks—Geese—Eggs—Smoked Meat

Mr. Nghiem turned the brochure over and pointed to a photograph of a white-haired Vietnamese man dressed in a business suit and tie. "Mr. Tu, boss."

"Where Mr. Tu?"

"Don't know."

She slid back into a speech pattern she'd left behind in Qui Nhon. "Why bus bring you here?"

"Phy-si-cals." Mr. Nghiem pronounced the word carefully, giving it three full syllables.

Pepper's heart sank. Fifty physicals would take a long time. Physical examinations for what? Hadn't US authorities given these people a complete going over before allowing them into the country? Considering the pandemonium she'd read about, maybe reception centers were so overwhelmed that they expected the health-care system at the receiving end to pick up the slack.

She opened the brochure. One of the photos showed two Vietnamese men in white uniforms, heavy aprons, and white caps standing behind a butcher's glass case. Rows of smoked ducks hung in the case. Pepper had seen similar ducks hanging in the widows of Chinese groceries in San Francisco. The caption under the photo read, "All of our employees have food handler certificates and are highly trained in health and sanitation." She pointed to the caption. "Food handler certificates?"

Mr. Nghiem grinned. "Food hand-lers phy-si-cals."

A food handler examination involved a chest X-ray, lab work, and an abbreviated physical exam. The clinic didn't have an X-ray, but she could fill out requests, and collect lab specimens. The doctor could do the quick exam.

She reached over the counter and pulled out packets of lab and X-ray forms, pens, and a yellow highlighter. She highlighted name, birth date, sex, and address on the top of the forms, to show that those blanks had to be filled in. Under reason for exam she wrote *Food Handler Certificate*.

She waved her arm in an arc that encompassed the room. "All do." She held up the example. "Like this. All do." She handed out blank forms and pens. Her small private army began to distribute them. People sat on the floor to fill in the forms.

From behind her reception counter, Lillian said, "I'll phone the lab and let them know that you will bring a lot of specimens to them this afternoon."

For once Lillian's super-efficiency was an asset instead of an irritation.

"Please. Phone the radiologist we use and tell them to expect a whole passel of people for chest X-rays tomorrow."

Pepper hurried back to her office. Anne was awake and appeared to be listening intently. Did she find the sound of all of those Vietnamese voices soothing?

"Stinky baby," she said, unbuckling Anne from the carrier, and laying her on the desk to change her diaper. She had a solution to Anne's adoption in her waiting room. She could hold a lottery: pick a number from one to fifty and the person who gets closest to her number went home with a new baby. If life were only that simple. Though maybe she did have a solution. This Mr. Tu might have connections that she could use to find adoptive parents for Anne.

She washed her hands, mixed a bottle of formula, and shoved the nipple in Anne's waiting mouth. When she walked into the waiting room, Mr. Nghiem fell to his knees; tears rolled down his cheeks. He held up his arms in a pleading gesture, *"Em bé. Em bé."*

Pepper stepped back. Some people turned away, other looked at the floor. *Trung uý* Bach and two other men went to Mr. Nghiem and pulled him to his feet. They herded him into a far corner of the room and made a protective circle around him. Mr. Nghiem nodded and made little animal noises.

Pepper called, *"Trung uý,"* and Mr. Bach came to her.

"What is he saying?"

He held up his index finger. "Him one here." With his hand he gestured four heights, one as tall as he was and three smaller stair steps, and then he shook his head sadly. "No here."

From which Pepper deduced that Mr. Nghiem's wife and children had either died or he hadn't been able to get them out of Vietnam. "I am so sorry."

Mr. Bach nodded. One of the women came to Pepper's side and held out her hands. Pepper was surprised how reluctant she was to hand Anne over, but she did it. The woman made clacking sounds and Anne smiled at her. For the first time since Edith Filmore showed up at her door, Pepper felt that Anne had a future in America.

CHAPTER 8

"Skoufalos Electronics. Mr. Kirkpatrick speaking."

The careful way Benny answered the store's phone gave Avivah a jolt. In the years that she'd known Benny, he'd swung from a rapid-fire "J.F.K. Special Warfare Center, First Sergeant Kirkpatrick. May I help you, sir?" to an abrupt, distilled, civilian "Kirkpatrick." Both greetings conveyed that the caller better have a good reason for bothering him. Getting used to Benny Kirkpatrick the customer's friend wasn't easy.

"It's Avivah. Your boss rented a car yesterday morning at ten thirty. He arrived at the rental agency alone, on foot. He had one suitcase with him and rented a car for seven days."

Benny's relieved sigh came clearly over the phone. "Did he say where he was going?"

"No, but he's supposed to return the vehicle here in Asheville. I'm sorry, but this means you can't file a missing persons report until at least next Wednesday."

"He's still missing." Benny sounded irritated.

"He didn't appear to be under duress, and he didn't attempt to hide who he was. He rented the car in his own name, and paid with a credit card also in his name."

"Yanni uses his credit card for emergencies."

"Based on the hurried way he left, let's assume this trip was an emergency. Emergencies aren't illegal. The best I can do is circulate a Call Home Notice."

"What's that?"

"North Carolina Highway Patrol will be alerted. If they spot his rental car, they'll stop it and ask the driver to call home. The same notice will be posted in high tourist traffic areas, places like entrances to national and state parks. Shall I list your name and home phone number on the circular?"

"Absolutely."

"I'm sorry; I wish I had more for you."

"At least I know that Yanni left under his own steam. It's something."

Not very much, Avivah thought after she hung up. It must have been a heck of an emergency to cause a man to leave his shop unlocked and keys in his apartment door.

Now that she'd taken care of Benny's business, it was time to get back to her own. She pressed the intercom button. "Please send Ms. Teague to my office."

A few minutes later, Pat Teague strode into Avivah's office. She didn't close the door behind herself. Today she wore tan cords, a pale-yellow ribbed cotton shirt, and an intricate hand-embroidered vest. Avivah picked up a pattern: simple clothes underneath and a costly vest that drew the eye. Ms. Teague was a woman who wanted to choose where attention was focused.

"I don't appreciate being kept waiting. I have a clinic to run."

"I have a murder to investigate."

"I gave you a statement last night."

Avivah got up and closed the door. "Today I have more questions. Personal questions. The usual procedure is to have a constable present as note taker during an interview. We have no female constables." She waited for the idea to sink in: having a male constable present when *personal* questions were being asked.

"I won't agree to an interview under those conditions."

"We are the police. You don't have a choice. The best I can offer is a secretary from the typing pool or I will take notes."

"You mean your word against mine."

"My notes will be typed into a statement for your signature. If you disagree with anything in that statement, you will be entitled to a second interview, with both a male detective and a constable present."

"I'm free to leave at any time?"

"Certainly."

"Let's get this over with."

"You agree to being interviewed with only me present?"

"Yes, anything. I want to get this over with."

Avivah jotted the date, time, and people present on her legal pad. "Last night, you stated that you left Laurel Ridge Clinic at four o'clock Monday."

"Correct."

"You drove home, where you remained all evening until returning to the clinic at the police's request."

Ms. Teague folded her arms. "Also correct."

Closed body language. A good sign. She had something to hide.

"You provided the name of a houseguest who could confirm those details."

"I did."

"Your houseguest provided us with fascinating details that you omitted." Thanks to Ash Morgan, who'd led Avivah in the direction of what questions to ask when she phoned the house-guest.

Pat leaned back, giving Avivah a hooded-eye stare. If that was how she did her fund-raising, Laurel Ridge Clinic's finances would always be in the black. Ms. Teague had mastered intimidating.

"How many people were at your house last night?"

"Why is that your business?"

Women in Avivah's family imbibed intimidating with their

mother's milk. "A woman was killed in a clinic where women are supposed to be safe. Has your phone started ringing? Are your financial backers having qualms? Would a clean bill of health from the city's only female detective help you? If so, I suggest you cooperate."

The big office clock ticked a full minute before Pat Teague said, "Thirteen people."

"All women?"

"Yes."

"Aren't thirteen guests a tricky seating arrangement?"

Ms. Teague's mouth curled in a ghost of a smile. "A round table is a wonderful asset."

Goddess-lore advocates ranged from silly to seriously spiritual to scams that interested bunko squads. Pepper was spiritually vulnerable. So was Ash Morgan, when you came down to it. It was not an overreaction to want to protect them. "A coven?"

"A dinner party of compatible women who came together to celebrate the arrival of summer."

"Summer doesn't arrive for another six weeks."

"Summer solstice celebrates mid-summer. For Wiccans summer begins at Beltane—May Day, if you prefer the modern name."

"May first was last Wednesday. Why did you wait five days to celebrate?"

"My houseguest couldn't be here until this week."

Wiccans, it appeared, were practical.

"Your clinic is open until five o'clock on Mondays. Why did you leave an hour earlier yesterday?"

"I wanted to be home when my guests arrived."

"If someone had required care between four and five, and the clinic wasn't able to provide it, would that have bothered you?"

"Stop baiting me. Laurel Ridge Clinic is not an emergency service, and the staff are allowed to have private lives."

"I would have thought having twelve witnesses to where you were last night would be to your advantage. Why did you mention only your houseguest?"

"Because if I mentioned the other women, you would have asked me for their names and addresses. I will not provide that information."

"This party happened at your home. Clinic confidentiality doesn't apply."

"I invited those women to my home because it was safe."

"Safe in what way?"

"From what Pepper has told me, you are neither naive nor stupid. You know that women who practice the Craft have always been harassed. I don't want these women's names and addresses in a police file."

"You don't have a choice."

She leaned forward. "I will make it a choice. I'll use every legal means at my disposal to protect those women. That includes going to jail on any trumped-up charge you decide to concoct. I will give interviews from my jail cell. Does the Asheville City Police's only female detective want that kind of publicity?"

She was throwing Avivah's opening argument back in Avivah's face. "According to your houseguest, while the other women wove May Day wreaths, you went into private meditation to, and I quote, 'prepare to lead the ceremony.' Are you a licensed minister?"

"Any Wiccan can lead a ceremony. I was the logical choice to lead this one."

"Most hostesses don't leave their guests during a party."

"How many hostesses spend all of their time during a party hiding out in the kitchen?"

Avivah had been at more than one party where the hostess

hadn't enjoyed herself. "How long were you away from your guests?"

"From their point of view, long enough to have returned to the clinic and killed Edith Filmore. That's what you're after, isn't it, opportunity?"

In the blink of an eye, any good lawyer could convert Pat Teague's bravado into Avivah's attempt to entrap. "I want to advise you of your rights. You have the right to remain silent. If you—"

"Skip it. I know my rights. I understand them. I don't want a lawyer present. Sorry, Detective, but what looks like opportunity from one point of view is actually an optical illusion. My partner checked on me during my preparation time. I was never alone for more than fifteen minutes."

Ms. Teague clamped her lips together; she knew she'd made a slip. Avivah asked, "Your partner?"

"Yes."

"You don't live together? She gave me a Colorado address."

"She has another eight months in graduate school. Beltane is our anniversary. That's why I waited until she could be here to celebrate."

Edith Filmore was a blackmailer, and Pat Teague a potential target. The entire US government, including the Army and the State Department, had a paranoid prejudice that gays and lesbians were ideal blackmail targets. It would be difficult to find out if Edith Filmore, as a State Department employee, shared their official paranoia. If she did, and if she had somehow learned about Ms. Teague's sexual orientation, or maybe even her Wiccan connections, then Pepper's boss had earned herself a place at the top of Avivah's suspect list.

"Have you ever been blackmailed because of your sexual orientation?"

"That is none of your business."

"In a murder investigation everything is my business."

Pat stood. "Not if I say it isn't."

In the reception area, Pepper heard Lillian tidying up after evening clinic. In ten minutes, she could close the clinic, bring the drug box to the pharmacy, and go home. It wouldn't be a minute too soon. She moved her right arm around in a circle. Her elbow still hurt.

Pat had barreled into the Vietnamese chaos about three thirty. She'd come to a halt inside the waiting room with her mouth open and her hands on her hips. After she'd latched on to Pepper's elbow, she'd dragged her into their office, slammed the door, and tore a strip off Pepper's hide.

Had Pepper forgotten that their dedicated grant money limited the clinic's services to women and children? Did she have any idea how much she had risked the clinic's future by providing services to men? Hadn't it occurred to her how much that the chaos in the waiting room would upset and disenfranchise their regular clients? What had she been thinking?

Pepper had apologized and promised never to do it again; she wasn't sure what she'd promised not to do. Refuse to provide care for confused people in need? That didn't feel right.

The penance Pat doled out would be that Pepper had to present Mr. Tu with a bill for providing services to the men. Pat had written out a whopping invoice; the final amount embarrassed Pepper. They would, of course, see the women for follow-up. The way Pat put it, they would insist on seeing the women for follow-up: complete physicals; Pap tests; breast exams; screenings for pregnancy, spousal abuse, and venereal disease; immunizations; mental-health counseling; stress-reduction classes; well-baby care; and complete examinations for all of their children.

Pepper had decided this wasn't the best time to point out

that their mandate of services for women and children included equal care for boys and girls until the age of eighteen.

Did Mr. Tu's refugees have children? Or had he picked people to sponsor who were either childless or who had, like poor Mr. Nghiem, lost their family?

After she finished her tirade, Pat had gone home, leaving Pepper and their volunteer doctor to contend with evening clinic alone. It had been an impossibly busy evening.

On Pepper's desk, Anne slept in her carrier with her thumb in her mouth. Pepper reached over and felt the baby's tiny toes through the foot of her sleeper. She was a sweetheart, all right. After seeing Anne's reaction to other Vietnamese, Pepper knew that finding Vietnamese parents for her would be the right thing to do.

Bringing Anne to work had been a mistake. Granted, this had been an unusual day, but all days were busy. If it hadn't been for one Vietnamese woman after another holding Anne, Pepper didn't know what she would have done. What Anne needed now—what they both needed—was a responsible teenage girl who was available during the day and in need of babysitting money. After school ended Pepper could find lots of babysitters, but she couldn't wait three weeks.

Randy Fulford wasn't a girl, but he was responsible and thanks to the broken water main, he was out of school for the rest of this week. He was also desperate for money. Maybe Benny and Lorraine wouldn't let him go to art camp this summer, but he could start saving for next year. He'd had first aid and CPR training in school. Frannie and Lorraine would be nearby to help him if things got dicey. She picked up the phone to call Lorraine, but Lillian knocked on her door frame before she could dial.

"There's a man here to see you."

Pepper replaced the receiver, not keen to see more men in

the clinic. "Who?"

"He won't give his name."

The man was Darby. He wore jeans and a black T-shirt. Unlike the Vietnamese in their pristine new clothes, his new clothes had creases. He'd also had a shave and a haircut. A few blond hairs stuck to his T-shirt. He'd tried to make himself presentable, but new clothes and a haircut couldn't disguise how tired he looked.

Pepper could swear that a faint odor of *nước mắm*—Vietnamese fish sauce—still permeated the reception area.

Darby winded the air like a hunting dog. His eyes unfocused for a second; he shook his head. He'd smelled it, too.

Lillian asked, "Should I stay?"

"It's okay. I know him."

Lillian watched Darby while she picked up her purse and scarf, but she left without another word. Pepper locked the door behind her and faced Darby. He seemed unsure how to stand or what to do with his hands. For the first time ever, Pepper was uncomfortable being with him. "Did you follow the doctor's instructions?"

"I took that vile-tasting medicine on time and ate white food. Mushroom soup and crackers for lunch. Baked chicken breast, mashed potatoes, and vanilla pudding for supper. I've drunk so much milk that I should be wearing a cowbell."

Pepper didn't laugh.

Darby handed a piece of paper to Pepper. "There's no easy way to say this, so I might as well get it over with. I'm resigning my commission. I've had it with the Army."

Reading the letter was like watching one of those films of a building imploding. One minute her life was standing, the next it collapsed inward in a cloud of dust. Her fingers brushed against his when she handed the letter back. Both their fingers were cold. "You're asking for a medical discharge?"

"I'm asking for a medical review in connection with resigning my commission."

"It's the same thing."

"It's a precaution. If I resign without going through a medical board, and I've got health problems later, it will be impossible to prove they were service-related."

"Avivah had problems when she got out and she didn't ask for a board."

"She should have. I tried to convince her to do that."

Pepper had, too. She'd used the identical phrase: a precaution. "The Army never promised us anything for doing our duty."

"You used your GI home loan to buy your property."

"It's not the same thing."

"It's exactly the same thing. A benefit is a benefit, whether it's education, buying a house or getting a medical rating. You don't give Kirkpatrick grief about his disability pension."

"That's different; he was wounded."

He shoved the letter into his pocket. "My two Purple Hearts don't count?"

"Three Purple Hearts—shot twice, stabbed once—they owe you one."

"Getting stabbed wasn't combat-related."

"It was blood spilled in a combat zone, at a time of active conflict. It counts."

"It was someone trapped in a fear-crazed crowd who knew that because I was an American I was getting out of Saigon, and that he—or she—wouldn't. I didn't even see who did it."

Pepper folded her arms. "It counts."

"Let me see if I've got this straight. I can get burned like Kirkpatrick; I can get shot or stabbed, and those are honorable wounds. But if I'm puking blood because of stress, it doesn't count. What offends you most, that I might have a disability, or that I might ask for money because I can't hack the Army anymore?"

"What offends me most is that you're quitting. So the past six weeks haven't been terrific. You've seen worse. The Army invested a lot in you, starting with a free education at West Point. You owe them."

"I owe them nothing."

He pivoted and fumbled with the door lock. When he slammed the door behind him, window glass rattled in its frame. Pepper jerked the door open. The moonlit street in front of the clinic was empty.

CHAPTER 9

Pepper automatically guided her car home through the familiar dips and twists of the narrow mountain road. For his own good she had to find a way to keep Darby from resigning his commission. Being a soldier was all he'd ever done; he was meant to be a soldier. He'd get over whatever had happened to him in the past few weeks. He'd always gotten over it before.

That little trick he'd used of disappearing the instant he'd left the clinic showed that he was still in soldier mode, even if he didn't realize it. It had taken her a few moments to figure out how he'd done it.

The clinic's wall extended a couple of feet farther than the store beside it. It would have been a second's work to slip into the corner formed by the two buildings and hide in the shadows. By the time she figured it out, he was gone.

She could already be too late to stop Darby's resignation. When he decided to do something, he did it. He certainly wouldn't mail that crumpled letter he'd shoved into his pocket, but what if that was a draft or a copy? What if he'd mailed his resignation before he came to the clinic? She couldn't phone his commanding officer in Japan and ask him to ignore Darby's letter because Darby was too sick to write a letter saying he was sick.

She had to find a way to stop Darby before he made a fool of himself, made a fool of both of them.

Her car crested a small hill. In the distance, coming toward her fast, with its lights flashing, was a Madison County sheriff's car. Pepper slowed and pulled onto the dirt verge. She expected the police car to whiz past her. When it didn't, she edged onto the road and picked up speed. Between where the patrol car had been and her car were two places to turn: Benny's driveway or her own.

Madison County had a lot of isolated geography. Sheriff, ambulance, and volunteer fire brigades monitored one other's radio traffic. When medical help was needed, the closest service responded. It wasn't unusual for the ambulance crew to arrive to find a sheriff's deputy or volunteer fireman already at the scene.

Lorraine being in labor was the one reason that Pepper could think of for a sheriff's car to be heading their way at such a speed.

Pepper's heart pounded. She hadn't set foot in a labor-and-delivery suite since nursing school. She remembered that an APGAR score of six or below meant the baby was in trouble. She couldn't even remember how to do an APGAR.

First babies were notoriously slow. Except this was Benny's first baby; it was Lorraine's third. Lorraine had said that Mark had come much faster than Randy had.

She sailed by her driveway and made a sharp right turn into Benny's place. From the baby carrier in the backseat, Anne protested the sudden jolt with a little mewing sound, but she didn't wake up. Pepper pulled to a stop in front of Benny's house, expecting to arrive in the middle of a high drama, and finding a still night, interspersed with cricket noises.

Benny's truck and Lorraine's car were parked in their usual places. There was no sheriff's car. The lights of the house on the lower floor were on, but the house was quiet.

Pepper ran up the front porch steps two at a time, and barreled into a locked front door. She pounded on the door. She punched the front doorbell in a staccato rhythm. Frantic, imagining Lorraine having progressed from labor to delivery, she dug in her pocket for her key to Benny's house, and opened the door.

"Benny? Lorraine? Anyone?"

The house smelled new. Pepper envied that smell. Lorraine's house was so clean and spacious. It was also empty. Papers and books—Benny's electrical engineering text, algebra for Randy, and a primary-grade science text for Mark—covered the dining-room table.

Pepper hurried through the kitchen. Clean supper dishes were stacked on the drain board. Off the kitchen was a small room that Benny planned to convert to a home office. For now, it was Benny's hope-not-but-you-never-know emergency delivery room. Weeks ago he'd asked Pepper to help him plan, step-by-step, what he should do if Lorraine went into labor and he couldn't get her to a hospital. Pepper had called another nurse who worked on maternity. Benny had followed every one of the nurse's suggestions.

The only thing in the small room was a cot, made up military-style with white sheets, a tight woolen blanket, and a single pillow in a white pillowcase at the head of the bed. In the precise center of the cot was a large, round-topped bundle wrapped in a muslin cover. Pepper half expected to see *Kit, Childbirth, Emergency, 1 each* printed in Benny's precise military hand. Instead, on top of the bundle was an old Red Cross booklet, *Childbirth at Home.*

Where was everyone? What if Lorraine had felt funny but wasn't sure if she were in labor? Had she gone to the homestead to ask Pepper's advice, and gone into labor there? The homestead was the only other place the sheriff's car could be.

Pepper stuffed the Red Cross booklet in her waistband. She scooped up the kit, almost dropping it because it was so heavy.

What had Benny prepared for, arrival of the Dionne quintuplets?

Hugging the kit to her chest, she left through the back door, and ran for the path that led to her property. Taking the path would be quicker than driving.

The waning moon was well over the ridge. In the cloudless night sky it provided enough illumination for Pepper to see where she was going. She knew this path even better than the highways dips and turns. Less haste, more speed she reminded herself when her toe caught under a root and she almost tripped. She slowed to a fast walk over the uneven ground, her heart pounding less now from adrenaline and more from a good workout.

If the ambulance hadn't yet arrived at the homestead, she'd phone her boss. Pat wasn't a midwife, but she'd worked for the Frontier Nursing Service and assisted with deliveries. Things would be fine. The ambulance had probably already arrived and Lorraine was on her way to an Asheville hospital.

She saw the reflection of blinking lights before she emerged from the path. The sheriff's cruiser was parked askew in the gravel driveway, its doors closed, but its light rotated lazily. The garage doors were up, with Avivah's and Saul's cars parked inside. Lights were on in her house. Her front door stood open. Pepper ran across her yard and in through the door.

"Where's Lorraine?" she yelled, not bothering to remove her dirty shoes. They could mop the floor later.

Randy came from the kitchen, carrying a large tray of mugs and coffee fixings. Lorraine was behind him, carrying a coffeepot. "I'm right here."

The muslin wrapping grew damp in Pepper's sweaty hands. Panting, she leaned against the arch between the hall and living room.

Her living room was full of people. Benny had stationed himself tight in a corner where he could both protect his back and see all entrances. Mark stood in front of him. Benny held him close, his arms protectively draped over his stepson's shoulders. Mark had his arms around his large stuffed rabbit, Mr. Ears. The three of them resembled a weird man-boy-rabbit version of Russian Matryoshka dolls.

Saul sat in a straight-backed chair. His eyes were bright, his face intense, his bony fingers clasped tightly in his lap. Pepper had seen that pose before when Saul was in a situation where he couldn't write notes. His whole body had become a recording machine, storing up data for when he could fly to his notebook or typewriter and disgorge everything he'd observed.

A sheriff's deputy sat at one end of Pepper's couch, and Avivah sat at the other. The deputy had a notebook open on his knee. Between them sat Kaye; at least, it was someone wearing Kaye's clothes.

She wore her usual faded housedress, but her eyes had lost their pale, blank-canvas appearance. Her skin had reattached itself to bone, and her hair was hair again instead of string.

Pepper had seen that spark before, particularly in Intensive Care. She'd leave work convinced that her patient would be dead within twenty-four hours. When she returned from days off, he'd be sitting in a chair, talking on the phone.

She's never been in the room when the will caught fire, when something kick-started a person's life. Pepper assumed that event had to happen in private, probably around four in the morning, the most vulnerable time of day, but Kaye appeared to have kick-started herself on a Tuesday evening.

The deputy paused with his ballpoint in midair. "You are?"

Pepper eased the emergency kit to the floor and moved it out of the way behind a large chair. "Elizabeth Pepperhawk. I live here."

Randy, having set the tray on the coffee table, plopped down on the floor in a corner. Pepper helped Lorraine serve coffee.

Lorraine finally eased herself into the one remaining chair. Saul started to stand so Pepper would have a place to sit, but Pepper waived him back down. She sat on the floor beside Randy.

He reached out and twined his right hand in her left. His skin felt smooth and boyish, but the hand itself had a man's bones. Randy ran his thumb up and down the base of her thumb. An electric shock ran through Pepper. He couldn't possibly be flirting with her! He was a child. Except that at almost fourteen, he hovered on manhood. Like Mark, was he seeking comfort? Aunt Pepper: large stuffed rabbit.

Kaye cradled her coffee cup in both hands.

"Miss Barley, you said you were sitting in your bedroom, and you saw a face at the window. Was it a man's or woman's face?"

Kaye Barley. Finally, she knew the young woman's last name.

"I don't know. All I could see was eyes in one of those black things that bank robbers wear."

"What happened next?"

"I screamed and ran to the kitchen, picked up an iron frying pan, and called the sheriff."

Kaye's voice had lost the first-grade singsong quality. Pepper heard no hint of the Blue Ridge Mountains in her accent. Wherever the strange young woman was from, it wasn't from around here.

"I heard someone moving around outside and then noise at the door. When I tried the door, it was jammed." Her voice wavered. "I used the frying pan to break the picture window, and climbed out."

The deputy frowned. "You knew the sheriff was on the way. Why didn't you stay in the trailer?"

"Trailers are fire traps. People are burned to death in them all the time." By the end of the second sentence, she was taking great gulps of air between words. Her coffee cup tilted precariously.

Avivah retrieved the cup and set it on the coffee table. She asked, "Did you see evidence that this intruder intended to light a fire?"

"I was afraid that's what he was going to."

Avivah tilted her head. "Why he? You said the person at the window wore a balaclava. Could it have been a woman?"

Randy winked at Pepper and let go of her hand. He had been flirting with her! Six years of adolescence ahead. Heaven protect them all.

Kaye squeezed her hands together. "After I climbed out of the window, someone grabbed me from behind. It felt like a man. He had on work gloves. I tried to hit him with the frying pan, but he pulled it out of my hand. He forced me into the toolshed and locked the door."

The deputy flipped back a page in his notebook. "Your call came into dispatch at nine forty-seven. How much time had passed from the time you made that call to when you were locked in the shed?"

"Five or ten minutes. Everything happened fast."

"What did you do after you were locked in the shed?"

"I stayed very quiet and smelled the air. For gasoline, you know, or kerosene."

What was this obsession Kaye had with fire?

"I felt around for a weapon. I found some kind of a big knife. It felt rusted and dull, but it was all I had. Going for his eyes would have been best, don't you think?"

The mousy woman who destroyed pottery was talking about slicing someone's face open with a rusty machete.

Pepper understood. It all hinged on that moment when Kaye Barley had decided to rejoin the world from wherever her soul had been hiding. Pepper was willing to bet it had happened when Kaye broke the window and got herself out of the trailer, but that Kaye hadn't realized it had happened until she was locked in the shed.

In Qui Nhon Pepper had had moments when—she felt a blush rising in her face—when she'd saved a man's life all by herself. It never seemed like a big deal when it was happening.

The weak knees and cold feeling in her stomach always came later. She'd need to be alone then, to sit and think, or more truthfully, not to think. Not think about what a close thing it had been. Not think that somehow she had touched something larger in the universe, or that it had touched her. Try to calm her racing heart and rapid breathing. Wait for the adrenaline tide to recede. Wait until her mouth stopped tasting like cold metal. Oh, yes, she understood Kaye sitting in that tool shed, cradling a machete.

Kaye said, "I knew Miss Pepperhawk would be home soon. On Tuesday nights she gets home between nine forty-five and ten o'clock."

Kaye knew her comings and goings. Pepper didn't like Kaye watching her.

"In a few minutes, I heard a car."

Saul raised one finger. "That would be me."

"I yelled. I figured the man would run away now that someone else had arrived."

Saul said, "I heard her screaming. Someone had jammed a branch through the toolshed hasp. After I freed her, I phoned Mr. Kirkpatrick."

Pepper realized that Benny was calling her name.

"What?"

"Where's Anne?"

"Anne who?"

Even as she said it, she pushed herself to her feet. "Oh, God! I left her in my car at your place."

Pepper ran down the path to Benny's land, her arms and legs pumping, the breath searing into her chest, but she couldn't keep up with either Saul's long legs or Benny's combat-hardened skill of moving through dense foliage at high speed. Both of them passed her on the trail. When Pepper emerged from the trees, it was straight into Benny's outstretched hands. "Stop." His arms encircled her to prevent her from moving.

She screamed, "What's wrong?"

"Anne is not in the car."

Pepper turned her face to the moonlit sky and howled, "Nooooooo!" Her fists beat on Benny's chest.

He said, "She can't have been gone long. Avivah and the deputy are here. We'll find her, but they won't want you to contaminate the scene."

Pepper gripped handfuls of Benny's shirt. "She needs me."

"The best thing you can do for her is to wait inside. I know that's hard, but do it."

Benny handed her off to Randy. Randy's arm around her had nothing to do with flirting now. Pepper stumbled up the front steps. How could this have happened in a few minutes? Had the kidnapper taken the diaper bag, too? Anne had to be fed. Were the instructions on the formula can clear enough? Would the kidnapper be able to figure out how to mix up formula for her?

Randy guided her to the living-room couch. In a few minutes, he handed her a cup of something hot. Pepper was sure her throat would close up if she tried to swallow anything, but holding her hands around the warm cup was comforting.

Lorraine, Kaye, and Mark arrived. Lorraine was panting and sweating. She held one hand to her side and tried to hug Pepper with her other arm. Pepper felt the baby kick. She shoved Lorraine away. "This is all my fault. I should have contacted child welfare. I'm not cut out to be a mother. My worst grade was in pediatrics. I never told you that."

Rapid footsteps sounded on the wooden porch. Saul burst into the room and bent double, his hands on his thighs while he caught his breath. "Found—her—safe."

The room spun.

Saul lifted his head. "I'm sorry, Pepper."

Pepper tried to get blood back to her brain. "Anne is okay. Why be sorry?"

"I'm sorry about where we found her."

The front door opened, hitting Saul on the bum. He moved out of the way. Avivah came in, carrying Anne.

Pepper raced across the room and pulled Anne out of Avivah's arms. She held the baby close to her chest and rocked her back and forth. Through the open front door, she saw the deputy escort Darby up the steps, with Benny close behind. Darby's hands were handcuffed behind him. Darby wore a black T-shirt and dark-blue jeans. All he would need was a balaclava. He owned several, like Benny did, along with belt knives and first-rate jungle boots, detritus from being in Special Forces.

Pepper backed away. She was never letting Darby near Anne ever again. "You bastard!"

The deputy said, "Miss Pepperhawk, be quiet. Miss Barley, is this the man who attacked you?"

Kaye studied Darby. "The man was shorter. Let me smell his hands."

The deputy took keys from a small leather belt pouch. "Sir, I'm going to release you. I want your word that you won't try anything."

Benny stood with his back against the front door, and his fists clenched. "You have my word that he won't try anything."

Darby said quietly, "You have my word."

The deputy unlocked the cuffs. Darby brought his hands to his front and rubbed his wrists. Kaye stepped up to Darby and turned around. "Grab me from behind."

Darby did so with great efficiency, but no pressure. Pepper realized how easy it would be for Darby to snap Kaye's neck.

After he released Kaye, she picked up one of his hands, which she smelled. She shook her head. "He grabbed me in the same way, but it felt different. The man who grabbed me was shorter, and his gloves smelled like salt, oil, and old fish."

Pepper handed Anne to Lorraine. "Let me smell."

Darby extended his hands toward her, palm up, in a supplicating gesture. She ignored the gesture, bent over, and sniffed. The familiar Darby-odor she associated with warm sheets and postcoital skin almost brought her to her knees, but even she had to admit she detected no fish odor. Pepper straightened slowly and said to Benny, "Salt, oil, and old fish. I know one thing that smells like that."

"*Nước mắm.*"

The deputy said, "That some new street drug?"

Pepper said, "It's a Vietnamese fish sauce. What happened to Kaye has a Vietnam connection."

Now Pepper understood why Darby had claimed to know nothing about Anne and why he had been so afraid to stay in the hospital. Someone wanted Anne; probably the same someone who had already caught up with Edith Filmore.

Sending Anne to her had been Darby's final fallback position. Pepper supposed she should be grateful that when he realized he absolutely had to pass the baton, or in this case, the baby, he'd chosen her.

He'd thought she was good enough to carry on after he was gone, but not good enough to play on his team now. After all, he was a real soldier and she'd only been an Army nurse. That's why he'd denied any knowledge of Edith Filmore or Anne. He'd decided he was the only one strong enough, smart enough, and tough enough to protect Anne. Pepper wasn't going to give him the satisfaction of seeing how much that hurt. She backed away. "Isn't it time you stopped lying?"

Chapter 10

Wednesday, for the third morning in a row, Pepper was awake at sunrise. Sun crested the mountain ridge, coloring the underside of banked stratus clouds electric red. Red sky in the morning, sailor takes warning. The one thing she didn't need was more warnings.

Mist rose from the creek in front of her and a fish jumped in the cold, flowing water. Pepper tucked a wool blanket tighter around her, but that didn't prevent cold from seeping through the worn chair seat into her backside. Someone should invent a battery-operated bum-warmer. But then, her chair was so old and ratty, it would probably go up in flames, like the rest of her life.

Benny walked into the clearing. He wore a navy peacoat and watch cap, which gave him the air more of a sailor than an ex-soldier.

Pepper said, "Go away."

He plopped down in a chair on the other side of a round wooden table and set his coffee mug next to hers. "You look like hell."

Pepper sank further back into her sweatshirt hood. "So kind of you."

"How much sleep did you get last night?"

"Sleep is becoming relative, isn't it?"

"I didn't think I'd be this tired until after the baby was born."

She blew across the top of her mug, watching steam wisps

dissipate. "After Vietnam, I promised myself I'd never be this tired again. So much for promises."

"Yeah, like I swore on Randall's memorial stone that I'd always listen patiently to anything Randy or Mark wanted to talk about."

"How are you and Randy?"

"He is grounded for the rest of his life. Lorraine and I put our foot down."

"Put our feet down."

"Don't start with me. Last night, when I was trying to get Mark to sleep, he said that it was okay if Lorraine and I loved the baby more than him because little babies needed more love than he did."

Pepper's eyes misted. "Where did he get that crazy idea?"

"Randy apparently told him that he'd better get used to being ignored once the baby came."

"You're right. Ground Randy for the rest of his life, or find out if one of Randy's buddies has a new baby in the family."

"What does that have to do with anything?"

"Maybe one of his friend's noses is out of joint, and he's sharing his pain. When does art camp start?"

"Three weeks from today."

"The same three weeks from today when you and Lorraine will be contending with a newborn, and Mark's reaction to being replaced as the baby of the family? You have plenty of love to go around, but time and energy are going to be in short supply."

Benny pursed his lips and studied the fast-moving creek. "Getting Randy out of the house would give us all a break."

Pepper knew about fishing. It never paid to set a hook too soon. She kept quiet.

Benny eventually said, "He committed forgery; that's a crime."

Pepper dismissed Randy's proto-criminal record with a wave of her hand. "He's a juvenile."

"Juvenile delinquent." Benny leaned back and stretched. "That's not fair. He made a kid's mistake. The scariest thing was how good he was. He didn't trace over our signatures; he made each one an art project, a line drawing. When he showed us his practice sheets, I believed it was my signature. Lorraine felt the same way about hers. I don't want my son becoming another Colin Blythe."

The warmth was almost gone from Pepper's coffee. She drained her mug and set it down. "He was a prisoner of war, you know."

"Blythe? Of course he was. That's what *The Great Escape* was about."

"Donald Pleasence, the actor who played Blythe, spent a year in a German prisoner-of-war camp. Would you do it?"

"Forge documents to get help other POWs escape? I'd be rotten at it. Randy got no artistic talent from me."

Pepper forbore reminding Benny that he and Randy weren't blood kin. "I meant, play a character in a movie about the worst experience in your life."

Benny's fingertips brushed the scars that covered his right side. "Not a chance."

"Me either. I've been kicking an idea around about a few people who know Randy chipping in for his fees, with strings attached."

"What strings?"

At least he hadn't rejected the idea out of hand. "Randy has to use what he learns to pay us back."

"He's good, but who would buy art from a fourteen-year-old?"

"I don't mean sell his art. Randy would have to come up with a business plan how he could work off his debt at so much per hour. It would be like a Junior Achievement project. Discipline him, ground him for the rest of the summer if you want, but after art camp."

"You mean when he gets back, send him to his room with art supplies for company?"

"Something like that."

"Some punishment."

"Don't allow him to go to the movies or watch television. Assign him extra chores. Reduce his allowance. Enforce a curfew. You and Lorraine have tons of ways to hold Randy responsible for his actions without penalizing his art."

"You don't have to do this. We're not charity cases."

"Benjamin James Kirkpatrick, when have I ever treated you like a charity case?"

"When you announced you were paying my mortgage next month."

Pepper studied the sky. The blood-red clouds had faded to a washed-out pink. "I said that was a graduation present."

"I'd prefer a fountain pen."

"You use ballpoints."

"I could learn to use a fountain pen if I had one."

"So can I start calling, collecting money for Randy?"

"I know you're trying to be kind, but Lorraine and I have to decide this together. I'll use your line about dealing with a two-week-old infant and a jealous seven-year-old. Since we so successfully put our feet down against him going, he'll think we're idiots if we change our minds."

"Tell him that it's okay for grown-ups to reassess complicated situations."

"He'll think we're idiots."

"He's almost fourteen. Parents are idiots if they breathe."

"You got that right."

"We'll have to do something special for Mark, too, so he

won't feel left out."

Benny picked up his mug and sipped his coffee. He made a face and got up, taking the mug with him. After kicking an indentation into the soft ground with his boot heel, he poured the coffee into it and used the toe of his boot to smooth the dirt back in place. Pepper watched, fascinated. She's never seen anyone fieldstrip coffee before.

Benny knelt beside the creek, his back toward her, and held his mug in the cold water. "I've kept up with a lot of ex-Berets. You want to know how many of them have died in hunting accidents, wrapped their car around a tree, or put a gun to their heads?"

They were talking about Darby. A bottle of bourbon and a winding Georgia road were a far too easy solution. Darby would become just another good-old-boy motor fatality at two in the morning. Pepper's heart did a flip-flop. "I don't want to know."

"Convince me that a senior Army officer who meekly submits to being handcuffed and riding in the backseat of a sheriff's car, without a word about calling the Judge Advocate, is behaving rationally."

Pepper couldn't. She searched inside herself for scraps of courage, but today the courage bin was so empty that even a church mouse would starve. "He's written a letter resigning his commission and asking for a medical board."

Benny straightened his back. "Written or mailed?"

"I don't know. He came by the clinic last night to show it to me. We fought. I agree that he's in trouble. What are you going to do about it?"

"Not me, not even we. This one is yours."

"I'm tapped out. You were a damned Beret; you know where his head is."

"And you were an Army nurse; you know where his wounds are."

"Was an Army nurse—past tense."

"It's like riding a bicycle. You don't forget what soldiers need."

"They didn't teach me a secret handshake in basic training."

"Ninety-eight percent of casualties who reached an evacuation hospital alive in Vietnam survived."

He'd learned that figure from her. Army medicine hadn't done some casualties a favor by keeping them alive. The drill had been to do her job and shove survivors down the medical evacuation pipeline. Next stop, Japan. Next stop, an Army hospital somewhere in the States. Next stop? Who the hell knew? By the time the casualty reached the end of the line, she'd have forgotten his name. Sometimes, she remembered his face. Sometimes she still did.

What happened down the line was SEP—somebody else's problem. Now that the buck had stopped at her front door, she had no idea what came next. "I agree that Darby isn't running on all cylinders. I vote we hog-tie him to the top of my car like a Christmas tree, deposit him at the VA Hospital, and convince a psychiatrist that his cornbread is no longer baked."

Benny stood, shoved his hands in his pockets, and began pacing in the small clearing. "Damn it, Pepper, for once be serious! You're the one person who stands a chance of convincing Darby to get help."

The previous winter, late on a very cold night, a passing pickup truck had thrown a tiny rock at Pepper's windshield. Her windshield had cracked. It had been one tiny crack at first, then it had branched and branched into a feathery pattern: Jack Frost running amok with a glass cutter. She'd been so busy appreciating the beauty that she'd come within a hair's breath of plowing into a rock facing. This time the tiny crack began in her heart.

She didn't want to be saddled with an ex-soldier who had his head screwed on wrong. She'd seen too many wives, mothers, and sweethearts like that when she worked for the VA. She lowered her head. "If I can't be his wife, I don't want to be his nurse. The first time we talked about Darby, you said he was dangerous. Why did you have to be right?"

"If it's any consolation, for four years you've come close to proving me wrong. He's not the same officer I served under in Vietnam, and I'm not referring to resigning his commission. He changed for the better after you two started dating. You changed for the better, too. I never realized that before."

"So I owe him and he owes me?"

"Army family. Brother in arms. You believe in that stuff the same way I do."

"He lied to me about Anne."

"About being her father?"

"About what happened in Saigon, and about finding her in a tree last night. How stupid does he think I am?"

"I don't know if he lied about Saigon, but I'm pretty sure he didn't lie last night."

"Why?"

"Pretend for a moment that you're Darby. You graduated from Georgia Military Academy and West Point, both times near the top of your class. For the better part of two decades you've been a Green Beret and a military intelligence officer. How likely are you to kidnap a baby without one iota of a cover story? The best you come up with is 'I heard her cry and found her in a tree'?"

It had been a piss-poor story, hardly worthy of Darby's imagination. Even she could have come up with better on the spur of the moment. "I would have said that I was angry at me—angry at Elizabeth Pepperhawk—that I found the baby left alone in the car and had taken her into my custody for protection. I'd confuse the issue by pressing charges for child abandonment. Elizabeth Pepperhawk would be the one in custody this morning instead of him. Are you saying that Darby chose the stupid-sounding truth over a believable lie?"

"That's how I read it."

Pepper ticked items on her fingers. "He bought a tent and camping gear. He set up what amounts to a forward observation post on my mountain. He was skulking around last night, spying on my house. Don't you find that creepy?"

"I find it completely out to lunch. But him camping on your mountain very likely saved Anne's life. Darby may be crazy, but he's crazy like a fox. That's what scares me."

Avivah went straight to Nate's office. She plunked coffee and his favorite bagel in front of him. He eyed the warm, oozing cream cheese. "I have a horrible feeling that this is a bribe."

Avivah sat down and unwrapped her own bagel. "What do you want first, good news or bad?"

"Good, by all means," Nate said around a mouthful of bagel.

"Ash was with her tutor and several other people all Monday evening. She can't have had anything to do with Edith Filmore's death."

Nate's shoulders slumped. "Thank you. I won't forget this. How bad is the bad?"

"Let's start with Sunday night, when Edith Filmore rang our doorbell at the homestead." When she finished outlining her and Pepper's involvement and Darby's protested noninvolvement with the baby from Vietnam fiasco, Nate asked, "Where's Colonel Baxter now?"

He should have been reading her the riot act, but he wasn't. Establishing Ash's alibi counted for something. So this was what the good old boy's network felt like from the inside. Except she wasn't on the inside. She was a woman, a northerner, and a Jew. She'd always be the outsider. "Madison County Sheriff kept him in custody overnight. They'll transport him here after they're finished with him. They're not charging him yet."

"Let me know when he gets here."

Darby arrived a few minutes before nine escorted, but thankfully not in handcuffs. He wore the same jeans and black T-shirt that he'd worn last night. A jailhouse odor clung to him.

Spending the past six weeks in hot Vietnamese sun had bleached Darby's blond hair almost white. This morning his hair looked dirty yellow, and his tanned skin had a greenish tinge to it. Nate called the police surgeon.

The doctor examined Darby, dosed him with Tylenol and vitamins, and suggested he be given food and water before the interview. Avivah's driver sneaked him into the constables' locker room for a shower. She rustled up breakfast, a toothbrush, and a disposable razor. The quiet, gracious way that Darby said "Thank you" made her heart ache.

Darby sat upright in the interview room, his gaze straight ahead, his fingers interlocked and his hands resting on the cold metal table in front of him. Avivah knew what she'd been looking at all morning, but until she sat down in a corner of the room and watched Nate and Darby face one another, she'd managed to avoid naming it.

Darby reminded her of the news clips of prisoners of war in North Vietnam. He had that same expectant, subdued body language. He'd been released from custody, but he hadn't been released from prison.

Nate Mirandized him and pushed a slip of paper toward him. "This is the phone number for the Judge Advocate Office at Fort Bragg. Do you want to call them before we begin?"

Darby didn't pick up the paper. "No, sir. Thank you, sir."

They got through his name, address and other necessary data in short order. Avivah could have filled in that information without asking Darby. Nate laid the Polaroid of Edith Filmore on the table. "Have you seen this woman before?"

"I have, sir."

All Darby had said yesterday morning was that he'd never seen Anne. Edith Filmore's name hadn't come up, and now Avivah wondered why. It would have been so easy for Pepper to say, "You mean you never gave this baby to a woman named Edith Filmore?" And yet, she hadn't asked. Why not?

"Do you know the woman's name?"

"She told me her name was Edith Filmore."

"When was the last time you saw her?"

"The last contact—the only contact I had with her—was on the top floor of the American embassy, in Saigon, the Republic of Vietnam, at or about twenty-three hundred hours, local Saigon time, on Tuesday, twenty-nine April, nineteen seventy-five."

He was spouting classic military jargon, what soldiers called baffling bullshit. Maybe Darby's Tylenol and breakfast had kicked in; maybe shreds of the old Darby were trying to reassemble themselves. If he managed to regrow his Army-green turtle's shell, Nate wasn't going to get a single straight answer out of him.

"What were you doing in the American embassy?"

"At the time, I thought I was dying. I'd been stabbed."

"Did Miss Filmore have anything to do with you being stabbed?"

"No, sir. It happened before I entered the embassy grounds."

"Describe this contact you had with Miss Filmore?"

"I had custody of a Vietnamese orphan. I believed I wouldn't live to make it out of Vietnam. I asked Miss Filmore to save her."

Avivah tried to stir up shock or indignation that Darby had lied to Pepper, but all she found was a cold, hard knot of resignation.

"You said you had custody. Was that legal custody?"

"No, sir. More accurately, the infant was in my care. I knew she was an orphan, because I'd seen her parents die."

"Miss Filmore agreed to take her out of Vietnam?"

"Yes."

"What was she supposed to do with the infant?"

Darby gave Avivah a brief, hard stare. "I suspect you already know that."

"For the record, I want you to go through it."

"Miss Filmore was to bring the infant to a friend of mine. Elizabeth Pepperhawk, who lives in Madison County."

"Had you offered Miss Filmore an incentive to do this?"

"Three thousand dollars to be paid out of my estate."

"What did you do after you gave her the baby?"

"Passed out. The next thing I clearly remember is waking up two days later in a Bangkok hospital."

"On Tuesday morning you stated that you had never seen this infant before."

Darby focused on the wall over Nate's shoulder. "I lied."

"Why?"

"Army protocol prevents me from answering that question."

"How far up your chain of command do I have to go to get that question answered?"

"Army protocol prevents me from answering that question."

Old military intelligence officers never lied, they bent the world to their truth. Avivah didn't try to untangle how much of his evasiveness and stonewalling was required by the Army and how much was Darby playing mind games. She was tired of military games. Tired of Pepper lapsing into soldier's jargon. Tired of Benny walking the perimeter around their land. Tired of Colonel Darby Baxter dropping in periodically to stir up their lives. She had left the Army, but she'd never left the military. It was time she did.

She and Saul would run away as far as Asheville, and she'd

use her GI home loan to buy a house. For the first time in years, she wanted to be a one-hundred-percent civilian. Good riddance to everything military!

"When you lied about the baby, did you know that Edith Filmore was dead?"

"Miss Pepperhawk had just informed me that the woman who brought her the infant was dead. I assumed that woman was Miss Filmore."

If Darby had killed her, he certainly knew she was dead.

"Did you know that Edith Filmore had demanded immediate payment of the money you'd promised her?"

For the first time that morning, Darby sat back in his chair. Someone who didn't know him would have guessed wrong that he was at ease with that question. Avivah knew him better than that. The feigned nonchalance was a cover. Darby's brain was scrabbling to process information he hadn't known before. "No, sir."

"Or that she'd threatened to turn the baby over to child welfare if she didn't get it?"

"No, sir."

"Or that Miss Pepperhawk secured out a loan in order to give Miss Filmore the three thousand dollars?"

"She what?" Darby resumed his up-straight, hands-on-the-desk posture. "Sorry. No, sir, I did not know any of that."

"You've had no contact with Miss Filmore since the embassy?"

"None whatsoever."

"How did you get from Vietnam to Bangkok?"

"On a plane. I can't give you details; I was unconscious at the time."

"How did you get from Bangkok to Asheville?"

"Military Air Transport out of U-Tapao Air Force Base, Bangkok, to Fort Lewis, Washington. I flew a civilian carrier from Seattle-Tacoma to Atlanta, with stopovers in Denver and Dallas, and then transferred planes in Atlanta for a commuter flight to Asheville."

"When did you arrive in Asheville?"

"Monday evening, around seventeen hundred hours." He faltered. "I'm sorry, I can't be more precise. The time is on my ticket."

"What did you do after you arrived?"

"Rented a car."

"Your rental car was found Tuesday morning in a feed-and-seed store parking lot near Fairview."

"If you say so." Darby rubbed his forehead with his fingertips. "I must have taken a wrong turn coming out of the airport. I got lost. Renting a car had been a mistake. I was ill, in pain. The second time I crossed the yellow line and almost hit a car head-on, I decided to stop driving."

The second time? He was a slow learner.

"What did you do?"

"I pulled off into the first parking lot I found. It must have been the feed-and-seed store. The building was closed. I wanted to call a cab, but I didn't find a phone. I hitched a ride into Asheville with a long-distance trucker."

Most trucking companies had rules about picking up hitch-hikers, but some drivers knew it was a long way to company headquarters.

Nate asked, "What was the driver's name?"

"I didn't ask."

"The company name?"

"I didn't notice."

How convenient.

"I hadn't eaten all day, so I asked him to let me off where I could eat."

"Where?"

He named a fast-food restaurant in the south part of town.

"After I ate, I phoned Miss Pepperhawk's house. The phone was busy. I waited a few minutes and phoned again. It was still busy. I waited fifteen minutes and phoned a third time. The phone rang that time, but no one answered."

Avivah asked, "What time was this?"

"Twenty-one hundred, maybe twenty-one thirty hours."

What was the probability that he'd phoned exactly when she and Pepper were on the phone, then again after Pepper had left for the clinic? On the other hand, how had Darby known that he would have gotten a busy signal, then one not answering?

"I started walking, and got a ride most of the way with a guy in a pickup. He dropped me off near Woodfin."

The Woodfin turnoff was about twelve miles from Pepper's house. Even sick and in pain, Darby could walk twelve miles. He routinely ran five miles before breakfast every morning. Or at least he had when he was well.

"What was this guy's name?"

"Fred, Frank, something that began with F."

"What color was the truck?"

"Bright. Red, maybe yellow. I wasn't interested in the color. I was trying to keep from throwing up on his upholstery. The truck smelled new; that smell on top of supper made me queasy."

Tracking down someone whose name began with an F, who had a new-smelling bright red or yellow pickup, wouldn't be easy, but it would be quicker than finding an unnamed truck driver who could be anywhere by now. And the people at the fast-food place were likely to remember Darby. At least that part of his story could be confirmed.

The times didn't fit. They knew for certain that Darby had rented the car at five twenty, and that he'd surprised Pepper and gotten kicked in the balls for his trouble, shortly after midnight. Even if she allotted generous times for driving around, being lost, parking, hitching two rides, having supper, and walking twelve miles, it was unlikely that those activities filled seven hours, the same hours that included when Edith Filmore had been killed. Bottom line, Darby had no alibi.

Chapter 11

At eleven thirty Wednesday morning, Pepper stopped her car beside a roadside sign partially hidden by tall vegetation. The sign had simple black letters, a white background, and a pale-blue frame.

Valley Forge Hatchery
Ducks ~ Geese ~ Eggs ~ Smoked Meat
Est. 1964

She'd driven this road many times. Either she'd never noticed the sign, or if she had, she hadn't paid attention to it, which amounted to the same thing. Obviously, Mr. Tu preferred a low profile.

He also didn't broadcast that his business had any connection to Vietnam. His neighbors must know. Gossip was an Olympic event in Madison County. She, Benny, and Avivah freely admitted that they were Vietnam veterans. Why hadn't someone asked, "Have you met the Vietnamese man at the hatchery?"

Valley Forge was a quintessential American name. Pretentious of Charles Tu to assume he could appropriate American heritage. It was pretentious to appropriate Charles, a name he almost certainly hadn't been born with. It was like Anne's name. Pepper hung her head; she'd done some appropriation herself. Anne's adoptive parents would have to choose a new Vietnamese name for her.

It was eleven forty-five. If lunch were at noon as she hoped, she would have fifteen minutes to deliver Pat Teague's bill and the message that women get health care, but men didn't. Pat Teague's world worked that way, but hers didn't. For all of Pat's ranting, Pepper couldn't believe that anyone had been hurt by what she'd done yesterday.

She shifted into drive, and turned onto the hatchery grounds, driving slowly down a curved graveled road bordered on the left by a large field that had gone to grass, and on the right by a tree-shaded stream. A large blue-gray metal building dominated the space where the property backed onto a mountain. Poultry noises came from that direction. That must be the coop or whatever the building was called where birds lived.

Next to it was a smaller building built of the same blue-gray metal siding. White smoke rose from multiple chimneys. Pepper smelled barbecue. On most days barbecue made her mouth water, but today the connection between those two buildings killed her appetite.

Scattered throughout the property were several brick or wood buildings and some military-surplus Quonset huts. She searched in vain for what would have been the original farmhouse, akin to her own house at the homestead. None of the buildings were houses, though a long, single-story building with multiple doors spaced along its front resembled a motel. She parked in a graveled parking area, got out of her car, and locked the door.

Chain-link fence surrounded a wooden building on her right. A dozen Vietnamese children, dressed in bright clothes, played in the grass playground beside the fence. Two small boys squabbled over a toy fire truck. Two Vietnamese women about Kaye's age sat on the building steps watching the children. One rocked a stroller back and forth with one hand.

Day care? Considering the number of school-age children,

more likely day care and homeschooling. Unless Mr. Tu didn't believe in kids going to school, in which case, the truant officer would be very interested in this place.

In Qui Nhon, children had played in dirt yards, surrounded by barbed wire. Black soot from explosions and bullet holes had pockmarked school walls. These children, and Anne, would have grass playgrounds and toys. Hair ribbons. Maybe even piano lessons. Whoever Anne was, whoever had written the last two pages in Darby's field diary, that person had made the right decision to get Anne out of Vietnam.

Darby hadn't said one word about his diary. He couldn't, could he? He'd closed that door when he denied knowing anything about Anne. "I've never seen Anne, never heard of Edith Filmore, but, oh, by the way, do you have my field diary?" wasn't on.

Five huge white geese waddled around the side of a building making goose noises. The lead goose stopped, spread its wings, and charged straight at her.

She flapped her hands at it. "Shoo! Go away!"

She had enough time to wonder if geese had teeth before she clambered onto the hot car hood. The geese circled the car, hissing and flexing their wings menacingly. Sharp ridges lined their mouths. A tooth by any other name could give a painful bite.

The children stopped playing. They wrapped their hands through the chain-link fence and yelled in Vietnamese. Pepper wasn't sure if they were offering advice, taunting her, or enjoying the spectacle of a round-eye perched on a car hood.

A Vietnamese man in his late twenties came out of a building about fifty yards away. He yelled the same thing the children had been yelling. The geese stopped honking. Pepper realized the children had been trying to shoo the geese away. He reached into a bin besides the building and scattered a handful of feed into the grass at his feet. The geese headed his way. Pepper climbed down from her car.

The man walked over to her, and bowed slightly. He wore gray coveralls, with a lab coat buttoned over them. "I am Mr. Lam. I hope you are not hurt. The geese were not told to expect visitors."

His English was perfect, but he spoke with a stilted rhythm.

Pepper dusted her clothes. "It's all right. They certainly do a good job of guarding."

"It is their nature."

"I'm Elizabeth Pepperhawk. I've come to see Mr. Tu."

"Do you have an appointment?"

"I'm sorry." It had never dawned on her that she needed one. Had she assumed that Mr. Tu would keep himself instantly available in case a round-eye decided to visit? That was exactly what she had assumed.

"Mr. Tu is away. I am his foreman. May I help you?"

"I'm sorry, it's Mr. Tu I need to see. Will he be back soon?"

"Perhaps. We are at lunch. Please join us while you wait."

The geese had finished their snack and were eying her. Even the chaos of fifty people eating lunch was preferable to spending the time sweltering in her hot car.

Pepper nodded her head in a small bow. "Thank you."

A loud bell sounded. One of the young women stood, ringing an old-fashioned brass bell. The children lined up, boys on one side of the building, girls on the other, arranged from smallest to biggest. Pepper hadn't seen lines like that since her own Catholic grammar school.

"You homeschool your children?"

Mr. Lam's brow furrowed. "Home is there." He pointed first to the motel-like building, then to the building where the children were. "School is there."

So he was good in English, but wobbly in idiom. And homeschooling explained why neither Mark nor Randy had come home full of news about Vietnamese kids in their schools.

Mr. Lam again spoke sharply to the geese and made a hand gesture. The geese waddled placidly away.

The building in front of them had screen-covered frames set in large square windows. White wooden covers, now extended in the open position, could be pulled down over the screens. Pepper had seen a lot of buildings like it in Vietnam. They were great in a tropical country, but how warm was that building in a North Carolina winter?

Mr. Lam opened the screened door. Pepper prepared herself for a repeat of yesterday's chaos. Her mama-sans had eaten their lunches squatting in a corner of the nurses' hootch. Pepper hoped the people here didn't do that. Yesterday had demonstrated that five years was a long time when it came to having flexible knees.

To her surprise, the dining room was quiet and almost empty. Framed photographs hung on the walls: the Statue of Liberty and New York skyline, a geyser in Yellowstone National Park, a New Orleans Mardi Gras scene, and a ubiquitous America farm featuring a red barn and ripe wheat fields. Three vending machines, one for soft drinks, one for chips and candy bars, and one for cigarettes, sat along one wall. The name of General Washington's winter encampment wasn't the only American culture that Mr. Tu had appropriated. Pepper felt that she'd wandered into a theme park.

Many large tables filled the room. The red-and-chrome chairs probably started life in a roadside diner. At one end of the room three tables had been pulled together into one long table. A yellow-and-red oilcloth covered the table. Several ashtrays were in use. Pepper adjusted her breathing to deal with more cigarette smoke than she cared for.

Four women and seven men sat at the table. Two places were

empty. All of the men stood. Pepper scanned their faces, trying to match each face with some detail of their clinic visit. She recognized Mr. Nghiem, Lieutenant Bach, and the woman who had offered to feed Anne.

Mr. Nghiem called out, *"Đại uý!"*

Mr. Lam spoke to him in Vietnamese, sounding sharp. Mr. Nghiem looked at the floor.

The woman who had fed Anne asked, "Baby?" in a disappointed tone.

Pepper said, "I work long today. Baby with babysitter," and immediately regretted it. In the face of Mr. Lam's perfect if basic English, she was embarrassed that she'd reverted to the pidgin English she was accustomed to using with Vietnamese.

People rearranged themselves, and added an extra chair at the table for her. A woman handed her a round, white cup containing clear green liquid. One of the men offered her a cigarette, which she declined.

Like Mr. Lam, everyone wore gray coveralls and lab coats. The clothes were clean, but their collars were frayed, and they had the dull appearance of clothing washed many times in an industrial washer. With their paper shoe covers and hairnets, they could be operating-room staff eating lunch in a hospital cafeteria. Instead of a lab coat thrown casually over the shoulders in nominal nod to hospital policy—what Pepper called the I-am-Doctor-Dracula look—all buttons were buttoned, hairnets covered hair, and shoe covers covered shoes.

An elderly Vietnamese woman came out from the kitchen wheeling a cart full of covered dishes and white bowls. The woman stopped her cart next to Pepper, and asked, "Would you like a cheeseburger deluxe, with fries?" Her English was less stilted than Mr. Lam's.

Pepper could have hugged the woman, but her Southern upbringing wouldn't let her accept. It was the height of bad manners to arrive at lunchtime. Expecting the hostess to cook special food was beyond rude. Pepper swallowed hard. "I'll have what everyone else is eating, if there's enough."

Please let her at least recognize what she was eating.

The woman distributed bowls of raw bean sprouts and lime slices around the table. "We have enough."

Pepper had never eaten Vietnamese food. The Army discouraged eating "on the economy" because food was scarce. There were health risks, too. Pepper's bottom line had been, considering what her mama-sans ate, Vietnamese food didn't appeal to her. She wished she'd remembered that before she accepted Mr. Lam's invitation. It was too late now; she'd have to make the best of a bad deal.

While the elderly woman served noodle soup, the other women moved many covered dishes from the cart to the table. Mr. Tu fed his workers well.

Pepper mimicked what everyone else did, adding bean sprouts, mint leaves, and lime juice to her soup. She picked up a shaped ceramic spoon, and poked tentatively at a piece of meat.

Vietnamese ate dog, didn't they? The small brown fragment smelled like beef. She glanced surreptitiously around the table. Some people were already halfway through their soup. They hadn't keeled over. She sank her spoon into the soup, allowing broth and a piece of bean sprout to fill the white well.

It was delicious! Unless dog tasted like beef, this was not dog soup.

Everyone ate silently. Her mama-sans had talked constantly through their meals in rapid-fire Vietnamese. Perhaps these people were being polite about speaking English in her presence. "I'm sorry I don't speak Vietnamese, but please continue your conversation."

Heads turned toward Mr. Lam. He said, "Our rule is to speak

English when a guest is present."

"I don't mind if you break that rule."

Mr. Lam smiled a tight, painful smile. "Perhaps on another day."

While people pushed empty soup bowls aside and uncovered dishes of rice and other food, Pepper noticed a sharp odor undercutting the odors of food and cigarettes. In Vietnam, chicken-shit had meant something worthless. She suspected that chicken-shit had a different meaning at a hatchery.

When one of the men reached for a plate of pickles, she saw on his coverall sleeve a stain suspiciously like blood. What had the sign said? Ducks. Geese. Eggs. Smoked meat. Before ducks and geese could be sold as smoked meat, a lot of things had to be done that Pepper would rather not contemplate at lunch. She decided to focus on something besides what those gray coveralls must be like under the lab coats.

She helped herself to plain rice, hoping it would be bland enough for her to keep it down. "I expected more people to be eating. Do you eat in shifts?"

Lieutenant Bach said, "*Đi-đi-mau* on bus."

Apparently they didn't have to speak good English, just English. *Di-di-mau* was a GI corruption of heaven knew what for "got the hell out of here."

"Where did they go?"

"Away." He ticked off on his fingers, "Iowa. Texas. Louisiana." He paused on his fourth finger. His face broke into a grin. "Wis-con-sin."

Mr. Lam said, "Mr. Tu's friends provided jobs. Mr. Tu drove everyone to the bus station. Mr. Nghiem and Mr. and Mrs. Bach were chosen to remain with us."

Mrs. Bach was the woman who had offered to feed Anne.

Nurse Pepperhawk inserted herself into the conversation. "Did everyone have their X-rays before they left?"

Mr. Lam said, "Everyone went for X-rays at six o'clock this morning."

Pepper suddenly felt better about presenting Pat's bill, but she wouldn't tell Pat that the clinic had been conned into using their resources for people going to work in other states. Finding jobs for almost fifty Vietnamese refugees was a big job. Who was Charles Tu that he had those kinds of contacts all over the country?

One of the men handed Pepper a warm bowl, which contained something fried, brown, and odd-shaped. Deep-fried chicken feet. Oh, God. She ran for the bathroom door marked *Women* and made it into a toilet stall in time to vomit.

She stayed on her knees for a long time until she had nothing left to throw up. All that lovely soup wasted. She pushed herself into a standing position. Mrs. Bach opened the door and peered in cautiously.

Pepper patted a wet paper towel against her forehead. "I'm so sorry, so embarrassed. It was an inexcusable lapse in manners."

Mrs. Bach stared at her. She doubted the woman had understood her apology. She pointed her finger to her chest. "Pepper." She pointed at Mrs. Bach, trying to remember if pointing was a rude gesture in Vietnam. "Mrs. Bach?"

The woman pumped Pepper's hand. "Bach Thi. Pleased to meet you." Each of the last four words sounded brand new.

"I'm pleased to meet you, too." Pepper felt ashamed. She'd only mastered a few Vietnamese words to sprinkle into conversations. Mrs. Bach was well on her way to mastering entire English sentences.

Thi gestured by flapping her hand, with her fingers pointed toward the floor. "Come." Bach Thi rubbed her stomach. "Tea."

She was either repeating her first name, or thought that tea would settle Pepper's stomach. Pepper stopped trying to decide which. She went with Mrs. Bach.

While she'd been in the bathroom, the three tables had been separated, oilcloth and dishes removed. Washed ashtrays lay in a neat arrangement on a dish towel. A fan blew fresh air through the room.

She recognized Mr. Tu from his photo on the brochure. Instead of his suit, today he wore slacks and a short-sleeved shirt. He sat at one of the tables, which was covered with a white cotton tablecloth. Apparently he rated higher than oilcloth. On the table were a teapot, two round cups, and a plate of small, irregular-shaped pieces of candy.

He stood. "Miss Pepperhawk, I apologize for your inconvenience. Had you made an appointment, I would have been here when you arrived. Thank you, Mrs. Bach. You may return to your duties."

She dipped her head in a proto-bow. "You are welcome, Mr. Tu. Good-bye."

Her words came out in staccato-like individual sounds.

Pepper dipped her head. "Good-bye, Thi. Thank you."

The woman smiled and left. Mr. Tu held a chair for Pepper. She sat down. Mr. Tu poured tea, and offered candy. "Candied ginger has a calming effect on the stomach."

She accepted both, and they helped. "I'm sorry. I feel so embarrassed."

"We are at fault. You should not have been served Vietnamese food."

She didn't want the older woman to be in trouble. "I was offered a hamburger and fries. I chose the Vietnamese food. The soup was delicious."

"Our cook is excellent." He refilled her teacup. "May I know the purpose of your visit?"

For the life of her, Pepper couldn't remember why she'd come to the hatchery. Oh, yes. It had been to present Pat

Teague's bill. If she'd learned anything here, it was that Valley Forge Hatchery functioned on rituals. "Ms. Teague asked me to convey how pleased we were to assist your people yesterday."

Why had she said that? They were not his people. They were people in their own right.

"But?"

Pepper suspected that very little got past Mr. Tu.

"Our clinic is for women and children." She handed over the now-wrinkled envelope. "We regret that we must charge for providing services to the men."

He opened the envelope, read the invoice, refolded it, and put it back in the envelope. His expression hadn't changed when he read the amount. "You will receive payment within thirty days."

Pepper bet that they would receive it on exactly the thirtieth day.

"We will be glad to see the women and children. Ms. Teague has directed me to assist you in finding other services for men, should they be needed in the future." She was putting words in Pat's mouth, but if Mr. Tu wanted her help, Pepper would help, on her own time. Pat didn't have to know.

"I will make other arrangements for the men."

In other words, thanks, but mind your own business.

"What about the women?"

"I will explain your offer at our next meeting. They will vote on what they want to do."

Mr. Tu seemed to keep a tight reign on everything that happened at Valley Forge Hatchery. How would her offer be presented and how free a vote would it be? She couldn't do a thing about it either way.

Mr. Tu said, "If the women accept your offer, Mr. Lam will phone your clinic to make appointments for them. When future groups arrive, I will make appointments for the women twenty-four hours in advance."

He hadn't asked her if that would be convenient.

"You expect future groups?"

Darkness colored his eyes. "I expect many such groups."

Mr. Tu escorted her to the door. Pepper asked, "Why do you require your employees to speak English when a guest is present?"

Mr. Tu stopped with his hand on the door frame. "My family came to Iowa in nineteen fifty-four. My mother still cannot speak more than a few English words. She cannot wait on customers or answer the phone. She cannot understand a movie or read her grandchildren a story. Merchants cheat her, and children torment her. If someone had encouraged her to learn English, her life would have been very different."

"You mean if someone had forced her to learn English?"

"You are a nurse. Do you not force patients to do things they must do in order to recover?"

Benny had expected her to force Darby to get treatment, and she'd been ready to do it. She didn't like the way Mr. Tu did business, but at this moment, she didn't have a moral leg to stand on.

CHAPTER 12

Avivah slit open the special-delivery envelope; she extracted a photograph and cover letter from the State Department. The letter was standard government-speak: stand ready to assist you, etc. Ready to create red tape was more like it. She tossed the letter on her desk and examined the back of the photograph. Embossed in gold in the lower left corner was *D.F. Portraits/ Madison, Wisconsin* and above the embossing a handwritten number—probably the negative code—and a date made by an adjustable office stamp. *Oct 11 1955.*

She propped the five-by-seven studio portrait against her stapler. It was a photo of a woman standing in front of a gray background with her right arm resting on a photographer's posing table. Add twenty years to that face and the State Department's Miss Filmore was their murder victim.

In the photo, Edith's pigeon-chest wasn't so obvious. Her black hair lay in tight waves that Avivah's mother called a Marcel. Her dress was made from the same impeccably tailored shirtwaist pattern that she'd worn on Monday, but that tweed fabric hadn't been popular for a quarter of a century.

What had possessed a middle-aged government employee to kick over the traces and resort to blackmail? What had possessed Avivah's own grandmother to write letters advocating compulsory sterilization for poor women? Avivah's sister was waiting for her answer on that one. Avivah had learned a long time ago that the reasons women did things were more

complicated than hormone surges. At least she hoped the trilling feeling she's had in her chest since Darby's interview was
more complicated than chemicals flowing through her blood-
stream, because she was about to change her whole life.

Ain't going to study war no more. She couldn't remember if
that was a line from a folk song or an alcohol-soaked aphorism
picked up at Army retirement bashes. Ex-military-police officer
Avivah Rosen wasn't going to study war no more; she had a lot
more interesting curriculum planned. She picked up the phone
and called home.

"Saul Eisenberg."

"Can you be in Schenectady on the weekend of December
sixth and seventh?"

"Why, are we celebrating Pearl Harbor Day?"

"Oh, shit. I'd forgotten the seventh was that anniversary. I
want us to get married, but I don't want our anniversary to be
on Pearl Harbor Day."

"Married? Us? Why? Wait a second, give me a chance to do
this right. I will be thrilled to marry you, in Schenectady or
anywhere else on Pearl Harbor Day, the Fourth of July, National
Pickle Day, or any day you choose. Why this sudden interest in
getting married?"

"My life is too full of veterans. I want my own space—our
own space. I want to be a civilian; I want to get pregnant."

"Is this the same woman I kissed good-bye a few hours ago?
You didn't mention anything then about getting pregnant. Are
we dealing with an Anne-effect here?"

"We had Darby in for an interview this morning. He played
military head games. I'm tired of him, and Pepper, and Benny,
and their constant preoccupation with the Army. I love them,
but I don't want to live in their hip pockets. I want us to pick a
wedding date, right now, this morning."

Saul asked, "Did the Army do anything memorable on

December fourteenth?"

"Nothing comes to mind."

"So let's get married December fourteenth: Schenectady, New York. Reception and dinner dance to follow."

The trilling in Avivah's chest erupted into a full symphony orchestra; this was definitely more than hormones. "Yes, yes, yes! But keep it a secret for now, okay?"

"We will have to break the news to Pepper eventually, unless you want to leave a note on the kitchen table when we leave for New York."

"I know, but I feel like I've been living in a hive for years: college, the Army, the homestead. For the first time in years I want one wonderful, private secret, something that you and I share. Oh, did I mention I love you?"

A loud, thumping sound filled Avivah's ear.

"Hear that? That's my heart. I love you, too. I am so excited; I can't wait to see you. I'll be at the police station when your shift ends. I'm whisking you away for an intimate evening of dining and dancing."

"Where are you going to find dancing on a Wednesday night?"

"I don't know, but if there's a dance in a fifty-mile radius, I'll find it. And if we can't dance, we will while away the evening drinking champagne, and making outrageous wedding plans."

When her driver came in half an hour later, Avivah's mind definitely wasn't on her job.

He held up an envelope. "Autopsy report."

She stared at him. "What?"

"Edith Filmore's autopsy report arrived from the medical examiner."

At least she stopped herself short of asking why she wanted an autopsy report on someone named Edith Filmore.

Cause of death: strangulation with her own scarf. She had injuries consistent with having fought her attacker. Her time of death was between four and seven o'clock Monday night. Edith had been a healthy forty-five-year-old woman, *virgo intacta*. The toxicology report wouldn't be back for a while, but based on stomach contents, and odor, she'd last eaten several hours before her death, and had consumed a large quantity of alcohol with the meal. It was also likely, from residue in the stomach, that she'd taken two Valium tablets shortly before she died.

Edith had been a big woman, but to fight hard enough to completely wreck the exam room when she had both alcohol and Valium on board would have been a feat. Edith Filmore had had a strong reason for living.

Avivah checked the items' list from Edith's purse and her motel room. Valium or pill containers weren't on either list. The ME was quite specific that the tablets had been taken whole. What was the chance that red toolbox the Laurel Ridge nurses carted off to the pharmacy each evening contained Valium? Or would that big jar of drugs that worried Ash have been even handier?

She tapped the autopsy report. "How many places in and around the mall serve alcohol?"

"A restaurant in the mall, and a couple of bars within walking distance."

"My guess is that Miss Filmore was more the restaurant than the bar type. See if anyone remembers serving her food and alcohol between about one and three thirty on Monday afternoon. When you've finished with that, phone Mrs. Katherine Wright. She's Colonel Baxter's grandmother. Here's her phone number. Verify the exact times she was with Miss Pepperhawk on Monday evening, and make a list of everything she did and who she saw on Monday. Get the name of the limo company she hired. Verify times with her driver, especially when they arrived and left Miss Pepperhawk's residence. Got it?"

"Mrs. Katherine Wright: timeline for Monday; limo driver to

corroborate details."

After he left, Avivah stared at the timeline they'd constructed, so far, of Edith's last twenty-four hours.

On Sunday evening, Edith Filmore hadn't rented a car or taken a taxi from the airport to the homestead. While Darby managed to get to the homestead by hitchhiking and a determined walk, Avivah couldn't see a middle-aged woman doing likewise with a baby in tow. From how Pepper described her, Edith didn't sound like a person who would cadge a ride with someone she met on the plane, though Avivah wasn't completely ready to discard that alternative. It was either that, or someone had picked her up at the airport.

Monday was more complicated. She'd had breakfast at a small diner a couple of blocks from her motel. Between nine and ten, she'd made long-distance calls from her room. The motel switchboard logged all out-of-town calls; Avivah's driver had verified most of the numbers. Edith had called the State Department Human Resources Office in Washington; Wisconsin Vital Records; Wisconsin Department of Transportation; a Racine, Wisconsin, bank, and a number that so far had not answered. All were calls that a woman would make if she'd lost her wallet and identification.

Edith hadn't been in her room when the housekeeper tidied up between ten and ten thirty. She'd surfaced again at the library, at twelve ten. Avivah bet that Miss Filmore had spent part of the time between ten and noon at Laurel Ridge Clinic. The question was, why?

After the library, she'd disappeared again, returning to her motel at four. She'd paid cash for one more night's stay, and asked for a seven-o'clock wake-up call for Tuesday morning.

Avivah wrote in the margin, *Ask the desk clerk if she appeared drunk?*

Boozer and blackmailer made a nice fit. So did boozer and

going to the clinic. Pepper hadn't mentioned that Edith had been drinking before their Sunday night meeting, and she certainly knew how to recognize the signs. Maybe Edith Filmore had sworn off booze long enough to get Anne into Pepper's custody. She could have been in full-blown d.t.'s by Monday morning.

In her room they found a second new dress, a change of underclothing, and toilet items. The shirtwaist dress Avivah saw her in Monday at the library had not been found. In her purse were receipts totaling less than two hundred dollars from stores in the Asheville Mall. What had she done with almost three thousand dollars?

The last time anyone had remembered seeing her alive was shortly before five o'clock, when she walked past the motel lobby, heading in the direction of the restaurant where she'd had breakfast. Apparently she'd never reached it. Three hours later Mr. Boniface found her body. Where had she been and with whom between five and eight?

She dialed the Wisconsin number that so far hadn't answered.

"*Sans Souci.* Madame Jelene speaking." The woman possibly had a French-Canadian accent.

"Madame, I'm Detective Rosen, from the Asheville, North Carolina, City Police. I'm investigating the death of a Miss Edith Filmore."

"*Oui?*" The voice sounded perplexed rather than shocked. Miss Filmore apparently hadn't been Madame Jelene's dearest friend.

"Did you know Miss Filmore?"

"No."

"She called this number shortly before ten on Monday morning. That would have been almost nine your time."

"An older woman?"

158

Avivah had never heard Edith Filmore's voice. "Middle-aged."

"You say she is dead?"

"I'm afraid so."

"What a tragedy."

"You said you didn't know Miss Filmore."

"I spoke with a woman who gave me her initials." Paper rustled. "E. F. measurements for a wedding dress at ten o'clock this morning. She failed to keep the appointment. I was not surprised."

Avivah scribbled: *0700 wake-up call for Tuesday morning = plane flight Asheville to Wisconsin? How paid for ticket? Ticket not in purse? Wedding dress?* Avivah underlined the last question hard three times. That had come out of left field. "Why weren't you surprised?"

"Lonely older women have fancies. *Ma grand-mère* believed that the butcher was secretly in love with her because he cut her bacon thick, and they shared a pew at Mass. It never came to anything, but we spent hours talking about what a lovely wedding it might be. These women come to me. I remember *grand-mère*. I do a few measurements. I give them tea. We talk about how wonderful love is. They go away happy, but I know they will not be back. The butcher, he did his good deed, and I do mine."

On the phone log, Avivah circled *bank*. Edith claimed to be short of walking-around money, but how much did she have tucked away in saving accounts or investments? Would she have been worth the attention of a scam artist who specialized in separating lonely women from their money? She also circled the *Department of Vital Statistics*. Maybe it wasn't a replacement birth certificate that Edith been after; maybe it had been a wedding license.

After Avivah completed Madame Jelene's statement, she

called Edith's cousin. The phone rang for a long time and when it was answered, the woman sounded so breathless that Avivah was concerned that further questioning might cause a serious medical problem.

"I hope you're calling—to say that I—can make—Edith's funeral arrangements—my heart can't—deal with this."

Now that the autopsy had been completed, Edith's body could be released. "I will talk to the medical examiner and have his office call you. I need to ask you a few more questions. Did your cousin have problems with alcohol?"

"Of course not."

Often families were the last to see or admit a problem existed. "You're saying that she didn't drink at all?"

"I didn't say that. She'd have a glass of wine or rum eggnog at Christmas."

"Was drinking a problem?"

"Never."

Edith Filmore had lived away from her cousin for a long time. Who knew what had happened after she left home? "Had your cousin written to you about getting married?"

"Cousin Edith?" The woman broke into a wheezy laughter that left her gasping.

Avivah waited until the gasps stopped. "Are you familiar with a shop called *Sans Souci?*"

"No."

"It's a custom dressmaker in Racine."

"Cousin Edith pay someone to make her clothes? Ridiculous. She even sewed her own undergarments. And she definitely was not getting married. Detective Rosen, someone has been pulling your leg."

She was barely off the phone when footsteps rang along the marble floor, coming toward her office. Pepper came in, brandishing a folded road map.

"Aren't you supposed to be at work?"

"I'm running an errand for Pat. I want to show you something." Pepper unfolded a pristine road map over Avivah's desk. The crisp paper crackled. Pepper ran her finger along a road. "Do you ever go home by Highway Twenty-five/Seventy?"

"Occasionally."

"Ever noticed the Valley Forge Hatchery?"

"No."

"White sign, blue frame? Ducks, geese, eggs, and smoked meat?"

"Doesn't ring a bell."

"Here's where we live; here's the hatchery. How far would you say it is between those two points?"

The distance looked small except for the substantial hill between them. Someone who had never seen the Rockies would call it a mountain. "Measured straight across?"

"As the crow flies."

"Three miles."

"How long would it take to walk from the hatchery to the homestead and back?"

"I'd have to check a topography map. There's a lot of up and down between those two points. It would be a darned tough walk."

"Have you ever seen the Ho Chi Minh Trail?"

"No, and neither have you."

"I heard tons of stories from my patients. A North Vietnamese soldier with nothing more than an AK-forty-seven and a bag of rice could walk the entire length of the trail. Not only was a lot of up and down involved, but he had to contend with triple-canopy rain forest, land mines, hostile patrols, and US Air Force bombings."

"Don't forget he'd be wearing sandals made from tires off US Army vehicles and carrying a copy of the Chairman's *Little*

Red Book in his hip pocket. I heard the same stories. Most of them were apocrypha."

Pepper frowned. "What's apocrypha?"

"Stories that get better in the telling."

"You think it's impossible to walk from the hatchery to the homestead and back?"

"More like difficult. Here's an easier route." Avivah traced her finger along Highway Twenty-five/Seventy up to where it met State Highway Two Five One and back down to the homestead. "Circling around and coming to our place from the north is about five miles. Why walk when you could drive?"

Pepper picked up the map and refolded it. "Because you don't have a car."

"Then why not walk along the road? Parts of the Ho Chi Min Trail were paved."

"Because neighbors would have noticed."

"People walk along the road all the time."

"Vietnamese people don't. Remember what Kaye said about the person who attacked her smelling of *nước mắm*? Last night Mr. Tu had fifty or more Vietnamese refugees at his hatchery. Their kitchen serves traditional Vietnamese food, loaded with *nước mắm*."

"How do you know this?"

"I had lunch with the ones that are left."

"What do you mean, the ones that are left?"

"This morning, poof, all gone. Shipped out to Iowa, Wisconsin, and a bunch of other places. Three were chosen to stay behind and work at the hatchery. Don't you find that strange?"

"I find it interesting. Is this hatchery a new business?"

"The sign says established in nineteen sixty-four."

"I can't believe that Vietnamese have been living that close to us, and we never found out about it. Our neighbors know we're

Vietnam veterans. Someone would have told us out of sheer perversity, to see how we'd react."

Some of their neighbors weren't keen on either the Vietnam War or veterans, whom they feared lived a heartbeat away from going off the deep end.

Pepper plopped into the chair beside Avivah's desk. "I didn't think anyone could keep a secret in Madison Country, but Mr. Tu managed. He keeps a low profile. He homeschools his employees' children. His workers wear American clothes, and he forces them to learn English. I'll bet he doesn't let them leave the hatchery compound unless he's with them."

In light of what had happened to Kaye last night, Avivah couldn't ignore a Vietnamese connection so close to home. Unfortunately, this Mr. Tu's place was outside of her jurisdiction. The Madison County Sheriff would have to be involved. Madison County would balk at tracking down dozens Vietnamese nationals, because one of them might have locked Kaye in a shed. She doubted the State Department would be interested either, despite their assertion that they stood ready to help. "What's the hatchery set up?"

"I had the feeling that Mr. Lam, the foreman, had been at the hatchery a while. There's an old woman who cooks, two teachers, a dozen workers, and another dozen or so kids. Mr. Tu is bringing in large groups of refugees, sorting them out, buying them new clothes, and shipping them all over the country. You don't think he's running a slavery ring, do you?"

"You know more about this than I do."

"Whatever he's doing, I don't like it." Pepper fell silent for a few minutes. Her finger traced the rubber desk bumper on Avivah's desk, stopping to worry her fingernail in a small gouged V. "What protected us more in Vietnam, our rank or our gender?"

Some bruises didn't show on the outside, but they still hurt.

"Where did that question come from?"

Pepper shrugged her shoulders. "It came up."

Avivah recognized a conversational land mine when she heard it. "You ended up in AA. I came within a hair's breadth of military prison. Is that a new definition of being protected?"

"We're alive. A lot of the guys we served with aren't?"

A sharp pain caught Avivah under the ribs. She might not want to study war no more, but while she lived with Pepper, the study was still on. "They aren't."

"Who do you think had it rougher in Nam, Benny or Darby?"

They wouldn't be having this conversation if Darby had behaved himself and not gone running off like a junkie for one last war fix. And she and Saul wouldn't have set a wedding date yet. Whoever said that every cloud had a silver lining has been right. "Until this week, I would have said Benny."

"Why?"

"General principles. Did you ever know an enlisted man who had it easier than an officer did?"

"Can't remember a single one."

"And because Darby is Darby."

"Meaning whatever happened to him, he popped back again like that toy clown."

"He was always good at that."

"He's not popping back this time."

Avivah twisted the diamond solitaire on her left hand. She wished that three o'clock would hurry up so that she and Saul could celebrate that they were now one hundred percent military-free.

"Benny thinks that Darby is headed for suicide and that because I've been an Army nurse, I've got magic that will save him."

"Benny and I talked about this yesterday morning."

"Do you agree?"

164

"Darby came to you. After he sorted himself out in that Bangkok hospital, he could have caught the first plane back to Camp Zama. He could have gone to his family in Georgia, or to that general who is his friend, but he didn't. Wounded animals go to ground in the safest place they can find."

Pepper's expression darkened. "Darby is not an animal!"

He was, but Pepper couldn't hear that right now.

"Besides, Darby coming to me had nothing to do with me being a nurse."

"How do you know that?"

"I just know it."

"I disagree. You were a good Army nurse, plus you and Darby are crazy in love with one another. You and Darby have military culture down pat, and you share Southern culture, and you both understand how Southern culture is enmeshed in the military. For the two of you, love, honor, and patriotism is like being in a room of mirrors. The way those three things distort one another drive you both crazy. In the eighteen sixties—when your and Darby's ancestors were busy seceding—my people were either New York abolitionists, or running from European pogroms. I come from a whole different heritage."

"You survived almost ten years in the Army."

"Your military experience and mine came from different places and played out differently." And she was ready to move on, but Pepper wasn't.

"You make Darby and me sound like macramé. I hate macramé."

"You hate anything crafty and fiddly. Darby is not a craft project."

"What is he?"

"The short list? Right now he's a truly screwed-up guy in a lot of pain. He's someone confused, hurting, and standing on a precipice. Darby is desperate for your help, even if he doesn't realize it. You're desperate for his help. Both of you have to help one another through this."

"You mean two can play at his game?"

"I mean that if both of you don't stop playing games, both of you will be destroyed."

"I hate being an adult."

"Saying that is part of that Southern airhead personality you concocted for camouflage when you were younger. It really is okay to be smart and tough, and right now, you're going to have to be both of those things. I have bad news, and I'd rather you hear it from me. Nate and I interviewed Darby this morning. He was in Asheville by five o'clock Monday evening, and he doesn't have an alibi for the time Edith Filmore died."

Pepper rested her elbow on Avivah's desk. Her hand cupped her forehead, with her thumb and fingers pressing into opposite sides of her temple. "He didn't do it."

"How do you know?"

"What you said. You're right, Darby and I live in a hall of military mirrors, but we both know our way around there. Darby and I have had long, serious talks about heavy, serious subjects, including killing. The way he feels about killing, he would never have murdered Edith Filmore. If he had killed her accidentally, he would have turned himself in."

Avivah wished she believed that. "How did you know that Miss Filmore told you the truth, that Darby gave her Anne to bring to you? How did you know that Darby promised her three thousand dollars, that it wasn't a scam to cheat you?"

Pepper hesitated far too long for Avivah's liking. Was she concocting one of her stories, or was she finally on the brink of telling the truth?

"We had a prearranged signal; like in the movies when someone brings the hero a signet ring, and he knows that his father has died, and it's time to return to his country to become king."

Pepper wasn't volunteering a lot of unnecessary information, and Darby was far too enamored with code words and secret symbols. What Pepper was telling her matched the way Pepper and Darby operated, but Avivah didn't quite believe it. She knew Pepper too well. "You and Darby prearranged a signal for 'take care of this baby and give this woman three thousand dollars'?"

"We had a signal for 'I didn't make it through this time. Trust the person who brings you this message.' "

That sounded exactly like Darby. "What was the signal?"

"The last two lines of a poem: *I could not love thee, dear, so much/Loved I not honor more.*"

English Lit had been a long time ago, but Avivah vaguely recalled a poem like that. The line encapsulated romance, honor, and death; a trilogy that was right up Darby's alley. "Edith Filmore knew the code words?"

"Yes."

"She didn't bring you anything in writing?"

"For God's sakes, Avivah, Darby was dying. What was he supposed to do? Write a letter of introduction? 'Dear Miss Pepperhawk, Allow me the honor of presenting to you Miss Edith Filmore of the such-and-such Filmores'?"

A man's slurred voice said from the doorway, "It would have saved a hell of a lot of trouble if he had."

Benny wove into the room with both hands jammed into his jeans pockets. Avivah smelled stale beer and cigarette smoke.

Pepper stood. "How much have you had to drink?"

"None of your business."

She strode across the room and held out her hand. "Give me your truck keys. Now!"

Benny slapped his keys into Pepper's hand. He collapsed into the chair she had vacated. He blinked and tried to focus on Pepper's face. "Why aren't you at work?"

Pepper peered back at him. "None of your business."

He burped. "I've been laid off."

In unison, Pepper and Avivah said, "What?"

"After class, I went over to Yanni's to open up. He was behind the counter. Shop open, wouldn't say a word about where he's been for two days. He paid me two weeks' wages, and shoved me out the door."

Benny tossed the recruitment brochure on Avivah's desk. "If that's the way Yanni wants it, that's the way he gets it. I earned a thousand-dollar bonus for signing a two-year contract. This time next month I'll be setting up a military communication network in Saudi Arabia."

CHAPTER 13

Pepper's client maneuvered off of the examination table and slipped her feet into her shoes. "Is this where that woman died? I heard that blood was everywhere."

Not for the first time since Edith Filmore died, Pepper wished for a completely separate annex to their clinic. A spare building that the police had rolled up and taken away for evidence would be so handy right now. "There's nothing to worry about. She died in another part of the building and the police have the investigation in hand."

If they did, that was going to be news to Avivah.

"Thanks for coming in today. I'd like to see you again in three weeks."

Pepper followed the woman to the reception area and watched her book an appointment with Lillian. If she'd been honest and said that her client stood on the exact spot where Edith's body had lain, would her client have made that appointment? Sometimes little white lies were necessary. Not mentioning Darby's field diary to Avivah had definitely been necessary.

The last line of Darby's letter had sounded vaguely familiar to Pepper, but she hadn't been able place it. Monday afternoon a research librarian had immediately found the Richard Lovelace poem. Pepper remembered that Darby had quoted it once when they were talking about war poetry. She and Darby hadn't fixed up the Lovelace signal, but they might have. It made a believable cover story, especially for someone like Avivah, who knew both of them.

What it didn't do was make it one iota clearer if Darby had or had not written the last two pages. Lots of people studied Lovelace's poem in school. Deep down she really wanted Darby to have written those lines to her, but she couldn't have that unless she accepted that he'd lied to her about Anne, and she really didn't want that. Avivah had been right. She and Darby lived in a house of mirrors, but it wasn't a fun house any longer.

Darby's diary—minus the last two pages—was between him and the Army. If he'd wanted Avivah to know about it, he would have told her. What if he had said something, and Avivah had been asking her for confirmation? Both she and Darby would be up a creek without a paddle.

No, Avivah knew her, and she knew Avivah. Avivah hadn't known the diary existed. What if she now went to Darby to confirm what Pepper had said about a prearranged signal? Darby might be lying about Anne, but he'd see the benefit in their stories matching. She'd have to trust that he'd cover for her.

Pepper locked the door behind the departing client and handed the woman's chart to Lillian, who said, "Your clinic logs are late. I expect you'll be staying late this afternoon to do them."

"Since I came in late yesterday, I thought I'd leave early today. You know, balance things out."

Lillian glared at her. She should be kinder. Lillian couldn't help it if she was a sour old lady, but something about the receptionist's prune-shaped mouth antagonized her.

She watched the receptionist close the chart grill and set their fake alarm. Why hadn't she thought of finding Edith's chart herself? Because every moment yesterday had been taken up by the Vietnamese refugees and Anne. She'd barely been at the clinic today.

Lillian picked up her purse and sweater. "In my time, it was a day's work for a day's pay." She slammed the door on her way out. In the Army the door slam would have been called dumb insolence.

Pepper looked at the chart grill. Tomorrow would be soon enough to check for Edith's chart. Right now, she had a pressing errand to do on Benny's behalf.

By the time she parked downtown and hurried to Yanni's store, it was two minutes before six. A man she'd never seen was flipping the door sign from *Open* to *Closed*.

Pepper stuck her foot in the door.

The man was taller than she was, paunchy, with thinning gray hair tied back in a ponytail. He pushed the door hard against her foot. "We're closed."

He was strong. Pepper's eyes watered from the pain in her foot. "Open this door or I scream!"

He hesitated. She pushed on the door, and stuck one hand in the opening, wrapping her fingers around the door edge. It would be a close thing. He could open the door enough to free her foot, and then slam it shut on her fingers. Which one of them had quicker reflexes? Nice to know she could still savor the feeling of a good adrenaline rush. "I need to see Mr. Skoufalos on personal business."

Ponytail pushed back. "He's not here."

"He'd better be."

They locked gazes and pushed on the door from opposite sides. Pepper won. She forced her way inside. The man locked the door behind her, and snapped off the shop lights. "Come through to the back."

She found her center of gravity and wrapped her hand around her car keys so that at least two keys protruded between her fingers. This man had a couple of inches and thirty pounds on her, but she'd bet he didn't work out. He walked with a rolling

171

gait from carrying too much fat around his hips and spending too much time sitting. A truck driver, she decided, though something wasn't quite truck-driverish about his slacks and short-sleeved shirt.

He turned on a hanging lamp over the workbench, and picked up the phone receiver.

When she saw how the dim light threw shadows on the man's face, a memory clicked into place. In the officers' club in Qui Nhon small groups of men sometimes sat in the bar's darkest corner. One of the things she'd absorbed by osmosis was that you left those men alone. The words Central Intelligence Agency were never spoken, but they hung in the air.

They always wore short-sleeved shirts and slacks that were Asian-made and Asian-bought. The clothes Darby had worn on Monday looked Asian. Whatever he'd had on when he arrived at the Bangkok hospital must have been a mess. He'd bought new clothes before he left Bangkok; this man also bought his clothes in the Orient.

The man said into the phone, "There's a woman down here to see you. Says it's personal." He held the receiver in her direction. "What's your name?"

"Elizabeth Pepperhawk."

He did a double take; he recognized her name. She suddenly recognized the narrow white line at the top of his forehead, the place where a baseball cap usually rested. The lines at the corner of his eyes said that he'd spent a lot of hours wearing aviator glasses. He wasn't a truck driver; he was a pilot. A pilot who'd bought his clothes in Southeast Asia.

The Central Intelligence Agency had its own airline, Air America. They must have their own pilots, too. What the heck was a CIA flyboy doing in Yanni's store?

He hung up. "That's an odd last name."

Good recovery, on the off chance she'd noticed something,

which she had.

"It used to be something else in German. My grandfather Anglicized it. Your name is?"

She expected him to reply, "None of your business," but he said, "Greg Lane."

That had to be an alias. Men who worked for the CIA weren't in the habit of giving their real names.

He picked up a tumbler lock and they walked outside. A new hasp had been installed on the store's back door, so new that wood shavings clung around where the screws had been inserted. Lane inserted the lock through the hasp and spun the tumblers.

He nodded toward the stairs that led to Yanni's apartment. "Go up."

Pepper backed up a step. In her pocket the key edges cut into her fingers. "You first."

He hoisted his bulk up the stairs, hauling himself up with a hand on each handrail. Pepper followed at a safe distance.

Soft Greek music played in the apartment. Yanni, who had a dish towel over his shoulder and a white apron tied over his black clothes, spooned broth over a leg of lamb in a baking dish, and then pushed the pan back into the oven. The kitchen smelled wonderful.

The small kitchen table was set for two people. A bottle of uncorked wine stood in the middle of the table. Whoever Greg Lane was, he rated lamb and wine.

Lane went down the hall towards the bedrooms. Pepper waited for the sound of a door closing, but didn't hear one. Oh, he'd be listening in all right.

Even Benny didn't know Yanni's age. He'd guessed somewhere between fifty and seventy. Yanni was one of those tight, muscular men who'd look the same age for twenty years, and then one day suddenly grew old. His hair and beard were black, with a few gray-hair grace notes. He always wore unrelieved black clothing and, when he went out, a Greek fisherman's cap.

"Miss Pepperhawk, how nice to see you again. Will you share a glass of wine with me?"

Pepper doubted he was at all glad to see her. His words were friendly; the tone, strained.

"I see you're about to sit down to supper. I'll say my piece and be on my way. Why did you lay Benny off? He's a good worker, and you know he needs the money."

Yanni appeared to be very interested in stirring a pot of rice. Pepper cooked lots of rice; she knew the pot didn't need stirring right now.

Yanni said to the pot, "Benny is smart. He's been to school. He knows too many new things for an old shop like this. He needs a real job, where they can pay him what he's worth. He's too stubborn to listen. Now he'll have to listen."

Benny had said that Yanni was always on him to "use that school you have." That didn't explain the man down the hall, listening.

"You laid him off for his own good?"

Yanni laid down his spoon. "It is better for him to be away."

Safer maybe, but not better. Pepper tore a page off the shopping list pad on the refrigerator door, and with the pencil hanging from a piece of string, scribbled, *Are you in danger?*

Underneath Yanni wrote, *No. Go, please!* He underlined *Go* three times.

Better not leave the paper for Lane to find. Pepper crumpled it in her fist, and raised her voice. She wanted Lane to hear her clearly. "It stinks that you fired Benny, but maybe another job would be better for him. I'll still do business with you. My toaster isn't working. I'll bring it in to you."

Yanni put his hands on both of her shoulders and turned her toward the door. "Buy a new toaster."

In other words, don't come back.

At the bottom of the stairs she glanced up at the apartment. Greg Lane watched her from a window. Pepper made sure she walked away slowly, stopping only when she was out of Greg Lane's sight. She leaned against the rough brick wall to catch her breath, feeling lucky to be in one piece. Yanni was obviously scared or worried or both. So why was he roasting lamb and opening a bottle of wine? None of this made sense.

Fifteen minutes later, she stopped in a loading zone in front of Pack Square Library and honked her horn. Benny came out of the library, tossed his books on the backseat, and slammed the car door.

She pulled into traffic. "Well?"

He sat in a sullen position with his arms folded across his chest, looking like Randy when he was too peeved to live. Benny and Randy weren't blood kin, but they certainly were rubbing off on one another. He growled, "Well, what?"

"Did you do it?"

"I did exactly what you told me to do. I ate and had coffee."

"Did you phone Lorraine?"

"You and Avivah promised not to get on my case about this."

"Are you planning to come downstairs one day, with your duffel bag packed and toss out a casual 'I'll be back in two years'?"

"Stop telling me how to run my marriage!"

Pepper's front tire bounced over a corner of the curb when she pulled into the lot where Benny parked his truck. She held the steering wheel with both hands and looked straight ahead. "Your keys are in my glove box."

Benny retrieved them. His hand hesitated on the door handle. "Do I smell all right?"

"You smell like the inside of a beer-soaked ashtray."

"Lorraine will believe that a few of us went out for end-of-term beers."

Pepper tightened her grip on the steering wheel. Benny and Lorraine would have to work this out for themselves. "Did Yanni ever mention a man named Greg Lane?"

"Not to me."

"Forties, paunchy, ponytail."

Benny shook his head. "No bells."

"Likely a Company pilot."

Benny frowned. "What company?"

"Company with a capital C. As in, there's nothing wrong with Air America except the Company it keeps."

It was the standard line in Vietnam about Air America.

"So?"

"Greg Lane is the reason Yanni fired you. I think he doesn't want anyone to know that Lane is staying with him. What's Yanni's connection to Vietnam?"

Benny flung open the car door. "Stop obsessing over Vietnam. The war is over. We've been back on the block for a long time now. Grow up, Pepper. I won't be here to watch your back much longer."

He got out, slammed the door, and strode toward his truck.

CHAPTER 14

The closer Pepper got to home, the more her head and shoulders ached.

She was not obsessed with Vietnam. So what if she occasionally dreamed she was in the emergency room in Qui Nhon? That was to be expected. She'd only been back from Vietnam three years, ten months and some odd days. She'd need a pencil and paper to figure out the exact number. Lots of veterans remembered the date they left Nam.

So what if Vietnam had been on her mind constantly since Sunday night? There were good reasons for that. Before Sunday night she hadn't thought about Vietnam more than—every day? Five or six times a day? Constantly?

The steel bands in her shoulders moved into stainless-steel territory. Alcoholics-Anonymous wisdom said that if something looked like a duck, sounded like a duck, and waddled like a duck, it was a duck. Pretty soon "obsessed with Vietnam" would start quacking like Mr. Tu's geese.

She was so obsessed that she'd lied to a police officer; worse, she'd lied to Avivah, picked a fight with Benny, and now she had to convince Darby to join her in the lie. But, because Pepper had made a detour to Yanni's place, Avivah might already be home and have talked to Darby. Supper was not likely to be fun.

Supper! Fiddle, Wednesday was her night to cook, and their larder was bare.

She managed a three-point turn without ending up in a ditch, and headed back to the general store she'd just passed. If she hurried, she could pick up a few things before the store closed.

Hubert Sprinkle, who ran the store, had been, in local parlance, "born wrong." He was four and a half feet tall, walked with a slight limp, and his face was permanently furrowed into a grimace. Strangers who regarded Hubert as a misshapen little man missed that they were in the presence of a local legend. The day Pepper bought the homestead, her real-estate agent had given her a tip along with the house keys: get on Hubert Sprinkle's good side and stay there if you want to survive in this part of Madison County. She'd taken the advice.

The bell over the front door tinkled when Pepper entered. Hubert climbed down from the ladder he used to restock his top shelves.

"Evening, Pepper. Bit of excitement out your way."

Had some new emergency happened while she was at work? She forced herself to slip into Madison-speak, a change in lilt rather than words. "Evening, Hubert. You referring to the rescue squad on Monday night, or the sheriff's deputies last night?"

"Both."

She let out her breath. At least the homestead hadn't been a further drain on public resources for the third day in a row.

Having lived on the homestead two years, Pepper was still considered "not from around here." She, Avivah, and Benny sharing a house; the three of them being Vietnam veterans; Avivah being Jewish and from New York, and the first woman police officer hired in Asheville; Benny moving out and Saul moving in; Frannie's women-only art studio that ventured beyond the traditional womanly hobbies of quilting and rug hooking were all fodder for the neighbors. She suspected that "those folks down to the homestead" were a popular local sideshow, providing hours of dinnertime conversation in houses all along the road. She counted herself lucky that in spite of the goings-on, the neighbors seemed to tolerate their antics. In some cases they acted downright friendly toward both her household and Benny's.

The rescue squad making a run to the VA hospital on Monday night was public knowledge. So was a prowler locking Kaye in a shed last night. Hubert expected details, or at least a plausible story.

Pepper opened the cooler for a jug of milk. "I got a friend visiting who took sick Monday night. Doctors down to the VA hospital say he has to watch what he eats for a while. That business last night is a right shame. I'm mortified that happened to a guest when she was staying on my property."

"Not your fault," Mr. Sprinkle said, with enough edge in his voice to say that a hostess was responsible for what happened to her guests.

On the counter, she lined up a carton of eggs and two loaves of bread. French toast would be a quick supper. "You ever heard of a Mr. Charles Tu?"

Hubert climbed the two steps to the worn wooden platform on which he stood while operating the cash register. "That hatchery man on the other side of the mountain?"

So Hubert knew him. Hubert also knew that Benny, Avivah, and Pepper had all been to Vietnam. Why hadn't he mentioned Mr. Tu to one of them? "That's him."

Hubert said, "I know him nodding well."

Meaning that Hubert and Mr. Tu would nod to one another if they met on the street, but had likely never shared a meal or a conversation. "How come you never mentioned him to me?"

"His people keep to themselves. They shop in Asheville."

In other words, Mr. Tu and the other Vietnamese were more "not from around here" than Pepper and likely to stay that way. Tu had snubbed Hubert's store; Hubert was returning the favor by ignoring him.

Hubert bagged her groceries. "How come you're asking about Mr. Tu?"

Pepper hefted the milk jug in her other hand. "After that prowler on Tuesday, I'm thinking of buying guard geese. Like to get them locally if I can."

He nodded. "Always buy locally, I say. Hope your friend feels better soon."

"So do I."

Pepper heard Anne squalling from the driveway. She'd promised Randy she would be home by six o'clock, and it was now a few minutes after seven. Randy was definitely on overtime. When Pepper got out of her car, Anne arched her back, tightened her arms and legs, and let out an unrelenting high-pitched squall. Pepper's heart raced. What if the baby had developed meningitis in the few hours since she'd been entrusted to Randy's care? But Anne's scrunched, beet-red face told Pepper the baby wasn't sick, she was pissed off. One day with a babysitter, and she was behaving like a spoiled brat.

Randy thrust the baby into her arms. He reeked of eau-de-infant. He pushed his fingers through his untidy hair. "I fed her and changed her diaper half an hour ago. My mom couldn't find anything wrong with her. She won't stop screaming."

She picked up the diaper bag. "Did she have a nap?"

"I tried, honest, but she wouldn't sleep."

Anne screeched again, making Pepper's ear hurt. She held Anne in both hands a few inches from her face and blew hard into the baby's face. Anne stopped screaming, and blinked.

Randy said, "Wow! Does that work all the time?"

"I wish."

"I can babysit tomorrow, can't I?"

Pepper saw dollar signs in his eyes. "You're game to do this?"

"I am, only I got to go now, okay? Mom is holding supper for me."

"Go. I'm sorry I'm late. I'll do better tomorrow."

Randy loped toward the path to his house. Pepper called, "Randy."

He stopped. "Yes, ma'am?"

"This art-camp thing will work itself out."

He shrugged. "I got no one to blame except myself. Daddy-Ben was right: never assume the enemy is dumber than you are."

It was terrible that Randy considered his parents the enemy. Unfortunately, they would be enemies until they all outgrew Randy's hormones. Benny was bugging out, leaving Lorraine with a new baby, a jealous second grader, and a bundle of raging teenage angst that walked like a man. All that Special Forces hero crap was well and good, but it was time that Benny stopped behaving like a soldier and start behaving like a responsible husband and a father.

She parked her car in the garage. The other two parking slots in the garage were empty. Maybe Saul and Avivah had gone out to supper. Balancing baby, diaper bag, and groceries, Pepper went into her house through the kitchen door. The house was silent.

"Saul? Avivah?"

She glanced at the household calendar and saw a note in Saul's handwriting. *Taking Avivah out to supper. Don't wait up.*

Anne rested on Pepper's shoulder while she one-handedly put eggs and milk in the refrigerator. The baby was red-eyed, with a tearstained face, but now seemed content with her thumb in her mouth.

"Missy, you and I have to have a talk about company manners."

Anne started to fuss again.

181

"It's you and me, baby. What do you say that I introduce you to the pleasures of a bubble bath?"

She laid Anne on her bed while she stripped out of her work clothes. A few minutes later she held the naked baby against her skin and looked in her full-length mirror. The dim bedroom light gave them a pale brown quality like a medieval painting. "Could we pose for a Madonna and Child Christmas card?"

She rested her chin on Anne's head. "Probably not. There's nothing blessed or virgin about me, and you're the wrong gender to save the world. Don't believe that crap, kid. Women have been saving the world for a long time." She stepped closer to the mirror, picked up Anne's arm and waved her hand. "The baby in the mirror is waving at you." She couldn't remember if a baby's eyes could focus on images in a mirror.

Anne's plastic bath seat fit into a corner of the claw-foot tub. Pepper let warm water flow gently over Anne's shoulders until the baby was belly deep. Anne squealed and splashed her hands. Pepper mixed bubble bath in a plastic bowl and decorated Anne with bubbles. Pepper nuzzled Anne nose to nose. "You need a rubber duck. You're a Pisces, like me, aren't you? A water baby."

Pisces people were born between February nineteenth and March twentieth. Pepper was a cusp Pisces, born two days before the fishes collided with Aries, the ram. Being both water and fire was the curse she'd lived with all her life.

She wished she knew Anne's birthday. The closest she could guess was the first or second week in March. Solidly in Pisces. Solidly conceived during that brief period last June when Darby had secretly been in Vietnam. Was she or wasn't she his daughter? Gestational calculators didn't lie. It was possible. "If he is your father, I promise you I'll make him to do right by you." If only she knew what right was.

Pepper heard a drawer open and close, a pause, then the same sound again. She dropped the plastic bowl into the tub.

Open. Close. She hadn't heard a car, but the bathroom was on the opposite side of the house from the parking area, and she had had the water running. Kaye better not be prying in her house. The other possibility was an intruder. The colors in the bathroom brightened. She didn't remember locking the kitchen door.

The bathroom door was locked, but Pepper doubted that fifty-year-old wood and an equally old lock would withstand a solid boot to the door. She scooped Anne out of the water, swaddled her in a huge bath towel, and laid her in the half-full laundry basket at the bottom of the towel closet. She closed the slatted door without a sound. Hopefully the warmth and darkness would send Anne to sleep, or at least keep her quiet.

The problem with bathrooms was that soap bars and almost-empty shampoo bottles made poor weapons. Pepper lifted off the four ceramic domes that covered the toilet screws and dumped them into one of Saul's socks, which he'd hung to dry on the door rack. The sock stretched to an impossible length. She'd buy him a new pair.

Pepper wrapped a towel around her body and eased the door lock open. It moved noiselessly. The doors were old, but all the hinges and locks in the house were well oiled. She had some pride of ownership.

From the bathroom doorway, she could see into the living room. It was deserted. She'd thought it would be. Drawers were found in the kitchen and bedrooms. She flattened herself against the wall and inched her way until she could peek into the kitchen. Empty.

Avivah and Saul always locked their bedroom door because Avivah's gun safe was in their closet. That meant the only place the intruder could be was in her bedroom. Pepper gauged her chances of phoning the sheriff from the kitchen. Too risky. In this old house private phone calls didn't exist. Could she get out of the back door unheard? What if she did? Being outside, barefoot, wrapped in a towel, and alone was a bad tactical choice. Besides, she wasn't leaving without Anne.

The elongated sock hung heavy in her hand. She stepped away from the wall and gave her homemade bolo a couple of gentle whirls, making sure that the heavy end wouldn't crash on the floor or ceiling.

Focus. If she saw a weapon, she'd go for a headshot. No weapon, a chest shot. She wanted this guy alive and talking. Pepper pictured herself succeeding; the marauder laid out cold at her feet. She took a deep breath, felt blood course through her body. With her free hand she inched open her bedroom door.

A dark figure stood in front of her dresser. He wore black pants, a black T-shirt, and a black balaclava pulled over his head, but what riveted her attention was that he had both hands around the cigar box where she kept Darby's letters. How dare he! Pepper sank into fighting stance, swished the bolo in a circle, and aimed for the center of his back. The instant before she let go, the sound of the back door opening and Darby's voice, saying, "You home, Pepper?" shattered her concentration. The bolo sailed past the invader's shoulder and through her bedroom window.

The man tucked the cigar box under his arm like a football and held his other arm out in front of him. He strong-armed Pepper aside. Her towel unwrapped itself when she fell to the floor. By the time she'd collected her towel and rewrapped herself, she saw through her broken window the man running across her yard.

She raced through the kitchen, where Darby was picking himself up off the floor.

"He's got your letters to me," she screamed. The screen door slammed against the house. She ran toward Saul's sock, which lay in the middle of shattered glass.

Freed from the confines of ceiling and floor, Pepper swung the ceramic-filled sock hard around her head. She let it fly. It caught the running figure on his right hip. He went down head over heels, and dropped the box. Letters spilled over the grass. A waft of evening breeze scattered them.

The man picked himself up and ran, limping. Pepper recognized the same awkward gait she'd followed up the steps at Yanni's apartment. Greg Lane. She ran after him, vaguely conscious of cold, hard-packed ground beneath her feet and cool breeze swirling around her bare legs.

Arms encircled her hips and she went down hard. The side of her face bounded off a round rock. Pain shot through her neck and left cheek. Darby landed on top of her. His hand covered her mouth. He whispered in her ear, "Where's Anne?"

Darby released his hand enough for her to answer. "Safe."

She shivered. Pain spasms radiated along her cheek. Likely she'd broken her cheekbone. Freezing and suddenly aware that she was dressed in a towel, Pepper curled into a fetal position. "You hurt me," she whimpered.

Darby untangled himself from her, sank to his knees, and wept.

CHAPTER 15

Saul met Avivah in the parking lot behind the police station with his hands behind his back. "Close your eyes."

She smelled the roses before she felt him pin something to her blazer. She opened her eyes and saw a huge corsage of six red rosebuds and baby's breath.

"I love you. I've been so excited since you called that I haven't done a thing except count two hundred, twenty-one days until December fourteenth. I've counted them forward, backward, by every other day, by every Saturday, and they still come out too many." He cupped his hands on either side of her face and they kissed. When she came up for air, a chorus of cheers and clapping reverberated off the brick buildings that surrounded three sides of the parking lot.

Five grinning constables, including her driver, lined the metal railing on the steps that led from the police department's back door into the parking lot. Avivah grinned and waved. Saul loved her every day, but this kind of response from "the boys" wasn't something she experienced often.

Saul interlocked his fingers with hers and held up their joined hands toward the constables. "Mine. Get your own."

He pulled her toward the parking-lot entrance. "We're taking my car. I don't want to let you out of my sight for one minute."

"What do I do about getting to work tomorrow?"

"I'll give you a ride. I'm sorry; I'm lousy at quests. I couldn't find a single respectable place to go dancing, but the newspaper's food editor recommended dinner at Rushing Creek Inn. It's out of the way, but it has two Cordon Bleu chefs, and a view to die for."

"Out of the way sounds terrific."

"It's too early for dinner. How about we go to the Grove Park Inn for drinks and appetizers first?"

Two hours later, when they passed the Valley Forge Hatchery sign, Avivah agreed with Pepper. The sign was so nondescript that, unless you were looking for it, you'd miss it.

Earlier, she'd phoned the Madison County sheriff's office. Their dispatcher, the county's repository of fifteen years of law enforcement history, remembered only one call to the hatchery, which was years ago. It had been a domestic dispute that never made it to court. "Ask Lawyer Ferguson. He represented the couple against that hatchery owner feller."

John Ferguson had been such a big part of her life through that awful time she appeared before the military tribunal judging her conduct in Vietnam, but the last time she'd seen him had been at Benny's and Lorraine's wedding. Funny how life changed and people slipped away. Maybe the next year she'd be saying the same thing about Pepper and Benny. She buried her nose in the roses and inhaled. Stop having regrets before they happened. It was time to move on.

Saul navigated another impossible dip-and-turn deep in the heart of Madison County.

"Almost there," Saul said, as he turned right onto a one-lane gravel road. Avivah heard soothing flowing water.

They were higher here than in Asheville, higher than even at the homestead, and spring still had a firm hold along Rushing Creek. Jonquils and low-lying pink rock flowers lined the dry-stone wall that flanked the road. On the other side of the wall dogwood trees had bloomed in riotous pink and white balls. Even if the food was terrible, the drive was worth coming here.

Just when she thought the ache in her heart from all that beauty couldn't be more intense, the land opened into a vista of lime-green trees, and row upon row of rolling mountains all the way to the horizon.

Avivah managed a throaty, "Ohhh."

Saul nodded. "That says it all, doesn't it?"

The road ended at a green-and-white two-story house. Large rectangular brick chimneys flanked either side of the house, and in the middle was a third-story cupola with a copper roof that had oxidized to green.

A familiar truck parked in front of the house sported a black-and-white bumper sticker that said *Not All POWs Are Home.* That truck belonged to Frannie's husband, Cody Doan.

Cody had started losing his right leg the day he stepped on a land mine; he'd finished the process two years later on Pepper's ward. Avivah could think of only one reason for Cody's truck to be here. "You set me up. Dawdling at the Grove Park Inn was a ploy to give our friends time to get here so they can pop out from behind furniture and yell, 'Surprise!' "

Saul stopped the car. "I promise I had nothing to do with this. We'll go somewhere else."

"Where else? We're in the middle of nowhere."

Cody Doan and John Ferguson walked out of the front door and stopped on the covered porch. The slanting afternoon sun highlighted bright blue curls of waste plastic and smears of orthopedic plaster on Cody's white pants and technician's tunic. He must have come here straight from his shift at the VA hospital. On the other hand, Lawyer Ferguson didn't have a hair out of place. His light-gray V-neck sweater, white shirt, and darker gray pants could have been on a fashion model.

The other way life was funny was that you thought about a person and he suddenly reappeared in your life. She could relax about losing Pepper and Benny; some bright pennies always kept turning up.

John handed Cody an envelope. "It's a standard contract. You and your dad are getting a sweet deal on that bass boat."

"Don't we know it? I appreciate you seeing me like this."

"I am always available to give a legal opinion on a fishing boat."

Ferguson's passion for fishing equaled his hard work convincing Madison County farmers that he was their poor ol' country lawyer, a description that belied his family connections and a *magna cum laude* law degree from Duke University.

Saul edged to the side of the narrow drive so that Cody's truck could pass them. Cody stopped with his window and Saul's a couple of feet apart. "Hey, guys. Frannie told me what's been going down the past few days. Is Pepper okay?"

Avivah said, "She's hanging in there."

"I'll call her."

"She'd like that."

He gave her the traditional mountain see-you hand wave and continued down the road. The sun's rim dropped behind a mountain ridge, and beams of sunlight began a slow color play across the house. Saul parked, they got out of the car, and John strode toward them with his hand outstretched to shake Avivah's hand. "Avivah, Saul, what a treat."

He held her hand briefly between both of his hands, trapping her in the warm standard mountain gesture of condolence. "I'm so sorry about Colonel Baxter. He was a fine man, and I know you treasured his friendship."

He let go. His handshake had been, like baby bear's porridge, just right. It offered consolation without being too familiar. She'd always insisted Lawyer Ferguson was heading for politics; he'd insisted he wasn't.

Saul came around the side of the car. "He's not dead."

"I beg your pardon?"

"Colonel Baxter was injured, not killed. A typical Army SNAFU."

Except Avivah knew this foul-up was anything but typical.

John shook Saul's hand. "That's—interesting."

Avivah's police radar came on. At the clinic Monday night, Pepper had known that she was in Darby's will. John Ferguson did a lot of will and estate work; he was the kind of man that Darby would want for an executor. "Since you're Darby's executor, the Army will probably get around to notifying you eventually."

"Let's go inside. I never liked discussing business in the open."

He hadn't batted an eyelash. She'd guessed right; he was Darby's executor. A phone call from John Ferguson would explain how Pepper knew that Darby had named her in his will. She was suddenly embarrassed for Pepper. What was it like to know that you stood more to gain from your lover being dead than alive?

They walked up the wide stairs and across the porch. A piece of paper taped to the etched-glass door said *Closed tonight for a private party.*

Saul hesitated. "We picked the wrong night to come for dinner."

John pushed open the door. "It's a family celebration. My sister-in-law cooks on the theory that the Army of Northern Virginia will drop by unannounced. If you're willing to settle for potluck, you can have the porch dining room all to yourselves."

The front door opened into an elaborately decorated hall that ran the width of the house. In a pale-yellow sitting room on their right, several people sat at ease with drinks in hand. Conversation stopped when John leaned into the room. "Old friends have stopped by. I'm going to have a drink with them. Ya'll go into dinner when the food's ready."

He turned left and walked through another sitting room to a glassed-in porch. Four tables were arranged down the long, narrow porch. The walls were painted a pale robin's-egg blue. Through the bay window at one end of the room was yet another mountain view to die for. John pulled out a chair for Avivah at the table nearest that window. Saul sat across from Avivah.

John opened three Cokes. "Shall I liven this up a little or ya'll want it plain?"

Saul said, "Plain for me. I'm driving."

John mixed two drinks. "Congratulations on being promoted to detective."

"Thank you."

"This is going to sound downright nosy, but do that ring on your left hand and the rose corsage indicate what I hope they do?"

"December fourteenth," Saul and Avivah said in union. They both laughed. She should have remembered that neither of them was good at keeping secrets.

He brought drinks to the table, kissed Avivah on the cheek, and shook Saul's hand again. *"Mazel tov."*

Saul said, "We'd appreciate it if you didn't pass the wedding date around. We haven't told anyone else yet."

John sat down, marked a cross on his chest and held up his right hand. "Consider it filed under lawyer-client privilege."

Avivah asked, "How are you?"

"Life's hard for a poor ol' country lawyer."

She surveyed the room. "It looks hard."

"This isn't mine. My little brother and his wife own it. The inn's governing board—me, my siblings, their spouses, and a cousin we snagged out of Colleton County—is celebrating being open six weeks." He studied his drink. "How seriously is Colonel Baxter hurt?"

Avivah ran her finger around her glass. "More damaged than he's willing to admit. Unlike Cody, he still has all his parts and they work."

"That's a blessing. Where is he?"

Saul said, "At the homestead."

"Being with Pepper is the best thing for him." John paused with his highball glass halfway to his mouth. "It is, isn't it?"

Saul said, "The jury's out on that."

"I'm sorry to hear it."

Wonderful food smells wafted into the room. Avivah salivated. A florid-faced woman in her thirties, wearing a chef's hat and a white apron over her clothes, pushed a cart into the room. "Welcome to Rushing Creek Inn. I'm Sadie Ferguson, one of your chefs. I hope ya'll like chicken."

Avivah loved chicken, especially when it was *coq au vin* with almond-and-raisin saffron rice, green beans in lemon-garlic sauce, fresh-baked bread, and a white asparagus salad.

Sadie moved the plates from her cart to the table. "Save room now for strawberry shortcake, you hear." She rested her hand on John's shoulder, "Come along to dinner soon, John."

"I'll be along in a minute."

After Sadie left, Avivah picked up her knife and fork. "What do you know about Charles Tu and the Valley Forge Hatchery?"

John borrowed her knife and buttered a roll. "Why are you asking?"

"I'm investigating a trespass and unlawful confinement with a Vietnamese connection."

"I doubt Tu's people were involved. He screens who he brings in; he has rules."

"My way or the highway?"

"In one case, literally. A few years ago he evicted a whole family—parents and three children—from his hatchery with nothing but the clothes on their backs. It was in February and colder than a witch's bottom."

Avivah stopped cutting her food. "Why did he evict them?"

"The father broke two of Tu's rules: he got drunk and attacked his wife."

"What happened to them?"

"Deported back to Vietnam."

Saul said, "Why didn't anyone go to bat for them? A photo of five people huddled on a frigid mountain road would have attracted the ire of everyone from the Civil Liberties Union to B'nai B'rith."

"Because it happened in nineteen sixty-eight."

That would have been during Tet of sixty-eight, when everyone from notable newscasters to the president knew how close the US was to losing the Vietnam war. It would have been the worst possible moment to try to garner sympathy for a Vietnamese family who'd blown their chance at the American dream.

"The husband hung himself two weeks after they returned to Da Nang. I tried to file an appeal to get the woman and her children readmitted to the US, but after a couple of months my letters to her came back marked *Not deliverable*. I don't know what happened to them."

Avivah could guess. Suddenly, she wasn't hungry.

CHAPTER 16

Aspirins and a cold soda tamed Pepper's pain long enough to chase Darby's letters around the homestead. By the time she retreated indoors to assure herself that she and Darby had recovered every page, her headache and blurred vision gained the upper hand.

Darby tried to help her sort pages, but she slapped his hand. "Go away. You've done enough damage for one day." The words trickled down to a whisper. Loud noises were a bad idea. She found a canvas bag for the cigar box and letters, lay down on the couch, laid an ice bag over her eyes, and surrendered to dark coldness.

When the pain didn't stop, Darby drove her to the Mission Hospital emergency room. The canvas bag rested between her legs. She wasn't letting it out of her sight until she knew Darby's letters were in a bank safety-deposit box.

At the hospital, the admitting nurse asked what had happened. Pepper said very carefully, "I fell and hit my face on a rock."

The nurse eyed Darby who held a squirming Anne.

Woman mumbling around an ice bag held to her face. Fussy baby. Muscular guy in a black T-shirt. Your typical domestic-violence family. "We were playing touch football and he tackled me a bit too hard."

The nurse said nothing but raised her eyebrows. Pepper realized that if she and Darby had been playing touch football, he shouldn't have tackled her at all. So much for a good cover story.

They waited an hour and a half. Her skull X-rays didn't show a fracture, but the doctor diagnosed a nasty bone bruise below her eye. Even Pepper was surprised at the number of bruises developing all along her left side. After the doctor loaded her up with painkillers and a tetanus shot, he scooted a wheeled stool close to her and said in a confidential voice, "It's okay to talk about what happened."

Through swollen face and pain medication all Pepper could manage was, "He didn't hit me."

The doctor's eyes said battered woman in denial. Pepper wanted to go home, and the quickest way to do that was to play the emergency room game. "Sometimes things get out of control."

"Violence always escalates. You need to get out now. I can call the woman's shelter for you right away, if you want?"

"Not tonight. We'll be all right. Really."

He handed her a typed list of resources for women. Seeing Laurel Ridge Clinic's name on the list jolted her. Pat would never buy the football tackle story.

"May I go now?"

The doctor handed Pepper a prescription for codeine, and a small paper envelope through which she felt the outline of enough pills to last until a drugstore opened tomorrow.

"Don't drink alcohol while you're on this painkiller. Take lots of soft food and liquids. For the next twenty-four hours, whenever you're awake, keep an ice bag on your face twenty minutes on and twenty minutes off. Does anyone help you with child care?"

Benny and Avivah believed that Darby was a basket case. When they saw her face, she wasn't sure she could tap-dance around the truth hard enough to convince them that he hadn't hit her. She recoiled from the noise of even imaginary tap dancing. "A neighbor babysits for me."

"Good. I want you on bed rest for two days; no lifting, no straining."

She gingerly lowered herself from the exam table to the floor. "I have to work."

He handed her a second prescription on which was written a sick note addressed *To Whom It May Concern.* "You have to take care of yourself so that your vision isn't permanently damaged. I want you to take a minimum of three days off work. Do you have a family doctor?"

"Yes."

"Check in with him before you go back to work."

Except that her family doctor was Laurel Ridge Clinic. She'd have to go to work to find out if she was well enough to go to work. She would have laughed, if that hadn't hurt so much.

Darby and Anne were waiting for her in the lobby. Darby held the canvas bag. Bother. He'd had enough time to read every letter while he waited. It wasn't like he didn't already know what was in them. Except sometimes when she read old letters she'd written, she found things in them that embarrassed her.

They passed a bank of pay phones. Pepper thought about calling her AA sponsor, but it was after midnight, and even without the codeine putting a damper on drinking, alcohol was the farthest thing from her mind.

Her sponsor had survived two abusive marriages. If Pepper couldn't get the ER staff to swallow a he-tackled-me-playing-football story, she could imagine what her sponsor would say. Her stomach rumbled. Food first; sponsor later, maybe a lot later.

When they were in the car, she said, "Drive around until you find an all-night coffee shop. I don't care where as long as it's a place that I've never been and will never go to again."

She didn't elaborate on how he was supposed to recognize some place she'd never been. He was the hotshot military intelligence officer; let him figure it out. She closed her eyes, so she wouldn't see where they were going, and allowed her body to flow with the car turns. Darby parked and Pepper opened her eyes. He pointed to two lit horizontal windows in a white stucco building. A red neon sign in one window said *Open All Night*.

"Okay?"

"It will do."

The small café was surprisingly busy for one o'clock in the morning. All of the stools and half of the tables were filled. Pepper groaned when she saw that cops occupied three of the stools. They studied her in the mirror behind the counter. She didn't recognize them, and hoped like hell she'd never met them at some official police function. Pepper matched them stare for stare; considering her left eye was swollen shut, it was more like stare for half stare.

The gray-haired waitress looked like she should have retired a long time ago. She wore a white uniform, with a flowered cotton handkerchief folded behind her nametag. *Mavis*. Mavis spoke to a big man in a cook's apron and paper hat who was at the grill. He came from behind the counter, and said in a low voice, "We don't want trouble here."

Pepper said, "We were playing football. He tackled me."

The man pursed his lips, considered for a moment, then beckoned to Mavis. "They can use the back booth."

The back booth was around a corner, private and enclosed. Pepper relaxed at the thought of hiding out even for a few minutes. Darby ordered coffee; Pepper let him. It was his ulcer. She ordered scrambled eggs, grits, and milk. The waitress offered to warm formula for Anne. Pepper handed her the bottle.

Darby added sugar and a huge dollop of milk to his coffee.

He tasted it, pushed it away, and stared at the table. For several minutes, his hands folded, unfolded, and refolded the little piece of paper that had been wrapped around his cutlery and paper napkin. In a thin, tight voice, he said, "Stop telling people that football story."

"Want me to say that you hit me instead? It's what everyone thinks. What's the matter, your martyr titer needs a boost?"

"Say nothing."

Military intelligence rule number something-or-other: silence was safer than a concocted story. Maybe he had a point. At least with silence, she wouldn't have to remember what she'd said to whom.

Mavis came around the corner with Pepper's food and Anne's bottle. Darby handed her his coffee cup. "I've changed my mind; I'll have what she's having."

Pepper tried to balance feeding Anne and herself. Darby reached for the baby. "Let me feed her. You eat."

She handed Anne over. The baby stopped fussing. Yesterday morning, she had screamed when she heard Darby's voice, had quieted only when she was in his arms. Pepper had thought it was because Darby had a deep voice, and in general, babies liked deep voices. Now she realized it was more likely that Anne had spent a lot of her first six weeks in Darby's arms. Pepper put down her fork and rested her forearms on the table. "Are you Anne's father?"

"Not unless her mother had a ten-year pregnancy."

The overhead fluorescent light dimmed. Her brain didn't have enough room for both blood and anger. "Ten years ago was nineteen sixty-five. It happened during your first tour in Vietnam?"

"About three months into it."

"You were married."

"So was she."

"What was it, collect the whole war set?"

Green Berets had a saying: stay in Special Forces long enough and you collected a divorce, a Rolex watch, and a dose of the clap.

"Some of us managed to stay away from the stereotypes."

She'd never seen him wear a Rolex and as for the clap, she wasn't going to ask.

Gradually the café's lights grew bright again. So he'd been to bed with a Vietnamese woman ten years ago. He'd never hidden from her that he'd been other women. She'd never pressed him for details, but because of Anne, this time was different. "Who was she?"

He tightened his lips so hard that small white lines outlined them.

"What is Anne's real name?"

"Dao."

That one whispered syllable had cost Pepper a lot of bruises, a codeine prescription, and a future hassle from her boss and her AA sponsor. It could also have cost Edith Filmore her life.

Darby's fingertips brushed back a few wisps of Anne's hair. "It means peach blossom in Vietnamese."

Darby was from Georgia, the peach state. Had Dao's mother called her baby that because Darby wasn't an ideal girl's name?

"What's her last name?"

He lifted Anne on his shoulder to burp her. "I don't know. Honestly, I don't. Her mother and father weren't married. Things got crazy the night she was born. I never found out which name she was to go by before her parents died."

"What were her parents' names?"

No answer.

"What's her birth date?"

No answer.

"Where was she born?"

No answer.

"How is Greg Lane mixed up in this?"

Darby's face paled. A moment later, Mavis arrived with his food, and he didn't thank her. Greg Lane had to be some kind of a bad guy if even his name had that effect on a man who had the stamina of a career military intelligence officer and the manners of a Southern gentleman.

Pepper took in a big breath, closed her throat and tried to forcefully exhale against her closed windpipe. The Valsalva maneuver slowed her racing heart and cleared her mind. She worked her way out of the booth and pried Anne from Darby's arms. "Now you eat before your food gets cold."

Her own food was cold, but eating had suddenly become important. "Passing out from hunger on a mission won't be a good idea."

He managed to weakly whisper, "Mission?"

Pepper leaned across the table and said softly, "Do you think Edith Filmore died because she brought Anne—Dao—to me?"

Darby made a quick *be quiet* gesture. He was right. Even if they were in a tall protective booth, a café wasn't the place to discuss Miss Filmore or use Anne's real name, not if the Central Intelligence Agency were involved.

Darby couldn't—or wouldn't—tell her the whole story, but she knew of one person who had a higher security clearance than either of them had ever held. If they were playing in the big leagues, it was time to bring in the big guns. She mouthed, "Tennessee," in overexaggerated lip movements.

Darby frowned. Pepper wasn't sure if he didn't understand her, or didn't want to do what she was suggesting.

Pepper tried to think of a way to say something without really saying something. "Richard Lovelace, sixteen eighteen to sixteen fifty-seven."

Darby clasped his hands together and, with his eyes closed,

rested his forehead on his knuckles. "I'm sorry. I know it was corny, but it was all I could think of."

Pepper dredged up a long-forgotten image. That was the posture she'd been taught to use in the confessional when she said, "Bless me, Father, for I have sinned." She reached out and put her hand around his. "It was beautiful."

He looked at her with bloodshot eyes. "Who knows about it?"

"You, me, and a man in Tennessee. You up for a road trip?"

Darby's answer was to mechanically shovel food into his mouth.

Pepper felt like an intruder in her own home when she and Darby sneaked into the homestead and packed three overnight bags. Anne required her own suitcase. Road trips were easier when Pepper was younger and unencumbered.

She left two notes on the kitchen table in sealed envelopes. The one to Avivah and Saul said, *We had an intruder yesterday evening. Darby is taking Anne and me to a safe place. Benny knows what's going on; what I told him yesterday afternoon is true. Destroy this note. Watch yourselves. Pepper. P.S. Get someone to fix my bedroom window. I'll buy Saul a new pair of socks.*

For Randy she left a check for what she owed him for Wednesday, plus what she would have paid him for babysitting Thursday and Friday, with a note that said, *You can work off the extra later.* She couldn't bear to shortchange him.

She left a third envelope taped to the door of Frannie's art studio. *I have to go out of town. Can you contact people about getting together a bursary for Randy?*

By false dawn—that faint touch of lighter sky in the east— she and Darby sat in her car in front of the Laurel Ridge Clinic. Pepper paused with her pen over a pad of paper. "I have to give some reason."

"It never pays to change a cover story."

Pepper wrote, *Pat, I got hurt yesterday playing football. Nothing broken, but I've gone to stay with friends for a few days. Back to work on Tuesday. Pepper*

She sealed her note and the doctor's excuse in an envelope and shoved it through the mail slot. In the door glass she had a clear reflection of Darby. He put his palm to his mouth, and briefly threw back his head. What in the world was he dry swallowing?

When she came back to the car, he asked, "Can we go now?" His voice was testy.

"I couldn't leave things undone, and I didn't want to wake up Avivah and Saul to explain things to them. We'd never have gotten away."

He shifted into drive. "You mean as opposed to getting away at dawn?"

"It's not dawn."

The first rays of sunlight struck the car windshield.

She closed her seat-belt buckle with a snap, leaned the seat back, and laid a small ice bag over her eyes. She hoped Darby wasn't going to be this irritating all the way to Chattanooga.

CHAPTER 17

At seven o'clock Thursday morning, Saul, carrying one sock, came out the homestead's back door. "Have you seen my other sock?"

Avivah stood from where she'd been crouching and slung her camera strap over her shoulder. She'd been photographing glass shards lying on the ground under Pepper's bedroom window. She handed him a piece of paper. "I have a feeling that Pepper knows where it is. The problem is, I don't know where she is, or what the hell is going on."

Saul read Pepper's note, blinked, and read it a second time. "Remember back when we used to say, 'She'll be all right, she's with Darby'?"

Avivah recalled having said that more than once. She couldn't imagine what had possessed her. That wasn't fair. Darby Baxter would lay down his life to protect Pepper; she choked at the thought of either him or Pepper being faced with that option.

"Where did you find the note?"

"On our kitchen table."

"How come we missed it last night?"

"Because it wasn't there when we came home."

"Neither were Pepper and Darby. You're saying that sometime between midnight and now, the two of them came home, wrote us a note, and left again? Even though we were here, and they could have woken us up and talked to us in person?"

"That's my guess."

"If she's so all-fired interested in us protecting ourselves, why didn't she tell us who to watch out for?"

Avivah pointed to *Benny knows what's going on.* "She did. All we have to do is ask Benny what he and Pepper talked about."

"I hate it when Pepper goes all need-to-know on us. I've got an interview after I drop you off at work, but I can reschedule if you want my help."

"Go to your interview. I'll talk to Benny and grow gray hair waiting for whatever comes next."

He kissed Avivah on the cheek and nuzzled her neck with his scratchy face. "I am so looking forward to the two of us living together like sane, normal people without housemates, cryptic notes, or smashed windows. We'll have quiet Shabbat dinners. And socks, like Noah's animals, will always be two by two."

She reached up and kissed him. "Sounds wonderful." Her tongue began to work its way around his lips, so her next words came out mushy. "How far away is December fourteenth?"

"Two hundred and twenty days, but who's counting?" He pricked a series of tiny kisses down the bridge of her nose.

Avivah laid her palms on his chest and gave him a gentle shove. "Go shave. You promised me a ride to work this morning."

He hesitated with his hand on the screen door frame. "Did I mention that the toilet's bolt covers are missing, too?"

By the time she phoned Benny's house, Lorraine said that he'd already left for school. She'd either have to pull him out of a class or wait until he got home. A hammering noise interrupted her reverie about which to do.

A woman in jeans, cowboy boots, and a gray sweatshirt was fitting a piece of perfectly cut plywood over the broken pane in Pepper's bedroom window. Avivah called out, "Who are you? What are you doing?"

"Frannie had this plywood in the storage room," the woman

said as though either Frannie having plywood or her using it or both were wrong. Avivah barely recognized Kaye's voice.

Her badly chopped hair had been evened out into a too-short haircut. Her boots looked new. The rest of her clothes, while old, were an improvement over faded housedresses. Being locked in the shed seemed to have shaken something loose in Kaye, or maybe Frannie's therapy was helping, or both.

"Did you see what happened here last night?"

"Miss Pepperhawk chased a man. She wore a towel. She threw something. He fell. Papers scattered. That blond man tackled her. She lay on the ground. She and the man chased the papers. They left with the baby."

Avivah remembered the night she'd met Pepper at Fort Bragg. Pepper was numb from Vietnam. Kaye's run-on narrative sounded like Pepper babbling on that night. Kaye was certainly dressing better, but Avivah suspected that she had a long way to go before her numbness—whatever had caused it—wore off.

"What time did all this happen?"

"Sunset."

Sunset was roughly at eight fifteen. "What happened to the man they were chasing?"

"He ran." Kaye pointed toward one of the trails that led up the mountainside.

"Did Pepper's friend go after him?"

"No."

"Was the man who ran the same man who locked you in the shed?"

Kaye wiggled her upper body in what might have been a shrug.

"Kaye, I need you to say something; *yes, no,* or *maybe* will do."

"No. Too fat."

That meant there had been two intruders, one Tuesday and a different one Wednesday. Avivah didn't like the sound of that.

"Show me where the man fell."

In the middle of a flattened grass tussock, Avivah found Saul's sock now stretched out of all useful proportions, and inside, the four missing toilet bolt covers.

Doing reconnaissance up the mountain trail gave Avivah a chance to work off the nasty taste in her mouth. Being dressed in a towel didn't sound like Pepper at all. Why hadn't Darby been the one in pursuit? What papers were so important that Darby had stopped to retrieve them instead of going after the fellow?

On the mountain she found a spot where a car had likely been parked. It was time to get Benny out of class.

Asheville-Buncombe Tech was a conglomeration of buildings, auto shops, and parking lots. Avivah parked in front of Administration, flashed her badge at a secretary and asked her to locate Benjamin Kirkpatrick, an electrical-engineering student.

Thirty minutes later, Benny came running down the corridor and shuddered to a halt like a cartoon character. "Lorraine?" he asked, breathlessly.

"Sorry, I forgot you were an expectant father. This isn't about Lorraine. Can we talk in private?"

He led her to a cul-de-sac where six dusty study carrels were haphazardly arranged. The place had a disused, stale smell. She handed him Pepper's note.

"Oh, crap. Where's Pepper?"

"With Darby; that's all I know. What did you and Pepper talk about yesterday?"

"Pepper went to Yanni's store after work. She said that Yanni has a guy named Greg Lane staying with him. She's convinced that Lane is connected to the Central Intelligence Agency. She wanted me to investigate him."

First the State Department, now the CIA. Avivah didn't know how much longer she could juggle the government alphabet soup that Pepper was stirring up.

"Did you say you would investigate?"

"You saw what shape I was in yesterday. By the time Pepper and I talked I'd reached my Pepper-limit for one day. I told her to leave me alone and to stop obsessing over Vietnam."

"Do you know Lane?"

"Yanni never mentioned him."

"Did Pepper describe him?"

"Something about a ponytail, and that he looked like a pilot, whatever that means."

Avivah read from Pepper's note, " 'Darby is taking Anne and me to a safe place.' Where would Darby feel the safest?"

"Fort Bragg," Benny said without hesitation.

Fort Bragg was the Special Forces' nursery. All Green Berets trained there and, like salmon returning to the same spawning grounds, most of them returned periodically through their military careers. The post covered two hundred and fifty square miles spread over four North Carolina counties. If you ignored sand in your shoes and chigger bites, an uncountable number of hiding places dotted the uninhabited piney woods that made up most of the post.

She'd have to contact the military police, the Criminal Investigation Division, and probably the J.F.K. Special Warfare Center. Just when she'd sworn off of all things military, she had to brew her own pot of military alphabet soup.

When Avivah reached the police station, her driver was waiting in the police station parking lot with the cruiser motor running. He opened the door for her. "Don't bother going upstairs. We have a riot on our hands."

Avivah got in and fastened her seat belt. "A riot in Asheville?"

He turned out of the parking lot with lights and siren blaring. "West Asheville strip mall."

The small mall was located on a bluff overlooking the French Broad River. Anchored at one end by a discount department store, the other shops were typical mom-and-pop businesses: barber, hair salon, café, cobbler, dry cleaner, bakery, insurance agency, and yarn shop. At eleven o'clock on a hot Thursday morning it should have been calm, but when the police car sped across the bridge, Avivah had a good view of chaos.

On the far corner of the parking lot, where the pavement ended and a dirt bank ran down the bluff to the river, a crowd of a hundred or more people was corralled between the bluff's edge and a police line.

"What happened?"

"A guy in the department store's garden center turned a fire hose on a bunch of gooks. In retaliation they wrecked the store."

Gooks. Her driver had never been to Vietnam, never even been in the military, but his use of that word told her where his sympathies lay. She looked at the people behind the police barricade again. Many of them were Vietnamese.

Where had they come from? Charles Tu was the obvious answer, but not the only possibility. The news was full of stories about thousands of Vietnamese refugees pouring into hastily constructed refugee camps in Manila, Guam, and as close to home as Arkansas. Appeals had gone out for people to sponsor them.

Bible camps and religious retreat sites surrounded Asheville. If a church had decided to sponsor a large group of refugees, one of those sites would be an ideal place to house the new arrivals.

Despite Pepper's and her own misgivings about the way

Charles Tu did business, his way of bringing in people in small groups had been peaceful, except for that one incident seven years ago. Bringing in large groups of Vietnamese refugees when the country was reeling from the Saigon debacle was a bad idea. Except that the government had run out of other options.

A number of police cruisers and ambulances lined one side of the parking lot. Avivah wondered who was guarding the rest of the city. Her driver pulled off the bridge and onto the road that led to the shopping mall. "Any fatalities?"

"The vultures didn't get that lucky," he said, pointing to where TV-news vans and a car marked *Asheville Citizen-Times* were parked. "Not that your guy is a vulture. I mean he's not a real reporter. He writes for magazines and shit like that, doesn't he?"

Avivah had given up trying to explain that an all-but-thesis PhD from Columbia School of Journalism was a real reporter. "Saul is a freelance *journalist*," she said, hoping her emphasis on the last would convey a message of sane and responsible reporting.

"That's what I mean."

So much for conveying a message.

The constables in the police line carried billy clubs and wore helmets. The heavy-duty protection—armored vests, Plexiglas faceplates, and riot shields—were locked in the armory at the police station. Either the people in charge had decided there wasn't going to be that much trouble, or the equipment hadn't had time to reach them. Avivah hoped for the first option. Corralled behind the line were the Vietnamese. In front of it, across a cleared space of about fifteen feet of pavement, was a group of about fifty onlookers. Right now, it looked like a standoff. She hoped it would stay that way.

Her driver stopped beside a Civilian Police Auxiliary, wearing a vest marked *APD-Aux* in reflective tape. He consulted his

209

clipboard. "Are you Detective Rosen?"

"I am."

"Lieutenant Alexander wants to see you in the department store."

Her driver parked where the auxiliary directed. Her driver's job was to be at her side, but Avivah remembered how she'd felt going through Military Police School at Fort Gordon. What she'd wanted most was to be where the action was. "You better join the line. I'll send for you if I need you."

When she stepped out of the cruiser, a wave of heat rolled over her. Real summer heat hadn't started yet, but even a May sun beating down on concrete for hours could raise the temperature.

She was grateful for the heat. The young men in the crowd wore jeans and T-shirts; tight-fitting clothing had the advantage of providing few places for concealed weapons. It didn't, however, do anything about knives hidden in boots and guns stashed under the drivers' seats in the parked cars and pickup trucks. She was glad to see two auxiliary constables patrolling the rows of parked cars. That made it less likely that someone would grab a weapon and return to the fray.

The crowd facing the police line was a typical collection of weekday shoppers: mothers and kids, guys with nothing better to do than hang out, and the retired. A knot of frowning older men stood to one side. Avivah bet they were World War II veterans and American Legion members. It was the young men, men the right age to have been in Vietnam, or had a brother or cousin who'd been there, who had faced off against the police. So far all that was flying were obscenities.

She'd earned the right to stand with them, if she agreed with their obscenities, which she didn't. She'd earned that right even if it would be impossible to convince them that she had.

Through gaps in the angry, sweating crowd, she caught

glimpses of wet, dirty Vietnamese corralled behind the police line. A paramedic was trying without apparent success to convince a blanket-wrapped woman sitting on the ground to let him examine her arm. In addition to the police and ambulance crews, a few civilians were on the other side of the police line.

The two nuns in navy A-line dresses and white wimples were a natural choice to be there. So was the man in a polyester sports coat and carefully combed pompadour that screamed preacher. Two gray-haired, grandmotherly women had charge of the children. They'd moved them to the most protected corner of the parking lot.

Avivah recognized Ash Morgan, dressed in navy slacks and one of those pink smocks that hospital volunteers wore. Ash sat on the pavement, put her arms around the hysterical woman, and whispered in her ear. The woman allowed the paramedic to examine her.

Did Nate know his wife was rendering aid and care in the middle of a potential riot?

The shift sergeant raised a bullhorn. "Clear this parking lot now. In fifteen minutes, anyone not in their car, making a slow and safe exit, will be arrested and have their car towed. If you don't believe me, look at what's pulling into the parking lot." He gestured to where auxiliary constables waived in a bunch of tow trucks. The trucks formed a line like a high-school marching band at a halftime show. The sound of their motors rumbled across the parking lot. The concrete shook.

Several young mothers shepherded kids toward cars. Auxiliary constables escorted them across the parking lot. Two gray-haired women marched into the group of World War II vets and separated two men from the group. The other men laughed, but they dug in their pockets for car keys.

A young man with sideburns and a scraggly beard picked up a rock, hefted it and threw it at the sergeant. It bounced off of the bullhorn. The man yelled, "Fucking gook-lover." Two police-men had him on the ground in seconds.

The sergeant was back on his dented bullhorn. "Thirteen minutes, and counting." The tow trucks revved their collective engines. About ten diehards, all young men, formed a line fac-ing the police. People tripped over their feet getting out of their way.

Those young men weren't going to obey orders from her, even if she flashed a detective's badge at them. She could have taken her legitimate place on either side of the line, but sometimes the sensible thing to do was get out of the way of testosterone. Avivah hurried along the sidewalk to the depart-ment store's main entrance. Both front doors had broken glass, circular impact points which baseball bats could have made.

A constable stood at the door. His boots crunched on broken glass when he opened the door for her. "Watch your step."

It seemed to be her day for broken glass.

For people "having wrecked the store" the place was in better shape than she'd expected. Two employees restacked a display of paper towels, and another woman with a mop made a mess of what smelled like strawberry bath oil. She spotted Nate to one side, talking to a middle-aged man.

Nate said, "Where have you been?"

She decided not to mention that Ash was in the parking lot, and sent up a quick prayer for Ash's safety, for the safety of everyone in the hot sun. "Sorry. I was doing an interview."

Benny qualified as an interview.

"This is Mr. Wescott, the store manager."

"Detective Rosen."

An employee brought him a folder. Mr. Wescott said, "Thank you, Kim."

He handed a piece of paper to Nate. "This is the authoriza-tion, what each person is allowed to charge."

Avivah peered over Nate's shoulder. The letter stated that each person who presented a voucher was allowed to charge a list of clothing items, toilet articles; a small toy for each infant and child; and a optional item, ten dollars in value or less, for each adult. The letter was signed in a round penmanship that Avivah remembered from cards posted around her grammar school classroom. *Charles Tu.*

"Mr. Tu's people have always arrived in small groups. We've never had a problem before."

These were Mr. Tu's people, and Mr. Wescott certainly had a problem now.

Nate consulted his notebook. "It appears that at or about ten twenty, two men argued over a plaster elephant in the garden center."

Avivah asked, "How much did it cost?"

Nate frowned. "I don't know. Why?"

Mr. Wescott said, "Clearance, nine ninety-five, marked down from thirteen ninety-five."

Avivah said, "According to that letter, each adult is allowed to buy one optional item, ten dollars or less in value. Elephants are prized in Vietnam. A lot of people believe that to have a statue of one in your house brings prosperity."

Goodness knows, the refugees could use a harbinger of prosperity.

Mr. Wescott said, "They broke the elephant, and a fist fight started. People came from everywhere. You'd think we'd announced the fight over the public address system."

Avivah had broken up enough street fights in Long Bien; she imagined high-pitched Vietnamese voices, shoving, and airing of old grievances and pent-up anger. All that would have been missing were rickety, top-heavy mini-busses; the whine of Lambretta motor scooters; and a background chorus of live chickens cackling from the top of the bus.

"It appears that their garden supervisor turned a fire hose on everyone in the garden center. The force of the water broke open fifty-pound sacks of peat moss, and knocked over a metal shelf full of clay flowerpots. People slid on the wet moss and the flower pots exploded."

Homemade shrapnel. Wonderful. Avivah asked, "Is the supervisor a Vietnam veteran?"

Mr. Wescott said, "Ex-Marine. It was all those hire-a-vet advertisements. We decided to hire him even if—"

Avivah tried to keep her voice neutral. "Even if he was a veteran?"

"Even if he was black."

Crazed, Black Vietnam Veteran Attacks Helpless Refugees with Water Cannon. The newspaper wouldn't have enough room to jam all the words they wanted into the headline. She said to Nate, "Let me guess; you want me to interview the vet?"

"You are the best person."

"Where is he?"

"In the lockup. I thought it was a good idea to get him out of here as quickly as possible."

Kim hurried up. Her face was white. "We found a man in the men's washroom. He's covered with dirt and blood. We think he's dead."

Given enough pressure, fire hoses could break bones and cause internal injuries. Even if the man was uninjured, but had died from a stress-related heart attack, the veteran behind the hose could still be charged with manslaughter.

Ex-Marine Kills Again. Now the headline would fit.

CHAPTER 18

Darby kept the speedometer pegged a few miles over the speed limit. Anne behaved. Pepper periodically changed and fed her at rest stops. She spent the rest of the trip washing codeine down with cold Cokes, renewing the ice pack on her face, and falling asleep. The sun beamed into their back window. Even in the mountains Thursday was going to be a scorcher.

Shortly after nine Darby stopped in a small town. He parked in a tree-shaded lot. "Give me your prescription. The drugstore across the street is open."

Pepper handed over her prescription, got out of the car and stretched. "Shall we come with you?"

He was already loping across the street. "You and Anne wait here where it's cooler. I'll just be a minute."

Pepper cupped her hand around her mouth. "Get half a dozen Cokes, diapers, and formula."

Darby stopped on the other side of the street. "We packed all that stuff."

"You always say never to pass up a chance to resupply. Get a yellow bath duck if they have one."

"A what?"

"A bath duck. One of those squeaky toys."

Darby shook his head and pushed open the drugstore's front door.

Near Knoxville they stopped for gas, and closer to Chattanooga, for a bathroom break and fast food from a drive-in window. Darby's hands shook when he tried unsuccessfully to drive and unwrap his hamburger. Pepper grabbed the sandwich from his hands. She thought back to what he'd done at the clinic. "What are you popping? Bennies? Black beauties? Diet pills?"

He retrieved the now partially unwrapped hamburger, and bit into it. "Diet pills. They're legal. Can't say they kill my appetite much."

"Here I thought, back at the drugstore, that you wanted me to wait in the car because you were concerned for Anne and me. Did you and the pharmacist have a chat about how your wife was desperate to get her figure back after having a baby?"

"You said it yourself: resupply."

She tried to turn the steering wheel with her left hand. "Pull over. I'm driving."

He wrestled the wheel out of her control. Remaining bits of hamburger threatened to fly in all directions. Darby stuffed the food in his mouth. Lettuce dribbled down his chin. He chewed for several minutes, and when he could talk again, he said, "I can see out of both eyes. Depth perception and a few diet pills beat being stoned on codeine."

"I've taken what the doctor ordered, two doses, four hours apart."

"You've had four doses since we left Asheville."

"Have not."

"Count the number of pills you have left."

Pepper fumbled for her purse, counted her pills, and then counted them again. "The pharmacist must have filled the prescription wrong."

She tossed the pill container in her purse, zipped it closed, and flung it on the backseat where she couldn't reach it. Anne had both fists in her mouth, watching what was happening in the front seat. "This is Anne's life and mine that you're playing with. Let's find a motel and sleep. This is not worth getting us killed."

Darby nodded toward the green road sign. *Chattanooga 15 miles.* "I want to get this over with."

Pepper balled her hands into fists. She didn't want to come face-to-face with Darby's mentor. Her hair needed cutting. Half her face was a mess. She had baby-stained clothes and a brain full of codeine. And Darby was strung out on amphetamines.

"Vietnam, was it bad?" she asked, feeling a tear rolling down her right cheek.

"It was very bad. Be quiet and let me concentrate. I don't want to give a sheriff's deputy a reason to pull me over."

On the outskirts of Chattanooga, Darby turned right and headed away from the city. The larger and further apart the houses got, the more panic gripped Pepper's throat. She couldn't breathe; she couldn't talk. "I can't do this," she gasped.

"Too late," Darby said, turning between two stone lions onto a winding drive.

He stopped in front of a single-story brick house that had round, sculptured camellia bushes under all the windows and a small white-columned portico sheltering the front door. Pepper gasped for air. Approaching this house was like climbing Mount Olympus. She'd expected Mount Olympus to be cooler, but the heat wave extended all the way to Tennessee.

Darby got out of the car and, without a backward glance, walked across the driveway, up under the portico, and rang the doorbell. Pepper wrestled with Anne's restraining straps. She rehearsed, "How do you do. I'm Elizabeth Pepperhawk. It's an honor to meet you."

A middle-aged woman opened the door. At least she wore a plain gray dress instead of a maid's uniform. A maid in a starched black-and-white uniform would have sent Pepper running and screaming down the driveway.

The woman hugged Darby's neck. "Colonel Baxter, the Army told us that you were dead!"

Darby hugged the woman, then removed her arms from around his neck and held both of her hands. "You know the Army, Fiona. Is he in?"

"They're sitting down to lunch. I'll get him."

Pepper crossed the sweltering driveway at a fast clip, least Fiona close the door before she got inside, too.

A wave of frigid air hit her when she stepped across the threshold into the air-conditioned house. A couple of feet in front of her, Darby stumbled, sank to his knees, and ended up swaying on his hands and knees.

Fiona exclaimed, "Lord help us!"

A tall, solidly built man Pepper recognized from photos in the military newspaper, *Stars and Stripes,* appeared in a doorway. He held a white napkin bunched in his right hand. "What's going on?"

His voice was the kind that could be heard across a parade ground. Pepper walked across the wide, tiled entrance, handed Anne to him, and said, "My name is Elizabeth Pepperhawk. This is Anne. Don't let her eyes fool you. Colonel Baxter is not her father."

The cold floor came up to meet her, and her world went dark.

There was a knock on the bedroom door. Pepper sat up in bed. "Come in."

A tall, slender woman in her early sixties came in carrying a tray. Pepper recognized her from a photo Darby had showed her. Mrs. General Fairclough had iron-gray hair like her husband.

In the Army, the closest Pepper had come to senior officers' wives like Mrs. Fairclough was to see them on the golf course or lunching at the officers' club. At Christmas gaggles of them toured the wards bearing punch, cookies, and small gifts for the patients. She'd never been sure if they were scary or mostly harmless.

Mrs. Fairclough said, "I've brought you a late lunch."

Pepper knew enough about Southern hospitality to know that when your hostess offered food, you ate it, even if you would rather sleep, even if you were dead embarrassed about passing out.

Mrs. Fairclough opened the heavy drapes. Pepper's bedroom looked out on a wide backyard, a wire fence, and pastures beyond. "The sun has moved to the other side of the house, so why don't we eat on the patio?"

Pepper glanced at the bedside clock. It was a few minutes before four o'clock. She'd slept the afternoon away. She got out of bed. "I'll be dressed in a minute."

"Our neighbors are horses. I often eat breakfast outside in a robe."

Pepper tied a robe over her pajamas and found her slippers. Courtesy required that she offer a nominal protest. "I hope you didn't go to any trouble."

Of course the woman had gone to some trouble, or Fiona had. Having two wobbly adults and a baby show up unannounced had likely caused the whole household trouble, but the rules of Southern hospitality forbade that Mrs. Fairclough say that.

"None at all," she said, right on cue.

The heat had broken, leaving the afternoon air mild and pleasant. Pepper sat beside the glass-topped patio table in time to see buried sprinklers start. Tiny rainbow arcs colored the mist covering the lawn. Mrs. General Fairclough ran a tidy household. At four o'clock we will have tea and rainbows.

Mrs. Fairclough placed a glass of iced tea and a bowl of

macaroni-and-cheese in front of Pepper. Homemade macaroni-and-cheese, the way Pepper liked it, with the cheese browned to a hard crust on top and little bits of white showing where eggs had been mixed in.

"Darby said this was your favorite comfort food."

Darby's favorite comfort food was chili relleno and guacamole. "About Darby's food—"

"He mentioned his ulcer. We compromised on his second-favorite food. Fortunately, he and Zachary share a passion for cherry-vanilla ice cream, so we had some in the freezer. Now, please, eat before it gets cold."

Pepper ate, savoring every piece of stringy cheese, every piece of pasta. She patted her mouth with a napkin. "This is wonderful, Mrs. Fairclough."

"Sibyl will do. I believe your friends call you Pepper?"

"Please call me that. I'm so embarrassed. I can't believe I fainted in front of a man who was a deputy commander in Vietnam."

"And held several of his own commands in other places," Sibyl said with a miniscule edge, like a sliver of broken glass, to her voice.

Of course having his own command would rank higher than being a deputy commander. Pepper felt herself blush, at least the parts of her face not covered with bruises. They were on a first-name basis, but it paid to have your facts straight with this woman. Scary, definitely scary. Pepper repeated, "And several of his own commands."

Having established the pecking order, Sibyl Fairclough relaxed. "We were devastated when the Army informed us of Darby's death."

The Army appeared to have informed everyone but her that Darby had died. Which version had the Army given General Fairclough? A man who retired with four stars on his shoulder rated the truth. If the Army had tried to pull the died-in-a-training-accident-in-Japan story, her letter would have set the general straight. If the general had learned the truth, would he have shared it with his wife? What did generals and their wives do for pillow talk?

Sibyl put her empty tea glass back on the tray. "I wanted to phone you, but since we'd never been formally introduced, I was afraid you wouldn't appreciate a stranger intruding on your grief."

"I hope you know you both would have been welcome at the funeral."

Except she wasn't sure what Darby's family knew about General and Mrs. Fairclough. Darby wasn't one to brag about his connections.

A small, dark shadow crossed Sibyl's face. "I'm relieved to hear that. Zachary was so upset, I'm afraid, that welcome or not, he would have crashed the funeral."

Pepper had a brief vision of General Zachary S. Fairclough of Signal Mountain, Tennessee, and the US Army War College and Katherine Wright (Mrs.) of Macon, Georgia, eyeing one another over Darby's closed casket. She drank the last of her iced tea to hide her smile.

Pepper touched her bruise. If felt smaller, and she could see fuzzily out of her left eye. "Did Darby tell you about this?"

"He said that you were injured when an intruder broke into your home."

"Something followed him home from Vietnam." That sounded like an unwanted stray. She doubted that Greg Lane had ever strayed anywhere. "He won't talk to me about it, but I hope he will talk to the general."

"Does what followed him home have to do with that adorable child?"

"Very likely. I'm sorry. I didn't mean to saddle you with

221

babysitting."

"Fiona's granddaughter will, to quote her, 'just die' if she doesn't get a certain dress for graduation. Her parents have refused to spend that much money on that little fabric, so she's delighted at the prospect of babysitting money. She'll stay over tonight with Anne, so both you and Darby can get a good rest."

Thank God for money-hungry teenagers. Pepper also heard the implied time line. General and Mrs. were thrilled that Darby was alive; glad that Darby and Pepper had come to see them, but tomorrow would be a convenient time for them to conclude their visit. It would never do to overstay their welcome.

After Sibyl left, Pepper set out to find Darby. He was behind the second door she opened, in a dark bedroom, wearing only his underpants, and keeping watch through a slit in the closed drapes.

Darby had good reason to keep watch. Pepper had told Sibyl that something followed Darby home from Vietnam. If it had followed him to the homestead, it could follow both of them to Tennessee. How secure was the general's perimeter?

The window air conditioner was off; the room, hot and stuffy. A quiet room was better for hearing intruders, though Pepper doubted that in this well-constructed house outside sounds could be heard.

Darby jerked around when she opened the door, but didn't give up his post by the window. She went to him and smoothed her hand over his back. His skin was heart-pounding-sweating-every-cell-soaked-in-diet-pills hot. A pitcher on a small tray beside him contained lemon wedges and the remains of melting ice cubes. From the size of the pitcher, he'd had a lot to drink. Lots of liquid was the best thing for washing amphetamines out of his system.

"Keep an eye on things," he said, heading for the bathroom.

He didn't bother to close the door. Pepper heard a waterfall of urine. Urine was a heat sink. The more he peed, the more he'd cool down. She wondered how long he'd needed to pee.

"Have a cold shower," she called to him, stripping off her own clothes before she, too, began sweating.

"Believe me, I don't have the energy to get up to anything."

"I meant to cool off. You're a little heat furnace."

While he showered, she tidied. It was a habit she'd picked up working intensive care at the VA hospital. Some of her coworkers were, frankly, slobs. She hated to come on duty at the beginning of a shift to find every surface in the room covered.

She locked the bedroom door and set the air conditioner on a moderate setting, which would avoid the huge temperature gradient that had felled both of them when they came into the frigid house. Listening for intruders be damned. Even if Darby didn't trust the general's perimeter, she did. She had to believe that nothing was going to get to them here, or she'd curl up in a ball and whimper, which wouldn't do anyone any good. She straightened the sheets and fanfolded the covers back.

Darby came out of the bathroom wrapped in a towel, using another towel to dry his hair. He fell across the bed with an "Uh!"

He didn't seem to notice that she'd removed her robe and was naked. Maybe cold showers did work. She sat on the bed next to him. "The problem with diet pills is you go up, and then you come down. Turn over."

He scooted his damp body around on the sheets. His twelve stitches stood out against pale skin. She'd remove those stitches in a few days. She reached for the lump of towel where he'd tied it to keep it on his hips. Darby watched her untie the knot.

She said, "Lift your bum."

When he did, she pulled the towel out and the sheet up at the same time. The two pieces of cloth crossed one another

223

briefly, so that he was never exposed.

"You're pretty good at that."

"I used to be better; I'm out of practice."

He stared at the ceiling. She knew that body language all too well from years of watching military patients. He was exhausted, but too tired to sleep.

She sat beside him with her chin on her knees. "How long since you've had a full night's sleep?"

He turned on his side, and drew his knees up, molding his body around hers. "First part of March."

"So we can add chronic sleep deprivation to an ulcer and getting stabbed?"

"If you say so."

It had taken effort to get him to even admit that Vietnam had been very bad. If she pressed him for details, Pepper knew he wouldn't talk about the bad stuff. She resorted to a technique she'd learned on the military wards even before she went to Vietnam. "What one thing did you accomplish in the past two months that you're proud of doing?"

Emotions flickered in his gaze. "I moved a fucking truck."

"You mean you drove it?"

"I mean I moved it. Picked it up by its rear bumper and dumped it on its head into a ditch."

She had read about people having incredible strength during an emergency. "That must have been some adrenaline rush."

"The truck had stalled crosswise on a narrow road, with steep ditches on either side. No one could get past. The driver kept cranking the starter, but I knew it wasn't going to start. Mama-sans were screaming; kids were crying. The North Vietnamese weren't that far behind us. I lined up six or eight of the women against the rear bumper and we pushed for all we were worth. We got the truck rocking back and forth, then it tipped and went into the ditch, and the road was open again."

Goosebumps formed on his arms. Pepper drew the sheet over him.

"When I was a kid, I watched Paw-Paw Wright lance a boil on one of his blue-tick hounds. It was this little-bitty white spot, nothing more than a bad pimple, but when he cut it with his pocketknife, horrible stuff poured out. I thought it would never stop. It was like that on the road. Vietnamese kept flowing around me. I was taller than most of them. They smelled like *nunoc-mam,* goats, and fear. Old mama-sans patted my arm, saying in that shrill voice they have, *'Cám on, ðại tá, cám on.'* "

Thanks for what? Darby had removed a roadblock, but where were these people going to go? "I know that *cám on* means thank you, but what does *ðại tá* mean?"

"Colonel." He closed his eyes. "I hear Vietnamese voices in my sleep. *'Dại tá,* we have a problem.' *'Đại tá,* wake up.' *'Đại tá,* you must look at this.' "

Because he'd taken a circuitous route from Japan to Vietnam, Pepper was certain Darby had gone into Vietnam covertly; that meant he went in wearing civilian clothes. She would love to know what his intelligence cover had been. It would have been innocuous: spare parts salesman or agricultural advisor.

In civilian clothes, he was a spy. The minute he wore a uniform—and he must have worn one for the Vietnamese to be calling him Colonel—he was a soldier violating a congressional order that there be no further American military involvement in Vietnam. When had he changed into a uniform, and why? The Vietnamese must have had to scramble to find a uniform that fit him. He was taller than most of them.

For a long time, the only sound was the window air conditioner kicking on with a shudder. "Nothing I did made a difference, not Georgia Military Academy, or West Point, or seventeen years of active duty. Nothing I knew how to do worked.

225

Everything I've done since I was fourteen has been a farce and a lie."

Pepper took his hand. The skin was soft and cooler. "You're wrong."

Darby pulled his hand away. "That's it? I expected protests, pithy aphorisms, advice to pull up my socks and get on with my life."

"You know me better than that."

"For weeks, I've been so jealous of you."

"Jealous of me? Why?"

"How many lives did you save in Vietnam?"

"The emergency-room staff worked as a team. One person alone didn't save lives."

"How many?"

Pepper knew exactly what he was talking about. The instant when luck or good nursing training or instinct compelled her to do the right thing. The moment when she knew five minutes later would have been too late. With a bottle of bourbon and a couple of quiet hours, she could recall the details of every one of those moments. Most of them had Simon-and-Garfunkel soundtracks. "Sixteen."

"I saved one, Anne."

"No sale, GI. You did two tours in Vietnam, a tour in the Dominican Republic, and you went all those places that you insist national security prevents you from telling me about. You've got my count beat by what? Double? Triple? A hundred times?"

He made a sour face. "It's like that old joke: what have you done for me lately? The only one that counts is the last one."

"Like hell it does!"

Pepper reached under the sheet and laid her fingertips to one side of Darby's belly button. She moved them in a small circle around his belly button, then pushed the sheet aside and gently kissed the circle she'd been rubbing.

He tried to pull away. "What are you doing?"

She pulled him back and kept kissing him. Between kisses, she said, "Unblocking your emotional chakra."

Under her lips, Darby's muscles tensed. She laid her hand on his abdomen so that the top of his belly button lay against the center of her palm. She concentrated on sending him a feeling of warmth and relaxation. "My boss is always going on about chakras and nodes. It sounds like mumbo jumbo to me, too, but I've seen her do this for women who are having problems letting go of guilt."

"You're telling me that your boss kisses other women's belly buttons in front of you?"

"The kisses were my idea. All she does is massage. Here," she laid Darby's right hand on his abdomen, and interlocked the fingers of her left hand with his. "I want you to breathe really slow, in and out, pushing your abdomen against our hands. You're supposed to concentrate on orange while you do this."

"Like the fruit?"

"Like the color."

"Pumpkins? Oranges? Fall leaves? Hunters' safety jackets? They're all different kinds of orange."

Pepper pulled her hand away. "You're hopeless."

"That crap makes me uncomfortable, but this felt good." He moved her hand back to his stomach.

Pepper visualized the brightest tropical orange sunset she could. Darby cooperated enough to breathe slowly and deeply. She sent waves of orange into his stomach. His muscles relaxed. Holy smokes, this stuff actually worked.

She climbed into his arms and rubbed her cheek against his stubbly face. He even had a five-o'clock shadow precisely at five o'clock. So much of him was about rules and protocols. "What time is supper?"

"You hungry? We could get up. Fiona would feed us."

"I wondered how long before we had to get up."

"In this house, supper is served at nineteen hundred hours."

She eyed the clock beside the bed. "I figure we can stay here until eighteen fifty, providing you can dress in ten minutes."

"My plebe-year record at West Point was under two minutes from bed to shower to fully dressed. Of course, my hair was shorter then."

CHAPTER 19

Avivah, Nate, and Mr. Wescott arrived at the men's room to see an EMS crew and store employees involved in a complicated dance during which the employees tried to get out of the bathroom and the EMS tried to get in. By the time they had traded places, the peat-moss tracks on the floor had been hopelessly contaminated. A live victim beat contaminated evidence.

The victim lay kitty-corner across the muddy tile floor, his feet in one of the stalls, and his head almost under the sink. The room smelled like urine, overlaid by industrial-strength disinfectant. A resuscitation airway and mask covered the lower part of the young Asian's face. He was dressed in cowboy boots, jeans and a striped cowboy shirt with mother-of-pearl buttons. A few small, bloody tears marked the sleeves and chest of his shirt. She hadn't seen clothes torn like that, from shrapnel, since she left Vietnam. Avivah asked Mr. Wescott, "Do you recognize him?"

"One of Mr. Tu's employees wears cowboy clothes. His name is Mr. Lam. It could be him."

Mr. Lam was dead on arrival at the Mission Hospital emergency room. By noon, the parking-lot riot, and the arrest of store employee and Vietnam veteran John Walter Boyd, thirty, of Asheville, was the lead story on every local TV and radio newscast.

Avivah suspected two things: first, that by six o'clock Thursday evening it would be the lead story on the national

news and second, the news was moving faster through the
veterans' community than it was on television.

At mid-afternoon, in her office, Avivah studied four photocopied
pages of names, addresses, and phone numbers, which the
auxiliary police constables had collected. Some of the information would be phony. In a crowd that size, there were always a
few people who didn't want to come to police notice.

The words *Valley Forge Hatchery* and a phone number headed
one page. All of the names on that page were Vietnamese; all
written in the same hand. The diacritical marks over the letters
were correct, and last names came before first names.

A person who knew Vietnamese had compiled that list. The
night Edith Filmore had died, when Pepper had mentioned
Anne's fake name, Pat had heard Ahn, a last name, instead of
Anne, a first name, and known that last names belonged first.

Avivah got up and checked the city map on her wall. The
northwest corner of the shopping center and the back of the
Laurel Ridge Clinic property were across an alley from one
another. Someone coming from the clinic would have to walk
the long way into the mall, past the discount store's delivery
docks, and around the side of the building to the parking lot. A
person running could probably cover the distance from the
clinic to the parking lot in less than five minutes.

She went back to the lists, this time sliding a ruler down the
four pages of names to help her see each name clearly. Pat
Teague, Lillian Hood, Ash Morgan. Their names one after the
other. It took her a minute to place Lillian Hood—the
receptionist at Laurel Ridge Clinic, who, so far, had successfully
resisted being interviewed.

Avivah had seen only Ash at the mall, but that didn't mean
anything. You could have hidden an elephant in that confusion.
She dialed an internal number. The duty sergeant answered.

From the rough way he growled his name, he was deeper in paperwork than she was and he hadn't had lunch either.

"It's Avivah. I've got a list of Vietnamese names here from the shopping center. Do you know who wrote them out?"

"Some guy volunteered to help. He said he spoke Vietnamese. I gave him a clipboard and let him go to it."

So Pat Teague hadn't written those names. "Did you get his name?"

"No."

"What did he look like?"

"White, mid-forties, beer belly, ponytail."

Benny had said something about a ponytail. A name near the end of the last page caught her attention. She folded the sheet so that name was at the bottom, and then compared it to the list of Vietnamese names. The handwriting matched. She dug out her Yellow Pages and checked for Skoufalos Electronics. The address and phone number matched what Gregory Lane had written beside his name.

Mr. Bad Penny "had come to the attention of the police" once too often in the past twenty-four hours. Lane was due a visit, immediately after Avivah could get free of her paperwork, and the jailhouse interview that loomed in front of her.

She wasn't sure if she'd drawn the short straw or the gold ring. Both Boyd and Charles Tu had to be interviewed. Nate had said, "Convince me that you can be in two places at once, and you can interview both of them. Otherwise, you interview Boyd and I'll see to Tu."

Half an hour later, Avivah signed herself and her driver into the jail.

The jailer said, "Interview room three. His lawyer's with him."

She'd already guessed who Boyd's lawyer might be. Cody Doan made a point of knowing every Vietnam veteran in the

Asheville area who wanted to be known. Likely, he knew John Walter Boyd; he also knew John Ferguson. It would have taken one phone call to match them.

She was right. Trying to keep her face neutral, she slid into the metal chair across the table from their prisoner and his lawyer. She nodded. "Mr. Ferguson."

He nodded back. "Detective Rosen."

The man next to Ferguson was a tall, solidly built black man. He had a fuzz of black kinky hair. An old scar cut through his right eyebrow.

"Mr. Boyd, I'm Detective Rosen from the Asheville City Police."

He sat with his hands clasped on top of the table. "Yes, ma'am."

Avivah nodded to her driver, who sat in a corner with his notepad and pen ready. "I note you've already been advised of your rights, but I want to repeat that anything you say during this interview will be taken down and may be used in court. The constable sitting behind me will take notes, which will be typed up into a statement that you will be asked to sign. I advise you to speak to your attorney at every opportunity."

What she really wanted to do was to send John Ferguson and her driver out of the room and talk veteran-to-veteran, but that wasn't going to happen. "For the record, state your name and address."

"John Walter Boyd." He gave an address in what was called "niggertown" in some circles.

"Where are you employed?"

"Right now, I'm unemployed."

Avivah wasn't surprised. Mr. Wescott had to be backpedaling hard to disassociate himself and his store from Boyd.

"Were you employed this morning?"

"I was a garden supervisor in a department store."

"How long had you been employed in that position?"

"Three months."

"You are a Vietnam veteran?"

"Gunny sergeant. Marines. An Khe."

His tone was flat, but Avivah also detected pride, akin to a flavor in a dish that you know is there, but can't quite identify. She remembered when she'd sounded like that. For all the bad times, going to Vietnam would be hers forever.

She familiarized herself with John Boyd's record: two aggravated assaults; one damage to property, restitution made. Enough driving under the influence to have his license suspended. "Did the store know you had a criminal record when they hired you?"

"Yes."

John Ferguson said, "If you check the dates of those offenses, Detective, you'll see that my client has had a clean record for two years. I can produce a number of character references for him."

Even men with impeccable references committed murder. "That won't be necessary right now." She hated playing tough-cop with a fellow veteran, but that was her job. "Reformed, have you?"

"I've joined Alcoholics Anonymous and a veterans' support group."

Did Boyd and Pepper know one another? If their connection was AA, neither of them would admit it. There were reasons the program was called anonymous.

"What time did you arrive at the department store this morning?"

"Nine thirty."

"Did you go straight to the gardening center?"

"I had to open up the outdoor display area and water the plants before we opened."

"What happened when the store did open?"

A fine sheen of sweat broke out on the prisoner's forehead. "The gooks came in when the manager unlocked the store. I could hear them out in the store, jabbering away in Vietnamese."

"How did you react?"

"I was nervous. When they came to the store before, they behaved themselves."

"What do you mean behaved?"

"Were quiet, like. I hardly knew they were there."

"Do groups of Vietnamese come to the store often?"

"Maybe four or five times since I started working there."

That would have been four or five times over a three-month period. "About every three weeks?"

"About that. In fact, it was so regular, I almost got used to it. I'd say to myself, they'll be in today or tomorrow and sure enough, they'd show up. I'd go for a long coffee break or hide out in the storage room until they left. Today we'd just opened, so I couldn't do that."

"Since you couldn't leave the garden area what did you do?"

"Kept moving. Protected my back. Watched."

Behavior Avivah knew all too well.

"How did the trouble start?"

Boyd swallowed. "About ten thirty, two men came in. They argued over a plaster elephant from the clearance bin. It slipped out of their hands and busted on the floor. One guy shoved the other, the other guy shoved back. A minute later they were at it. Gooks came running from everywhere. They be running and yelling at one another. They had me backed into a corner. I just—I just—"

He just had a flashback.

"The fire-hose cabinet was pushing against my back. I uncoiled the hose and turned it on."

"What did you hope to accomplish?"

"I wanted them to stop that racket. You know, like you throw a pail of water on two fighting dogs."

"What happened?"

"I'd been fixing to unload a pallet of peat moss. That fire hose, it be strong enough to pick up sacks right off the pallet. They busted open. People were slipping and sliding. When I saw that, I aimed the hose to the ceiling. We had this metal shelf, with extra-big flowerpots on it, way up high. The bottom shelves were empty because that's where I be putting the peat moss. That water it done hit the shelf. I knew those pots were going to break something awful, but I couldn't do nothing about that, not nothing at all."

"What did you do?"

"I yelled, 'Incoming!' I let go of that hose, and dove to cover two women who were closest to me."

Sweat had beaded up on his forehead. "It sounded like a rocket attack, all that crashing. People were crying and bleeding."

"Did you try to help them?"

He hung his head. "I wanted to, but I couldn't, I purely couldn't. My head said I should hep them, but all my body would do was crawl under the counter and hide."

Nate had said the first officers on the scene had found the place awash from the still-running fire hose, and Mr. Boyd curled up under the cash register counter, holding a set of pruning shears like an M16. They'd had to pry them out of his hands. But that was almost half an hour after the pots had broken. None of the store staff remembered seeing him in that half an hour. He would have had had plenty of time to go to the men's washroom.

"You never left the garden department?"

"Not that I recollect."

"Do you recollect the whole time between the time you yelled 'incoming' and the time they found you?"

Avivah wasn't surprised when Mr. Ferguson said, "My client declines to answer that question at this time."

It had been a fishing question and both of them knew it. The core of Boyd's defense depended on exactly what he could or couldn't remember for those thirty minutes. She wished she had a photo of Mr. Lam, but the morgue hadn't been forthcoming yet. "Did you know Mr. Lam? I understand that he's been in with groups of Vietnamese before."

"I purely don't recollect anyone by that name. I never talked to the gooks if'n I could hep it."

"Maybe he was one of the people slipping and sliding on the wet peat moss? He was wearing cowboy boots, jeans, and a striped shirt with mother-of-pearl buttons."

"Ma'am, the gooks I was seeing this morning weren't dressed in civilian clothes."

Avivah imagined not.

CHAPTER 20

Pepper lay with her stomach curled against Darby's backbone. Small heat ovals radiated from each place where their skins touched, but the rest of his skin felt cooler. Both of them were in precisely the same position they had been when they fell asleep; a testament to their exhaustion. The warmth of his skin and faint rhythm of his chest rising and falling against her arm assured her that Darby was alive.

Did the Army know that he was alive? The question sent a little electric shock through Pepper. Darby hadn't phoned his parents until she'd bullied him into it, but had he notified his commander at Camp Zama? He must have. She wished she'd been able to listen in on that conversation. It would have been instructional, maybe even funny, in a dark, military-humor way.

She reached over his smooth hip curve and brushed her hand over his belly button, willing his ulcer to disappear like dust. He stirred, mumbling, "Is it time?"

"Almost."

With his eyes still closed, he turned over and pulled her into his arms. "I feel like I've been run over by a truck."

"That's because you have been. Diet pills are nasty things. Are you AWOL?"

He opened his eyes and blinked a couple of times. "I don't think so."

"Did you notify your commanding officer in Japan that you were alive?"

"I reported to the military attaché at the Bangkok embassy, and filled out a request for medical leave."

She could relax. Darby was safe in the arms of military clerks who, even now, were batting his paperwork around the system. At least having his name on the right piece of paper covered his tail. They could worry about details later.

Resolutely she pushed herself to a sitting position. "If we expect to be presentable for supper, we'd better get up."

During supper, Pepper rummaged in her convent-school memory trunk until she found Deportment 101. Sister Mary Margaret: sit up straight; elbows belong at your side. Sister Consuela: tailor compliments to fit your hostess.

She picked up a gold-rimmed water goblet. Her mother would have a fit at the idea of using crystal like this for an everyday supper. Considering that the Faircloughs had found out that Darby was alive, maybe today wasn't an ordinary day. "What lovely stemware."

Sibyl smiled. "A gift when we left Panama." She leaned toward Pepper. "He'd drink out of jelly glasses, if I let him."

General Fairclough muttered, "Man's got a right to be comfortable in his own home."

Despite the old-married-couple banter, Pepper couldn't let go of remembering who the man at the head of the table was. She'd seen a photo in *Life* magazine of West Point plebes sitting ramrod straight on the edges of their chairs during a meal. She knew now what they felt like. She hoped she wouldn't forget herself and accidently salute the general over dessert.

Anne, bathed, sweet smelling, and dressed in a pink dress, with pink bows in her hair, made a brief appearance after the meal. The general bounced her on his knee, and Anne sucked a tiny amount of whipped cream from his fingertip.

"One of the fortunate ones," Sibyl sighed when Fiona carried

Anne from the dining room.

The general frowned and crumpled his napkin beside his plate. "Best not to dwell on it."

Sibyl stood, and the two men also rose. Pepper planted her feet and crossed her fingers. If Sibyl suggested that she join her, leaving the men to themselves, Pepper intended to break every rule of Southern hospitality by flat-out refusing. Sister Consuela would spin in her grave, but Anne's future and her own future with Darby depended on her hearing what Darby told General Fairclough.

"They've had a long day, Zachary. Try to make it an early night." Sibyl said in a mock whisper in Pepper's ear, "If they start talking boring Army stuff, you have the general's wife's permission to leave."

Relief flooded through her. "Thank you, I will."

Pepper suspected that her definition of boring Army stuff was very different from Sibyl's.

The three of them retired to a book-lined room, dominated by a large wooden desk. She half expected a red telephone connected to the White House, but what she saw was a plain, boring black one. On the wall over the television was a large framed photograph of four men in slacks, golf shirts, and caps, leaning casually on their clubs, with palm trees in the background. Pepper recognized all of the men: General Zachary S. Fairclough, General Dwight D. Eisenhower, General James J. Gavin, and golfer Ben Hogan. It was your typical waiting-for-a-Saturday-morning-tee-off photo. Right.

One corner of the office had been fenced off with baby gates. Inside were a child-size table, two chairs, and a full toy box. A stuffed rabbit had been left at the table with a picture book and tea set.

The general said, "My daughter's idea. Since I'm retired with nothing to do—her words—I'm expected to babysit whenever she feels like it."

His voice sounded gruff, but his eyes twinkled.

Pepper said, "I suspect she feels like it far less than you would prefer."

"Let's keep that our secret, okay?"

She threw him a salute. "Sir, yes, sir."

He straightened and gave her a crisp salute. "Carry on, pretty lady. I'll be in the area all evening."

Breath caught in her throat. She wondered if Darby had taught the general that phrase, or vice versa.

More important, she'd saluted and had the salute returned by a soldier she'd admired for years. Civilians assumed that saluting was a military way of saying, "Hi, how are you?" They didn't get that it was an exchange of respect. Pepper collected that salute, wrapped it carefully, and saved it in her mental memory chest.

The general asked, "Coffee?"

A coffee service sat on a side table. Pepper recognized it from the Pacific Post Exchange catalog. She'd considered getting one like it, but even with a military discount, it cost more than she could justify for a few pieces of exquisite Japanese porcelain. Apparently a general's salary stretched farther.

He wouldn't have had to buy the set himself. Even if you disliked the man in charge—General Fairclough had not been universally loved—protocol said that you gave a gift when he moved to another posting.

Collecting money for a group gift was the kind of thing Pepper could see Miss Filmore doing: calculating to the penny how much a coffee service, card and wrapping paper would cost, entering donations in a steno pad, and giving exact change from an old-fashioned black coin purse. She wondered if the general's time in Saigon and Edith's time had overlapped.

The general poured her a cup of coffee. "Darby tells me he's off coffee and alcohol for the duration."

Her cup wiggled slightly. Was that a tactful way of saying that he knew she was off alcohol permanently? Not permanently, just for today. "Darby might manage one cup of coffee, if he wanted."

General Fairclough handed Darby a cup with one hand, and the cream pitcher with the other. "Permission straight from the Army Nurse Corps. I assume by now, son, you've learned to never, ever countermand an order by an Army nurse."

The two men grinned at one another and Pepper's head swam. Henry Kissinger had been right. Power was the ultimate aphrodisiac.

The general settled himself into a recliner. She and Darby sat on opposite ends of a small sofa that felt like sinking into a leather pillow. For several moments the only sounds were expensive porcelain clinking.

Darby was the first to set his cup aside. "How did I die?"

General Fairclough set his own cup on the small table beside his chair. He made work out of taking a cigar from the box on the table, and trimming the end. "According to the call I received from Japan, you were observing a field exercise. A deuce-and-a-half rolled, trapping men inside. You got them out, but died when a live electrical wire struck the vehicle. Attempts to revive you at the scene were unsuccessful. You died a hero's death."

In that alternative world, Darby had gotten what he most wanted. He'd saved people. A lot about life—and death—was never fair. The skin around Darby's eyes tightened. "I see. Were you aware that I left Japan for Vietnam on March fifth of this year?"

The general lit his cigar and drew in a long breath that made the tip glow orange. His words came out in a swirl of smoke. "Congress has specifically prohibited further US military intervention in South Vietnam. Should I be aware that a colonel intended to make a lengthy ground tour of South Vietnam, and I didn't report that information to appropriate people in Washington, my failure to disclose would jeopardize my commissioning oath."

In other words, son, we are friends, but I've played this game a lot longer than you have.

"But you doubted the report of my death?"

"I asked for the names and home addresses of the men you saved. Your commanding officer was remarkably evasive. I became suspicious enough to call in a few favors. A very tired and slightly incoherent Marine officer was convinced that you'd died of a stab wound in the US embassy. The Graves Registration Unit in Hawaii had your personal effects, including a nasty pocketknife, but they appeared to have lost your body. The officer commanding that GRU spent the past week jumping through himself trying to find you. I gave him permission to stand down from searching this afternoon, after you showed up on my doorstep."

Whatever time it was in Hawaii right now, a Graves Registration officer was haunting the bar of the Schofield Barracks Officers' Club. Or perhaps, he was already back in his quarters, sleeping it off.

Darby said, "I want my things back."

"Minus the pocketknife, I assume?"

"With the pocketknife."

"I'll see what I can do."

"I'll need my field diary, too."

"If it's with your things, you'll get it. Unless Graves Registration has managed to lose that, too."

Pepper spoke quietly, emphasizing every word. "I mailed Darby's field diary to you on Monday afternoon: special delivery, signature required."

She counted the general's pause. One-one-thousand. Two-one-thousand. Three-one-thousand. He flicked ash into a cut-glass ashtray, and judiciously examined his cigar. "I never received a special-delivery envelope."

How had she fucked up? The wrong address? Not enough postage? She hadn't fucked up. She visualized standing at the postal counter Monday afternoon. The special-delivery envelope in her hand had the correct address, return address, and correct postage. Either the post office had screwed up or General Zachary S. Fairclough lied.

The one place she and Darby had believed was safe, wasn't. Should she call Fairclough's bluff; tell him that she had a tracking number for the package? Pepper envisioned large black cars, men with dark glasses, and a convenient accident on their way back to Asheville. That was the way it happened in the movies.

Darby suddenly doubled over in a sudden spasm, his closed fist pressed hard against his stomach. It took him a moment to catch his breath. "Anne is Hang Nhu Gaudet's daughter."

The general leaned back against his chair. He didn't pause this time, didn't use his cigar as a weapon. Darby had delivered a stomach blow, too. "I see."

Pepper didn't see. She racked her brain trying to remember a Vietnamese public figure named Hang Nhu Gaudet. Maybe the point was that she wasn't supposed to recognize the name; someone's mistress or a shadowy figure like the Dragon Lady in that old adventure comic strip.

She said to Darby, "I'm lost."

"Hang was the woman who shot me in Na Trang in nineteen sixty-eight."

Her head and stomach did a free fall. She half expected the rabbit at the child's table to sport a top hat and pocket watch. "You went to bed with her on your first tour, and she ended your second tour by almost killing you?"

Too late Pepper realized she could have been more discreet than to mention Darby's bedroom antics in front to the general.

"It was a firefight. My men killed her husband. She was justifiably upset."

The general stubbed out his cigar. "We'd all do better here, son, if you started at the beginning. Miss Pepperhawk, you had the usual Army nurse security clearances?"

The commanding officer had replaced the genial grandfather. If the gloves were off, so be it. "You know my security clearance and a lot more about me. You started a file on me the day Darby and I started dating. When you groom an officer to become a general the way you've groomed Darby, you have to know if the future general's potential wife will pass muster. Did I?" she asked Darby.

"I never—"

"Don't pretend that you don't know he checked me out."

Darby hung his head. "You passed muster."

"So, General, if you're asking me if I believe in my country, right or wrong, my country, I don't. I heard too many outright lies, and I saw what those lies did to people. I share a house with a well-respected investigative journalist, a fact I'm sure you know. If you're asking me if I'm going to blab to that journalist or anyone else about whatever Darby is about to say, that's an insult. You already know that's not my style." She stood. "Darby needs to tell you his story; I'm not sure anymore that I need to hear it. I'll be in my room."

Assuming those men in dark glasses didn't kidnap her. Maybe she and Anne should run for it. Run where? They had run here, and see how much good it had done them.

Darby reached up and tightened his fingers around her wrist. "Stay. I plan to say this once. National security isn't an issue here, sir. What happened between me and Hang is a private matter."

Except that Darby had been in a place where he shouldn't have been, following orders he shouldn't have followed. Again. That was what had, in 1968, gotten him shot in the first place.

Through the window, Pepper watched twilight fade into darkness. General Fairclough reached up to the switch on the standing lamp beside his chair. His hand hesitated and he withdrew it. "I regret that this evening is too hot to use the fireplace. Some stories go down better by firelight."

Darby got up and pulled the drapes over the window, double-checking that the slit between them was closed. The only light in the room was the faint bar of light from the hall that shone under the door. It was enough that he found his way back to the sofa without banging his shins. He intertwined his fingers with Pepper. The side of his wrist pressed into her skin. His pulse was racing, too.

"When the brass-heads—no offense, sir—advised me that Vietnam was likely to go down the tubes within six months, I made a list of Vietnamese who had worked for me, people I considered friends. I knew that anyone who had helped us would be in danger. I couldn't go to Vietnam officially, but I had some crazy idea about taking leave; going in unofficially. At least I could warn my friends to get out before it was too late, maybe even charter a plane for them if I could manage it."

He wanted to create a version of the Baby Lift, only this would have been the Darby Baxter Emotional Air Lift.

"Was Mrs. Gaudet on your list?"

"I didn't know or care if she was in Vietnam. Then a chance to go in-country fell into my lap. Heaven helps those who help themselves. Maybe God was testing me; offering me a chance to prove I was serious about getting people out."

The last thing Pepper needed added to this mess was a messianic complex. She asked, "Did you find Mrs. Gaudet, or did she find you?"

"We literally ran into each other during a rocket attack on Ban Me Thuot."

Even Hollywood could come up with better than a pregnant woman running full tilt into a man she'd both made love to and tried to kill, while rockets whistled overhead. On second thought, maybe they couldn't.

"Her lover, an ARVN officer, was trying to find a way to get her to Saigon."

The general said, "You offered to escort her?"

"She wanted me to; I refused."

So that was where part of his guilt came from. A humanitarian desire to help, conceived at a desk in Japan, fell apart when real life and past indiscretions got in the way.

"It wouldn't have made a bit of difference if I'd agreed to escort her to Saigon. The North Vietnamese attacked before any of us could get out. I delivered Anne the night before Ban Me Thuot fell. Her father died later that same night, Hang the next day."

No wonder Anne homed in on Darby's voice; it was the first voice she'd heard. Here was real life complicated by childbirth, an orphan, and Darby's Southern-gentleman programming about protecting women and children. She wondered how many times he'd watched the burning of Atlanta sequence in *Gone with the Wind*.

"Before she died, Hang wrote a letter in Vietnamese in my field diary. She made me promise to give that letter to Anne when she was older."

Pepper remembered seeing three separate Vietnamese handwritings in Darby's diary. She touched her cheek. The swelling had gone down and she could see out of both eyes. What if Greg Lane had broken into her house to retrieve something written in Vietnamese? Why had he tried to run off with the cigar box? Maybe all Lane knew was that what he was after was in writing, but not where it was written.

The general sat silent for several minutes. Eventually, he turned on the lamp, got up, opened one of the baby gates, and unceremoniously plopped armloads of toys and children's books from the toy box onto the floor. He laid the box on its side and squatted in front of it. His body hid what he was doing. Pepper heard a metal door slide open. Before he stood, he replaced the fake bottom, turned the toy box right side up and replaced all the toys. The rabbit was back having tea. The nice, innocent rabbit was really standing guard. He had to earn those imaginary teacakes.

General Fairclough flapped the notebook in his hand. "If I were you, son, I'd be on my knees every morning thanking God that this pretty lady had the wherewithal to send me your diary."

"Yes, sir."

"I want to be sure that I've read this diary correctly. You put on ARVN uniform, and led Vietnamese troops into battle?"

"Yes, sir."

"Even though you knew that Congress had specifically voted against such involvement by the American military?"

"Yes, sir."

"Do you know what that's called?"

"The congressmen who voted against further US involvement would call it treason, and would have me court-martialed."

"Damned straight they would."

"It would never come to a court-martial."

The room suddenly felt cold. Darby wasn't saying that he was too smart to get caught, but that he would make sure that he never lived to be court-martialed.

General Fairclough said, "A dead officer wouldn't be any better than a live one."

"But a dead rogue officer would be; it gives the Army more

options on how to play it without that officer contradicting you."

Meaning that after he was dead, the military could do what they needed to with his reputation. Darby's loyalty to the Army extended to the grave.

General Fairclough handed Darby his diary. "We can't brush under the rug that you were in Vietnam; too many people saw you. Every day that goes by without someone blowing the whistle on you will be a victory for our side. Can you live with that pressure?"

"Yes, sir."

"Can you, Miss Pepperhawk?"

Where did he come off asking if she would fail where Darby would succeed? "Darby said I passed muster. That should give you your answer."

"Good woman. In five years, Colonel Baxter being in Vietnam will hardly matter. In ten years, no one will care. In fifty years, military historians will salivate over a field diary from the only American officer to be present at every major event during the last six weeks before Saigon fell. Son, my advice is to find a way to bury that diary for fifty years, and on the off chance that natural causes catch up with you before the half century is up, will it to the West Point archives. It's far too dangerous to exist right now, and far too valuable to destroy."

Darby nodded. "What about the accident in Japan?"

"It's amazing how a bit of hand-waving turns up clerical errors."

Pepper hoped a nameless clerk now stationed in Japan hadn't planned on making the Army a career. She wished it were otherwise, but that saying about having to break eggs to make omelets held some truth. She had enough pride in having held a commission that she knew General Fairclough was right on both counts: right now, Darby's diary was deadly, and in fifty years it would be almost worshiped. She suddenly hoped his grammar and spelling were all they should be.

Beside her Darby fidgeted. "You'll find out soon enough, sir. I intend to resign my commission and apply for a medical board."

"I see. How long have you been an officer?"

"Including West Point?"

"Including West Point."

"Sixteen years, seven months, and eight days."

He was one up on her. He could do the exact number of days without pencil and paper.

"That you know those figures to the exact day is, by itself, unhealthy."

It was? Maybe she was one up on him, after all.

"You've managed to outgrow that brashness you showed at the Academy, and eventually got over your I-know-what-is-good-for-the-Army-better-than-they-do attitude. You became a damned fine officer."

Darby dropped his gaze again, but this time Pepper recognized that blush creeping up his face. He recognized a compliment when he heard one. He said, "Almost dying has a way of reorganizing priorities."

"However it happened, it did happen, but when you decided to go to Vietnam for a personal reason—"

"Personal reasons weren't the only reasons I went."

"I didn't say they were, but you admitted it was part of your reason. When you did that, you broke one of the first rules of good command. You let your iron head overrule your eggshell ass. By my calculations, this is the second time that you are, by the grace of God and military medical intervention, still with us. How does the saying go, Captain? The one you Army nurses use to keep us guys alive."

She hadn't thought about the saying in years, but the words

came back to her. "Die if you must, but not on my shift. I don't have time today to do the paperwork."

"Baxter, you've got a university degree from one of the finest schools in the country, the GI Bill if you want more education, a chest full of medals, and a slightly spotty Army career. And you have a pretty lady who is more precious than rubies. I'm sorry, my Sunday school days were a long time ago, but you get my drift. I'm going to be real curious to see what you make from all of that. I retired three years ago after thirty-six years on active duty. You think plebe year at The Point was hard? Wait until you survive plebe year in civilian life. Civilians are so—disorganized."

Darby stood. "I hear you, sir."

Pepper got up too and faced the general with her back straight and eyes front. "I want my file destroyed."

He went to one of the filing cabinets, unlocked a drawer, removed a folder and fed the pages into a shredder. He handed her the empty folder, which had her name neatly printed along the top. "You have my word that no one else has seen this file."

The people who collected the information for him had seen it.

"I'm sorry. I apologize to both of you. Old habits, unlike old soldiers, don't fade away. That's another thing you'll learn. If I can help with your board hearing, I hope you'll ask."

Darby shook the general's hand. "Thank you, sir."

Pepper was exhausted, but she couldn't leave without knowing one more thing. "May I ask where you got your coffee set?"

"It was a gift to Sibyl from the officers' wives club in Okinawa."

"Meaning no disrespect, sir, but can you prove that?"

He frowned, and removed containers from the tray, which he handed to her when it was empty. An engraved brass tag read, *To Sibyl Fairclough, with thanks from the Okinawa O.W.C., 1970.*

"Of course, I could have had that tag engraved today on the off chance you'd ask me about the set."

She examined the tray in the lamplight. "No, the engraving is old."

He threw back his head and laughed. "Baxter, you have completely corrupted this woman."

"I tried my best."

Pepper handed the tray back. "Did you ever meet a woman named Edith Filmore? She was middle-aged and worked in the financial department in the Saigon embassy."

"I don't recall ever meeting anyone by that name in or out of Vietnam."

"Where were you Monday night?"

"We had family over for an early supper, then went into town with our grandchildren to see a magician. We were home, in bed, by eleven. Is it important?"

"You just established your alibi for a murder."

CHAPTER 21

At eight thirty Friday morning, Avivah's driver escorted into her office an elderly woman, dressed in a straight skirt and a sage-green cardigan twin set. A generous swath of white, fluffy bangs overshadowed the woman's wrinkled face; the overpowering face powder odor made Avivah sneeze. From the heavy-handed way the woman applied powder, she must buy it in bulk.

Her driver said, "Miss Lillian Hood."

Avivah stood. "I'm Detective Rosen. Please be seated." She nodded for her driver to close the door and squelched an urge to add, "So nice that you could finally join us."

Miss Hood arranged herself carefully on the wooden chair. "Sending a policeman to my workplace is intolerable."

"You've cancelled three interviews with us this week."

"They were inconvenient."

"Murder investigations are not conducted on convenience."

Miss Hood's jewelry consisted of a gold sweater-guard, nurse's lapel watch, and a single strand of pearls. The close pattern of tiny pricks on her sweater suggested that she'd pinned her watch in the same place for a long time. This was not a woman given to experimentation.

Miss Hood consulted her watch. "I can give you exactly one hour; forty-five minutes would be preferable."

Avivah already knew three things about Miss Hood: one, she hadn't worked at the clinic more than a few months. Avivah had met their previous receptionist, a very pregnant black woman. The second was that either Miss Hood didn't know or didn't care that Avivah and Pepper shared a house, and the third was that Pepper had never mentioned Lillian's name. She was most curious about the last one.

"I'll keep your time concerns in mind."

A frown furrowed the powdered forehead. "Are you going to read me my rights, like on television? I don't have a lawyer."

Avivah removed a phone book from her desk drawer. "If you feel more comfortable with a lawyer present, I'll give you time to locate one."

She hoped Miss Hood would realize that impromptu lawyer shopping wouldn't get her through the interview in forty-five minutes.

"May I take the Fifth if you ask me an impertinent question?"

Avivah replaced the directory back in her drawer. "Simply saying, 'I prefer not to answer' will be fine. To begin, please state your full name and address."

She was Lillian Maud Hood, with an address in West Asheville. Avivah glanced at the city map on her wall. Laurel Ridge Clinic, Miss Hood's address, and the shopping mall formed a perfect Iron Triangle. She blinked. She'd imagined an isosceles triangle, but in her head changed it to Iron Triangle, which had been a tunnel-laced Viet Cong stronghold near Cu Chi. She had to stop seeing the world in military metaphors. "You work at the Laurel Ridge Clinic?"

"I do."

"How long have you worked there?"

"Four months."

"In what capacity?"

"Office manager and records supervisor."

Two titles for a three-person office were impressive, especially since Pat Teague had called Miss Hood their receptionist.

Avivah handed Lillian a legal document. "This is a court order for all records held by Laurel Ridge Clinic for Edith Filmore. Do you have a chart for her?"

Lillian removed a pair of half-moon glasses from her handbag, and unwound a gold-and-seed-pearl chain from around the nosepiece. The chain clinked against her sweater guard.

Lillian read the document carefully. She gave a painfully thin smile when she handed it back to Avivah. "I prefer not to answer that."

"You are the records supervisor. You must remember if you started a file for Edith Filmore."

"You may have a court order, but I had forty-seven years in the Mission Hospital Medical Records Department. I am conversant with the protocol for making records available on court order. My instructions to disclose must come from Ms. Teague."

Lillian Hood, one; Avivah Rosen, zero. "Let's talk about Monday, May fifth. What time did you arrive for work?"

"Eight o'clock."

"The clinic didn't open until nine."

"I always arrive an hour early. The nurses depend on me to have everything in order by the time we open."

"Was Monday a normal workday?"

Miss Hood frowned. "One of our nurses waited until the last minute to book off absent. That put us behind all morning. My first break was when I went home for lunch."

"When was that?"

"From twelve to one."

"You were short-staffed; the work was behind schedule, yet you went home for an hour? Most people eat at their desks on a day like that."

Miss Hood sat very straight. "I am entitled to an hour for lunch, and to go home if I wish. Unlike in a hospital, where the medical records area is properly secluded, I am forced to work in a germ-laden environment. I never eat or drink anything at the clinic."

Properly secluded. Ha! When Avivah had worked security at the VA Hospital, her opinion about finding the medical records department was that no one should attempt it without a compass, ball of string, and packed lunch. If Lillian Hood hated germs so much, why was she working at the clinic?

"You returned to the clinic at what time?"

"Precisely one o'clock."

"Did anything unusual happen on Monday afternoon?"

"By dint of effort we managed to complete our work."

Avivah was beginning to see why Pepper never talked about this woman. The phrase "oil and water" came to mind.

"Did you close on time?"

"Ms. Teague had a social engagement. We closed early." Her mouth made a little moue.

"You didn't approve of closing early?"

"Our posted hours for Monday are nine to five. People expect us to be available during those hours."

"What time did you leave the clinic?"

"Four o'clock."

"Pat Teague was at the clinic when you left?"

"She was about to leave."

"Ms. Teague mentioned a drug box that is taken to the pharmacy each evening. Did you take that box to the pharmacy?"

"The drug box is the nurses' responsibility. I saw it on the counter next to Ms. Teague's purse, but saying what happened to it after I left would call for a conclusion on my part."

Avivah heard a certain TV district attorney's voice. This

woman watched a lot of television. "May I see your keys to the clinic?"

Lillian dug in her handbag and produced a key ring. One key looked similar to the one that Pepper and Pat Teague had showed her; the second was a smaller bronze key. The key ring smelled like powder. Avivah handed it back to her. "What is the smaller key for?"

"The grill in front of the chart rack."

"How many sets are just like yours?"

"None."

"Ms. Teague mentioned duplicate key rings."

"You asked me how many sets are just like mine. I have the only key to the chart grill, so my set is unique."

"What if one of the nurses needs a chart when you're not there?"

"If the clinic is open, I'm there. During my lunch hour, I leave those keys with a nurse."

Pepper occasionally went to the clinic on weekends to catch up on paperwork. "What if a nurse needs charts on the week-end?"

"The clinic is closed on weekends."

In Lillian Hood's view of the world, that was that. Pepper's view of the world included what you don't know won't hurt you, and, for important things, have not only a backup, but also a backup to the backup. Darby had taught her both things. Avivah knew that somewhere in Laurel Ridge Clinic a duplicate key to the chart grill existed.

"While we were at the clinic Monday night, I noticed a large glass jar of pills in the nurses' office. What is that?" She hadn't noticed the jar, but it was better not to bring up Ash's name.

"The nurses' dead-drug jar."

"You see a lot of children at the clinic. Is it safe to keep a jar of pills where children can get to them?"

"Children are never left alone in the nurses' office. My job doesn't include anything to do with that jar."

Avivah could believe that. What wasn't between the covers of a brown Manila folder made little inroads on Lillian Hood's mind.

Avivah handed her the State Department photograph. "Outside of the clinic, had you ever seen this woman? She would have been about twenty years older, with more gray hair, and a stouter figure."

"I never saw this woman outside of the clinic."

Which could be construed to mean either that she had seen her in the clinic or she was answering Avivah's question in the precise way it had been asked. "What did you do after you left the clinic Monday afternoon?"

Miss Hood rewound the chain around her glasses. "Being forced to leave early broke my routine. When I arrived home I remembered that I needed milk and bread. The place where I shop is across the street from the clinic. I had to walk all the way back."

She made it sound like a trek across desert wastes, when it wasn't more than a few minutes' walk. "What time was that?"

"I arrived at the grocery between five twenty and five thirty."

"That's an hour and a half from the time you left the clinic."

Lillian Hood glanced at the constable. A faint blush rose on her powdered cheeks. "Personal needs must be met when one has been at work all day."

Miss Hood's self-imposed abstention from food or drink at work probably extended to avoiding the clinic's washroom, too. Germs positively gamboled on toilet seats.

"I met those needs, changed out of my work clothes, made a cup of coffee, and set the sprinkler to water my bedding plants." Her hand went to her throat. "Oh."

Avivah leaned forward and slowed her breathing. Interviews

were like panning for gold, and she'd spotted glitter at the bottom of her pan. "Continue, please?"

"If I mention something I overheard, would that be perjury?"

The glitter grew brighter. "That's called hearsay."

Hearsay wasn't admissible in court, but, like preferring not to answer a question, it often led to interesting places.

"Could I be sent to jail for hearsay?"

"Hearsay is not a crime."

Miss Hood readjusted her position in the chair. "Laurel Ridge Clinic is not universally liked in the neighborhood."

"Why?"

"Ms. Teague welcomes women who—well, women whom my mother would never have allowed in her home, and neither would I."

Prostitutes? Drug addicts? Lesbians? Wiccans? Women of color? Unwed mothers? There were so many possibilities.

"If you're so concerned about your work environment and you dislike the clients, why do you work at the clinic?"

Another faint blush colored Miss Hood's cheeks. "My pension is not generous. I can assure you that at work I adopt a welcoming and professional demeanor. I simply prefer not to socialize with certain types of people."

Avivah didn't care to socialize with the people she interviewed, either. Except, this week, a lot of the people she'd interviewed had been people she lived with. "You mentioned overhearing something?"

"Two women in the grocery store. One of them was irate about a woman pounding on our clinic door."

"Did she say when this had happened?"

"I assumed it was after we closed. I was mortified. I'd told Ms. Teague that we had a duty to stay the course of our posted hours."

"Did she say what happened to the woman?"

"She said she was about to call the police—the woman at the door appeared intoxicated—but before she could do so, the clinic door opened and the woman went inside."

"Why have you waited four days to come forward with this?"

"I assumed that either Miss Pepperhawk or Ms. Teague had mentioned it to you. It had to be one of them who opened the door for the woman."

Except that Pepper had an alibi and Pat Teague and her partner said she had one. "Did you check the clinic on your way home?"

"It was none of my business, and I had to hurry if I wanted to watch my six-thirty program."

"What did you do after you got home?"

"Made supper, watched television, and went to bed at my usual time, which is nine thirty."

"Can anyone verify that?"

"I don't entertain guests on a work night."

"There was a disturbance yesterday morning at the mall behind the clinic."

"There certainly was."

"You, Ms. Teague, and a Ms. Morgan went to provide help?"

"We did."

"Why?"

"People were hurt."

"How did you know that?"

"I go to the store every Thursday morning for the clinic's coffee supplies."

"Were you in the store when the problem with—"

The intercom buzzed and kept on buzzing.

"Excuse me." Avivah pushed the switch. "What is it?"

The dispatcher's voice said, "Sorry to bother you, but I've got a disturbing-the-peace report in front of me. One of the names on it is Benjamin Kirkpatrick. He apparently was the instigator."

What was Benny involved in now?

Avivah stood. "Please excuse me for a moment. Constable, perhaps Miss Hood would like coffee, or a chance to use the ladies' room."

She left her driver to deal with the question of whether Miss Hood would find police-station coffee or their sanitary facilities more acceptable than those at Laurel Ridge Clinic.

The dispatcher was half right. Both names on the report interested her; she didn't like seeing either one of them there one bit.

Avivah applied excessive force to the emergency-room curtain. Metal rings rattled on along the rod. "I don't want to hear that he started it."

Benny zipped his jeans. "He threw the first punch."

"I read the responding constables' report. A slew of witnesses say that all Lane did was defend himself. If Lane had decided to press charges, those would be the arresting constables. You're damned lucky to end up at an emergency room instead of in jail."

He picked up his jacket from the gurney. "Pepper wouldn't have been hurt if I'd gone to see Lane in the first place like she asked me to do."

"Accosting a guy in a threatening manner in the middle of a public sidewalk and demanding to know what the hell is going on lacks finesse."

"Lay off, Avivah." He tried to brush past her, but she stopped him with a hand against his chest. She turned his head at an angle. He had three stitches under his left eye. "Another scar?"

He brushed past her. "I've had worse."

She watched his retreating figure, hunched over with his

hands in his pockets, then walked down to the nurses' desk, and flashed her badge. "I need to see Greg Lane."

The unit clerk thumbed through papers on a clipboard. "Cubicle eleven, but you can't go in right now. The doctor is with him," she said to Avivah's back.

At the entrance to cubicle eleven, behind another closed curtain, she heard a metal chart close. A man's voice said, "I want to admit you for observation and more tests."

"In the past ten months, I've had four complete physicals in four different countries. I'm not in the mood for a fifth one."

The accent was nine-tenths vanilla-flavored American, with a couple of touches of someplace else. The man sounded like a boy Avivah had known in high school. He'd attended fourteen schools in ten years; his father had been in the Air Force. Greg Lane's accent said that he moved around a lot.

"If you develop further symptoms, I want you back here immediately."

"I know the drill."

The curtain opened. She was face-to-face with a sandy-haired man in surgical scrubs.

She flashed her badge again. "I'm here to see Mr. Lane."

"All yours," the doctor said, brushing past her.

Greg Lane's gray hair was pulled back in a greasy ponytail. Sweat covered his forehead. Both hands gripped the examination table. He peered at her. "Who the hell are you?"

She showed him her badge. "Detective Avivah Rosen, Asheville City Police."

His head reared back. "They sent a detective to investigate a street fight?"

"I want to interview you about the riot yesterday at the shopping mall."

"I figured someone would get around to me eventually, but how did you find me here?"

"I read the disturbing-the-peace report, and recognized your name."

He got up, winced, and stood for a minute, swaying. "Fine, you can give me a ride home."

"All right."

He cocked his head. "You serious?"

"Sure. You don't look good. You want coffee or something?"

"I want out of here. Hospitals make me nervous."

They picked up coffee at a fast-food drive-in. Avivah parked at the far corner of the parking lot. Lane closed his eyes, leaned his head back against the seat, and sipped his coffee.

She still hadn't placed his accent. "Where are you from?"

"That's an unusual question in a police interview."

"I don't have a stenographer in the backseat. For now, we'll talk, okay?"

"Okay. I'm from Shanghai."

"American parents?"

"Yes."

"Where did you learn to fly?"

"From a bush pilot in Tahiti after the war." He pulled his head up slowly from the headrest. His color was better and the sweating had stopped. "You're no ordinary detective, are you?"

"I share a house with Elizabeth Pepperhawk, and I live next door to the man who picked a fight with you."

"Oh, Christ."

"I don't have jurisdiction over crimes committed in Madison County, but I know plenty of deputies who do. Pepper believes that you're the man who broke into our house Wednesday night. You've built up quite a tab: trespass, breaking and entering, theft, and unlawful confinement. Pepper's homemade bolo must have hurt like hell. If she remembers exactly where she hit you, will that emergency-room doctor confirm that you have a spectacular bruise in that same spot?"

He rubbed his hand over his right hip. "How do you make a homemade bolo?"

"Ceramic toilet bolt covers in a sock."

"I'll remember that."

"Can I see photo ID?"

He lifted his bum, groaned, and got out of the car. While he dug for his wallet, Avivah put their empty cups in a refuse bin.

He handed her an Australian driver's license. The ten-year-old license had been issued to Gregory Lane, and the photo was a younger version of the man sitting beside her. She handed it back to him. "It's expired."

"Only photo ID I have."

"Your passport?"

"Don't have it on me."

"What are you doing in Asheville?"

"Vacation."

"What's your connection to Yanni Skoufalos?"

"He knows my parents."

"Mr. Skoufalos left his business in a hurry Monday morning. He rented a car and wasn't seen again until Wednesday. You know anything about that?"

He massaged both sides of his temples with his fingertips. "I'm embarrassed. I was on my way to see Yanni, but I collapsed at a gas station in Georgia. Just my luck to end up in a rural hospital where the doctor wouldn't allow me to leave unless someone picked me up. I phoned Yanni and asked him to come get me. I wasn't well enough to travel back to Asheville until Wednesday morning."

He'd obviously rehearsed a cover story that would be easy enough to check. "What's wrong with you?"

"You tell me and we'll both know. Doctors in Australia, Japan, China, and Georgia haven't figured it out. Strangely enough, tai-chi, Chinese food, and herbal medicine have helped, so maybe there's something to inscrutable Oriental wisdom after all."

"Ever been to Vietnam?"

"Nice weather you have here in Asheville."

"When was the last time you were in Vietnam?"

"I forget." He tapped his forehead. "Short-term memory loss. It's one of my symptoms."

"Before I became a city detective, I spent nine years in the Army. I was a captain in the military police and did a tour in Vietnam. I have connections. You know what comes to mind when I look at you? *Anything, Anywhere, Anytime, Professionally.*" That was Air America's motto. "When was the last time you were in Vietnam?"

"I'm glad I got to see dogwood season here."

"I don't like people who invade my home and threaten my friends. Nothing would please me more than spending time with an atlas and a telephone, until I find every jurisdiction that ever issued you a pilot's license. Do you think that a report on your health would give them reasons to pull your pilot licenses— hear the plural—until you pass a flight physical?"

Lane pressed his lips together and stared out the car window.

Avivah tucked one of her business cards into his shirt pocket. "You and Yanni Skoufalos had better be in my office at nine o'clock Monday morning. Bring your passport."

CHAPTER 22

Friday morning, outside of Chattanooga, Darby stopped beside a mailbox. He reached past Pepper and removed two envelopes from the glove box.

Her cheek had shrunk enough that she saw out of both eyes, but her vision was blurry. One envelope was addressed to Darby's commander in Japan. She didn't need to ask him what it was. After General Fairclough had given thumbs-up to Darby's resignation what was left to do but mail it? In a way, she was relieved that the would-he/wouldn't-he suspense was over.

He handed her the second envelope. It had her name and address on it; the flap was unsealed. Fiona's lovely breakfast congealed in her stomach. "What's this?"

"Read it."

She unfolded a single sheet of paper.

I bequeath my final Army field diary, dated 5 March to 30 April 1975, to the West Point Archives, West Point Military Academy, New York. I ask Elizabeth Pepperhawk that she, or a representative of her choosing, deliver this document to those Archives on or after 1 May 2025.

Darby Randolph Baxter
8 May 1975

General Fairclough had witnessed it. Wouldn't that send the

military historians into a tizzy-fit! The general must have figured that in fifty years, he wasn't likely to be around to answer questions.

Calculating her age in the next century always left her feeling like a dried prune. "In twenty twenty-five, I'll be seventy-eight. I might not be around."

"Me either."

Darby was seven years older than she, and women in general lived longer than men. Her good Catholic upbringing—always be prepared to face God's judgment—argued that they could die on the way home. She didn't want to deal with either option. "Where's your diary now?"

"I'm wearing it."

She ran her hand over his body. Her fingers traced the outline of a money belt. A world traveler like Zachary Fairclough would have had one handy. "You can't wear it for fifty years."

"I haven't decided what to do with it."

"Are you going to cut out Anne's letter?"

All her efforts had gone for nothing if he was prepared to chop up his diary.

"I'll copy what Hang wrote to a separate piece of paper."

"And have it translated?"

"That's up to Anne to decide when she's older."

She looked at the backseat. Anne's attention focused on a set of plastic keys hung from her baby carrier. It would be a long time before she was interested in letters or translations. "What's in that letter?"

He stared straight ahead. "I don't know, but I imagine the things a dying mother would say to her daughter."

"Why is Greg Lane desperate to get his hands on your diary?"

The sun crested a hill. Pepper threw one hand in front of her eyes to block the glare; with the other she fumbled for sunglasses in her glove box. By the time her eyes stopped watering, Darby was out of the car, dropping both envelopes in the mailbox. The flap clunked closed.

She leaned out the window. "Why waste a stamp?"

Protecting his stitched side, he inched himself back behind the wheel. "Zachary instructed me to mail it. When it arrives, leave the envelope sealed and make sure it goes to that safe-deposit box with my other letters."

"This seems needlessly complicated."

"Zachary told me to do that. I couldn't think of a good reason not to do what he said."

For the first time, Pepper had an inkling that Darby and the general were no longer joined at the hip. She liked that idea. "You haven't answered my question. What's in that diary that Greg Lane is so desperate to get?"

Darby started the car. She knew that set of his eyebrows and pursed mouth; one of his need-to-know moments. They had a five-hour drive. She was well-rested, well-fed, and ready for bear. "It's a long way home. Want to guess how many questions I can ask about Hang Nhu Gaudet before we get back to the homestead?"

"Too many."

"Talk now and save us both aggravation."

He pressed his lips tighter.

Pepper removed her sunglasses and stared at him, concentrating on her breath going in and out in a steady rhythm and not letting Darby catching her blinking. He cracked about the time they crossed the county line.

"Hang was one of my interpreters during my first tour. The Vietnamese kidded us about being brother and sister because we had the same color eyes. Hers came from a French father. Youth. Hormones. War. Connect the dots."

She could. If she'd shaken off twelve years of convent school by the time she got to Qui Nhon, she'd have invited several men to join her in that youth-hormones-war triangle. "I need more dots to get from bed-hopping horny to she tried to kill me."

"On my second tour, I made a point of finding Hang."

"To play musical triangles again?"

"I was older, divorced, more focused on my career. I just wanted to know if she was all right."

"Was she?"

"She'd have been a lot better if she hadn't spent her life in a war zone. She was different, too."

"That doesn't answer my question."

"She was more beautiful and desirable; but I didn't sleep with her again. I'm not sure we were even still friends."

"The dots are closer together, but I can't get to *she tried to kill me.*"

"Six months into my second tour, I became the first member of my graduating class to go on the promotion list for lieutenant colonel."

"That focused you even more?"

"It obsessed me. I wanted to do something so spectacular that I wouldn't fail to be noticed."

"In other words, you fucked up."

"I intervened in a local black-market power play. Hang's husband was one of the players."

Intervening in local politics ranked as slightly less stupid than getting involved in a land war in Asia. "Ouch!"

"I've been reamed out by the best. I doubt you can add anything new to what's already been said."

She reached over and laid her hand on this thigh. "How about never second-guess an officer on the ground?"

He removed her hand with an irritated gesture. "I know you're trying to be kind, but you said it. I fucked up. The saving grace was that I was the only casualty on our side, for which I will be eternally grateful."

He steered with two fingers and held both of his hands with the palm up. The car wobbled slightly. "Benefits. Risks. The lesson I learned was that the first one has to outweigh the second."

She copied his hand movement, without the restraints of driving at highway speed. "Keep Pepper away from Greg Lane. Keep Greg Lane away from Pepper. All risk, no benefit that I can see."

Darby opened his mouth, but she filled in words before he did. "What you don't know can't hurt you; release information only on a need-to-know basis. Correct me if I'm wrong. Edith Filmore was killed in my clinic less than twenty-four hours after she brought Anne to me. Kaye was locked in a storage shed. Anne was kidnapped and abandoned in a tree. Greg Lane invaded my house while Anne and I were naked in the bath. I've come up with a pretty good idea of what I've gotten myself into. Anything. Anywhere. Anytime. Professionally. We've got four hours left on the trip home."

"Traveling with you is like anticipating a trip to the dentist."

She resisted the urge to say, "Open wide," substituting, "When did you meet Greg Lane?"

"First tour in Nam."

"Is Greg Lane his real name?"

"Likely."

"Is he a pilot?"

"Yes."

"Fixed wing or helicopter?"

"Both."

"Flying for whom?"

"If he likes your offer, he flies for you."

"Including—?"

"For, but not of, if you catch my drift."

She did. Lane would fly for Air America if the terms were right, but he wasn't a spook. A youth-war-hormone candidate if she ever saw one, even though he was probably twice her age. Maybe youth was a state of mind. War certainly was.

"Did he know Hang?"

"I don't know. He'd flown in and out of Vietnam for a long time. It's possible they met."

"Was he in Ban Me Thuot when Anne was born?"

"He dropped me off and got the hell out of there before the shooting started."

"Was that the last time you saw him?"

"We ran into each other again in Da Nang, just before he bugged out to fly a private charter out of the country."

"How did he know where I lived? Let me guess. In Da Nang the two of you made one of those if-anything-happens-to-me pacts."

"His parents are elderly and he's an only child."

"You gave him what? My name? Address? Phone number?"

"All of that."

"That doesn't answer how he knows about your diary."

Darby raised his hands in a frustrated gesture. A new possibility occurred to Pepper. He didn't know. Grade-A career military intelligence officer Colonel Darby Baxter had come up blank as to why Vietnam had come home to roost in his own backyard, or rather, her backyard. "Not knowing must frustrate the hell out of you."

"More like scares the hell out of me. Lane knew I kept a field diary; he saw me write in it. I have no idea why he wants it or how he knew I sent it to you."

For a while, Pepper sat and thought. She didn't have any more of a clue about Lane's motivation than Darby did. The farther north they traveled, the hotter it got. Pepper closed her eyes and sank into the rhythm of traveling on mountain roads.

Halfway home, her hindbrain kicked in. She didn't bother staring menacingly at Darby this time. Either he would answer her question or he wouldn't. "How would you do it?

He stared straight ahead at the road. "Do what?"

"How would you not be around for a court-martial if things come apart about you violating a congressional order?"

He worked something out of his jeans pocket. "Hold out your hand."

He dropped two .45-caliber bullets into her palm. They were warm from his body. To Pepper, they weighed a ton.

"I doubt you'd need two," was all she managed.

Darby shrugged.

She pried the fingers of his right hand from the steering wheel, pulled his hand toward her, and rested hers, cupped around the bullets, in his palm. "If you do this, I will be devastated. So will your family; so will Benny. Avivah and Saul, probably less so, but they will be sad." She left the bullets in his palm. "At least promise me that you'll arrange things so none of us find you."

His voice wavered. "I promise."

He put the bullets back in his pocket.

Pepper let him alone for the rest of the way home.

It was mid-afternoon when Darby turned the car off the highway into the homestead. Fannie's car, Cody's truck, and a car Pepper didn't recognize were parked in the graveled parking area beside her house. "Oh, blast. I thought Fannie's Art-Do wasn't until next weekend."

"What's an Art-Do?"

"An all-weekend art class. Art all day; wine and frivolity in the evening: it gets noisy."

She unbuckled her seat belt and got out. The driver's door on Cody's truck stood opened. He stood, balancing on one foot, with his jeans dangling over his empty right pants leg. He wasn't wearing his prosthesis. "Leadbelly is in jail."

Huddle Ledbetter or Leadbelly, a Negro blues singer, had spent his share of time in jails. He died about the time Pepper was born, so it was highly unlikely that he was in jail today. That left an ex-Marine gunny Sergeant Pepper had met at a veterans' support group and occasionally saw at AA meetings. He went by the nickname of Leadbelly.

She could figure out the charges all too well: driving under the influence or a knife fight in a bar. Leadbelly had had problems with both knives and alcohol. She tried to remember who his AA sponsor was, and wondered if anyone had notified him.

She walked over to Cody's truck. He pivoted to sit on the seat, and frowned. "What the hell happened to your face?"

"An accident. Why is Leadbelly in jail?"

"Mr. Ferguson says the charge will be manslaughter."

The bottom fell out of her stomach. "DUI or a bar fight?"

"Neither. A bunch of gooks started a riot yesterday in that shopping mall in West Asheville. Haven't you seen the news?"

"We've been on the road."

At least this couldn't have anything to do with Mr. Tu's employees. He'd never have allowed his people to cause a riot.

Cody grabbed a flyer from a stack on the seat beside him. It was a homemade poster, with a badly photocopied picture of Leadbelly in his Marine uniform. Handwritten underneath was

> Veterans' Rally to support John Walter Boyd,
> US Marine Corps veteran
> and to protest Vietnamese refugees taking jobs
> from North Carolina veterans
> 1:00 PM, Saturday, May 10, 1975
> Lawn in front of the Asheville City Jail

"What's all this about?"

"It's about supporting one of our own and about gooks coming here and taking our jobs. There's a hatchery and meat-processing plant practically spitting distance from here. The owner has been sneaking gooks into the country illegally for years. He's probably in the country illegally himself."

Tu was too obsessive-compulsive to break the law. "When was the last time you, me, or anyone we know wanted to gut ducks for a living?"

"It's the principle."

Darby, with a fussy Anne in his arms, walked over to the truck. Pepper handed him the flyer and took Anne in return. She jiggled Anne to quiet her. "What about her? When she's sixteen, she can't babysit or flip hamburgers after school because she was born in Vietnam?"

"Not if an American wants the job."

"By the time she's sixteen, she's going to be an American."

"Not if I have anything to say about it. Are you and Avivah going to march with us?"

"I can't speak for Avivah, but I won't."

Cody's face was red. "I thought I could count on you. Fine then. What about you, Colonel? Will you support us?"

Darby handed back the piece of paper. "Active-duty military personnel are prohibited from participating in public demonstrations reflecting a political position."

So Darby could hide behind his commissioning oath, even though he'd mailed in his resignation. How convenient.

Cody hoisted himself into his truck, starting the engine with such force that Pepper feared the key would break off in the ignition. He slammed the door, and Pepper stepped away. He yelled at her, "Wait until some gook takes your job. Don't say I didn't warn you."

Pepper yelled at the truck, "Why aren't you wearing your prosthesis?"

She didn't get an answer.

Darby stood beside her. "That young man has a bad case of NIMBY."

"What's NIMBY?"

"Not in my backyard."

She shifted Anne's weight. "I have to see Benny. If Cody asked me to support the demonstration, I'll bet he asked Benny, too. I don't want Benny involved in this."

"You can't forbid Kirkpatrick from demonstrating. He's not on active duty; he has a right to follow his conscience."

"I want to know what he plans to do."

"You want him to do what you think is right."

Anne didn't like bumping along a mountain path in Pepper's arms. She let go the floodgates and made it clear that she wanted to go home, now! Pepper came out of the path at Benny's place, winded, sweating and, thanks to Anne, announced ahead of time. Darby was right behind her.

She was in time to see Lorraine's car drive away at the same breakneck speed Cody had used. Mark leaned out of the left back window, his arms reaching. He screamed, "I want to stay with Daddy. I want to stay with Daddy," until someone pulled him inside. The car disappeared down the drive.

Benny stood in front of his house. He hung his head.

Pepper barely had enough breath left to ask, "What is going on?"

"My new employer phoned from New York City to confirm flight details. Lorraine answered the phone."

"She's some mad?"

"I thought she was going to have a stroke."

"Where is she going?"

"I don't know."

Darby said, "Is this a private catastrophe, or does someone want to fill me in?"

"Benny signed a two-year contract to be an executive civilian advisor: technical communication support, discreetly delivered by ex-military personnel."

Benny was a civilian, and Darby was on the downside of being subject to his commissioning oath, but they had spent a lot of years being sergeant and colonel. When Darby bellowed, "Kirkpatrick!" Benny came to attention. Darby stood with his feet apart and both fists on his hips, leaning in slightly toward Benny's face. "Are you out of your mind? You have an education, a new house, and a family. I know guys who would kill for that. You're going to throw it all away on some two-bit foreign contract?"

Pepper tugged on his shirtsleeve. "What about that 'Kirkpatrick has a right to follow his conscience' speech you gave me?"

"That was when I thought he knew what common sense was."

"Back off, Colonel. I don't answer to military discipline."

At least until he got off that plane surrounded by sand and heat. Pepper assumed Benny had figured that part out for himself. Pepper stepped between the two men and faced Benny. "Did Cody talk to you about his idiotic protest tomorrow?"

"So Cody's mixed up in that, is he? A couple of ex-Berets in Fayetteville phoned to ask what the hell was going on. I told them I didn't know." Benny unlocked his truck. "Keep an eye on the house. I'll be gone a couple of days."

Pepper yelled to be heard over the revving truck motor. "Where are you going?"

"To do what Special Forces taught me: capture the high ground."

The truck kicked up gravel when Benny drove away.

Pepper asked Darby, "What the hell does that mean?"

"It means Ex–First Sergeant Kirkpatrick is going to war."

"Against whom?"

"I don't know. I hope it's not himself."

Risks and benefits. Pepper knew Benny well enough to know that, unlike Darby, he wasn't at risk of doing himself harm. What he needed was a chance to blow off steam. It was a small consolation.

A few minutes later Pepper locked Benny's front door with her key to his house. He had a key for her house. They lived in one another back's pocket, the same way they had at Fort Bragg. For the first time, she wasn't sure that was a good idea.

By the time they walked back to the homestead, Anne had cried herself out, an exhausted, tear-streaked baby who laid her head on Pepper's shoulder and whimpered. Pepper felt like whimpering, too. At least today Darby could stand guard while she and Anne bathed.

At Kaye's trailer Frannie, Kaye and—surely not, but it was—Ash Morgan sat at a covered patio table in the shadow of the trailer. Frannie yelled, "Come over here."

They went. Pepper waited for Frannie to ask what had happened to her face.

Frannie shaded her eyes with her hand. "Did Cody talk to you?"

"He did."

"Did you agree to protest?"

"Of course not."

Frannie moved aside and made room for the two of them at the table. "Good. Sit down. We can use your help."

"Maybe later. Anne needs baby maintenance in the worst way. Ash, are you here for the Art-Do?"

Frannie said, "The Art-Do is next weekend."

Pepper had remembered the date correctly after all. "Then why are you all here?"

Ash said, "I called you yesterday and today, to see how you were feeling. When I didn't get an answer, I got worried. I came to see if you were okay. Frannie and Kaye invited me to stay for supper."

Frannie said, "I'm not going home until Cody gets over this stupid idea that America isn't big enough for both him and Vietnamese refugees. Kaye and Ash are keeping me company. A mini-Art-Do is a great idea. I can work out my hostility pounding clay. What do you say, ladies?"

Kaye said, "I'll pound clay."

Ash said, "I've never done ceramics, but if you'll show me what to do, I'm game."

Pepper heard a car turn onto her road. She hoped it was Saul and Avivah; the last thing she needed now was more company. "Let me get Anne settled and I'll come pound clay, too."

The nose of a large, black car appeared. Pepper had to be hallucinating. She wanted to be.

The limo stopped. Dave got out and opened the back door, assisting Nana Kate from the car. Darby grabbed her hand. He whispered, "Pepper."

It's amazing how much angst distilled into one word. Brought it on yourself, she thought. She's your grandmother.

Nana Kate, dressed in dove gray instead of unrelieved black and a gray hat with two feathers instead of a veil, stomped across the lawn. Each snick of her cane dug a divot from the grass. She came to a halt directly in front of her grandson. Nana Kate looked exactly like Darby had looked when he chewed out Benny.

"Young man, you'd better have a plausible explanation why you've allowed your family to believe that you are convalescing in Japan."

CHAPTER 23

The three women rose from the table and stood beside Pepper, forming a shield wall between Darby and Nana Kate. Frannie was on Pepper's right, Ash on her left, and Kaye on Ash's left.

Frannie stepped forward and held out her hand. "You must be Darby's grandmother. I regret that we've never been formally introduced. I'm Mrs. Francesca Maddox-Doan." In one smooth movement, honed by years of working with geriatric patients at the VA hospital, Frannie turned the handshake into a let's-go-this-way movement, with her right hand in Nana Kate's hand and her left hand clasped around Nana Kate's elbow. "I've heard so much about you. Perhaps you've met my friend, the sculptor Felicia Farrisee? She's active in historic preservation in the Macon area."

Nana Kate didn't appear to notice or care that she was being led away from the confrontation and toward the umbrella-shaded table. Excellent start.

Ash said, "I'll find us something cold to drink." She headed for the kitchen door.

Always assume your guest is perishing of thirst. Maybe a well-watered, well-fed octogenarian would be more amenable to explanations. Then again, considering the stories Darby had told about Nana Kate, maybe not. All the sisterhood could do was buy him time.

Kaye started across the backyard toward Dave and the limo. "I'll see to your chauffeur. He'd probably like something cold to drink, too."

Always see to the hired help.

Pepper's actions were more of a military bent: get off the firing line. She grabbed a handful of Darby's shirt and led him toward the car. "I need Anne's things now! Unload the car." For once Darby obeyed orders instead of giving them.

As Avivah washed lettuce, she watched early-evening shadows crawl across her backyard. One anemic cloud sulked alone in the sky. So much for hoping that bad weather would keep Cody and other demonstrators at home tomorrow.

The backyard was blissfully empty. Saul and Frannie had taken Darby's grandmother on a leisurely stroll around the homestead. She wasn't sure a woman in her late eighties should be touring mountain terrain, even leisurely, but she wasn't Nana Kate's keeper. Having Darby's grandmother out of the house sure beat having Nana Kate, Pepper, and Darby glowering at one another.

She heard a familiar clunk when Pepper turned on bath water. Living in an old house meant that housemates knew who was doing what in the bathroom. The tepid water flowing over her hands turned cold.

The oven timer dinged. Ash hurried out of the pantry, carrying their largest baking dish covered with foil. She grabbed pot holders, removed apple crisp from the oven, and shoved the foil-covered dish into the oven in its place. A heat wave raced across the kitchen, bringing with it odors of baked apples, caramelized sugar, and cinnamon. Avivah sweated and salivated. It had been a long time since lunch.

Ash laid a folded towel carefully on top of the refrigerator and hoisted the hot apple crisp up to rest on it.

Avivah said, "We cool hot dishes on the counter."

Ash replaced the pot holders back on their hooks. "There's a child in the house."

Avivah snapped off lettuce leaf ends. "It will be a long time before Anne can pull hot dishes off the counter."

A chair grated over the linoleum floor; Ash sat down. "You don't like me, do you?"

Avivah concentrated on tearing lettuce into small pieces. "I don't know you. I only know what Nate has said about you."

"What would that be?"

"That since your daughter's death, living with you has been like living with a stranger."

Ash said nothing. Avivah glanced at her, watching her studiously unscrew the saltshaker lid. Salt fell on the table. Ash screwed the lid back on, and swept every spilled grain into her palm.

Avivah said, "I'm not going to tell Pepper that you're Nate's wife, but one day she will find out. Whatever we don't want the world to know is exactly the information that gets out. That's the way life works."

She stopped, a perfect cone of tomato stem poised on her knife tip. She had the answer to her sister's question. The one thing she and her sister didn't want the world to know—that Miriam Schneiderman Altman advocated compulsory sterilization of poor women—was exactly the thing that would get out. That's the way the world worked. Her sister's only possibility of mitigating repercussions was to make the letters she'd found public. She'd better do it soon, before Miriam's biography was published. Once her sister hit the book tour circuit, that wasn't the kind of thing you wanted someone to bring up unexpectedly at a book signing.

Ash asked, "Are you and Nate lovers?"

Avivah's breath caught in her throat. The ripe tomato slid from her hand, landed in the sink, and split open along one side. She laid the sharp knife on the counter, grabbed a dish towel, drying tomato juice into her hands. Too late she realized she should have rinsed first. "No."

Ash sat still, both hands clenched into fists. "I don't just mean are you lovers now? Have you ever been lovers, ever kissed, ever held one another? Even once?"

Pepper pulled the tub plug. Water ran down the drainage pipe. Pepper always dressed quickly after a bath. She'd be in the kitchen in a couple of minutes. Whatever you didn't want the world to know about, that was exactly what would get out, and Avivah didn't want Pepper to know about this conversation she and Ash were having. "Nate and I have never kissed, never held one another. We shook hands once, for the photographers at my promotion ceremony. You think I slept with Nate in order to be promoted to detective."

Tears spilled from Ash's blue eyes. "I think he slept with you in order to be promoted to lieutenant. His career was going nowhere. He's waited years for a promotion. Then you showed up: the first female constable, the first female detective, and his protégée. Suddenly, he's a lieutenant."

Ash wiped at her tears, squealed, "Ow," and wiped more furiously. Avivah pulled Ash from her chair. She weighed hardly more than a child. Avivah practically carried her to the sink, shoved her face under the faucet, and turned on the water full force. Water rebounded, sending blobs of squishy tomato over both of them.

"Stop fighting me! You had salt on your hands. I have to wash it out of your eyes."

A minute later, Pepper, wearing jeans, a T-shirt, and a towel turban came into the kitchen. "What's going on?"

A sodden Ash, her white-blonde hair plastered to her face, extricated herself from under the running water. Avivah handed her a clean dish towel. Ash wiped at her eyes and face. "I got salt in my eyes. Silly of me."

Ash's partial truth and the fishy smell now filling the kitchen were a nicely ironic combination, one that Avivah wouldn't share with Pepper.

Ash continued quickly, "I found canned tuna, mushroom soup, and egg noodles in the pantry, and green peas in the freezer. I made a casserole. I hope that's all right. I figured fish, in case Mrs. Wright follows the Friday abstinence."

"How did you know that Nana Kate is devout Catholic?"

Avivah said, "She wears a gold crucifix."

Ash said, "Protestants wear a cross; Catholics wear a crucifix. There's ice cream and apple crisp for dessert and Avivah is making a salad. All that's left to do is make iced tea and set the tables. We're using a couple of the long tables from Frannie's workshop."

"You're marvelous. You're wasted at the clinic. You should be running the governor's mansion."

Ash blushed.

"Let me check on Anne, then I'll make the tea."

Both women slumped when Pepper's bedroom door close. Ash handed the wet dish towel back to Avivah. "I feel like such a fool."

Avivah tossed the towel on the counter. "Nate got his promotion because he's good at what he does."

"He was good at what he did for years before you showed up."

"Maybe working with me did move Nate into the spotlight. Call it Affirmative Action fallout."

"I'm so jealous of you."

"You probably always will be. Do us both a favor. Talk to Nate."

"About you and him?"

"If you need to hear his version, too. I meant talk about the two of you."

"Should I tell him everything?"

"Dancing sky-clad with twelve other women Monday night can wait a while."

"I think you're right."

Pepper sat next to Darby on her living-room couch listening to silence. Nana Kate sat across from them in the same chair Edith Filmore had occupied five days ago. Anne was asleep. Avivah and Saul had beaten a tactful retreat to sleep at Benny's house, taking Dave the Chauffeur with them. Through the window, she saw a dim light in the trailer's living room. Frannie and Kaye were having themselves a late night.

Darby planted both feet on the floor and leaned forward with his clasped hands between his knees. "How did you know I was here?"

"An Asheville policeman phoned to enquire about my activities Monday. He let slip that you were here."

Oops.

Nana Kate rested gnarled hands on her formidable cane. "You owe your parents and me an explanation."

"It's a long story."

"I am eighty-nine. Perhaps you can condense it?"

Pepper pressed her lips together to keep from smiling. She'd never imagined that Nana Kate owned a sense of humor.

Darby said, "Not this time."

Nana Kate hesitated, laid her cane beside her chair, and folded her hands in her lap. "I see. You may have whatever time you need." Her voice had changed, become softer.

Night settled into late night while Darby talked. He started with leaving Japan in March, and went straight through to his reasons for resigning his commission, leaving out the existence of his field diary, Anne's real name, and that Anne's mother was the person who had shot him on his second tour of Vietnam.

Pepper stopped worrying about national security. An eighty-nine-year-old woman who knew secrets dating back to Reconstruction could probably keep a few more.

When he finished, Nana Kate said to Pepper, "Richmond was burning when my grandfather escaped. The last letter we have from him—saying he was out of the capital alive—was written on the back of a blank dry-goods receipt from the Richmond Emporium."

By 1865, the Richmond Emporium, like all Southern stores, would have had precious few dry goods to sell.

"The paper was folded into quarters, with directions to his parents' home in Macon written on the outside. By the time it reached his family, the Confederacy had surrendered. The letter reached home, but he never did."

Pepper entertained a brief fantasy that Darby's great-great-grandfather, like Huck Finn, had "headed out for the territories." Maybe he raised a family in Wyoming, but never got around to letting the folks back in Georgia know about them. From what Darby had told her, she knew that if Darby Randolph Mahoney could have come home, he would have.

Darby pushed past Pepper, mumbled, "Excuse me," and ran for the bathroom. Behind the closed door, Pepper heard retching sounds.

Nana Kate's eyes narrowed. "Should you see to him?"

Pepper stood. "Perhaps I should. Excuse me."

Pepper opened the bathroom door. Darby flushed the toilet, rinsed his mouth at the sink, and dried his face. The room reeked of tuna and vomit. "At least it's just food. That medicine must be working. I guess I shouldn't have had second helpings."

She smoothed her hand over his back. "I guess you shouldn't have barreled through the past six weeks at one go."

He closed the toilet and sat on the lid. "Once I got started, it was easier to continue. My senior thesis at The Point was on the fall of Richmond. The research was so good that the paper was published."

Pepper leaned her rear end against the cold tub lip. "Did you find any mention of Darby Randolph Mahoney?"

"No. The name Darby Randolph isn't bantered around in my family; I'm the second person to carry it. The first was born in eighteen forty; I was born in nineteen forty. Nana Kate named me. Him and me, both officers, separated by a hundred years. I wanted to know how he'd spent his last days."

"When things got dicey in Vietnam, did you ever see his ghost?"

Confederate ghosts held a special place in Southern lore.

"I wanted to. A couple of times I said, 'Come on, Gramps, now would be a good time,' but I suppose after a hundred and ten years even ghosts lose their taste for war." He paused. "I always believed he wrote a second letter to his wife, a letter that never reached her. She died believing he was on his way home to her."

Waves flooded through Pepper. Cold. Warm. Cold again. She rubbed the goose bumps on her arms. "The three thousand dollars wasn't about Anne, was it? You promised that money to Miss Filmore to make sure she'd deliver your diary to me."

"Have you ever had a high fever, where everything is disjointed and sentences like 'Kumquats roundel through the demijohn' make sense?"

"I've had a few nights like that." Most of them had been alcohol-soaked.

"That's what it was like. I was vibrating. I smelled things I couldn't identify. People jabbered words that I should understand, but didn't. The thing I remember clearly was, 'I'm catching the milk-train to heaven.' "

"At least you were going to heaven. Was my letter like that?

Kumquats rondeling through the demijohn?"

"I was confused before I wrote and after, but I had absolute clarity for every word of that letter. I was frantic to keep you from going through the rest of your life not knowing what had happened to me. When I handed my diary and Anne to Edith Filmore, I thought, 'I've held until relieved. I can go now.' I'm sorry you had to take out a loan. I'll pay you back as soon as I cash in some bonds."

The homestead wasn't going to be hers, free and clear, but paying off the loan would be enough. "Why hadn't you listed me as your next of kin? The Army would have notified me."

"I meant to get around to it. Considering what happened, it was good that I'd let that chore slide. The Army would have you believing that I died in that training accident or some other cockamamie story."

Pepper pulled him into an embrace. Her hands slid over his warm, real back. She traced every vertebra down his back. "If they had made it romantic enough of a story, I'd have believed it."

"The hard part is over. I've got it all out of my system, in more ways than one. Nana Kate will either give me absolution or she won't."

"What if she doesn't?"

"What's a little more guilt?"

They went back into the living room and sat on the couch.

Darby said, "Sorry. I have temporary stomach trouble."

"I assume you have consulted a doctor and are following his orders?"

"I have and I am."

"Indisposition is not discussed in polite company. We will not speak of it again. Nor will we speak of anything said in this room tonight."

Somehow that felt more like an order when Nana Kate said

it than it had when General Fairclough said it.

Nana Kate asked, "Your resignation. How much time remains for you?"

She made it sound like a terminal illness; perhaps it was.

"A few weeks, maybe a few months."

That long? Pepper had assumed that Darby would be out of the Army a day or two after his letter arrived on his commander's desk. This was going to be like a lingering illness.

"Are you required to return to Japan to do—what is it you call it—out-processing?"

"No, the Army can ship my things home."

"Tomorrow morning you will call your parents and inform them that you are returning to the States and that you will make a short visit to Miss Pepperhawk before coming to Georgia. When you've spoken with your parents, we will consider this matter closed."

He'd received absolution. For a moment, Pepper actually liked Nana Kate.

"What are your plans?"

"I have none."

"Find some." Nana Kate paused. "What will happen to the infant?"

Darby said, "Pepper and I know a good lawyer in Marshall. We'll ask him for advice about how to find adoptive parents for her."

After that good lawyer got through defending Leadbelly on a manslaughter charge.

"The prospective parents are not to incur expenses related to the adoption. We will cover all of the costs."

Darby frowned. "We?"

"You may rely on me for a contribution. Elizabeth, you are welcome to contribute."

"I'll do what I can."

"The adoption agreement must include a provision to keep us informed of her progress until she reaches her majority. Whether we allow her to learn the true circumstances of her birth must be negotiated between us and her adoptive parents."

Darby nodded. "I agree to all of that."

"This Miss Filmore, the woman who brought the baby to Pepper, what progress have the police made in finding her killer?"

"I don't know. I've been busy," he added, apologetically.

"You will ask Detective Rosen for a progress report, and you will offer the police whatever assistance you can in bringing her killer to justice. Debts of honor must be paid."

Nana Kate really was handing out penance along with her absolution. Avivah was going to love it when Darby told her that he was supposed to horn in on her police investigation because his grandmother said that he had to.

"May I assume that you and Elizabeth will publish your marriage bans soon?"

Darby reached over and took Pepper's hand. For the first time, she saw him in a clear, clean light unencumbered by a military halo. He was handsome, and fun, and she was incredibly grateful that he'd been part of her life, but somewhere on that trip back and forth to Tennessee, something had died between them. She knew Darby's answer before he said, "Bans and marriage aren't in our futures."

It was a relief that Darby had said it for her. Some time soon the realization that she and Darby weren't going to marry would smack her in the heart. She'd handle that part when it came.

Nana Kate picked up her cane. "I regret that." She stood. "At my age, one doesn't often entertain the prospect of a new playmate."

Darby pulled Pepper to her feet, still holding her hand. "You mean like a cat plays with a mouse?" She was trying to swallow the compliment that Nana Kate considered her a potential playmate.

"Don't be impertinent, young man."

Darby grinned. "I've answered all of your questions, now I want one answered. Where do my parents think you are this weekend?"

"I've been called to the side of a dear friend whose daughter faces a delicate and dangerous operation."

Darby waggled his index finger at her. "You'd better hope my mother doesn't phone your dear friend to express her concern."

"Lilly and I have covered for one another since the Roosevelt administration."

No doubt that would have been Theodore rather than his fifth cousin, Franklin Delano.

"Then you'd better hope Lilly's daughter doesn't answer the phone."

Nana Kate smiled. "Her daughter is in Peru for a year."

Pepper turned to Darby. "You come by what you are honestly, don't you?"

"I'm afraid so. The Army worked with the raw material I brought to it."

On that note, the three of them went to their separate beds.

CHAPTER 24

The phone woke Pepper Saturday morning at six fifty. She padded to the phone in her robe and slippers. "Hello."

Saul's voice sounded close to hysterical. "Come to Benny's house now. Run. Don't waste time dressing." He hung up.

Benny was back? Lorraine was back? Lorraine was in labor? Lorraine was minutes away from delivering?

Pepper hurried back to her bedroom, scooped up Anne, tucked her under her arm in a football carry, and ran. Darby met her on the path and plucked Anne from her arms in a football handoff. "You don't want to miss this. Run."

Of course she didn't want to miss it. She was almost to Benny's porch before it dawned on her that she should have asked Darby if the rescue squad had been called. She stopped at the bottom of the porch stairs. "I am a professional; I can handle this," she said to herself and bounded up the steps.

Avivah and Saul sat on the couch, watching television. On the screen a Red Cross public service announcement urged people to donate blood. Saul wore a robe and pajamas. Avivah was half dressed in a white T-shirt and her uniform pants.

Pepper asked breathlessly, "Where's Lorraine?"

Saul said, "We don't know."

Pepper collapsed into a chair, with her slipper-clad feet sticking out straight in front of her, and her hand over her chest. She inhaled great gulping breaths. "I thought you called me because Lorraine was about to deliver."

Saul said, "I saw a promo for this program when I turned on the TV for a weather report."

Pepper pushed herself into a sitting position, already feeling the lactic acid collecting in her muscles. "You called me for a television program?"

Saul said, "We had to; you don't have a TV."

The mountains played havoc with reception. The homestead's reception was too piss-poor to make having a set worthwhile. Benny Kirkpatrick—budding electrical engineer and field communications expert—had calculated where to run up wires on his side of the mountain to an antenna that brought in two stations. Randy and Mark considered him a genius.

Pepper got up and flopped next to Saul on the couch. "This has better be some program."

The word *Proactive* filled the screen backed by up-tempo background music. Behind the letters, on a dark stage, backlights outlined four people. One sat alone on the left and three were grouped together on the right. The words faded and lights came up, and a camera panned left to a distinguished man in a gray suit, white shirt, and dark tie. "Good morning. I'm Andrew Morrise. Welcome to *Proactive*, where we focus on people who are doing something positive about today's issues."

On the wall behind him was a small screen. Familiar bits of recent newsreels showed on the screen. Pepper had seen most of the images, some repeatedly. She didn't know if her heart raced because of running or because her heart broke again every time she saw them.

"In recent weeks we've seen photos of terrified Vietnamese and Cambodian men, women, and children fleeing the North Vietnamese troops rolling over South Vietnam. By whatever means possible, often at great risk, some people managed to escape. They are now being housed and processed in hastily established refugee stations at military bases overseas, and closer to home in places like Fort Chaffee, Arkansas. Government experts predict that a hundred and fifty thousand Vietnamese will seek refuge in this country in the next six months. This morning our guests are three men who are already doing something proactive for these refugees."

The camera pulled back to show the other three men sitting on molded plastic chairs. She recognized all of the men. Oh, shit.

Another camera cut in for a close-up of the first man, a muscular, crew-cut priest in clerical collar, black shirt, and black suit coat.

"Our guests are Father Thomas Clarke Devoy, a former Army chaplain, and founder of the Interfaith Asian Refugee Center in Orange County, California."

The camera panned. Benny wore a sports shirt and jacket that Pepper had never seen. He'd also gotten a haircut. His exposed white scalp looked very military.

"Ex–Green Beret Benjamin Kirkpatrick served two tours in Vietnam."

The camera panned again. Father Lincoln wore his usual cassock, with a long string of buttons down the front. Avivah's old friend had gotten, if not fat, softer around the edges.

"And Father Ronald Lincoln is a Jesuit priest, teacher, and social-justice advocate."

Pepper blinked, opened her eyes, and blinked again. The three men were still on Benny's television screen.

The moderator folded his hands and settled back in his chair. "Father Devoy, you founded the Interfaith Asian Refugee Center earlier this year. What prompted you to do that?"

Father Devoy sat with his left arm across his knee and his right hand resting on his right knee. He could have been a football player waiting for the coach to send him in. "After I left the Army . . ."

Saul had chronicled Tom's story in a three-part *New Yorker* feature: from burnt-out, shaved-head, tattooed Special Forces chaplain suffering a crisis in faith, to pastor of a Vietnamese parish in California, to founder of the Interfaith Asian Refugee Center. Pepper felt like hitting herself in the forehead. In all of her stewing about how to find adoptive parents for Anne, she'd never once thought of contacting Father Tom. He could find prospective Vietnamese parents in a heartbeat. One problem solved. "Benny rolled out of here yesterday afternoon. How did he get on a New York talk show in less than twenty-four hours?"

Saul said, "If he went straight from here to the airport, and phoned Tom and Ron while he was waiting for a flight to New York, it would be doable."

"How did he wangle his way onto a national television show?"

Avivah said, "Ron and Andrew Morrise are old friends. They co-teach positive-social-action workshops."

"Do people actually watch this show?"

Saul said, "I'd say their audience is half a million, maybe six hundred thousand."

"Half a million people get up at seven o'clock on a Saturday morning to watch a talk show about social issues?"

Saul laughed. "Half a million people is a drop in the bucket when you're talking television."

The moderator spoke again. "Sergeant Kirkpatrick—may I call you Sergeant?"

"I've been out of the military a while; Benny will do."

"Benny, what's your stake in Vietnamese refugees coming to the United States?"

For an instant Benny had a deer-in-the-headlights expression on his face. Pepper bet she'd had the same expression on her face when she'd stopped outside, thinking she would have to deliver a baby. She could almost hear Benny saying to himself, "I'm a professional, I can handle this."

He cleared his throat. "My honor and gratitude are at stake."

Avivah murmured, "Ron coached him well."

Benny sat up straighter. "I want to speak to anyone who served in Vietnam, but especially to Green Berets and former Green Berets. I want you to remember every ARVN, every Montagnard, every Mike Force, every LLDB who fought beside us. Every translator and scout. Every cook's helper who fed us. Every mama-san who cleaned our hootches and did our laundry. Every child who played in our compounds. Every family who invited us into their homes. Every person who befriended us."

Memories and faces flooded Pepper's brain. She had one more group to add to Benny's list: Vietnamese patients she'd cared for.

"If we didn't care what happened to the Vietnamese people, what the *bleep* were our MED-Caps and SAR-Caps projects all about? Why did we work so hard building dispensaries, orphanages, and schools?"

And immunizing kids? And ask our families to send books, blankets, and clothing for those same schools and orphanages?

"If you feel the slightest debt to one Vietnamese person, here's your chance to pay up. There's a man who lives over the mountain from me who has singlehandedly sponsored dozens of refugees. I know I can't do anything that big, but I know one person can make a difference, and that's what I intend to do."

The moderator said, "Thank you, Benny. Father Lincoln, from a social-justice perspective . . ."

Avivah switched off the set. "I love Ron dearly, but nothing he will say is going to top that." Tears rolled down her face.

Pepper felt tears running down her own cheeks. She went to Avivah and enfolded her in her arms, smoothing her hands over Avivah's back. The cotton T-shirt felt warm and smooth under her hands. "Benny said fuck on national television."

"He said bleep."

"He said fuck. I watched his lips."

Darby inserted himself gently into their hug. "Any soldier who was watching knows he said fuck."

Pepper hadn't noticed him come into the house.

On the other side of the room, Saul held Anne. He said, "Come with me, sweetheart. I'll teach you to serve coffee."

Anne gurgled.

The three veterans stood with their arms wrapped around one another, their foreheads touching. Their collective breaths steamed the small space among them. Pepper felt their embrace grow from warm to hot. They separated, but didn't move away from one another.

Pepper rubbed the side of her thumb over her eyes. "Oh, crap. We fucking lost. I hate losing."

Darby said, "So do I."

Avivah said, "We've lost the war, but we've got one more battle to win: finding Edith Filmore's killer. Like Benny said, one person can make a difference. Imagine what three people can do."

She laid both hands on Darby's shoulders and looked him in the eye. "Even if I allow the maximum time for everything you told Nate and me you did on Monday night, there is still a gap. Where the hell were you?"

"In the cab of a parked eighteen-wheeler with a former Dust-off Radio Telephone Operator who had been stationed in Pleiku. We held a private wake for Vietnam."

"The guy who picked you up was a vet?"

"That's why he picked me up. He said he could still spot an officer, even in civilian clothes."

"Why didn't you tell us that?"

"Substances were involved."

"Unless we can find this guy and he'll confirm your story, substances and all, you still look like a suspect."

"I swear on my beret that the first, last, and only time I saw Edith Filmore was in the American embassy."

"I believe you. Now I have to prove it."

The phone rang. Saul came to the kitchen doorway. "Avivah, it's Nate. He wants to talk to you."

Pepper and Darby trailed behind Avivah to the kitchen.

She picked up the phone. "It's me."

"I woke up some old woman at your house."

"How did you know to call me here?"

"She gave me this phone number."

Benny's phone number was on a card beside the kitchen phone at the homestead.

"Along with a lecture on telephone etiquette. She's unhappy with me."

"I imagine so. What's shaking?"

"What do you want first, good news or bad?"

Cody's demonstration was hours away. How much bad could have happened overnight? Her stomach did a free fall. "Let's get the bad over with."

"John Boyd overdosed on sleeping pills."

Avivah set her cup down hard. Coffee sloshed over the counter. "When? How?"

"How we're working on. When was sometime between lights out and four this morning. My guess is earlier rather than later."

"Is he all right?"

"He's far from all right; he's in intensive care at Mission Hospital."

"You'd better have a lot of good news to balance that out."

"Boyd didn't kill Mr. Lam."

"Are you sure?"

"The autopsy report was on my desk when I got to the station this morning. Lam had tissue damage consistent with being hit with high-powered water from a fire hose, but the cause of death was strangulation. According to Boyd's statement, he was never closer than ten feet from Mr. Lam. It's impossible to strangle someone from ten feet away, though I suppose he could have followed Lam to the bathroom."

"Hang on." Avivah covered the receiver mouthpiece. "Assume that John Boyd is in the middle of a full-blown Vietnam flashback. He turns a fire hose on a group of Vietnamese and then (A) he drops the hose, follows a Vietnamese man across a store to a washroom, strangles him, walks back to the garden center, picks up a set of pruning shears, and wedges himself into a miniscule space, with a death grip on the shears like they were an M-sixteen. Or, (B) he drops the hose and wedges himself into a miniscule space, with a death grip on a pair of shears like they were an M-sixteen?"

Everyone, including Saul, said, "B."

Flashbacks were weird, unpredictable things, but Avivah agreed. She removed her hand from the receiver. "Nate, we are in a shitload of trouble."

"I want you in my office in half an hour. Break the speed limit if you have to."

CHAPTER 25

Avivah missed Nate's deadline by five minutes. He sat at his desk, using a compass to draw a circle on a road map. A stained brown paper bag sat to one side. The office smelled like chocolate.

Street uniform was the order of the day for constable and officers alike. Avivah's constable's uniform had sat in her closet for four months. It fit.

Nate's uniform strained. Avivah had never seen one like it. It was made from thicker cloth than hers. His brass buttons gleamed. The hat on top of Nate's filing cabinet came straight out of old movies about moonshine and fast cars. She didn't care to speculate how many decades it had been since he'd been on the street.

Nate said, "What kept you?"

"Finding parking. Every constable we have is downstairs."

He shoved the paper sack towards her. "Have a brownie."

"Breakfast?"

"Five o'clock this morning the phone wakes me. It's the jail telling me about Boyd's overdose. Ash is already in the kitchen, baking. Do you know how long it's been since she baked? I felt like she was sending me off to war."

Avivah wanted to say, "She's making love, not war, you idiot," but she restrained herself. Ash and Nate would have to work this out for themselves, but Avivah hoped that Ash had sampled some of her own baking. That woman was too thin to be healthy.

She dug in the bag and pulled out a black, crumbly square. Around a full mouth, she said, "What are you doing?"

"Figuring out from how far away a person could start driving at five in the morning and reach Asheville by one in the afternoon."

"It sounds like one of those word math problems. Is a train leaving Cleveland involved?"

"Worse, we could be in the middle of a lot of protesters from God knows where."

She multiplied eight hours by an average highway speed limit. Her heart rate rose with every number. She tapped the circle, leaving a chocolate fingerprint on the map. "You've pegged it: every Southern state except Mississippi, Louisiana, and Florida, plus bits of Ohio and Indiana are within driving distance."

She pulled a tissue out of the box on Nate's desk and cleaned her fingers. "Why pick five in the morning?"

"Boyd was taken to the ER at four thirty. One of the eleven-to-seven hospital staff—ex-Navy corpsman—recognized him and phoned Cody Doan. By five o'clock, people were carrying signs and lighting candles outside the emergency room. You know Doan. Is he likely to have an organized phone fan-out?"

Avivah sat down. "Yes. He's heavy into vet networking."

Nate said, "So we've got an innocent, black, ex-Marine, Vietnam vet in a coma."

"And a white, female, New York Jew, Vietnam vet, and ex-military-police officer with a less than perfect military record in charge of the investigation against him. Civil rights, anti-Semitism, gender politics, police brutality, and the Vietnam War. *Oy vey,* we've hit it all with this one."

Nate folded the map. "The chief doesn't want you in the plaza; I'm to tell you to go home."

The slow burn in Avivah's chest had nothing to do with the brownie she'd eaten. A dark, heavy feeling immediately quenched the quick white-hot flair. "Am I going to take the fall for Boyd's arrest?"

"There is no fall. It was a good arrest, knowing what we did at the time."

"If you were going to send me home, why did I drive all the way here from Madison County? You could have told me this on the phone."

"I prefer to deliver bad news in person."

She slumped. "Every cop in the department will know that I'm not on the line."

"You wouldn't have been on the line anyway. You and I were sidelined for crowd control."

"I would have been in the plaza. I would have been visible."

"The problem is that you're too visible." Nate wadded the paper bag and tossed it in the trash. "Some constables are being held back to work night shift. You've been reassigned to night duty for one shift. Go home and get some sleep; report back for roll call at ten thirty tonight."

Avivah sat down. "I hate this."

"Forgotten how to take orders?"

"Forgotten how to enjoy taking orders. How was your interview with Mr. Tu?"

"He's devastated. Lam Trong Tri worked for him for years. Apparently he was more of a partner than a foreman. Tu relied on him to run the hatchery."

"What about Mr. Lam's relatives?"

"None in this country. What do you think the possibility is of getting a message to his aunt in Vietnam?"

"Right now not good."

"That's what Mr. Tu said, but he will try."

"Edith Filmore and Mr. Lam both have connections to Vietnam, and both were strangled. What's the possibility that we're dealing with two killers?"

"To quote you, not good."

"If we're going to interview people at the hatchery, we're going to have to involve the Madison Country Sheriff."

"Not today."

"How about if instead of working night duty, I get out of this uniform and do some detective work today?"

"Go home. Humor the chief, okay? For my sake?"

"The first forty-eight hours of an investigation are the most important."

"The first forty-eight hours have already passed."

Avivah stood. "I don't like it."

"Neither do I, but I have to take orders just like you do. Monday morning we hit both murder investigations full blast."

Avivah left through the back way, hoping to avoid anyone asking her why she was leaving when everyone else was arriving.

City crews were arranging wooden sawhorses to cordon off three sides of a large rectangle. The square, flat-roofed jail that no longer housed John Walter Boyd formed the fourth side of that rectangle. The protest didn't start for hours, but a crowd was already gathering. A few toddlers rode on their father's shoulders. What kind of parent brought a toddler to a potentially violent demonstration? The same kind of parent who would scream about police incompetence and child endangerment if things got nasty.

At the edge of the plaza, ten elderly women huddled together. They wore identical sun hats, name tags, and nervous glances. Avivah was considering asking them if she could help when a harried woman corralled them and headed them off to another tourist attraction more to their liking.

The weather was already stifling. Dark thunderclouds raced over the mountains. Working in killer heat and humidity or a gully-washer thunderstorm didn't offer good choices, but she would have welcomed either if she could be out on the plaza with her fellow constables. That might have been taken away from her, but there was still one thing she could contribute. Good reconnaissance beat speculation every time. Nate was worried about how big Cody's phone out was. The way to find out was to ask Cody.

The first thing she noticed when she got to Mission Hospital was that two groups had gathered in the parking lot. About twenty blacks stood in a group away from the front of the building. In spite of the heat, most of the men wore suits and ties. A few skinny bucks flaunted natural Afros and brightly colored shirts. The women wore Sunday dresses and hats. Many of them held black-and-white photos of Boyd. It was the same photo from which Cody had made his posters. Cody must have convinced Boyd's family to give him a copy.

Another copy of the picture had been taped to a hospital wall above a flowerbed. Flowers were piled under the photo. A line of votive candles burned in front of the flowers.

About thirty protesters including Cody walked or rolled in wheelchairs in a circuit near the hospital's doors. They carried homemade signs that said, "John Boyd is innocent," and "Vets are praying for you, buddy." Many of them wore faded fatigue jackets with the sleeves cut or ripped off, and boonie hats or rolled bandannas around their heads.

One of the two police constables on duty saw her and walked over to her. She nodded at him. "How you doing?"

"Good, outside of having been here since five this morning."

Meaning that he'd been on night shift last night, and was coming up on twelve hours on duty. "Long shift?"

"Feels about a week long right now."

The hospital doors opened and three people came out: a middle-aged man in green hospital scrubs, an elderly black woman, and John Ferguson.

John climbed up on the flowerbed wall. He yelled, "May I

have your attention, please?" several times before the vets stopped walking their circuit; many of the blacks moved closer.

"My name is John Ferguson. I'm John Boyd's lawyer, and I've been asked to read a prepared statement from his family." He indicated the two people standing at his right. "This is John's mother and his doctor."

John cleared his throat. "John remains unconscious. His breathing is assisted and he is being closely monitored. A highly skilled intensive-care nurse is with him at all times. A complete medical update will be issued Sunday morning at eight o'clock. The family is deeply grateful for your support, but they ask that you leave now, so that patients, staff, or visitors may use this busy hospital entrance. Please keep John in your thoughts and prayers."

He stepped down from the flowerbed wall, and began working the crowd, shaking hands and talking with people. It was always a pleasure watching pure, golden poor ole' country lawyer—no way I'd ever run for office—Ferguson in action.

The two groups—blacks and vets—merged cautiously in front of the flowerbeds to extinguish candles and pick up flowers. Cody went to talk to John's doctor and his mother.

The constable said, "Does that mean we can go home?"

"As soon as they clear out."

"Great. My partner and I have to be back for night shift tonight."

Wonderful. Maybe the three of them would meet for coffee. Avivah muttered, "We few, we happy few."

"Huh?"

"Doesn't it bother you that you'll miss all the excitement this afternoon?"

"It's one demonstration, and from the look of that sky it's going to be one soaking-wet demonstration. What I want more than anything else is a good day's sleep. I love sleeping on a rainy afternoon, especially after a spell of hot weather."

He was missing the demonstration and he wasn't in a snit. Was she a good-enough cop to get over hers? Nate hadn't sent her home because she couldn't do her job, or because she was a woman. He pulled her because she was a liability. He would have done the same thing if the liability were male. "I have to come back for night shift, too."

"You're working night shift?"

"Tonight I am."

"Whose tail did you step on?"

She dredged up her over-the-top New York accent. "So yuh wanna do it by yuhselves? Whaddayuh, crazy?"

He grinned. "Welcome on board, *Constable* Rosen."

She checked his name tag. "Thank you, *Constable* Harris. Let's have coffee after roll call. I'm buying."

Cody had finished talking and was heading for the parking lot.

Avivah said, "Excuse me, I have to talk to someone. See you at roll call." She called, "Cody!"

He wore jeans, a faded Army Engineers T-shirt, a shapeless boonie hat and the same sullen expression he'd had the day she'd met him on Pepper's ward at Fort Bragg. He folded his arms and stood so that his left leg bore his weight. "What do you want?"

Avivah held up both of her hands. "I come in peace? My boss and I are worried about how big this demonstration is going to be."

"None of your business."

"Wrong. You've got your permit. The police aren't going to stop your demonstration, but we've got people bringing small children to the plaza; little old ladies are scared witless. All we're interested in is public safety. We need to know how many people you're expecting."

He stuck out his lower lip, shifted his body weight to his artificial leg with a jerky movement and leaned toward her. "I don't know, okay?"

"Can you guess?"

"Maybe."

"Will you call Lieutenant Alexander?"

He looked at the place where John Boyd's photo, flowers, and candles had been. "This isn't what I wanted to happen."

They went into the hospital lobby and found a bank of pay phones. She handed the receiver to Cody and dialed Nate's office.

In a few seconds he said, "It's Cody Doan. Avivah asked me to call you."

Avivah was too keyed up to go home. If she went home, she wouldn't sleep; being around Nana Kate would drive even the chief crazy. She found a phone book, looked up a number, and made a call.

Pat Teague answered.

"It's Detective Rosen. I have more questions for you. Meet me at Laurel Ridge Clinic in half an hour."

Chapter 26

The large gift basket on Pepper's lap blocked her view of the mountains. Cellophane wrap poked her in the ear when she craned her neck to see the billowing dark gray clouds. "Are you sure this is a good idea?"

Frannie kept her eyes on the road. Her colorful silk scarves fluttered in the cloud-driven breeze. "If I stay at the homestead, all I'll do is stew over being mad at Cody. This is healthier."

Maybe it was and maybe it wasn't. "Convince me again that it was a good idea to leave Anne with Nana Kate. She's eighty-nine years old. What if she has a stroke and dies?"

Kaye, in the front seat, fighting with her own basket, said, "Then Dave will have to care for Anne while he makes funeral arrangements."

"What exactly do we know about Dave? He could be a kidnapper or a child molester."

Kaye's voice had the quality of a master-of-ceremonies announcing a pageant contestant. "Dave is a third-year student at Emory. He hopes to be a lay minister, focusing on youth work. His favorite food is fried chicken, and his hobbies are photography and playing the guitar."

Kaye had a sense of humor? Something Frannie had done had worked a miracle. Or perhaps aliens had replaced the mousy woman in drab clothing with the vibrant person dressed in a denim skirt and silky, white-fringed cowboy shirt. All three women stared at her. "You said to keep Dave occupied."

Ash Morgan, prim in a pale-green shirtwaist dress, repositioned the stack of cookie tins on her lap. "Occupied, not get engaged to him."

Engaged. An unexpected tightness caught in Pepper's throat. By the time it made it to the surface, she'd managed to turn it into a cross between a ragged sigh and, "Huff."

Frannie said, "You okay?"

"This basket wrapping poked me in the eye."

Frannie drove slower around the next winding curve.

Kaye said to Ash, "If you want to keep a person occupied, ask them about themselves, then be quiet, and listen."

That was what Darby had done the first time he phoned Pepper. His warm Georgia voice had said, "My name is Darby Baxter; Sergeant Kirkpatrick gave me your phone number. He said we'd met at Fort Sam Houston, and that you wanted to talk to me."

Pepper, her knees weak, had sunk to the floor beside the phone table. "August sixty-nine basic class intake. I wanted to thank you. What I learned from you helped me in Vietnam."

She'd figured he'd say that teaching was his job; they'd hang up. That would be that. Instead he'd asked, "Where you were stationed?" and listened until she ran out of steam.

Two hours later they'd agreed to meet in Atlanta. They drove to Stone Mountain Park where the nearly completed bas-relief carving of Jefferson Davis, Robert E. Lee, and Stonewall Jackson—and their horses—had just gone on public display. It wouldn't do to forget Thunder, Traveler, and Old Sorrell. She should have realized that a first date looking at icons of The Lost Cause was an omen.

She would have to forget about a military wedding or a honeymoon, though goodness knows where they would have gone, probably on a tour of Civil War battlefields.

A weight rose from Pepper's shoulders and fluttered away.

Except for last Monday night, when she'd tried to cold cock him, every time Darby phoned, or when they came together after a long absence, butterflies always filled her stomach. The lightness she felt was the departure of a whole squadron of butterfly rubble that she had collected over three and a half years. She rolled the car window all the way down to make sure nothing blocked their escape.

The butterflies' departure left a cold gray spot in the middle of her chest. She curled her hand around the window crank. Maybe she could convince a few butterflies to stay. She and Darby could stay friends; she'd heard that some people who had been engaged did that. Who was she kidding? She and Darby had never been engaged; they'd meant to get engaged. He'd meant for them to go to Georgia to meet his family. He'd meant to name her his next of kin. We meant to get around to it would be their epitaph.

Pepper's hand covered the cold, sore spot where her heart should be. Warmth was good for shock. She'd have to be very careful the next few—days, weeks, months? She'd leave it at having to be careful. Treat the shock. That was the important thing now.

Frannie slowed the car. "Uh-oh, what's this?"

This was a Madison County sheriff's car parked beside the road, and two deputies lounging with their butts against the side of the car. One of them stepped into the road and held up his hand. Frannie stopped. The deputy leaned down to window level and touched his fingertips to his broad hat brim. "Morning, ladies, where are you headed?"

Frannie kept both hands visible on the steering wheel. "Valley Forge Hatchery."

"I can't allow that."

Ash said, "We're from Nice 'N Neighborly. We welcome new women to the community."

Good recovery. It made them sound as unthreatening as they could get.

The deputy pulled on his ear. "Those people are in no fit state this morning for a social call."

Pepper leaned forward. "What's the problem?"

He stooped to look in the car. "Don't I know you?"

Probably he did, from one of the frequent calls to the homestead.

Ash popped a cookie tin lid. Odors of lemon extract and shortbread crust wafted through the car. She held the tin out the window. "Lemon bar? Take one for your partner, too."

"Ma'am, those good-smelling cookies are not near enough of a bribe for me to let you into the hatchery. They got hit by vandals last night; the owner has turned the place into Fort Apache."

"Meaning?" Pepper asked.

"Meaning my orders are to stop anyone from setting foot on the property. Them hatchery folks are nothing that lovely ladies like you need concern themselves with. Let us men handle it."

Ash drew the tin into the car, and replaced the lid without a sound.

Frannie shifted into drive, but kept her foot on the brake. "You have a legal right to block a public road, but to quote you, the hatchery is private property. I intend to drive into the grounds, and your authority doesn't extend to stopping me."

He touched the brim of his hat again, this time more formally. "I wouldn't advise that ma'am, because if you do, when you're back on this here public road, I'm going to charge the lot of you with trespass, disturbing the peace, failure to follow the lawful commands of a peace officer, and creating a public nuisance."

Frannie moved her foot from the brake to the accelerator and the car shot forward. Gravel sprayed under the tires when she swerved into the hatchery's driveway. Behind them, Pepper heard the deputy curse.

Pepper had a split second to read the obscenity scrawled over Mr. Tu's neat blue-and-white sign. The brief manure scent flooding through the open window made it obvious what material had been used to write the words. Considering Mr. Tu's fastidiousness, why hadn't his employees scrubbed the sign?

Frannie slammed on her brakes. Her car skidded sideways. They ended up with the right-front tire wedged in a draining ditch and the car angled across the road with one tire up in the air. Pepper wiggled herself out of her seat belt. She and her basket exited the car without an ounce of decorum.

Two metal-cage flatbed trailers blocked the drive. Puny coils of barbed wire stretched from the flatbeds across the road. A good sapper would be around the wire in an instant, but Pepper assumed that Mr. Tu had had a limited supply of barbed wire on hand. About fifteen feet beyond the flatbeds and the wire, a small square building had been constructed of sandbags, rough lumber, and a piece of tin for the roof. It was a typical Vietnamese guard post.

On either side of the driveway black, burned ground cover extended to the trees that lined the road. On Wednesday, those same areas had been green meadows. A faint gasoline odor hung in the air. Pepper couldn't remember if burning fields was illegal. Even if it wasn't, a gasoline fire could have gotten out of control, burned all the way to her homestead.

Sheets of plywood covered every window in the compound. Graffiti spray painted on the dining-room walls read, *Next time, we'll come for your women.* Underneath was a lewd drawing showing what they'd do to the women. Swings, ripped from the swing set in the play yard, lay broken in a heap on the ground. Along the crosspiece of the swing set, five white geese hung, their necks broken.

Pepper saw no Vietnamese, heard no background poultry

sounds. Either the vandals had killed more birds than just the geese or Mr. Tu had ordered the birds killed. A cacophony of background bird noises would diminish the ability to hear intruders.

She muttered, "Welcome to Vietnam," as she laid her basket on the backseat. This was not the time for scented bath products.

Mr. Bach popped up inside the guardhouse. The top third of his body was visible; sandbags hid the rest. He wore a short-sleeved shirt, but he carried himself as if he were in uniform. Lieutenant Bach formerly of the Army of the Republic of Vietnam had a new stateside command. Pepper knew what else the sandbags hid: more men sitting out of sight. Everything she'd learned in the Army said that those men would be armed. Would it be with a ragtag collection of hunting rifles and target pistols, or with automatic weapons?

The two deputies on the road were too old to have been in Vietnam. Sooner or later a deputy Pepper's age, a man who'd done his time in jungles and rice patties, would show up. When he saw the burned field and the guardhouse he'd recognize that a perimeter plus a guardhouse equaled armed men.

Pepper stepped forward, holding her hands where Mr. Bach could see them. Thank goodness she'd worn a sundress. Clothing loose enough to conceal explosives would make the men in that guardhouse nervous. "Mr. Bach, I am so sorry. My friends and I came to bring gifts to the women. We didn't know this had happened. Can we do anything?"

"Go away."

Frannie stepped forward beside Pepper. "My name is Frannie Maddox-Doan. I know a lot of lawyers. Shall I call one for you?"

"Go away. We will do this ourselves."

Ash wrapped her arms tightly around her cookie tins and slowly walked toward the guardhouse. With every step, Pepper's heartbeat ratcheted up a notch. If there was burned ground cover and barbed wire, why not land mines?

Ash stopped an arm's length from Mr. Bach and made a slight bow. "My name is Ash Alexander. Please accept these. The top tin is lemon bars, brownies in the middle, and cheese puffs in the bottom one. The cheese puffs taste best if you heat them for five minutes in a three-twenty-five oven."

Pepper remembered a photograph of a hippie putting daisies in a soldier's rifle during a Washington antiwar march. Mr. Bach accepted the tins with the same confused expression that soldier had. She's forgotten how surreal the nuances of war could be.

Ash Alexander? Why had Ash suddenly changed her last name?

Frannie got into her car and restarted it. The other three women stood shivering in the breeze while she tried unsuccessfully to rock her car out of the ditch. Mr. Bach and two other men came from the guardhouse and sat on the rear bumper, which gave enough traction that the car righted. Frannie turned the car around so it was headed toward the highway.

The thing I did that I'm most proud of is that I moved a truck. Darby's voice echoed in Pepper's head.

The women got into the car. Frannie said, "When our tires hit the highway, we will be in a shitload of trouble. Deputy Let-us-men-handle-it will love making life miserable for us. Cody is at the demonstration. So are Avivah and Saul. Who does that leave on our side that we can call?"

Pepper hadn't seen Darby after she'd left Benny's house this morning.

Ash said, "My husband is at the demonstration, too."

Kaye said, "My family doesn't know I'm in North Carolina."

The women looked at one another. Frannie suggested, "Dave and Nana Kate?"

Pepper groaned. "Anyone but them. I vote for John Fergu-son. Of course, if fishing season has started anywhere around here, we won't be able to reach him until late Sunday night. We're going to spend time at the sheriff's office, maybe even in the jail, until someone comes to our rescue. I hope no one had plans for tonight, maybe for the rest of the weekend."

Kaye got into the car. "We're on private property. Let's do what we came here to do: show these people that we care about what happens to them. From the looks of those clouds, we should be grateful that we have shelter from the storm." She slammed the car door. "In the words of other women who have gone before us, we shall not be moved."

CHAPTER 27

Pat Teague met Avivah outside the clinic. Cold air blew around Avivah's feet. The storm was closer.

Ms. Teague's grass-stained gardening pants and yellow T-shirt reminded Avivah that some people had other things on their mind today besides a demonstration. The scowl reminded her that Pepper's boss was a hostile witness and a possible murder suspect. She greeted Avivah with, "I didn't expect you to be in uniform; emblems of the paternalistic hierarchy aren't allowed in my clinic."

"What you see is what you get."

"My partner and I spent hours yesterday evening restoring the clinic's energy balance. You may not bring that gun into this sacred space."

"Sorry, not an option."

Two elderly women walked past them. One stared at Avivah so long that she almost ran into a light post.

Avivah touched the brim of her cap. "Morning, ladies." To Pat Teague she said, "If you're concerned that I'll track emotional mud all over your floor, we'll talk here on the street instead. I've come to accept that a woman constable in uniform draws quite a crowd."

Pat opened the clinic door. The reception area smelled of sweetgrass. When Avivah followed Pat into the clinic, a wave of something she couldn't name washed over her. She felt calm and at peace for the first time that day. The feeling evaporated like water on a hot sidewalk. Whatever Pat and her partner had done yesterday she'd undone it.

Ms. Teague said, "Come into the nurses' office."

Avivah followed her down the short hall. She sat at Pepper's desk; Ms. Teague sat at her desk. The desks were back-to-back, so that the nurses faced one another. Avivah didn't see the drug jar.

Lightning flashed around the edges of closed blinds, and thunder rumbled in the distance. Ms. Teague said, "Lillian mentioned that you have a court order to see Edith Filmore's chart. Let's get it over with."

Avivah handed over the court order. Ms. Teague opened it. "I may wish to consult with our lawyer."

She leaned back in Pepper's chair and clasped her hands over her gun belt. "Be my guest."

Amid the usual desk detritus on Pepper's desk were two framed photographs. The larger was a standard US Army post-exchange color portrait of Darby in starched fatigues and his beret. From the cherry blossom background, Avivah deduced it had been taken in Japan. She wondered how long that photo would stay on Pepper's desk.

The smaller photo was more casual. Benny. Lorraine, her pregnancy not yet showing. Randy. Mark. Avivah. Saul. Frannie. Cody. Pepper grinning in the middle. Pepper had organized a white-water rafting trip to celebrate the Kirkpatrick family's return from Alaska last year. Pepper gathering her family-by-choice around her, a family that understood her and accepted her a lot better than her family-by-blood did.

She and Saul were moving to Asheville. They would see Pepper and Benny all the time. Why did she feel like she was abandoning her best friends?

Ms. Teague folded the court order into thirds and handed it back. She leaned forward, straining to reach under her desk.

Sharon Wildwind

She withdrew her hand holding a magnetic key box, the kind in which people hid a spare car key behind their bumper, thinking that was safe.

So there was an extra key to the chart area.

Avivah followed Ms. Teague to the reception area, where she turned off the fake alarm and unlocked the chart grate. It clanked when she shoved it aside. She pawed through files and extracted a thin folder, which she handed to Avivah.

The neat printing along the top said *Filmore, Edith/May 5, 1975.*

Avivah sat at the reception desk and opened it. The three pages of neatly written notes began, "Client arrived at clinic at 1000 hours in a highly agitated state. Demanded immediate medical attention. Near faint in reception area . . ."

Lillian Hood wouldn't have liked that, particularly on a morning that the clinic schedule had already gone to heck in a hand-basket.

Pat Teague knew her business. The three-page chart was engaging and lucid, like reading a well-crafted short story. A couple of plot turns made Avivah's heart thump. She continued to the end, which was, "Offered immediate referral for psychiatric consult: declined. Is aware of and accepts risks of not seeking immediate assistance. Following the standing order for anxiety: Valium 10 Mg (po) stat. Rx: Valium 10 Mg (po), dispense 3; sig. 1 every 8 hours as needed. Return to clinic tomorrow. Cab called at her request. Left clinic in cab at 1145 hours. P. Teague, RN, MSN, NP."

Avivah closed the chart. "It appears that she was having a mental breakdown."

"I deal in symptoms rather than medical diagnoses. She was tearful, highly agitated, with pressure of speech, and flight of ideas."

That sounded like a breakdown to Avivah, but it didn't sound like the woman she'd met in the library. "Did you expect her to return on Tuesday?"

"I try not to anticipate clients' behavior based on one visit."

"Did you say anything to her like, 'Come back at any time'?"

"I explained what our hours were—including that we were closing at four o'clock that day—and that if she needed assistance when we weren't open, she was to go to an emergency room."

"Essentially you allowed a highly agitated, distraught woman, whom you'd recently medicated, to leave with instructions that amounted to have a nice day."

"I allowed a woman who was capable of making her own health-care decisions to do that."

"Someone saw a highly agitated woman pounding on this clinic door at five o'clock Monday evening. Would Miss Filmore have run out of Valium by then?"

"Not if she was taking them according to instructions."

"Highly agitated women don't always follow instructions."

"Don't patronize me. My caseload is full of women who have trouble following instructions."

Avivah went back to the first item that had caught her attention. "Item number two on your stressor list: 'Bereavement visit.' What was that all about?"

"She'd promised someone who died in Saigon that she would see his family. That was why she came to Asheville."

Anne wasn't mentioned anywhere. Had Edith concocted a cover story that omitted Anne because she knew Pepper worked at this clinic? Had she come here on Monday morning to see Pepper, perhaps to increase her money demands? Or had coming here been a random choice because Laurel Ridge Clinic was near her motel? How random a choice was it that she'd picked the motel closest to where Pepper worked? Avivah had stopped believing in coincidences a long time ago. "What did she say about that visit?"

"She didn't volunteer details, but she seemed relieved that she'd kept her promise. Completing that task gave her a sense of closure and control. She'd had very little of either in the past weeks."

Three thousand dollars could have gone a long way toward closure and control. It hadn't worked out that way.

"What about item number six: 'Recent engagement? (Not wearing a ring).' Did she talk about being engaged?"

"Briefly."

"Did she mention her fiancé's name?"

"Mr. Lindberg. She was returning to Wisconsin to join him."

"Did you believe that she was really engaged?"

"A woman of her age and sensibilities would have required an engagement ring from a suitor."

"Could she have left her ring in Saigon?"

"How often do you remove your ring?"

She hadn't had it off once since Saul slipped it on her finger, and she wasn't in the middle of a war zone, faced with fleeing for her life at any moment. If Edith Filmore had had an engagement ring, it would have been on her hand. "Do you think she lied about being engaged?"

"She'd had many losses. A fantasy suitor could provide comfort, be the grown-up equivalent of a teddy bear."

Or could it have been a sign that Edith Filmore had completely lost touch with reality? At least now she had a name to ask Edith's cousin. Lindberg sounded Swedish. Didn't a lot of Swedes live in Wisconsin, or was she confusing that with Minnesota?

Avivah stood up and handed back Edith Filmore's chart. "I'll need a copy of this chart."

Ms. Teague went to the photocopier and turned it on. "The machine takes a couple of minutes to warm up."

"While we're waiting show me your dead-drug jar."

"My what?"

"Lillian Hood told me about the jar of pills that you use to il-lustrate waste in the medical system."

Ms. Teague tilted her head like a hawk studying its lunch. "I don't have that jar any longer."

"Since when?"

"Since yesterday evening. When we were doing the cleansing ceremony, my partner identified that jar as a nexus of negative energy. Drugs are linked to illness, not health. I don't know why I didn't see that before."

Sudden behavior changes in the middle of a murder investiga-tion were suspicious, even if a suspect dressed the change up with folderol. Especially if she dressed it up. "What did you do with the jar?"

"Gave it to the pharmacist down the street for disposal."

"After you copy the chart, let's go see if he still has it."

A few fat, wet drops splattered on the pavement. The two women hurried two doors down to the pharmacy. A middle-aged man in a white lab coat stood behind the pharmacy counter. "Good morning, Ms. Teague. You don't usually work on Saturdays."

"It's an unusual Saturday."

Avivah stepped up. "I'm Constable Rosen, Asheville City Police."

Too late she realized she should have said Detective Rosen. Put on a uniform again and she bought into the constable persona. "Did Ms. Teague bring you a glass jar of pills?"

"Yes."

"Do you still have it?"

"Yes."

"Please show it to me."

He unlocked the cabinet behind him and opened the door.

On the shelf was a large glass jar, the kind in which restaurants bought bulk pickles or olives. It was two-thirds full. About half of the pills were arranged in colored bands, but the top half was higgledy-piggledy.

Packing tape surrounded where the lid joined the bottle. A red-bordered paste-on sticker had been attached so that it extended from the glass jar, over the rim and onto the lid. It would be impossible to open the jar without tearing that sticker. Avivah read yesterday's date, a time—"6:00 P.M."—presumably when the jar was sealed, and two signatures on the label. A large Manila tag *For disposal* was attached to the jar.

The pharmacist folded his arms across his chest. "What's the problem, Constable?"

Chain of custody had been broken. The pharmacist couldn't say what had happened with the jar's contents before he received it, and even the tape and sticker didn't guarantee that the jar hadn't been opened after it left Ms. Teague's possession. And if she had the jar removed to the evidence locker, moving it would rearrange the pills. She had a feeling that the pills being arranged in a pattern was important evidence.

A rack of cheap cameras and film stood beside the pharmacy counter. Avivah paid for a preloaded camera and a package of flashcubes and shot twelve photos of the glass jar. "Are you open tomorrow?"

"Not on Sunday."

"Before you close this evening, a constable will pick up that jar. Please don't touch it, don't move it around, and keep the cabinet locked."

They got wet going back to the clinic. Once inside, Pat Teague asked, "Are we through?"

"Not quite. I have reason to believe that a distraught woman pounded on the clinic door at approximately five o'clock Monday evening, and that someone opened the door for her.

Four people have clinic keys. Mr. Boniface and Pepper were with other people at five o'clock. That leaves you and Lillian Hood. You stated that you went straight home. Do you want to change that statement?"

"No." It would be interesting to see whether Pat Teague's partner agreed.

"It must have driven Miss Hood crazy."

"What must?"

"You and Pepper randomly dumping pills into that jar. Will I have to get another court order to see Miss Hood's medical records? Don't waste time saying she doesn't have a chart here. What is her diagnosis? Obsessive-compulsive behavior? Depression? Is this job a work/therapy program for her?"

Ms. Teague frowned. "You know I can't answer those questions."

"You already did when you pulled that hidden key from under your desk. You allow Miss Hood to believe that she has the only key to the charts. Her retirement must have been like yanking an underground creature out of her burrow into the sunlight."

"You should be a poet instead of a police officer."

"Sometimes what I do is poetry."

Ms. Teague ran her hand through her hair. "I should have stored that jar where she couldn't see it."

"She wouldn't have been able to leave it alone."

"Probably not."

"You knew you couldn't stop Lillian from rearranging those pills. I don't imagine you wanted her messing with drugs unsupervised. How did you arrange it?"

Pat Teague sat in one of the waiting-area chairs. "We did nothing illegal or unethical."

"I didn't ask you that. I asked you how you arranged it."

"When I work late clinic on Tuesday and Thursday evenings, I allow Lillian to rearrange the pills under my supervision."

Pepper had colored their refrigerator calendar with highlight-ers. On yellow days Pepper opened for early clinic; on pink days she worked evening clinic and closed late. Pepper had had the early duty this week. "When Pepper booked off Monday, this week's schedule changed, didn't it? You had to open early for her on Monday and, in exchange, she'd do the evening clinics for you."

"That's our agreement."

"That meant you weren't going to be in the clinic on a Tuesday or Thursday evening for three weeks in a row. Lillian couldn't wait, could she, especially after how bad Monday was?"

"She finds putting things in order soothing."

"Would she have come back in the evening and sorted the pills without your supervision?"

"She would have felt terribly guilty about doing it, but I'm afraid that's exactly what she would have done."

CHAPTER 28

Avivah and Pat Teague went back to the nurses' office. Pat called her lawyer; Avivah called the duty desk. The demonstration was scheduled to start in forty-five minutes. It was probably already impossible to get into the police station, and she didn't want to try to conduct an interview with chaos going on outside the building. "I have to interview a suspect in a murder investigation, and I need a constable to be present for the interview."

"Where are you?"

"West Asheville."

"You need brains or brawn?"

"Brains would be nice. The suspect is a highly anxious woman in her sixties."

"I can give you a rookie who seems bright enough."

"I'll take him. I also need an evidence pickup this afternoon before five o'clock." She gave him the details and addresses for both the clinic and the pharmacy.

She and Pat hung up their respective phones at almost the same moment.

Ms. Teague said, "My lawyer is on her way. How are you going to get Lillian here?"

"I'll interview Miss Hood at her house."

"Would you mind some advice?"

"That depends on the advice."

"Lillian's house is her one safe place. Strangers in that private space will rattle her so much that your interview will go down the tubes."

A gust of wind shook the clinic windows. Likely Lillian's house was compulsively neat. Muddy shoes and dripping raincoats wouldn't make them welcome. "How would you get her here?"

Pat replaced the key in its magnetic box and leaned under her desk. The magnet snapped to the metal with a sharp click. "I'll phone her and tell her that I need her to open the chart gate so you can see Miss Filmore's chart."

It was their best shot. The lawyer arrived before the constable did. She was a tidy middle-aged woman, probably closer to Miss Hood's age than to Avivah's.

"I don't do criminal work," she said, when she shook Avivah's hand.

Pat said, "You're an advocate, and that's what Lillian needs."

"Just so you don't expect to get Perry Mason."

The constable arrived minutes later. He was young and wet. Avivah handed him a towel. "Have you ever taken notes for a formal interview before?"

"Only in training. My spelling isn't very good."

Her driver could spell like a champion, and he knew shorthand. "Do the best you can."

They arranged themselves around the waiting room, with the constable sitting unobtrusively in a corner. Avivah and the lawyer sat in two of three chairs, which had been pulled into a triangle in the middle of the room.

When Pat phoned Lillian, she'd offered her a ride to the clinic. Lillian had preferred to walk. She arrived wearing a gray raincoat, hood, boots, and carrying a gray umbrella. She shook out the umbrella so that the water droplets landed outside the front door, removed her raincoat and rain hood and hung them on a coat rack beside the door.

Even on a Saturday, she was neatly dressed in linen slacks, a casual blouse and full makeup. Neither autopsy report had mentioned powder on the victim's clothes. Avivah didn't see how Lillian could have strangled two people and not gotten powder on the victims.

Ms. Teague said, "I appreciate you coming over."

Lillian's mouth was set in a thin line. "Needs must." She looked at Avivah. "I didn't think detectives wore a uniform."

"I'm wearing one today."

Miss Hood turned on the copier, deactivated the alarm connected to the chart grill, opened the grill, located the file, made a photocopy, sealed it in an envelope like the one now residing in Avivah's trunk, turned off the photocopier, replaced the chart, locked the grate, and reactivated the alarm. The entire process had taken her under five minutes.

Pat guided Lillian to the third chair, and squatted beside the chair. "Lillian, Detective Rosen wants to ask you a few more questions. Detective Rosen won't allow me to stay for your interview, but this is my lawyer, Gretchen. She's agreed to stay with you."

"I don't have money for a lawyer."

Pat stood. "Since this is clinic business and you're being interviewed here at the clinic, we will pay for today."

Avivah wondered if Lillian noticed the qualifier. Laurel Ridge Clinic would pay today, but if Lillian turned out to have committed murder, it would be a whole new ballgame.

Pat left quietly and locked the door behind her from the hallway. There was an outside chance that Pat Teague was headed home to pack a bag and go on the run. If that happened, at least it would tell Avivah what she wanted to know.

She read the Miranda warning to Lillian, who squared her shoulders. "Yes, I understand my rights, and I wish Gretchen to be present as my lawyer."

"I know that we did this in my office, but I need you to state your full name and address again."

Lillian did.

"Ms. Teague explained to me how the early and late clinic schedules work. How did you feel when you realized that Miss Pepperhawk would be working late clinic three weeks in a row?"

"It was very irritating."

"Ms. Teague also told me how much she appreciates you arranging the pill jar for her."

"She has an important presentation next week."

"How soon after Ms. Teague left here on Monday did you come back?"

Lillian said to her lawyer, "Do I have to answer that?"

Gretchen said, "It would be a good idea if you did. As an employee, you had every right to come back here."

Lillian clasped and unclasped her hands several times in her lap. "Half an hour."

That would have been about four thirty. "What did you do when you got here?"

"I got the jar and my sorting bowl and poured all of the pills into the bowl. Then I started to arrange them in pretty layers."

That's why the bottom half of the jar was neatly arranged.

"Were you working in the nurses' office?"

"I never work in their office. My place is here at reception."

"So you were sitting at the counter sorting pills. What happened?"

"That horrible woman pounded on the door. She scared me so much that I almost upended the bowl." Lillian scrunched her eyes closed and covered her ears with her hands. "I yelled at her to go away!"

Avivah reached over and removed Lillian's hand from one ear. "Did she go away?"

"She kept yelling, 'I know you're in there.' She couldn't have known. I'd locked the door and turned on the little lamp here at my desk."

"Did you open the door?"

"I had to. She was making so much noise."

"She came in, and—?"

Lillian sat up straight. "She accused me of stealing drugs. I tried to explain what I was doing, but she wouldn't listen. She threatened to report me to the police unless I gave her something for her nerves."

Avivah could imagine the scene: Edith and Lillian both near hysteria, a bowl of pills between them. Nothing but Valium and alcohol had shown up in the autopsy. Edith had been lucky that Lillian hadn't reached into the bowl and offered her a handful of pills.

"What did you do?"

"I checked her chart to see what Ms. Teague had given her. I was so relieved that it was Valium."

"Because you knew you had some in the jar?"

"Valium has a street value; the nurses never put anything with a street value in the jar. I was relieved because I had Valium in my purse."

"Do you have it with you today?"

"I always have it with me."

"May I see it, please?"

Lillian opened her purse and removed two half-filled vials of pale-yellow pills. Avivah studied the labels: two different doctors, two different pharmacies. Pepper called it doctor shopping.

"Your prescriptions aren't from this clinic."

Lillian leaned in confidentially. "Ms. Teague pretends to be a doctor, but she's really only a nurse. Sometimes she doesn't understand what I need. I get Valium from my real doctors."

How many doctors and how many prescriptions did Lillian

have? However many it was, Pat Teague wasn't going to like it one bit when she found out.

"How much Valium did you give Miss Filmore?"

"Ten milligrams. That's what the chart said, ten milligrams; Sig: one every eight hours as needed. Sig is the abbreviation for signature. That's what the pharmacist types for directions to the patient. I followed the chart exactly."

Monday morning, Pat had given Edith Filmore ten milligrams of Valium. She'd sent her away with another thirty milligrams. Avivah had to assume that Edith had taken all of that Monday by the afternoon or she wouldn't have returned to the clinic in such a panic. Lillian had given her another ten milligrams. That equaled fifty milligrams of Valium and an unknown quantity of alcohol in seven hours. Edith had been a hefty woman, but even so, she had remarkable stamina still to be on her feet.

"Did the Valium work immediately?"

"No. I told her to lie down in the exam room with a cool cloth on her forehead. I would go out and buy her a cold drink."

Lillian believed that germs contaminated all food and drink in the clinic. Even for a woman she didn't like, she had to go out to buy her something safe.

"Was this when you went to the store across the street?"

"Yes."

"Did you lock the clinic door when you left?"

"I left it unlocked, in case she wanted to leave."

Meaning that Lillian had hoped that Edith would leave and that Lillian took her time returning to the clinic to give Edith lots of time for that to happen. "How long were you gone?"

"Forty minutes."

More than enough time for the murderer to enter the clinic, especially if he or she had been outside, watching. The murderer had to have been desperate to risk everything. "What happened when you came back?"

Lillian whimpered. "I don't want to talk about it."

"Would it be simpler if I asked yes or no questions?"

Lillian's knuckles were white. "Yes."

Lillian's lawyer nodded for Avivah to go ahead.

"Were the lights on?"

"No."

"Was the photocopier on?"

"I didn't notice."

"The clinic was dark and quiet?"

"Yes."

"But it wasn't empty?"

Lillian's voice wobbled. "She was on the floor in the exam room. It was horrible."

"Did you call the police?"

"No."

"Why not?"

"I watched her for three minutes. She didn't breathe. An ambulance wasn't needed."

"The room was a mess. What did you think had happened?"

"That she'd died from a seizure. They tell you all the time not to share your medicine with anyone else. I was so relieved when I learned that she'd been strangled."

Viewed through the prism of Lillian Hood's world, being relieved that Edith Filmore had been murdered made sense. "Because that meant that the medicine you gave her hadn't killed her?"

"Exactly."

"What did you do after you decided not to call an ambulance?"

"Poured the rest of the pills back in the jar, replaced the jar in the nurses' office, and scrubbed my bowl and my counter before I left."

That accounted for the top half of the pills being a mess. At least now Avivah knew how Edith Filmore had gotten into the clinic, and why she'd come, but if she believed Miss Hood's story, she wasn't one bit closer to finding the killer and she was running out of suspects.

"Did you lock the front door when you left?"

"Both locks, the door and the dead bolt."

"I have some questions about Thursday morning. Were you in the discount store when the trouble started?"

"I was at the till, waiting to pay."

"What happened at the store?"

"I heard something break. I thought a salesgirl had dropped a set of dishes. People started yelling in a foreign language. They ran and screamed, too. I was frightened; I abandoned my cart and ran to the clinic. Ms. Teague would know what to do. We gathered some blankets and the first-aid kit because people were likely to be hurt."

"When you went back to the mall, did you go into the store?"

"I'm never going back in that store again."

"Please answer the question I asked?"

"I stayed in the parking lot."

"Had you gone into one of store's restrooms at any time that morning?"

Two spots of color appeared on the heavily powdered cheeks. "Public restrooms are filthy."

Faced with two autopsy reports that didn't mention face powder, and Mr. Lam dead in a men's public washroom, a place that Lillian could not have brought herself to enter, Avivah doubted that Lillian Hood was their killer.

The phone rang. Miss Hood got up and answered it. In a calm voice she said, "Reception, Laurel Ridge Clinic." She reached for a pink pad of phone message slips.

This woman had one heck of an ability to dissociate.

"Miss Pepperhawk will be at work on Tuesday. Do you wish to leave a message?"

Avivah got up and took the receiver from Lillian's hand. "You're looking for Miss Pepperhawk?"

Darby's voice said, "Avivah? What are you doing there?"

"Working. Why are you calling Pepper here?"

"I didn't get an answer at either the homestead or Benny's. I thought maybe Pepper had gone to the clinic to get a break from Nana Kate."

"I haven't seen or heard from Pepper since I left Benny's house this morning. Maybe she and your grandmother went shopping or out to lunch."

"Maybe. Greg Lane and I have had a word of prayer. Can you come to Skoufalos Electronics? He's prepared to give you a statement."

CHAPTER 29

Another gust of wind buffeted Frannie's car. The four women shivered. Pepper sat up and peered out the window at the slough of muddy water running alongside the car. Any more rain and the road would become a stream. She tried to keep her teeth from chattering. "You think the demonstration is over?"

Frannie pulled multiple scarves tighter around her shoulder. "For all his faults, Cody has enough sense to come in out of the rain. He better not catch cold and expect me to nurse him."

Ash rubbed her hands over the goose bumps on her arms. "I wonder what happened."

Frannie said, "I don't know, and I don't care."

"I'm sorry. We're going to freeze to death in this car and it's entirely my fault for suggesting a sit-in. I am so stupid."

Ash rubbed again. "Kaye, if you say 'I'm sorry' or call yourself 'stupid' one more time, I'm going to beat you to a pulp."

All of the women stared. Our Lady of Baking threatening to beat someone to a pulp? Pepper's emergency-room background kicked in. Crankiness was a sign of hypothermia.

"Frannie, turn on the heater again."

Frannie pointed to her gas gauge. "I can't. We're out of gas."

Pepper looked at the seemingly empty guard post, where the men remained hunkered down out of sight. "I could ask Mr. Bach for a can of gas."

"What have we accomplished so far?" Kaye held up her hands defensively. "I didn't say I'm sorry or call myself stupid. I'm asking what we're accomplishing?"

Pepper pulled her hands around her bare arms. "The sheriff hasn't arrested us yet."

Frannie tied a silk scarf tighter over her head. "We said we'd come to support the Vietnamese and we're showing that we mean business. Saving face, which is important to the Viet-namese, right Pepper?"

"I suppose so." She wasn't sure what would happen to face if they all died from being under clothed.

Ash asked, "Has anyone but me asked herself where Mr. Tu is in all of this?"

Frannie stopped trying to arrange her scarves. "What do you mean?"

"Pepper said that he's fanatical about everything being just right. Teaching his employees about good manners and always speaking in English. Face sounds important to him. How come he hasn't come out here to see if we are all right, invited us to come inside and warm up, or called the sheriff to forcibly remove us?"

The wind changed direction, bringing a whiff of a lot of dead poultry.

Pepper managed to keep from gagging. "Ash is right. Killing the birds was a military decision. You can't hear an enemy sneaking up on you if ducks and geese are making a gosh-awful noise. It was also one hell of a bad business decision. Valley Forge Hatchery will be out of business temporarily, maybe permanently. So, where is the boss while this is going on?"

Frannie said, "Maybe something happened to him last night when the vandals came. Maybe he tried to stop them and got hurt or even killed."

Pepper felt sick, and it wasn't just the smell. She started to get out of the car. "I'm going to talk to Mr. Bach."

As she got out of the car, a movement near the tree line by

the road caught her attention. Saul, protecting himself from the rain with Pepper's patio umbrella, slogged across the wet, burned ground toward them. He also carried a green garbage bag and a white Styrofoam cooler. In a few minutes he planted the sharp end of the umbrella pole in the gravel beside the car.

Not that it did much good. Pepper was already soaked from standing in the rain. "What are you doing with that?"

"It was the only umbrella I could find in the whole homestead."

They got in; Saul squeezed Pepper into Ash. She was grateful for the warmth of skin contact.

He opened the plastic bag and handed gray blankets all around. The women wrapped them around themselves. In the cramped space, Saul managed to wiggle a thermos and four Styrofoam cups out of the cooler. The odor of hot chocolate filled the car.

Frannie asked, "How did you know we were here?"

"A sheriff's deputy was waiting for me at the homestead. He wasn't necessarily waiting for *me*, just the first person who got home. The temperature has dropped fifteen degrees in the past two hours, and the sheriff is terrified you're going to die of hypothermia on his watch."

Saul surveyed the barricade, burned ground, and dead geese hanging from the swings. "What the hell happened here?"

Pepper said, "The war followed us home."

Kaye said, "Vandals broke in here last night. Mr. Tu's employees reacted by securing a perimeter and clearing a fire zone." She dropped the level of her voice, so that her words were barely more than puffs of air. "Mr. Bach wants us to leave. Pepper says that he might have automatic weapons in the guardhouse."

"I gather Ex-Captain Pepperhawk has been giving you a military briefing?"

Pepper had started to warm up. "Lay off, Saul. Wait a minute. Did you say that the sheriff's deputy was waiting for the first person to come home? Where are Dave and Nana Kate?"

"I don't know. I guess they went out, and took Anne with them."

"You don't *go out* in bad weather with an eighty-nine-year-old woman and a six-week-old baby. Did they leave a note?"

"I didn't see one."

She grabbed his arm. "Oh, my God, they've kidnapped Anne."

Saul pried her fingers from his arm. "I assume Anne is with them, but I doubt it was a kidnapping. Her diaper bag was gone, but they left the rest of the baby stuff. The sheriff wants you out of here. It sounds like Mr. Bach wants you out of here. I want you out of here. Sometime soon, the rest of the press is going to discover that you are here, and this whole situation is going to go to hell in a hand basket."

Ash asked, "What happened at the demonstration? Is everyone okay?"

"*Macbeth*, act five, scene five."

Kaye said, "A tale told by an idiot, full of sound and fury, signifying nothing."

Saul said, "What happened was that it rained. About a hundred demonstrators marched. Cody made a brief speech about John Boyd and asked people to pray for him. It was over in twenty minutes. The four of you are going to be better copy than the demonstration was. That's why I have to get you out of here."

In the guardhouse, Mr. Bach stood up.

Pepper tried to crawl over Saul. "Let me go talk to him."

By the time they were both out of the car, Mr. Bach had crossed the driveway to stand under the umbrella. He gave Saul a small, hurried bow. "Go home now!"

Pepper said, "Mr. Bach, this is our friend Saul Eisenberg."

Saul towered over the Vietnamese man. He bowed and the men shook hands.

Mr. Bach said, "Leave!"

Saul frowned. "I agree."

Pepper planted her feet on the wet gravel. "Not until we talk to Mr. Tu. Mr. Bach, don't you realize that all of that dead poultry constitutes a health hazard?"

From his puzzled expression, she doubted that Mr. Bach had learned enough English to understand a word she'd said.

Mr. Bach made the indistinct guttural sound that Pepper had heard many times when talking to Vietnamese hospital workers in Qui Nhon. That sound could mean anything from "I agree" to "I have no idea what we're talking about, but I'll keep nodding."

She pointed her finger at the hatcheries. "You kill birds?"

He waved both hands back and forth in protest. "Night. Men come." He pointed to the hatchery buildings. "Hot. Die." He dropped his head to one side and closed his eyes, imitating, Pepper guessed, ducks and geese falling over dead.

Where was Benny when she needed him? He knew more Vietnamese than she did, and he'd grown up in farm country. He probably knew something about the life and death of poultry.

"Saul, you come from Indiana. What he's talking about?"

"I come from downtown Terre Haute, but if someone cranked up the heating system full blast in the hatchery buildings, birds would die."

Sabotaging a heating system would have been simple: reset the thermostat, and disarm the alarms.

"Where Mr. Tu?"

Mr. Bach pantomimed walking fingers toward the hatchery, put his fingers to his eyes like binoculars, then the fingers walked very fast away from the hatchery. Mr. Bach rolled his hands around one another faster and faster. "Mr. Tu angry over angry."

"Furious?" Pepper offered. "Enraged?"

He rolled his hands again. "Angry over angry."

She tried GIspeak for bad. "Mr. Tu, number ten?"

"Number ten-thou."

Very, very angry.

She walked her fingers. "Mr. Tu go where?"

Mr. Bach pantomimed holding a phone receiver to his ear, and made "Brrrr, brrrr, brrrr" sounds. He hung up the pretend receiver, picked it up again and repeated the sounds.

They'd tried to call Mr. Tu more than once, but he wasn't answering his phone.

From somewhere across the compound, a muffled child's cry was quickly silenced.

"Dead birds make children sick." She pantomimed an imitation of vomiting.

Mr. Bach went back to the guardhouse. The other men inside stood up and they went into a huddle bent over like football players, jabbering in Vietnamese. Every so often one of them would glance at Pepper.

Each time, Pepper yelled forcefully, "Dead birds. Children sick."

Finally the men nodded and stood up. Mr. Bach said, "Women, children go."

Pepper had a brief image of Darby's description of Vietnamese flowing around him somewhere in Vietnam. Would that deputy dare to arrest them if they came out surrounded by Vietnamese women and children like Moses leading his people to the promise land?

"Good. Men go, too."

Mr. Bach surveyed the burned grass and desecrated buildings. "Home. Stay."

From the tree line somewhere on her left, a double-thunk sounded faintly, followed by a whistling sound. It was the same sound that brought Pepper awake some nights, drenched in sweat. Pepper and Mr. Bach locked gazes. He yelled in Vietnamese at the same instant that she threw herself on the ground, screaming, "Incoming!"

Chapter 30

By the time Avivah and her constable-in-tow got to Skoufalos Electronics, the rain had downgraded itself from a downpour to a steady soaker.

A bell tinkled when she opened the shop door. Darby, Greg Lane, and Yanni Skoufalos—all dressed in black—were gathered around a small black-and-white television. Avivah recognized Yanni from the photo Benny had given her.

She and the constable shook out their rain slickers at the door and walked around to where they could see the television. The men moved to make room for them.

On the screen a group of men dressed in an assortment of fatigue and boonie hats, marched through a downpour. Cody led the group holding up a soaked homemade poster that had originally said, *Your best bet, hire a vet.* A red line had been drawn through *hire,* and over it written *don't fire.* The red marker had bled down the poster.

A whistle sounded, and a strong voice, likely an ex-drill instructor, sang out, "I don't know, but I been told."

The protesters' voices raggedly repeated, "I don't know, but I been told." It must have been a long time since any of them marched in formation.

"Asheville streets ain't paved with gold."

Yanni said, "Pfff," pressed a button, and the protestors shrank to a white dot in the center of the screen, then blinked to darkness.

Avivah asked, "Was that live?"

Darby said, "A recap. What happened here today? What does it mean? The answer is nothing and nothing."

Lane leaned close to Yanni and said something in a low voice. Yanni nodded and slapped him lightly on the cheek. It was a gesture Avivah had seen European men use to express fondness.

Lane said, "Let's go to Yanni's apartment."

Darby tried to follow them. Avivah restrained him with her hand on his chest. "Go home."

He started to say something but pointed at Greg Lane instead. "One hundred percent cooperation with Detective Rosen, and Wednesday night never happened."

Avivah rounded on him. "I can do without you threatening people. If you want to make yourself useful, go find Pepper and your grandmother."

So these two experts in hand-waving obfuscation had cut a deal. She was going to get a story from Lane, but not necessarily the truth. She didn't know whether to thank Darby or charge him with obstructing an investigation. It was Pepper's home that had been invaded. Had Darby consulted Pepper before he promised to forget Wednesday night? Pepper and Darby would have to sort that out for themselves.

A few minutes later Greg Lane unlocked the apartment door and stood aside for her and the constable to enter. The apartment wasn't what she'd expected, given the condition of the downstairs work area. She liked how the white walls and curtains made the space appear bigger.

Lane asked, "Would you like coffee?"

She was cold, damp, and had missed lunch. "Coffee would be appreciated."

"I'm afraid it's instant." He picked up a small copper pot with a long handle. "I can make Greek coffee, if you'd prefer?"

If Greek coffee required a special pot, it was sure to take

longer than instant. "Instant will be fine."

While Lane worked, the constable carried a straight-back chair from the living room and set himself up in an unobtrusive corner. In a few minutes, Lane distributed coffee mugs all around. He opened a round tin. "Koulourakia?"

Avivah limited herself to three cookies. They had a faint orange scent. She would gladly have eaten the entire tin.

Lane sat down and wrapped his hands around his mug. He paid polite attention to Avivah's telling him his Miranda rights, but she suspected he thought it some arcane native ritual rather than anything that applied to him.

"Do you understand your rights?"

"Yes."

"Do you wish a lawyer present?"

"We can skip the lawyer, but we have to agree on one ground rule: there's a fence around national security."

Those had to be Darby's words. "It better be a very small fence."

"I'll keep it as small as I can."

"Let's start with your name, address, and a look at your passport."

"My name is Gregory Lane." He gave a Hong Kong address and an overseas phone number. "My parents' place. They usually know how to contact me." He got up, took a passport from the top of the refrigerator, and handed it to Avivah.

"You travel on an American passport?"

"I'm an American citizen."

Avivah thumbed through the well-worn pages. "Who doesn't spend a lot of time in the States."

"Other places are more interesting."

She turned to the last entries. "Manila on March twenty-eighth of this year; San Francisco on May third. You flew from the Philippines to California?"

"Vietnam and Thailand were in between."

"You were safely out of Vietnam, but you chose to go back?"

"I had things to do."

"You seem to be missing entry stamps."

"The South Vietnamese government was too busy to stamp passports."

"The Thai government?"

"Have you read Antoine de Saint-Exupéry?"

"*Night Flight*?"

"It's a good book; I can lend it to you."

The constable printed laboriously, his brows drawn and the tip of his tongue between his teeth. Antoine de Saint-Exupéry probably exceeded his spelling capabilities. "Constable, indicate that Mr. Lane answered that he entered Thailand on a night flight by special permission."

If Lane's Wednesday night visit to the homestead wasn't going to show up on a police blotter, she'd wasn't going to waste time asking about it. Going straight to her murder investigations suited her fine. "When did you meet Edith Filmore?"

Lane worried at a small irregularity in his mug's glaze. "Fifteen months ago."

"What was your relationship with her?"

"Social."

"I'm good at extracting details, but like dental work, the sooner this is over, the easier for both of us. Work on more detailed answers, okay?"

"She lived in a State Department building on Gia Long Street. Air America had a crash pad in the same building. She liked to cook. When you're living off the local economy and ration packs, a home-cooked meal is a treat."

"Didn't you find her a bit rigid?" And a calculating blackmailer. And a woman possibly given to symptoms of mental illness. "I thought pilots like 'em hot and horny?"

The constable blushed, but kept writing.

Lane slammed his mug on the table. "Sometimes people take a chance on being kind to one another, especially in a war."

"What did *kindness* entail?"

"Sharing meals; listening to music; talking."

"Did she ever mention a Mr. Lindberg? Someone from her past?"

"I'm Mr. Lindberg. Lindberg Lane. It's my nickname."

The repressed spinster and the aging flyboy matched Pepper's fascination with bad boys. War, loneliness, and kindness made a hell of a triangle. That poor, misguided woman had parlayed kindness and shared meals into a fantasy that she and Lane were engaged. Or had it been a fantasy?

"When did the two of you become engaged?"

Lane played with his spoon. "On the evacuation helicopter between the roof of the American embassy and the USS *Blue Ridge*."

Engagement rings being in short supply over the South China Sea would account for Edith Filmore not wearing one. "That must have been a hell of an engagement party."

"Don't make fun of something you know nothing about."

Please let this precipitous engagement be something more than exhaustion and "we both thought we were going to die." She was desperate for a thick, solid motive that made sense. "Why did you get engaged?"

"It gave me a reason to follow her to the States; she had a letter that I was desperate to get."

"Get or get back?"

"I don't write letters that I would be desperate to get back. Edith had stumbled upon a way to make me rich."

"Where does this start?"

"On the embassy roof. It was my last flight. I had enough av-gas left for one more trip to a Navy ship, and then I planned to ditch the helicopter in the sea, and hope like hell for a pickup. The minute I landed, Marines shoved this woman with a baby into the copilot's seat."

"You were flying without a copilot?"

"I hadn't exactly had time to interview applicants."

"Did you know the woman was Edith Filmore?"

"You were in Nam. I assume you've been in a helicopter cockpit?"

"I have."

"Then you know room is a thing it ain't got. Of course I knew it was Edith. A Marine medic handed me a personal-effects envelope and told me they'd loaded an American's body onboard. I almost crapped in my pants when I read Darby's name. We went back a long way."

"I also know that a helicopter is too noisy to hear a marriage proposal."

"Saigon air traffic control was dead. I had a few minutes before I'd tie in to naval air traffic, so I gestured for Edith to use the headphones, and switched over to intercom. While people were freaking out in the back, and I was paying attention to the engine, listening for it to sputter from lack of fuel, Edith and I had this bizarre chat over the headsets. The first thing she said was 'Are you well, Mr. Lane?' "

If Edith Filmore had resolved to hold herself together until she delivered Anne to Pepper, that kind of remark made a lot of sense. Edith had wallpapered over all of her feelings.

"I'm flying for my life—our lives—and she shoves papers in my face and asks me if I read Vietnamese."

"Do you?"

"Yes."

"What did the letter say?"

"I could tell right off it was from the baby's mother. It started with stuff about her loving her daughter always and waiting for her in heaven."

"I gather it ended differently?"

"With instructions to bank officials to allow the bearer to open a safe-deposit box."

"Did the letter say what was in the safe-deposit box?"

"Diamonds."

Diamonds qualified as a motive; diamonds for Anne spun this investigation in a whole new direction. "Did you tell Miss Filmore what the letter said?"

"I told her that the letter gave her permission to legally care for the infant; that the letter was all that would stand between her and a kidnapping charge, and that she must keep it with her at all times."

Edith Filmore had been a bureaucrat; she understood documentation. "How did you know that Edith was bringing the baby to Asheville?"

"I handed her my kneepad. She wrote down everything that Darby had told her, including where she was taking the baby. You ever play slot machines?"

"I wasted a few quarters before the Army took the machines out of O-club bars."

"When I read where she was taking the baby, it was like hitting the biggest jackpot in the world. Darby had made me promise that I'd contact his lady if anything happened to him, so I knew where she lived. Yanni lived in Asheville, too. Visiting my parents' friend gave me an alibi for why I was in Asheville. I'd have a place to stay where I wouldn't show up on any motel's records. Meeting Edith here would give me a chance to sweet-talk her out of the letter long enough to make a photocopy."

"Banks don't accept photocopied authorizations."

"Forging an original wasn't going to be a problem. I have contacts."

"You planned to steal from an orphan?"

"Only enough to make sure my parents will be okay if I'm not around. I'm their only child. You want to know the kicker? The bank is in Hong Kong a few blocks from where my parents live."

"You decided the way to soften up Edith was to ask her to marry you?"

He rubbed his hand over his forehead. "I'm not proud of that."

"Would you have married her?"

"I would have sent her money."

"After you broke her heart."

"I'd already given her money to buy a plane ticket to Asheville." He said it as if it made up for a fake wedding proposal.

"Where did you get that kind of cash?"

"I'd been carrying around a wad since I was paid for that private charter to Manila."

"So you landed on the *Blue Ridge,* your passengers got off, Edith was on her way to Asheville, you were on your way to ditch your helicopter and make a beeline to get to Asheville before Edith. What happened?"

Lane pushed himself away from the table, stood, and stretched. "Sorry, my hip's killing me." At the sink, he downed three aspirins with water. "I was sitting on the deck, scanning the sea for a place to ditch, when naval air traffic screamed in my headset to 'get the fuck off the deck.' When an air traffic controller says *fuck* on air, you know it's time to move. Land, off-load, take off. I could do it in my sleep, but this business with Edith distracted me."

More likely he was half dead from exhaustion.

"The chopper coming in behind me was so close that the prop wash shook my machine." Lane moved his hand in a sharp up-and-right arc. "I went up and right. My prop tips should have caught on the deck and cartwheeled me into the sea. They didn't."

His hand shook.

Avivah said, "Thank you."

"For what?"

"For all those flights; for all the people you got out."

Lane's skin looked gray, his face exhausted. "No one's said that to me before."

"Somebody should have."

He came back and sat at the table. "Next thing I knew, I was on course back to the embassy. Reflex. That wasn't where I wanted to go. I knew I didn't have enough gas to get there and I'd already overshot where I could ditch and expect an American pickup. My only chance was the rumors that had been floating for weeks about a turn-off-the-light site."

"You mean as in, 'Will the last American out of Vietnam please turn off the lights?' "

There had been a handmade sign that said that in the Long Bien military-police office.

"All I'd heard was that it was an airstrip without lights or radio somewhere south of Saigon. An Air America plane would stay on the ground until the North Vietnamese were coming over the hill."

Coming over the hill was a figure of speech. The delta country south of Saigon was flat and wet.

"I was flying on fumes when I found it. Prettiest gooney bird I'd ever seen sat at the end of the runway. I was out of my seat fumbling for my logbook before my rotor stopped moving. That's when I discovered two things: those Navy fuckers hadn't off-loaded Darby's body bag, and the bag was moving."

"That must have given you a turn."

"I thought my heart would stop. A couple of guys helped me haul him from the chopper to the plane. One of the few Vietnamese on the plane was a doctor. He had six bottles of IV fluid crammed into plastic shopping bags. A couple of hours later, while I sat on the floor trying to keep Darby's IV bottle from smashing itself, I realize that if Darby made it, the first thing he would do was phone North Carolina. If he called before Edith got to Asheville, she could be in a shitload of trouble."

So he did care about her. Or did he care about the letter?

"After an ambulance carted Darby away to a Bangkok hospital, I headed for a safe house. I fell asleep in the shower and almost drowned, but I made it to a bed and crashed."

"When did you wake up?"

"Thursday evening. Darby was 'resting comfortably.' The hospital operator didn't know if he'd regained consciousness. I headed for Asheville; by Saturday I'd gotten as far as Atlanta."

"Had you had any contact with Edith Filmore since the ship?"

"No, but I managed to pry out of an airline employee in Atlanta that an Edith Filmore was listed on a flight into Asheville the next day. I rented a car."

"Why didn't you fly from Atlanta to Asheville?"

"I was almost out of money. I could afford to rent a car or buy a plane ticket but not both, and a car gave me more mobility."

"You met her at the airport Sunday night?"

"Yeah."

"How did that go?"

"We weren't over the South China Sea anymore. She couldn't believe that I was serious about marrying her. I knew she'd never give me the letter that day, even for a few minutes, so I dropped into low-key mode: took her to supper, didn't make any demands on her."

That accounted for the time between when Edith's plane landed and she showed up at Pepper's. "You drove her to Madison County?"

"Yes."

"Where were you while she was in the house?"

"On the road pretending to change a tire."

Pepper couldn't see the road from her front door.

"What happened after she came back to the car?"

"She said that she'd left both the baby and the letter with Pepper."

"Did you believe her?"

"I'd stressed to Edith how important it was to keep that letter with her at all times. She was fanatical about good filing. She said it was the bedrock of good business."

"You decided there was a possibility that she'd photocopied the letter for her files?"

"Ever have that hopeful expectation when you'd already lost more money than you'd planned in those slot machines?"

"You mean that the machine had to be due to pay off; that it would be a crime to walk away without putting one more quarter in the slot?"

"That one. Besides, Edith was acting funny."

"What kind of funny?"

"Excited. Hyperactive. She'd concocted a plan for me to go with her to Wisconsin so that I could meet her cousin. She didn't shut up all the way to Asheville, and Edith wasn't a motormouth."

What was the term that Pat Teague had charted? Pressure of speech. Anne was safely with Pepper. Edith had prospects of blackmail money, and Lane really had met her in Asheville. The pressure was off. The problem was that when pressure came off something that had been tightly wound, that thing often flew apart. "What did you do when you got to Asheville?"

"Drove her to a motel. I agreed to meet her in Wisconsin at the end of the week."

"Were you really going to do that?"

"Yes."

"Who picked the motel?"

"I did."

"Why that motel?"

"Darby told me all about Pepper. I knew where she lived and where she worked. I had time to kill Sunday waiting for Edith's plane, so I did a little reconnaissance."

"On Pepper's house, too?"

"Complete reconnaissance is the best kind."

Avivah had spent Sunday buried in work, trying to bury her feelings about Saigon. Not that being at home would have made a difference, but it felt like it would have. "What did you do after you dropped Edith at the motel?"

"Started back to Atlanta."

"Why?"

"My parents were wiring me money in Atlanta, but it wouldn't be there until Monday."

"I thought your parents didn't have money."

"It was my own money; my parents have signing authority for my bank account."

"Had you seen Yanni when you were in Asheville?"

"No."

"Why not? You said you had time to kill."

"I never could keep a secret from Yanni. An hour with him, and he'd be on the phone to my parents telling them what I was up to. I didn't trust myself to see him."

"Yanni got a phone call Monday morning and left in a hurry. Was that to meet you?"

"I lied about collapsing on the way to see Yanni; actually, it happened on the way back to Atlanta. Next thing I know, I'm in this country hospital, with a doctor who won't release me unless someone picked me up."

"Signing yourself out against medical advice didn't occur to you?"

"I would have done just that, but I no longer had a car. My doctor's buddy, the sheriff, towed my rental and called the company to pick it up. I was desperate. Yanni was the only person I could think of to call."

"When did you get out of the hospital?"

"Tuesday about noon."

He couldn't have killed Edith, but he was still in the running for Anne's attempted abduction and Mr. Lam's murder. Of course, that blew her and Nate's theory that they were looking for one killer.

"Where were you Tuesday night?"

"Yanni and I shared a motel room in Greenville, South Carolina."

She'd have to find out how heavy a sleeper Yanni was, but it looked like Lane was out of the running for attempting to kidnap Anne. "When did you find out that Edith Filmore was dead?"

"Wednesday, when I saw Tuesday's Asheville paper."

"Why didn't you come forward?"

"In my line of work, coming forward to the authorities is a bad idea." Lane reached into his sweatpants pocket and pulled out a small velvet box. "I need a favor."

"I need answers."

He held out the box. "Trade?"

Avivah opened it. Inside was a gold-and-diamond engagement ring. "This is a nice ring for someone who wired home for money."

"I'll pay Yanni back. I want this on Edith's finger when she's buried."

Avivah closed the box and buttoned it into her uniform pocket. "I can make sure it goes with her personal effects, along with a letter to the funeral home stating that it was her wish to be buried wearing it."

"Good enough."

"The two of you would have been a disaster."

"I agree, but I owe her something. Edith's cousin was always holding it up to her that she'd gotten married but Edith hadn't. I can do two things for Edith now. One is put her cousin's nose out of joint with that ring."

"What's the second?"

"Tell you everything I know about Lam Trong Tri."

CHAPTER 31

Pepper pressed her face into wet gravel. She whispered, "The first round is always wide. The first round is always wide." To her it sounded like a prayer.

The ground shook. The last things she heard before the world went quiet were breaking glass and shattering wood. Then, only her heart pounded in her ears.

She turned her face to the right. Fifty feet away, a corner of the little school had turned into splintered wood and glass shards. A piece of white-painted lattice swung in the opening; it held vines with a couple of glass jars attached. A tan-and-white guinea pig wiggled its way through a tiny space between two pieces of wood.

Pepper agreed with the guinea pig; being a moving target appealed to her more than being a still one. "Follow me," she screamed as she pushed herself off the ground and ran. They darned well better follow her. If anyone was too terrified to move, she couldn't do a thing about it.

Her blanket flowed behind her like a wet cape. She turned loose of it, and the wind grabbed it from her shoulders. Cold rain quickly soaked her dress and skin. She made a brief zig, grabbed for the guinea pig, and to her complete surprise, caught it. She held it close to her chest. The animal's claws raked her skin. Wearing a sundress had been a bad idea.

She'd just reached the guardhouse when another double-thunk sounded. She stood aside to allow other people to pass

Sharon Wildwind

her, and when they were all behind the sandbags, dove in herself. The second round landed on the burned ground, throwing up great gouts of mud.

Mr. Bach grabbed her dress. With his other hand pointed to the school. "*Một.*" To the burned ground. "*Hai.*" Straight down. "*Ba.*"

She got the message. The idiots with the mortar had fired bracketing shots to zero in on the guardhouse. *Ba* was not the place to be.

Mr. Bach said something sharp in Vietnamese, maybe his version of "Follow me." He ran toward the motel-like building, pulling her along by her dress. Behind her Pepper heard the sound of feet crunching gravel at a run.

She and Mr. Bach half ran, half slid down concrete stairs at one side of the building. Bach pounded on the door. A bolt slid open. He pushed her inside. Just before the door slammed shut behind her, she heard the sound of wood shattering. The third mortar round had hit something solid, likely the guardhouse.

Wet and shaking, Pepper bent over with one hand on her thigh and the other holding the squealing animal. She gasped for air. She'd probably just learned to count to three in Vietnamese. *Một, Hai, Ba.* Hell of a language lesson.

One of the women took the guinea pig from her hands and held it up. The younger children clapped their hands and cried, "Piglet!" Apparently, Mr. Tu's required English lessons included *Winnie the Pooh.*

Another woman draped a towel around Pepper's shoulders. Pepper pulled it over where the guinea pig had scratched her. Mrs. Bach thrust a warm mug into Pepper's hands. "Tea," she said, rubbing her stomach. Tea seemed to be Mrs. Bach's remedy for everything. Mrs. Bach, the Tea Lady, and Ash Alexander, the Queen of Baking, would be a great team.

Ash Alexander? Avivah's boss was Nate Alexander; what an

odd coincidence of names.

Ash, Frannie, Kaye, and Saul huddled, drying themselves, in a far corner of the room. Ash's shirtwaist dress had survived the best. Saul's clothes were grubby. Kaye's cowboy fringe was matted and limp, and Frannie's scarves resembled lumps of wet tissue paper. Pepper collapsed on the floor beside Saul.

He said, "You're bleeding."

Pepper slapped away solicitous hands. "The guinea pig scratched me. It's nothing; it's already stopped bleeding."

Gradually her breathing and heart rate returned to normal. Two battery-operated lanterns gave the basement laundry room a dim glow. Industrial-size washers and dryers lined one wall; three home-size washers and dryers lined another. The room smelled of detergent and mustiness.

One of the women pulled a plastic liner from a tall metal bin. Piglet went into the bin. Pepper heard him—her—squealing and scratching on the metal sides.

Sounding far away, another shell landed. How many rounds could those guys have? Why hadn't the sheriff arrested them? Because it took time to slog through rain-drenched ground cover.

Ash asked, "How come we are over here and everyone else is on the other side of the room?"

Frannie said, "We have a different status, but I don't know if it's higher or lower. They haven't asked us to join them, so maybe it's up to us to make the first move."

Several loops of string hung from a nail in the wall. Kaye took one of them. She walked across the room and sat on the floor in the middle of the children. With a few hand movements she wove the string into a design, which she held out to a child. Tentatively, he put his finger in the middle of Kaye's string pattern.

Kaye dropped her thumbs and pulled her hands apart. The

string was now below the boy's hand. He giggled. Kaye reformed the string and held it out to a little girl.

Frannie said, "I'll bet you that she's a teacher."

Pepper thought so, too.

Frannie and Ash got up and went to sit among the women. The women offered them more tea. Pepper wanted to join them, but exhaustion kept her rooted. She'd survived her first mortar attack in years and rescued Piglet in the process. The second accomplishment pleased her more. Now she understood Darby's truck. It was one human-size gesture in the middle of chaos.

Saul said, "Where are all the Vietnamese who were at the mall?"

There didn't seem to be any more women and children here today than on Wednesday.

"Mr. Tu moves people through here fast."

She hoped he'd moved them through, that they weren't somewhere in another building, exposed to the mortar fire.

"Avivah isn't going to like that." He cupped his hands around Pepper's ear. "The autopsy showed that John Boyd couldn't have killed Mr. Lam. Avivah is going to have to find every person who was at the mall on Thursday morning."

Pepper didn't envy her that task.

Someone pounded on the door. The children became quiet; Kaye put her arms around as many as she could reach. The women hustled them into a corner and formed a line in front of them. Frannie and Ash stood with them. A couple of the women held baseball bats.

Mrs. Bach opened the door. A wet and joyful-looking Mr. Nghiem said something in Vietnamese. People babbled at one another. All of the adults ran outside. Saul and Pepper followed at the end.

The rain had slowed to a mist. Two Vietnamese men were

slogging across the muddy ground lugging a mortar between them. Near the shattered guardhouse two skinny guys in fatigues, with bandannas tied around their heads lay facedown in the mud. Their hands were tied behind them with cord. The sheriff's deputies might not have known what to do during a mortar attack, but ex-ARVN soldiers certainly had. They'd attacked and secured the mortar position.

The old cook booted one of the guys in the side and spat on him.

Pepper opened her mouth to protest and shut it. She walked away and turned her back on Vietnamese and Americans alike. Saul or Frannie would have to stop them if things got out of hand. She had no energy left for fighting.

I will lay down my sword and shield. Was that from the Bible, or was it a book title? Maybe she'd even made it up herself. It didn't matter. Wherever it came from, it sounded good to her. She'd had enough of war to last a lifetime. All she wanted was to go home.

Pepper looked up to see more sheriff's cars than she'd ever seen in one place turning, one after another, into the hatchery drive. The cars stopped at skewed angles, and deputies poured out like clowns out of tiny circus cars. Darby was in the third car. He swept Pepper into his arms and held her so hard she couldn't breathe. "I am so proud of you."

"I didn't do anything except run for cover."

And save Piglet, but she didn't feel a need to share that with him.

"You did the most important thing; you yelled, 'Follow me.' "

Yeah, she had and people had followed her. For thirty seconds she'd had her own field command. It wasn't the same thing as having the guts to go after the people who had been shooting at them, but it was enough. "How do you know what I yelled?"

"You screamed it so loud, the deputies heard you all the way out on the road."

"I guess I was excited."

"I guess you were. Should I be concerned that you've got blood on your dress?"

"No."

"*Đại tá* Baxter! *Đại tá* Baxter!"

Darby winced. He spun around to the sound of the voice, and screamed, "*Nghiem!*" He ran toward the Vietnamese man, scooping him up in a bear hug.

He released Mr. Nghiem from the hug, but didn't let go of his hand. He pulled the man across the muddy yard.

"Pepper, I want you to meet Anne's uncle."

CHAPTER 32

Avivah and her driver arrived at the police station's front door about suppertime. "For a man who was roused out of a comfortable recliner to do overtime, you looked remarkably cheerful."

"Can't have an easier collar than the person we're looking for turns himself in."

Avivah had learned a long time ago to suspect any police work that came easy. The real question was why had Charles Tu turned himself in *now*.

"Here's the Miranda translation in Vietnamese that you asked me to get. I thought this Mr. Tu spoke English."

"Like you said, he's made this too easy for us. I'm not taking any chances."

The same elderly women whom Avivah had seen earlier walked past, talking enthusiastically about their day. For them Saturday had been another day in a tourist town. They would be tucked in their beds before Avivah went on night shift.

When Avivah and her driver entered the interrogation room, both Charles Tu and another Asian man stood. The men wore dark suits, white shirts, and gray ties. The other man handed Avivah a business card. "I am Mr. Pham, attorney-at-law." They waited until Avivah was seated across from them before sitting down. Mr. Tu folded his hands on the metal table. "I am here to make a statement."

Avivah pushed the piece of paper with the Vietnamese Miranda toward him. "You have the right to remain silent . . ."

After she'd finished, Mr. Tu glanced at the paper. "Thank you for your consideration. I understand my rights and I am making this statement of my free will. Mr. Pham is my attorney, and I desire him to be present each time I speak to the police. I regret the delay in coming forward; Mr. Pham advised me not to contact you until he could be present."

Pepper had been right: the combination of Mr. Tu's Vietnamese features and Midwest American accent were disconcerting. "Let's start with your name and address"

"My birth name was Tu Canh Cuong; I legally changed it to Charles Tu." He gave an Asheville address.

Mr. Pham opened his briefcase and removed two pieces of paper. He offered one to Mr. Tu, who shook his head. Mr. Pham took a small gold pen from his suit pocket.

Mr. Tu sat very straight. "On Sunday, May fourth, nineteen seventy-five, I became aware that a woman was to visit Asheville. She carried a letter that might be of benefit to me. I was at the airport when she arrived and followed her Sunday evening and the next day, Monday, May fifth. I attempted to speak with her on Monday afternoon, but she rebuffed me. I continued to follow her. I approached her a second time in the Laurel Ridge Clinic at approximately five thirty on Monday afternoon. She became hysterical and attacked me. In defending myself, I strangled her. Subsequently I learned from a newspaper report of her death that her name was Edith Filmore. I regret what happened and am willing to submit to the legal consequences arising from my action."

While he spoke, Mr. Pham had made a meticulous tick at the end of each sentence.

Her driver was right; police work didn't get easier than this, or more complicated. An easy confession meant that she was treading barefoot on broken glass. She had to sew up every detail in case Tu later reneged on his confession or contended that it was made under duress. She laid four black-and-white photographs of middle-aged women on the table. "Do you recognize any of these women?"

Mr. Tu laid a well-manicured finger on Edith Filmore's dress. "This is the woman who died."

Avivah collected the photos. She wouldn't tell her three aunts that they had been part of a police lineup.

"How did Edith Filmore and her letter come to your attention?"

"My associate, Mr. Lam, told me about them."

"Mr. Lam knew her?"

"He'd learned about her from a man he'd worked with in Vietnam."

"What man?"

"Greg Lane."

"Have you ever met Mr. Lane?"

"No."

"Have you ever spoken to him, perhaps on the phone?"

"No."

"When did Mr. Lam talk to Greg Lane?"

"Sunday afternoon. Mr. Lam was at the airport doing business for me. Mr. Lane was also there."

That matched what Lane had said. He'd gone into the airport to confirm that Edith's plane was on time. Running into Mr. Lam had been more of that slot-machine payoff, the last cherry dropping into the window before everything turned sour. "What did Mr. Lam tell you about their meeting?"

"That the outcome could be beneficial to us."

"Us?"

"I am president of the American-Vietnamese Businessmen's Association."

Interesting that he put American first.

"Part of our work is to sponsor Vietnamese refugees. Several years ago, we decided that it would be more efficient to have an employee representing our interests in Vietnam."

Had that been after the debacle John described? Tu had gotten away with no publicity that time, but he couldn't count on Tet and public sentiment protecting him again.

"Mr. Lam had found Mr. Lane helpful in conducting our business in Vietnam."

That was Greg Lane, helpful all around. "In your interview with Lieutenant Alexander, you stated that Mr. Lam was foreman at your hatchery."

"I sponsored him several months ago and made him my foreman."

Had that been a reward for a job well done, or did he want to keep an eye on Lam, who must have known a heck of a lot about Tu's business? "You no longer needed a representative in Vietnam?"

"I anticipated a time would come very shortly when I would not. As things turned out, I was right."

The catch in his voice was the first flicker of emotion he'd shown. US government officials claimed not to have seen the debacle coming, but maybe the American-Vietnamese community had. "How would the outcome be beneficial to your group?"

"Mr. Lam was skilled in procuring appropriate papers for some people we sponsored."

In other words, he was a forger. Cody had been right: Mr. Tu had brought in at least some people who didn't qualify for immigration. Mr. Pham looked on edge. This case was going to be complicated enough without immigration violations. For now, she'd let that issue slide. "What did Mr. Lane want?"

"An opinion about a letter written in Vietnamese. He said that time was of the essence."

Lane had told Avivah he'd asked Lam to forge a letter that

Hong Kong bank officials would accept. "You agreed that this letter might be beneficial to your association?"

"Yes."

"More beneficial if Mr. Lane wasn't included?"

"Yes."

"You went to the airport. How were you going to recognize this woman?"

"Mr. Lam described Greg Lane to me. I waited to see who he met."

"Once you'd seen the woman, you followed her through Sunday night and all day Monday?"

"Mr. Lam and I took turns watching her."

"We know that Lane took Miss Filmore to visit someone in Madison County. Were you following her then?"

"Yes."

Lane said that he'd parked on the road near the homestead, but where had Mr. Tu concealed himself? "How did you prevent Mr. Lane from noticing you?"

"I drove past where he stopped, turned around in the Baptist Church parking lot, and drove back to wait at a small store down the road. I knew he would have to come back that way."

A dark grove of trees bordered one side of Hubert Sprinkle's store. A car parked between the building and those trees wouldn't be seen at night.

"When was Mr. Lane bringing the letter to Mr. Lam?"

"Mr. Lane was to phone when he had the letter in his possession."

Everything turned on that visit to the homestead. By the time Edith Filmore and Greg Lane drove past Tu's hidden car, Lane didn't know if Edith or Pepper had the letter, but he was going to Wisconsin in case Edith still had it. "Did he phone?"

"No."

"Did you draw any conclusion from him not phoning?"

"We decided that the only way to find out if the woman still had the letter in her possession was for me to talk to her."

"So you continued following her?"

"Yes."

"Where did you approach Miss Filmore on Monday afternoon?"

"Outside of a travel agency at a shopping mall. She ran from me."

By that time Valium and alcohol were the only things holding Edith's shaky mental health together. Tu had been lucky that she hadn't screamed or called a security guard. "Tell me about going to Laurel Ridge Clinic."

"Mr. Lam had reported to me that she'd spent several hours at a clinic Monday morning. I saw someone let her in, but the place appeared to be closed. When I saw a woman leave, I decided to take a chance. If there were other people inside, my excuse would be that I was inquiring about the process for obtaining food handlers' certificates. The front door was open. The woman was at the photocopier. I said, 'Excuse me, I must speak with you.' She became hysterical and fled into one of the rooms."

In dim light, groggy from alcohol and Valium, Edith Filmore had heard an American's voice and turned around to see the same Vietnamese man who had approached her at the mall. What better trigger to hysteria for a woman who had gone through the fall of Saigon a few days before?

Mr. Tu bowed his head. "I could have walked away, but I followed her to apologize for scaring her. She grabbed glass jars and threw them at me. She ended up between the door and me. I tried to push my way past her and she attacked me. My hands became entangled in her scarf. I did not mean for her to die."

Avivah didn't buy it. Strangling someone took several minutes. If the scarf had accidently tightened around Edith's neck and she'd become unconscious, Tu would have had a chance to untangle his hands. Edith wouldn't have died.

Nate would realize that also. So would the prosecutor. Any smart reporter could figure it out. What no one in the court system or the newspapers would understand was that the real struggle in that dark clinic was between events and memories from half a world away. John Boyd wasn't the only one subject to flashbacks.

Tu had stalked Edith Filmore. He admitted that when she ran into the exam room, he could have walked away. In the cold light of jurisprudence, she had no idea if the prosecutor would accept Tu's confession and agree to a manslaughter plea or would want to try him for first-degree murder. If this went to trial, Darby would be called as a witness. Not answering questions because of national security would not go down well in court. He'd likely end up in jail for obstruction. "You said that you found Edith Filmore standing at the photocopier. After she died, did you check the copier?"

"Yes. There was a copy of a letter on the machine, and she was making a second copy. I took both with me."

One copy would have been for Edith's files; likely the other copy was for Lane. His slot machine had almost paid off.

"Did you do anything else?"

"I wiped my handkerchief over the places I touched on the photocopier."

That accounted for there being lots of prints on some parts of the copier and none on others.

"I need both copies."

"I burned them."

They would have to search Tu's house, hatchery, bank, and any other place that he might have hidden those copies, but Avivah doubted they would find them.

She picked up Mr. Pham's business card. His office was in

Raleigh. Edith died on Monday; today was Saturday. It wouldn't have taken him five days to travel from Raleigh to Asheville, but it could have taken that amount of time for him to come here from Raleigh, pick up a forged letter, take it to a Hong Kong bank, and return. Tu had waited until his association had retrieved the diamonds before turning himself in. "Where are the diamonds?"

A brief confused look flickered in Tu's eyes. "Ah, Greg Lane made a statement. That's how you know about the diamonds."

"Where are the diamonds?"

"My people are desperate. I must do anything that I can to help them."

Including murder. "Had Mr. Lam outlived his usefulness to you?"

"I did not kill him. I deeply regret his death. He would have been invaluable to me in the coming months, but more important, he was my friend."

"You'd better have a convincing alibi for Thursday morning."

"I was in a meeting with Immigration and Naturalization Services."

"When?"

"From nine o'clock until noon."

"Where?"

"At Brevard College."

Brevard was a forty-five-minute drive from Asheville: she had a second killer to find, few clues, and a hundred Vietnamese refugees scattered over the entire country. She was going to spend a lot of time taking to Immigration and Naturalization herself.

It took another hour before she was satisfied that Tu had told them everything. Her driver and another constable took him to the jail for processing. Avivah sat in the empty interrogation room. The room smelled old and used, or maybe that was the way she felt.

If Edith had only a copy of the letter, she must have given the original to someone. Pepper was the logical person; that meant Pepper had lied about Edith not giving her anything in writing. That farce about a coded poem had been smoke and mirrors.

Pepper had never lied to her before. But then, how would she know? The best she could say was that she'd never caught Pepper in an outright lie to her before. Didn't Pepper have any idea how serious a murder investigation was? Didn't she have any appreciation of how important their friendship was? They had to talk. She didn't know if the police officer or the house-mate would open that conversation.

Who knew what law applied in Hong Kong; it certainly wasn't North Carolina law. Tu's story had a big enough hole that the prosecutor could decide to bring a first-degree murder charge. That would mean a trial.

The secrets Darby carried weren't welded shut enough to resist a trial and the accompanying newspaper frenzy. Whatever you most didn't want people to know was what came out. When those secrets came out, Darby and likely Pepper would be in serious trouble. And a trial was bound to affect Anne when she was older.

If the prosecutor accepted Tu's confession and settled for manslaughter, Tu would still go to prison. Justice would be done, but with a lot less publicity, and a lot less damage to all of her friends. She had to get Nate on her side before they presented Tu's confession to the prosecutor. Nate would listen to her, especially if she convinced him that she understood Vietnamese psychology better than he did. He would lean on the chief, and the chief would lean on the prosecutor.

When she signed off shift, the desk sergeant came from his cubbyhole. "Should I take your name off the night-shift roster?"

Saying yes was so tempting. "Constable Harris and I have a coffee date after roll call."

"Aren't you engaged?"

"Public relations. We detectives feel it's important to keep in touch with the constable on the beat." Not to mention that she looked forward to straightforward Saturday night drunk-and-disorderly arrests and sleeping in the patrol car.

"Your choice. Oh, there was a phone message for you."

It was from Saul. *Darby found his grandmother. She's on the Maternity Ward at Mission Hospital. Come as soon as you can. If it's not too much trouble, bring a world atlas.*

CHAPTER 33

Mark, Randy, and Dave sat in the hospital's lobby. Dave was explaining to Randy an article in a photography magazine. Mark bounced his legs against an overstuffed couch. He did that when he was bored.

He jumped off the couch and ran to her. "Aunt Avivah, Aunt Avivah, we have a baby sister. Her name is Madison Kirkpatrick. She weighs six pounds, four ounces, and she's sixteen inches long. The nurses took her picture for me because I'm too young to go up to the nursery. Now I get to be a big brother, too."

He thrust a Polaroid photo into Avivah's hand. A pink baby blanket and stockinet cap filled most of the photo, leaving enough room for a small red face.

"Isn't she beautiful?"

She resembled every other wrinkled newborn that Avivah had seen. "She sure is."

"Randy drove us to the hospital. Dad said he did a great job taking care of us."

"Your dad is here?"

"He came here straight from the airport."

Dave and Randy joined them. Randy blushed, gazing steadfastly at his shoes. Avivah wasn't sure if his embarrassment came from driving without even a learner's permit, or if it was all this talk about babies. Randy knew the basics of how his parents had produced Madison.

"It's all right, Randy. People do what they have to do." She wasn't sure if she were giving him absolution for driving or apologizing for Benny and Lorraine's indiscretion.

"Times I reckon they do."

A mountain lilt was replacing the not-from-anywhere accent that Army brats carried. It was about time all of the Kirkpatricks found a place to call home.

She asked, "Where is everybody?"

Dave said, "Colonel Baxter and Miss Pepperhawk are taking Anne to her uncle."

Poor Mr. Nghiem. Pepper would insist on telling him everything about baby care that she'd learned in the past five days.

"Mrs. Wright, Mr. Kirkpatrick, and Mr. Eisenberg are upstairs. If someone can give Mrs. Wright a ride home, I'll take the boys to supper and then home. I don't know about them, but I've had about all of today I can take."

"Saul and I will see that Mrs. Wright gets home. You guys okay going with Dave?"

Both boys nodded. She handed Randy money. "Supper is on me to celebrate Madison's birthday."

Avivah asked a pink-coated hospital volunteer how to find the maternity unit. Saul sat on a couch a few feet down from the elevator. He was sound asleep with his head thrown back.

She kissed him lightly on his eyelids, which fluttered open. Every time she did something like that she was grateful that he'd never been to war. He was so unconditioned. He pulled her to him and kissed her properly. That was nice, too.

She collapsed on the couch. "Where is everybody?"

"I beat a hasty retreat when Mrs. Wright started lecturing Benny on a husband's responsibility to pace the waiting room when his wife was in labor. The boys are somewhere with Dave."

"I saw them downstairs. Dave is taking them to supper. We have to give Mrs. Wright a ride."

"Oh, joy."

"She's not that bad." Avivah held out the atlas. "The library was closed, but I found a cheap kid's atlas at the drugstore."

Saul opened to a map of Southeast Asia. "It will do. Anne's uncle stared us in the face all the time, and we missed it. We should have looked at a map." He pointed to Vietnam. "Ban Me Thuot is here; Saigon is here. You know the geography better than I do, but those cities are what? About a hundred and fifty miles apart?"

"I was never in Ban Me Thuot, and barely in Saigon, but that's a good guess."

Saul spread his fingers into a large C-shape. "See the distance between Ban Me Thuot and Da Nang? Ban Me Thuot falls. The whole country is unraveling. What's Darby's best chance to get out of Vietnam?"

"Get to the American embassy in Saigon."

"But instead of heading south he goes north into the face of the enemy, on a journey that's what? Four, five times longer than getting to Saigon? Darby by himself, okay, I'd buy it—all his soldier genes kicked in—but with a newborn baby? We never asked ourselves why."

"Sometimes in Nam you hopped whatever transport was available. It was an all-roads-lead-to-Rome theory. Eventually you'd find someone going in your direction."

"Darby's incapable of procuring something with four tires and a full gas tank?"

It didn't even have to be that elaborate. Even a bicycle would have been an improvement over walking, and there were thousands of bicycles available for *procurement*.

He said, "We should have asked ourselves what was so all-fired important about getting to Da Nang. The answer was because Anne's—sorry, Nghiem Dao's—only remaining relative was in Da Nang."

"Is that Anne's real name?"

"I gather her parents weren't married. She would have been either Dao Gaudet or Nghiem Dao depending on which parent's name they decided to use. Mr. Nghiem has chosen to go with his family's name."

"What happened in Da Nang? Had Mr. Nghiem and his family already left by the time Darby arrived?"

"It's more complicated. Mr. Nghiem's wife refused to have anything to do with Anne."

"Because she was illegitimate?"

"Maybe. Or because she was afraid for her own children; they were about to run for their lives. A newborn baby would have been a terrible burden. With Mrs. Nghiem dead, we'll never know."

"Mrs. Nghiem refused to take Anne; she and her children die. Mr. Nghiem ends up with Anne half a world away. Stories keep falling into your lap today, don't they?"

Saul closed the atlas. "Not this one."

"What's the matter, an embarrassment of riches?"

"Saul Eisenberg, human being, convinced Saul Eisenberg, premiere journalist, to sit this one out."

"You talked yourself out of a story?"

"Being around you people is catching."

She got up and reached for his hand. "Come on, I want to see this baby."

They found Benny with his forehead pressed against the nursery glass. Avivah smoothed her hand over his back. "It's not a candy store, Benny. They're going to let you take her home."

Benny pointed at one of the bassinets. "That's her in the middle row, second from the left. Her name is Madison Elizabeth Avivah Kirkpatrick. We're going to call her Maddy."

Avivah had always assumed that, if the baby were a girl, Elizabeth would sneak into the baby's name somehow. Pepper and

Benny had hit it off from the day they met. She was thrilled with second billing.

Saul groaned. "Don't do that to her."

"Do what?"

"Her initials will be MEAK; it sounds like meek. Do you want to saddle her with that all her life?"

"I'll have to teach her how to stand up for herself; the nurse already made out her birth certificate." His face grew sad. "I tried, Avivah, I really tried. I went to New York to see the recruiter. I hoped we could negotiate."

"No luck?"

I called and called the number I had, but there wasn't any answer. The address was a mail drop in a dinky convenience store. A courier picks up the mail. The convenience-store owner knew nothing about the recruiting company. It's probably run out of the guy's apartment, which makes me skeptical that job conditions are going to be what he promised."

"What you need is a good lawyer; I might know where to find one."

She went to the nurses' station and asked the nurse to phone ICU. They were in luck: John Ferguson was sitting with Boyd's mother. He came down a few minutes later. After a whole day at the hospital, he was still looked fresh, his shirt crisp. One day she'd have to ask him how he did that. She suspected he kept spare shirts and ties in the trunk of his car.

"How is Boyd?"

"The doctors are optimistic."

"I'm glad. We have a new problem for you."

"You always have a new problem for me."

They went down the hall to an empty conference room. Benny explained his contract. When he finished, John asked, "Do you have a phone number for these people?"

"I doubt anyone will answer on a Saturday evening."

"If he really works out of his apartment, Saturday evening could be a good time to catch him at home. Give me his phone number and five dollars as a retainer."

Benny handed over the money, which John Ferguson pocketed. "Mr. Kirkpatrick, is it your intention to vest me with a power of attorney?"

Benny hesitated. Saul and Avivah said in unison, "Do it, Benny."

"It is my intention to vest you with a power of attorney."

Mr. Ferguson dialed the hospital operator. "I'd like to place a long-distance call and charge it to my business number." After a minute he held up his hand in a thumbs-up gesture. "Good evening, I'm glad that I caught you at home."

Score one for Lawyer Ferguson. They guy on the other end knew right off that John knew something about how the business was run.

"I'm an attorney in North Carolina, and I'm in the process of registering a power of attorney for Mr. Benjamin Kirkpatrick in the areas of personal decision-making, mental-health care, and veterans' benefits. I've recently learned that Mr. Kirkpatrick signed a contract with you. Is that correct?" He waited for an answer. "That's unfortunate."

He clicked his ballpoint pen very close to the receiver. "I'll need to know the civil jurisdiction in which your office is located, and an address where someone in your organization can sign for a registered letter."

He pointed at Benny, and then made a little circular motion at his temple, the motion people used to suggest someone was crazy. Benny looked blank for a minute, and then sank into a crouch. "Get away from me with that needle!"

John grinned and circled his hand in a ramp-it-up motion.

Avivah channeled for Pepper. "Hold still; this is for your own good."

"Stay away from me!"

Mr. Ferguson didn't make an attempt to cover the mouthpiece. "Somebody close that door before he gets away again."

Saul slammed the door with enough force that the sound surely carried to the telephone.

John drew his finger across his throat, and the three friends went silent.

"Sorry, where were we? I want to review a copy of the contract that Mr. Kirkpatrick signed. When is he due to report for work?"

A pause.

"That soon. All right, if that's what we have to work with, it will have to do. I'll give you my office address so that you can mail me his contract."

Another pause, longer this time.

"Are you sure? Considering the current circumstances, that is your safest option. I will mail the check back, but I still want to see that contract." He gave his office address, and then hung up. "Benny's future employer has suddenly discovered that all positions have been filled. Benny's sign-up bonus is in the mail. I promised that I would send it back."

The three friends whooped.

Avivah said, "Was that legal?"

Mr. Ferguson ticked on his fingers. "Benny retained my services. You and Saul witnessed his intention to vest a power of attorney. I never said I held such power, but that I was in the process of registering it, which would be the next step if Benny decides to pursue the matter. I voiced no opinion on his competency or his legal ability to enter into a contract. All I said was that his future right now was uncertain—new babies add a lot of uncertainty to life—and that it was unfortunate he had signed a contract under current circumstances."

Saul said, "What about that theater the three of us performed?"

"A hospital is a poor place to conduct business. I am not responsible for unrelated distractions happening in the background. Benny, come by my office on Monday so we can fill out the power-of-attorney application."

Benny said, "I've reconsidered."

"I thought you might."

"Can I have my five dollars back?"

"My secretary will mail you a receipt and a bill for services." John handed Benny a business card. "If you're offered further employment, I would be glad to review the contract before you sign. I offer competitive rates and convenient office hours. My office is open late on Thursdays, closed at noon on Fridays during fishing season."

CHAPTER 34

Late Sunday afternoon Avivah and Pepper, with Anne-Dao on her lap, sat on Benny's front steps watching Saul and Mark set up Mark's new tent. The tent and camping gear were from Darby's aborted Night on Weird Mountain. Between the excitement of a baby sister and Benny's promise that he and Mark would sleep in the tent tonight, Mark didn't care one whit if Randy went to art camp.

Pepper picked up Anne-Dao. The baby wore red overalls, a striped T-shirt, and socks with lace on them. "Maddy is coming home tomorrow. You better behave yourself, kid. I won't stand for you bullying her because you're so much older than she is."

She brought the baby very close to her face. Anne-Dao locked eyes with Pepper. Pepper turned her head slowly and Anne-Dao stayed right with her. "I'll be! That's the first time she's done than. Watching her and Maddy grow up is going to be so much fun."

"She's not a toy for your amusement."

Avivah had been in a rotten mood all day.

"I'd forgotten how crabby you get working night shifts."

"I am not crabby."

Pepper nuzzled the top of Annie-Dao's head. "Are so."

"You lied to me."

"About what?"

"That cock-and-bull coded-poem story. Flat out, did Darby send you a letter via Edith Filmore? I'll get my badge from the house if that's needed to make that an official question."

Oh, shit. Avivah's investigation had turned up the diary. Wait a minute, she was asking about a letter, not a diary. "Why are you asking me this?"

"If I can't trust you, who can I trust?"

Stay calm. She still had wiggle room. "Darby sent me a letter."

"What did it say?"

"That he was dying; that he loved me; that I was to find Vietnamese parents for the baby; and that I was to pay Edith Filmore three thousand dollars from his estate for bringing her to me. I lied to you because that letter was too private to share."

Please don't let her ask to see the letter now.

"Was Darby's letter in English?"

"Of course it was."

Avivah said more to herself than to Pepper. "There were two letters. What did Edith do with the other one?"

"Am I supposed to know what you're talking about?"

"Forget it."

It would be a good idea to turn Avivah's attention away from letters. "Darby and I aren't getting married."

Avivah looked sad. "Oh, love, I'm so sorry."

"For the best and all."

"I feel like a rotten person telling you this after what you just told me, but as long as we're back to being honest with one another, I want you to know that Saul and I have set a wedding date. December fourteenth, in New York."

"Yes!" Her excitement dipped. It would be a Jewish wedding. That meant she would be on the sidelines. "I guess I can't be part of the wedding party because I'm not Jewish."

"The ceremony itself will be only a small part of the day. We'll find a way to include you."

Leaves rustled as Kaye, wearing a denim skirt and white

blouse, came from the path. Pepper and Avivah moved away from one another to make room for her on the steps. "I came to say good-bye."

Pepper said, "How long are you staying in Atlanta?"

"Long enough to help Dave's church organize a work party to rebuild the school. Frannie says rebuilding a school will be good therapy, give me memories of a school being built instead of going up in flames."

Avivah said, "You don't sound convinced?"

"I don't blame myself for the fire, only for pretending to be sick so I could stay home and work on pottery. I wish I had been sick that day, even dying."

"You dying wouldn't have brought back your first graders."

"But maybe I'd have been there when they arrived." She brushed away tears. "You know, lined them up and told them to mind their manners in front of Saint Peter."

Pepper said, "I don't think it works that way."

"I guess I don't either, not really. Mr. Nghiem apologized for locking me in the shed. All he wanted was to see his niece."

They had learned a lot about the hatchery in the past twenty-four hours. The people at the homestead might not have known about the hatchery, but people at the hatchery certainly knew about the homestead. At supper Tuesday night, when Mr. Nghiem had told everyone about the miracle of seeing Dao at the clinic, Mr. Lam had known exactly who Pepper was and where she lived. He'd given Nghiem a ride to the homestead.

Mr. Lam had also taken Dao from Pepper's car. Pepper wasn't sure whose idea it had been to leave her in the tree. Had Lam gotten cold feet, or had Nghiem persuaded him against kidnapping? She didn't completely trust Nghiem yet, but as long as he took good care of Anne-Dao, she'd give him the benefit of the doubt.

Benny opened his front door. "Pepper, can you come in here for a minute?"

Now that the Kirkpatricks didn't need an emergency delivery room, Benny had moved a rickety card table and four chairs into the small room off the kitchen. Pepper wondered how much a desk cost. She still hadn't gotten Benny a graduation gift.

Benny, Yanni Skoufalos, and Greg Lane sat around the table. Benny pulled out the fourth chair for Pepper. "Sorry that you had to wait, but we had a lot to sort out. Mikhel has something to tell you."

"Who is Mikhel?"

Yanni said, "I am. My real name is Mikhel Skoufalos. The real Yanni drowned in nineteen forty-nine. He was my older brother."

Greg Lane said, "My birth name was Gregorios Skoufalos. I'm the third brother."

Pepper's gaze flitted between the two men's faces. If she imagined Lane forty pounds lighter, dressed in unrelieved black, and sporting a Greek fisherman's cap, there might be a family resemblance. "I don't understand."

Mikhel said, "The rest of our family died during World War Two and the Greek Civil War. The three of us ended up in a displaced persons' camp. I had tuberculosis; Yanni and Gregorios didn't. They were able to get visas to come to America."

Greg/Gregorios said, "I came down with polio a few days before Yanni and I were to leave."

Like tuberculosis, polio had been an illness that disqualified a person from immigrating to the United States. Pepper said, "And after you recovered you couldn't get another visa."

"Even if I could have, Mikhel was sicker than he had been when Yanni left us. I wouldn't have left him. When Yanni stopped sending money from America, we became desperate. We stowed away on a freighter. A seaman named John Lane found us. Together we smuggled Mikhel off the ship when it reached America. He was going to look for Yanni. I worked passage back to Singapore alongside my dad."

"Dad?"

"All of us thought that Mikhel was dying. John Lane said that he and his wife would adopt me. I've been Greg Lane a lot longer than I was Gregorios Skoufalos. But, deep down, I always knew I was still Gregorios."

Pepper asked Yanni—it was hard to think of him as Mikhel— "You found Yanni?"

"He had become a drunk. One day he went fishing and drowned. I took his papers and his identity."

Mikhel needed papers; Yanni had papers. Yanni drowned. How convenient.

"I had heard that the air in Asheville was good for tuberculosis. I came here."

"The mountain air cured you?"

"It kept me alive until streptomycin was available."

Benny said, "Mikhel is going to Hong Kong with Greg."

Mikhel put his hand on Greg's shoulder. "For thirty years all I have had of my brother was a photo that I pinned in a shrine. We want to spend time together."

Greg said, "I don't know how this thing I've got is going to play out. If anything happens to me, having Mikhel there to take care of my parents will mean a lot."

"Are you selling the store?"

Benny said, "Bach Anh Dung and I are going to manage it. He and his family will live in the apartment."

"Bach knows electronics?"

"I'll teach him what I can until he learns enough English to get him into A-B Tech."

Pepper detected in this the fine hands of Father Tom and

Father Ron. Do what one person can do.

After Mikhel and Greg had left, Pepper said to Benny, "It's none of my business, but why didn't you offer Nghiem the job of managing the store? He's almost family."

"I did, but Nghiem and I agreed that if Mr. Tu's father continues to bring new refugees into this country through the hatchery, it will be safer for the Bachs not to be there."

"Why?"

"The more Vietnamese through there, the more likely someone is to recognize him. Bach Anh Dung wasn't an ARVN Lieutenant."

"You mean he lied about being an officer?"

"No, he was an officer, but not ARVN."

Pepper dredged her memory for Vietnamese military units. Each time she named another unit Benny shook his head. He wore a pained expression. She opened her mouth, but all that came out was a rush of air pushed by a spasm of her stomach. Pepper moved her mouth without making a sound. "The other side?"

Benny nodded.

"Who knows this?"

"Nghiem."

"It's okay with him?"

"Bach did everything he could to try to keep people, including Mr. Nghiem's family, alive on the boat from Da Nang. Nghiem and Bach made a separate peace."

"You're okay with it, too?"

"I've set my sights on my own separate peace."

"What if someone finds out?"

"The Bachs have crossed the biggest hurdle. They have sponsorship and legitimate papers. Everything builds from that."

Just like everything had built for Yanni—Mikhel—once he had his brother's papers.

CHAPTER 35

Pepper and Darby sat side by side on the couch in stupefied silence. The living room looked so empty stripped of baby stuff. Outside a green-and-gold Sunday evening edged its way from late spring to early summer.

"When are your parents expecting you?"

"Any time in the next five days. I didn't know how long you'd want me to stay."

Pepper didn't know either. "You will come back occasionally, won't you?"

"I'll come back to check on Dao."

It was and it wasn't the answer she'd wanted. She wasn't sure what she wanted, though whatever it was involved Greg Lane being safe. He might be a rogue, but once she stopped being afraid of him she liked him. "What's that thing called that allows one country to send a suspected criminal back to another country for trial?"

"An extradition treaty."

"Does Hong Kong have an extradition treaty with the US?"

"I imagine so. The British control Hong Kong and the cousins are tight, even if they do squabble."

"What cousins?"

"That's how British Intelligence refers to the CIA. It's a shorthand for American-British relations." He frowned. "Why do you want to know this?"

"Who do you think killed Mr. Lam?"

"I think Vietnam caught up with him. If he were as good a forger as Lane said, Tu wouldn't have been his only employer. I think someone in Tu's refugee pipeline had old business to settle."

"Greg Lane was at the mall on Thursday morning. Lam contributed indirectly to Edith Filmore's death. Maybe Lane had old business to settle. I don't want him to have done it."

"Neither do I. Lane has always been out for the main chance, but I've never seen him violent. Do you have any idea what's wrong with him?"

"I think he's prodromal."

"What's that in English?"

"He's got something bad wrong with him, only it isn't developed enough for doctors to pinpoint it yet. Fifty-fifty chance that he's going to get sicker."

"Before he gets better?"

"If he gets better."

"That's too bad. I think I'll keep in touch with him."

"If you'll give me his address, I will, too. He saved your life; like Nana Kate said, debts of honor must be paid."

Darby was quiet for a long time. That was okay with Pepper. They seemed to do better when they were just being quiet together.

Darby said, "Do you know what Stonewall Jackson did before he joined the Confederate Army?"

"He taught science at The Citadel."

"I studied science at West Point. For a while it was a toss-up if I would go Engineers or Infantry. Nana Kate told me to find something to do. Maybe I could follow in Jackson's footsteps."

"Teach at The Citadel?"

"Teach science, maybe in a high school."

"You graduated in nineteen sixty-two. Science changes. You'd have to catch up, and you'd need a teaching certificate."

"Hell, Pepper, I have enough GI Bill that I could change my major every year for a long time. Maybe I could learn to fly. I've heard that the GI Bill pays for that, too."

"In other words, you don't have a clue what you want."

"I want to get up every morning without lying awake half the night wondering if I'm going to be able to get up."

Pepper remembered a few nights like that. Benny still expected her to help Darby, and the only thing she'd come up with that might work went all the way back to the first day they had met at Fort Sam Houston. "Explain to me how to walk a map course."

"Why?"

"Explain it to me, the way you did in front of my basic class."

"I don't see the point."

"Have you forgotten?" She hoped he hadn't. She hadn't. "You will take a compass reading—"

He fixed his gaze on the opposite wall. "You will take a compass reading on the most distant objective you can reach safely. Once you reach that objective, you will locate yourself on the map and take another compass reading. You will repeat those two steps until you have successfully completed the course. You will learn to do this without reference and without error. My students do not fail."

Pepper raised her hand. "Sir, please, sir."

Darby swallowed. "What is it, Lieutenant?"

"What if I find an obstruction like a bog between me and the objective?"

"Then, Lieutenant, you will locate a closer objective on this side of the bog, and achieve that objective."

"Suppose the only objective I can identify is five feet away?"

"If it's two feet away, you would do the same thing."

"Why bother moving two feet?"

"Because moving slowly is better than standing still and dying fast. If you travel two feet repeatedly, you will eventually find a way around that bog. Now sit down and let someone else have a chance to ask a question."

"You were so full of yourself."

"I was, wasn't I?"

"When you asked me to sit down and give someone else a chance to ask questions, I was afraid that I'd asked the stupidest question in the world."

"I was afraid that you'd keep asking questions, and I'd keep answering them until the janitor locked the auditorium. You were a pest. You always had your hand up to ask another question."

"They were good questions; I lay awake nights thinking them up."

"They were great questions. I was impressed."

"They were great answers. I was impressed, too. Stop stewing in your own juice. Pick an objective, something on this side of the bog. What do you want most?"

"You mean something I'm likely to get?"

"Something two feet away."

"I want my stuff back." He picked at his new shirt. "I'm tired of going to the store every time I change clothes. I want my clothes, my books, my record collection, and most of all, my coffeepot."

A car rumbled slowly over the cattle guard at the end of Pepper's driveway. It was a dark-green Army car with white numbers stenciled on the side and a Fort Bragg bumper decal.

Pepper tensed. General Fairclough had said that in five years Darby being in Vietnam would hardly matter. Pepper had taken that as a half promise that no one would come looking for Darby for five years. The Army had broken another promise. She pulled Darby to his feet and shoved him hard toward the kitchen. He careened into the door frame.

"Go. Now."

He held his hands out to her in a helpless gesture.

"You said it yourself. Things weren't supposed to end like this: not us, not the war. But it's the way they are ending. I'll do what I can to distract them. Go!"

In an instant he was gone in the sound of a slamming screen door. Pepper thought that her heart would explode in her chest.

The doorbell rang.

"Just a minute," Pepper yelled. She waited as long as she dared before going to the door. "Yes?" she said, opening the door.

The young Beret who stood there looked barely old enough to have completed the lengthy Special Forces training. From the way his beret wasn't quite molded to his head, he hadn't had it long.

"Good evening, ma'am. Are you Miss Elizabeth Pepperhawk?"

Pepper felt a hand on her shoulder. She jumped. Behind her, Darby said, "She's Miss Pepperhawk."

She hadn't heard him come back into the house.

"Good evening, ma'am, sir. Compliments from the John F. Kennedy Special Warfare Center at Fort Bragg. It is my privilege to inform you that Colonel Darby Baxter's status has been upgraded from Missing in Action, Presumed Dead, to Wounded in Action."

Upgraded made Darby sound like an airline reservation. Missing in Action, Presumed Dead, sure didn't sound like Died in a Training Accident. Had General Fairclough worked his clerical-error magic, or was the Army running so many files on Darby that they didn't know what was going on anymore? She covered her mouth with both hands to keep hysterical laugher from bubbling out.

Darby said, "Are you sure?"

"Colonel Baxter is safe in a Bangkok hospital. His condition is stable."

Darby stable? That would be the day.

Darby shook the man's hand. "You can't imagine what this means to us, Sergeant. We'll never forget this moment."

The sergeant's face turned red. He extracted his hand from Darby's grip.

Darby said, "How long have you been a Green Beret?"

"Three weeks, sir."

"God speed."

"Thank you, sir."

Pepper had recovered enough to offer in her best Southern voice, "Would you like coffee?"

"Thank you, but I have kin down to Weaverville and overnight leave to visit them. I'd best be on my way." He pulled his heels together. "Sir, ma'am." He nodded to both of them, pivoted smartly on his heel, and traced his route back to his car. Darby closed the door behind him. Both of them collapsed against the door, hands intertwined, laughing so hard that tears rolled down their faces.

"Why did you come back?"

"One Baxter martyr to a lost cause is enough."

"When did you decide this?"

"Halfway across your backyard."

"What if that car had been filled with burly military police sent to take you into custody?"

"One of your housemates is a shoe-in for a Pulitzer Prize, as soon as he finds a story that isn't classified. The other one has a mother and aunts who hang out with the American Civil Liberties Union, Amnesty International, the National Organization for Women, and the rest of the liberal alphabet. I figured we'd mobilize the troops."

"What about me? Don't I have any troops to mobilize?"

"Die if you must, but not on my shift. There's too much paperwork. I'd hold you to that promise."

A small lump formed in Pepper's throat. She would have kept that promise to the best of her ability. "They execute people for treason."

"The Army hasn't intentionally shot a soldier in thirty years. By the time the Pentagon, Congress, journalists, public opinion, the American Legion, the Veterans of Foreign Wars, and all of those organizations Avivah's family belong to finish fighting over me, I won't end up in front of a firing squad. Prison time maybe, but I was in jail this week and I survived."

"Fort Leavenworth Military Prison wouldn't be anything like overnight in the Madison County Jail."

"If it comes, I will survive." He reached in his pocket, and deposited two bullets in Pepper's free hand. "Ask Avivah to get rid of these."

"What if she asks where they came from?"

"You found them in your Army souvenirs; you have no idea where they came from."

"Why did he come here? I thought I wasn't on your next-of-kin notification?"

"You aren't, but when I filled out my request for medical leave, I gave your name and address."

"So the Army sent notification saying that you are alive to the place you would be staying. That young man had no clue who you were."

"That young man has no clue about a lot of things."

They walk down the hall. Darby leaned against her for support.

"You're tired."

"I'm exhausted."

"Will seeing your family likely take a lot of energy?"

"Likely it will."

"Do you want me to go with you?"

"A little private duty nursing?"

Benny was wrong. Darby didn't need an Army nurse; he needed a friend. "A little friendship."

"What about your job?"

"I have vacation."

"I'd love for you to come with me. While we're there do you think we might go on a date? A civilian date?"

A voice in Pepper's head said, "Don't even consider it. Not for one minute."

She recognized that voice, except maybe Captain Elizabeth Pepperhawk wasn't in command of her life anymore. "What's a civilian date?"

"I have no clue. I started military school before I was old enough to date. Maybe I could ask my brothers and cousins what they do on dates."

"All right. One civilian date."

"Everyone is going to be on our case about our lack of wedding plans."

"Are plebes allowed to marry?"

"No cadet is allowed to marry."

"Tell everyone what General Fairclough said about your plebe civilian year being tougher than West Point. Tell them that you need time to decompress."

"What do we tell them a year from now?"

"Stick to moving two feet at a time. A year from now will have to take care of itself. How do we get your things here from Camp Zama?"

"Hell, Pepper, I can't remember anymore how the Army works."

"Some nineteen-year-old military clerk remembers. What time is it in Tokyo?"

"I don't know what day it is."

"Let's phone Japan and ask."

"Lead on, pretty lady, lead on."

ABOUT THE AUTHOR

Sharon Wildwind is originally from Louisiana. More decades ago than she cares to admit, she spent a year in Vietnam as an officer in the US Army Nurse Corps. She can still remember exactly where she was the day that Saigon fell. When she's not writing, Sharon keeps a journal, is a mixed-media artist, and teaches writing workshops. Her Web site is www.wildwind author.com.